'*The White Room* is essentially a powerful family saga written with all the techniques of the classic noir crime novel, as well as the anger and passion of someone who really cares for his subject' Mike Ripley, *Birmingham Post*

'A gripping read; Waites juggles a complex plot with astute urban commentary' *Jack*

'Waites' writing is lean and taut, while his eye for detail gives his prose a vivid immediacy' *Ink*

'Lean, mean and machine-like, with a pacy narrative and sharp, staccato dialogue . . . His male characters are tough and complex, a throwback to the no-nonsense, near-mute charisma of *Get Carter* or *Point Blank*' *Scotsman* on *Born Under Punches*

'An ambitious, tautly-plotted thriller which offers a stark antidote to PD James' cosy world of middle-class murder' *Time Out* on *Born Under Punches*

'Not so much a crime novel as a furious study of the social spoilage which makes crime inevitable . . . Waites' book has a reckless energy which demands attention and respect' *Literary Review* on *Born Under Punches*

'An evocative, gripping and angry novel' *Newcastle Evening Chronicle*

'Waites is successful in creating a feeling of menace – of something manipulative and calculating out of shot: ordinary folk trying to live their lives are set up to be trampled on' *Weekly Worker*

BY THE SAME AUTHOR

Born Under Punches

Born and brought up in Newcastle-upon-Tyne, Martyn Waites has worked as a market trader, bar manager, stand-up comic, professional actor and, most recently, as Writer in Residence at Huntercombe Young Offenders' Institution and HMP Chelmsford.

The White Room

MARTYN WAITES

**POCKET
BOOKS**

LONDON • SYDNEY • NEW YORK • TORONTO

First published in Great Britain by Simon & Schuster, 2004
This edition first published by Pocket Books, 2005
An imprint of Simon & Schuster UK
A Viacom company

1 3 5 7 9 10 8 6 4 2

Simon & Schuster UK Ltd
Africa House
64–78 Kingsway
London WC2B 6AH

www.simonsays.co.uk

Simon & Schuster Australia
Sydney

A CIP catalogue record for this book
is available from the British Library

ISBN 0 7434 4952 5
EAN 9780743449526

Typeset by M Rules
Printed and bound in Great Britain by
Cox & Wyman Ltd, Reading, Berks

In memory of my late father
Derek Waites

Acknowledgements

This has been a difficult book to write. Inspired by real people, real events and set in real locations, when you're dealing with a past that is still pretty fresh in certain people's minds, it's a thin line to walk between giving offence to the survivors, being libellous to the innocent bystanders and being obliged to tell the truth as the writer sees it. But it is fiction. I've just reimagined everything to suit my story and myself and that includes dates, places and events. All the main characters (with the exception of the late T. Dan Smith) are entirely fictional.

People who assisted in one way or another: Deb Howe, Councillor Nick Kemp, Councillor Joe Hattam, Pat McCarthy of Amber Films and Dave Douglass.

Reference books: *Newcastle Upon Tyne, a Modern History* edited by Robert Colls and Bill Lancaster; *Geordies Wa Mental*, Dave Douglass; T. Dan Smith's Autobiography; *Cries Unheard* by Gitta Sereny. Also two photo collections: *Scotswood Road* by Jimmy Forsyth; *Byker* by Sirkka-Liisa Konttinen.

My editorial team: Kate Lyall Grant at Simon & Schuster, Caroline Montgomery at Rupert Crew and my wife Linda.

And just in case you were wondering, the Jungian archetypes in the last chapter is an established psychological test.

PART ONE

The Old Country

At night he dreamed the city.

The same dream, the same city. The old city. Built on calculated malice, constructed with hatred, governed by fear. More than a city, a factory, a machine.

In the dream he was back there, alone. It was empty now, not full as he had found it. Full of life, half life, death. He walked up to the gates, the road now cleared, heard the echoes: the crunch of bone underfoot, the slap and slip of boot on sun-dried leathery skin. The moans, cries and shrieks, pleading for help, some beyond help. The flies, dust clouds of them, droning and buzzing like approaching doodlebugs. It was all still there: in his ears, his nose, his tongue, his eyes, on his hands. In all his dream senses.

He approached the gates, pushed them open. They swung slowly back. He looked around, breathed in. He was alone.

The world was in black and white, the buildings black against the dead pearl-grey sky. Mist hovered, hung and clung like persistent ghosts to the low flat buildings, permeated the wood, brick and concrete, rolled up against the walls and fences, curled around the barbed wire. Left untouched the guntowers.

He saw his breath before him, cold and steaming, turn to clouds and join the mist. He called out. No one replied. He called again. Again, nothing.

He felt he was there for a purpose: to help, to save. He had to find someone, anyone, lead them away from this place. Help them to a future.

He moved quickly from hut to hut, flinging open doors, calling. Nothing.

He knew there was someone there, someone he had missed, a life unfound. There must be. But he couldn't move fast enough, shout loud enough. His dream self was slow, near-mute.

He found no one. He slumped, exhausted, down by the side of a hut, heart like a large rock in his chest, defeated. They were all gone. He was the only one left.

His dream body closed his dream eyes, tried to will himself away from the huts, the fence. The cold mist. He tried to imagine a world beyond the city, untouched by this place, tried to go back to a time before. A simpler time, a gentler world. A place of moral absolutes. He tried to re-create that place, will it to spring up, burst rumbling through the earth, obliterating this city of hate, taking its place.

And from that gentler, more honest place, build the future. Find the blueprint for tomorrow in the fairness of the past.

He stood up; made to go to the gates, let himself out. Get as far away from this place as possible.

Yes.

Get out of here, make the future happen. All things were possible. Heart daring to rise, mind daring to hope, for the first time in ages, he reached the gate.

And found it closed.

He rattled it; it stayed firm. He pulled hard, but his dream self lacked the strength. He tried to climb it but his dream legs stayed rooted to the ground.

The small kernel of hope he had been nourishing withered and died.

He slumped to the ground before the gate, bereft, trapped. He closed his eyes, tried to will the place before him to disappear. Told himself it was only a dream.

Threw himself around, rolled and writhed in the dirt.

But to no avail. He stayed where he was.

Then, slowly at first, he began to hear. The moans, cries and shrieks, pleading for help, some beyond help. He covered his ears with his hands. The sound came through. The flies, dust clouds of them, droning and buzzing like approaching doodlebugs. He closed his eyes: his eyelids became transparent. He felt the mist curl its ghost-like tendrils around his body, the city trying to reclaim him as one of its own. Another ghost in the machine.

He told himself it was all a dream, that he would wake up soon.

But he didn't.

He was stuck in the dream.

Stuck in his past.

June 1946:
Slaughterhouse Newsreels

The bull was terrified.

Eyes and mouth wide open, muscles straining, hide chafing against the rope, hooves digging in to the ridged stone floor, scraping along well-worn grooves. Pulling away, pulling back. Fighting for its life.

It took four of them to move it, Jack Smeaton on the back left flank. Head down, arms pushing hard, biceps straining. Legs firm but feet ready to jump, to dodge another load of bovine fear-shit or a potentially bone-breaking hoof blow. Two others pushed equally hard, the fourth pulled from the front, played tug o' war on the noose-like rope strung around the bull's neck.

The three other men were used to their work; Jack was not. Concentration allowing, he stole glances at them, looked into their faces, their eyes. He didn't know what he was searching for, couldn't articulate it. But couldn't find it either.

To them the bull was just meat. Walking meat.

Then the bull jumped, took them by surprise. The noose holder slackened his grip. The bull took its chance, lunged forward. A desperate escape bid. The others were on it, pushing, pulling, forcing the animal into the direction they wanted, to break its spirit, take its life. Jack joined them, put his back into it, pushing, pulling, hands firm on the hide, but fingers trying not to mark or tear.

Noise came from the pens around them, like spectators at a wrestling match: grunts and moos, howls and squeals, cheering on the unfancied contender, knowing what the ultimate score would be, knowing any of them could be next.

Grunts and moos, howls and squeals. Communicating their fear, their terror.

They pushed and jostled, tried to escape, threw themselves against their bars, tried to force bolts and hinges to spring free. Tautened their necks against their ropes, choking themselves, stretching, trying to pull the metal tethering rings from the walls, the ground. Stumbling, legs quivering, collapsing from terror and exhaustion.

The men pulled, pushed. Muscles straining, faces frowning. The bull fought on but was weakening. The men were regaining control, guiding, manoeuvring the bull to where they wanted it.

The killing shop.

Jack and the other three held the bull firm. Another man stepped up holding a heavy dark object. It looked like a starting pistol but was more a finishing pistol. The bolt gun. He held it hard against the back of the bull's neck, felt around with the nozzle to find the right spot, used his other hand to steady and guide, and fired.

Two inches of heavy metal were punched into the bull's brain.

The bull staggered. Pained and confused, its body closing down, dead but not yet realizing it.

Nerve signals ceased. The bull shivered and shook, collapsed. Dead.

The noise from the stalls and pens increased. Grunts and moos, howls and squeals. Communicating their fear, their terror. Knowing one of them would be next. They pushed harder, stretched further, panic ratcheting up their actions.

The men were inured to the sounds. They ignored them, carried on working. A metal rod was pushed into the bleeding bolt hole, connecting with the bull's spinal column. Its legs spasmed.

Now just meat, bone and organs in a heavy bag of skin, it was hoisted on to a meat hook. The men sharpened their knives, ready for the bleeding.

This was the time they came alive, Jack thought, the only time they had betrayed emotion in their work. Metal sparking off metal as anticipation increased. Eyes lit by butchers' gleam.

Jack looked at them. Slicing carcasses, hefting trays and buckets of innards. Mostly middle-aged, with strong arms and big bellies, red-faced with greased-down hair. Their abattoir coats, once white, now ingrained with blood and guts. The secretions of dead animals formed a map of the world. Their world. Past, present and future. Jack looked at the designs, saw countries he had yet to visit, territorial boundaries he had yet to cross.

One of the men, Alf, looked over at Jack, smiled, held his knife aloft.

'What d'you think, Jackie lad? Reckon you're ready to have a go yet?'

Jack looked at the knife, the dead bull, the smiling butcher. His stomach began to rollercoaster, his legs to shake. He shook his head.

'No . . . not yet . . .'

His voice sounded weak, sapped of resonance.

Alf shook his head, turned to the carcass, slit it open. Organs, guts, stomach spilled steaming out. Others moved in with trays and buckets to collect the entrails and blood, splashing and catching them as they did so. Waste hit the floor trough, was carried away to the drain.

Jack looked at the blood, mesmerized. In that spurting and swirling, he saw other scenes, other slaughter. Other carcasses. He closed his eyes to block out the images but they remained, playing against his inner eyelids like a Pathé horror newsreel.

Other slaughter, other carcasses. Grunts and moos, howls and screams. Communicating their fear, their terror.

He felt his hair turn white all over again.

His head began to spin, pins and needles fracturing his vision. His legs shook further. He reached out to steady himself, found the top bar of a pen, caused a mini stampede as the animals inside jumped away from him, thinking they would be next to die.

Heat prickled his skin, blackness took his vision. His legs quivered and buckled as if the bolt gun had been used on him.

He dimly heard a voice, Alf again: 'How, Jackie lad.'

Then another: 'What's up wi' Chalky?'

'Get 'im, he's ganna fall.'

Jack felt arms, strong, smeared with and smelling of blood, beneath his armpits. He fell into them, felt himself being dragged beyond the killing shop. The air changed, the noise abated. Calm fell on him. Now sat on a chair, he opened his eyes.

'Y'all reet, young 'un?'

It was Alf.

Jack breathed fast, shook.

'Aye, gets you like that, sometimes. When you're not used to it, like.'

'Thought you would be,' said the other man, 'you bein' a soldier an' all.'

Jack said nothing. Just breathed, shook.

The men looked at him, waiting for him to speak.

'Think I'll knock off early,' Jack said.

The two older men looked at each other, looked at him, nodded.

He knew what they were thinking about him. He didn't care. Let them. They weren't there.

He stood up, legs still unsteady. Began to remove his apron, walk away.

'See you tomorrow, Jack.'

Jack nodded, threw down his apron.

He wouldn't be back.

Monica Blacklock walked down the street, coat buttoned up to her throat, hat pulled firmly on her head. Her eyes were down, looking at the pavement; she watched her shoes, old but shinily made up, step on the slabs, avoiding the cracks. It was important to avoid the cracks. Something bad would happen to her if she stepped on the cracks. She knew it.

He pulled on her hand, gently guiding her in the direction he wanted her to go. She crossed roads, went around corners, holding hands all the while. Sometimes he looked down at her, smiled. She avoided his face, looked straight ahead or down at her feet. Neither spoke. Monica felt cut off from the others on the street, like she was inside a bubble, one where she could look out, reach people, but no one could see or reach her.

She skipped her feet around a cracked paving slab, tried to keep safe, giving a tug on his arm as she did so.

'Watch where you're walkin',' he said, grasping her hand more firmly in his, as if to protect her, keep her upright or stop her from bolting.

She didn't reply, just nodded and kept on walking, looking for safety in the path.

Scotswood looked drab and ordinary to Monica. It was the world, all she had ever known. She looked at the other children playing in the streets. Skipping, running, chasing each other. Laughter coming from their throats in uninhibited screams. From within her bubble they looked a hundred, a million miles away. Alien and strange. She wished she could have been with them but wouldn't have known what to do, how to join in.

He guided her around another corner. They came to a stop before a terraced house with a green door. It looked like any other in the street, but she knew it wasn't. He knocked, waited for a reply. She looked up at him. He looked down, smiled.

'You goin' to be a good girl, eh?'

She nodded, eyes widened.

He smiled again.

'That's it. I'll get you somethin' nice as a present.'

The door opened. A middle-aged man stood there. Fat and balding with glasses. Braces and vest stretched over an expanded stomach, trousers dark and old, unpleasant-smelling. The smell coming from the house wasn't much better: old food and a filth that went deeper than surface dirt; dingy with closed curtains, only the smallest chinks of light breaking through.

'Evenin', Jim,' said the man. 'This her, then?'

'Aye.'

The man looked down at Monica, smiled.

'By, you're a pretty one, aren't you?'

Monica said nothing. She looked at the ground, checked for cracks. Moved her feet away from the paving slab edges, tried to force her feet to shrink to stand safely within the protective lines.

'How old are you?'

She kept staring at the ground.

'Answer the man.'

She looked up at her father's voice.

'Seven,' she said.

'Seven, eh? You're a bonny lass for seven, aren't you? You just come from school?'

She said nothing.

The man looked away from her and back to her father.

'Quiet one, eh?'

His smile disappeared. He dug into his pocket, handed over some notes and coins. Her father took them, counted them, pocketed them.

'Right,' he said, 'I'll be off, then.'

He dropped Monica's hand.

'Aye,' said the man. 'You leave her with me. You know when to pick her up.'

The man went to take Monica's hand. She didn't move. He pulled at her, rougher than her father had been.

'Come on, then.'

Monica didn't budge.

'Monica,' said her father, 'come on. Be nice. Hey, I'll buy you a present, eh? An' we can have fish and chips on the way home. You like that, don't you?'

Monica stared at the ground. All the paving stones around her were cracked. There was nowhere to stand. There was nowhere she could be safe. Reluctantly, she allowed herself to be led into the house. The green door closed behind her.

Her father looked at the door for a few seconds after it had closed behind his daughter. Then, patting his pocket, smiled and walked off, surreptitiously adjusting his trousers so his erection wouldn't show.

Jack walked out of the slaughterhouse and on to Scotswood Road, his steps halting, tentative, as if he had just been given his freedom and didn't know what to do with it.

He walked, with no particular destination in mind, just wanting to move his legs, breathe in the air.

He breathed. The air was fresh with soot from the factories by the Tyne. He had the smell of industry in his lungs, but he couldn't erase the deeper smell from his nostrils. His mouth. Clothes, skin and hair, hanging on him like a carcass on a meat hook.

He had been in the job for less than a week, work being hard to come by for returning soldiers in the North-East. He hadn't had a hero's welcome. By the time he had been demobbed the novelty had worn off, the celebrations ended. He had been given his suit, his money, but no job. He had had to find that for himself. His brother had got him a job at one of the Scotswood slaughterhouses. Jack hadn't wanted it, but it was that or nothing. Now he had nothing.

He was conscious of the way he must seem to the outside world: his walk too hesitant for a young man, his hair all wrong. He pulled his cap further down on to his head, trying to cover his hair. Unnaturally white, leached of any tone or hue, lifeless, like thin fibres of bleached bone.

He took another deep breath, smelled carcasses, blood, skin. Skin was the worst. He had been sick the first time the skin lorry had turned up at the slaughterhouse. Bovine hide expertly cut, pig skin blowtorched to remove hairs then stripped from the dead animal. Waste, meat by-products, turned into coats, shoes, watchstraps, belts, anything. There was no limit to human ingenuity. The smell of the skin as it was loaded on to the skin lorry, the smell of the lorry from years of accumulation was rank. He had piled them in, gagging as he did so, vowing never to do it again.

He shook his head, tried to trade blood air for industrial air.

Scotswood hadn't changed. It looked just as it had when he had left three years previously. The river's-edge factories and gasometers still fronted a dark, sluggish Tyne. Chimneys still pumped out clouds, cloaking and choking the city, turning red brick to black, white paint to grey. Street cobbles worn and dusty, like seaside pebbles awaiting the splash of waves to shine them up. The lines and blocks of uniform, flat-fronted terraces stretching from factories upwards to Benwell and the West Road as if trying to escape.

Nothing had changed.

Except the world.

And Jack.

The lambs. They affected him the most. They arrived in vans, small and lost-looking, scared to leave the stinking metal shell, waiting to be led. The men would walk up to them, stick their fingers in their mouths. The lambs would suck, expecting milk, food. Trusting. The men would lead them to the pens, then the killing floor. Bleating and screaming too late.

Lambs to the slaughter. True enough.

He walked. Street after street, around corners, along roads. Trying to lose himself. Trying to find himself. He was hungry, empty inside, but he could think of nothing he wanted to eat.

Places triggered memories. Brought back an earlier life. He let the memories come to him, hoped they would replace the mental newsreel footage he had experienced at the slaughterhouse.

Lights flickered, film whirred. A corner shop where an eight-year-old Jack and his friend had shoplifted a quarter of black bullets, earning himself a strapping from his father. He had never done it again.

A back alley where Molly Shaw lifted her skirt and took down her drawers to show Jack and six of his friends what was underneath. They had looked on, confused, as she pulled them up again, laughed and ran off.

Topper's front door. His best friend, now gone. Eighteen years old, blown up by a German landmine. He sighed, shook his head and walked on.

The memories continued. The films unspooled. It was watching a life from the back of a deserted cinema, unable to join in with the rest of the audience, unsure of what his responses should be. The images were familiar, yet the language of common, shared experience was completely alien to him. Foreign with no subtitles. No one there to explain the meaning. A life of simple definitions: good and bad, right and wrong, black and white. A life lived in a far-distant country, a long time ago. A life Jack couldn't relate to any more.

He walked on. People nodded, sometimes spoke: a small greeting. Jack nodded, sometimes spoke in return. He walked on.

He knew the way they looked at him. Surprise, shock. He felt their stares, could almost hear what they were thinking: no nineteen-year-old should look like that. Should walk like that. Not when you think what he was like before. And his hair . . . He knew they wanted to ask him about the war, what he'd seen, where he'd been, but he knew they wouldn't. They didn't want to hear the answers. So they would stay behind their windows and nets scrutinizing him, reaching their own conclusions. If they met him and had to say hello, they would do so quickly, just enough to catch the hollowness of his cheeks, see the ghosts lurking behind his eyes, before looking away fast and excusing themselves, hoping that whatever he was carrying wasn't contagious.

Among them but no longer of them, he was able to see Scotswood and its people objectively. What he saw was poverty. A lack of nourishment in all areas. A community badly housed and badly educated, dressed in old clothes made drab through repeated washing, pressing and repairing. The make-do-and-mend ethic shot through every aspect of their lives. A cold, hard life lived in cold, hard houses. Just bodies piled upon bodies. Existing, not living. No heating or water. Children playing in the streets dirty and ragged.

Jack found it hard to believe they were on the winning side.

He walked on with no direction.

He didn't want to go home, back to the house he had grown up in and in which his mother, father, brother and sister still lived. It was too small and no longer a home to him, just a place he slept, usually uncomfortably. He needed something to do, somewhere to go.

He put his hand in his pocket. His fingers curled over a piece of paper. Finding it unfamiliar, he drew it out and unfolded it. It was a flyer. He read:

MEN:

WHEN YOU RETURNED HOME VICTORIOUS FROM FIGHTING FOR YOUR COUNTRY, DID YOU EXPECT SOMETHING MORE? WE AGREE. WE ALSO BELIEVE IN THE ENRICHMENT OF LIFE. IF YOU ARE LIKE-MINDED, JOIN US TONIGHT AT 7.30 AT THE ROYAL ARCADE.

THE SPEAKER WILL BE MR. DANIEL SMITH.

SOCIALIST SOCIETY

Men had been handing out leaflets as he had entered the slaughterhouse that morning. He had absently accepted it but never looked at it. He looked at it again, read it slowly, picked out what were, to him, key words:

Socialist Society. Enrichment of life. Did you expect something more?

He stopped walking, looked around.

Poor, badly housed and badly educated.

He folded the paper, replaced it.

Did you expect something more?

Seven thirty, Royal Arcade.

He would be there.

Monica walked down the street, absently pushing chips into her mouth. The chips were hot, salty and vinegar-soggy. They burned her mouth as they went in, blistered her gums.

She didn't care. She wanted them to hurt, wanted to feel something that would block out the earlier pain.

Her tears had stopped. The man had given her a handkerchief to wipe them away before her father picked her up. She had cleaned herself up all over with it. It stank. She obviously wasn't the first person to have used it.

Her father walked alongside her, eating his chips and fish from old newspaper. They walked slowly: he to make his meal last, she because she hurt. They said nothing to each other. Under his arm he carried a boxed doll. She had looked at it once when he had picked her up, but she hadn't touched it. She wasn't in a hurry to play with it. It seemed small and inappropriate, like a bandage that wouldn't cover and didn't heal a wound.

She opened the battered fish with her fingers. Hot steam escaped. She picked a piece up, fat and batter burning her fingers, and shoved it in her mouth. More pain.

'Hey, careful,' her father said. 'You'll burn yoursel'.'

She chewed, ignoring him. Tears came into her eyes, whether from the pain of the food or the earlier pain she didn't know. She didn't care. She fought them back, swallowed. There were no children playing on the street now. They had all gone home. Home, she thought.

Her father finished his meal, threw the grease-sodden newspaper in a bin.

'Good, that,' he said. 'Always nice to have a treat.'

Monica looked down. Her shoes were scuffed and there were bruises developing on her legs. Her feet hit the pavement indiscriminately. She no longer avoided the cracks. She walked on as many as possible. The paving stones wouldn't protect her.

She felt a hand on her shoulder, looked up. Her father was looking down at her, smiling.

'You're a good lass, you know that?'

Monica said nothing. Smelled the beer on his breath. Beer and whatever was in the hip flask in his coat pocket.

'A good lass. You know, you're special. A special little girl.'

Monica said nothing.

He squeezed her shoulder.

'Sometimes people have secrets. Things that other people shouldn't know about. They wouldn't understand. You know that, don't you?'

Monica said nothing.

'I know you do. Your mam . . . well, it's best not to say anything to her about where we've been. Understand?'

Monica said nothing.

'I know you won't. You're a good girl.' He gave a little laugh. 'What we've got is special, you know that? What we've got—' he looked around quickly '—is love. Real love. I know men aren't supposed to say it, because it sounds sloppy, but I love you, Monica. You're a special girl.'

Monica swallowed the hot potato in her mouth.

'I love you too, Dad,' she said, her voice a small, caged thing.

Her father smiled.

'Good.'

He squeezed her shoulder again. Monica put more burning food into her mouth.

They walked home in silence.

Later and the streets of Newcastle were damp and dark with night and drizzle. Jack didn't care. He was elated. Those streets seemed transformed in his mind into avenues of possibility. What he had seen and heard in the Royal Arcade had, he felt, changed him.

He had been nervous about going in, thinking the people there would have all been better read, better educated than him. But he had been welcomed unequivocally. For the most part they were just ordinary working-class men and women, coming along after finishing work or taking time off from household chores. He tried to remember names: Jack Common, Billy Beach. They had talked, even argued quite heatedly, violently, but Jack sensed it was a healthy argument; they were all on the same side.

Jack had become lost at times trying to follow the conversations and had had just to sit back and accept the incongruity of the situation: in the rarefied and genteel atmosphere of the old Victorian Royal Arcade, shipworkers and bakers talked knowledgeably and at great depth about social justice, equality, politics and the arts. Admittedly, some of the plays and films he had never heard of, but he tried to catch some of the names: *The Cabinet of Doctor Caligari* was one, *Battleship Something or Other* was another. He sat there, nodding occasionally, sometimes offering a small opinion when asked. He was asked if he had been in the war. He had nodded, given rudimentary answers, not elaborating. There had been glances at his hair following that, but no questions, none of the staring, the fear he had encountered in Scotswood. These people seemed to know what had happened to him, or at least understood. There, in that company, he began to relax for the first time in months.

More than that: it was as if windows and doors, long barred and boarded inside himself, had been flung open, allowing him access to inner places he had only suspected existed. He knew what wasn't right within, where he didn't belong. Now he felt he was beginning to discover where he did belong.

Halfway though the evening, Jack Common had stood up and introduced the speaker: Mr Daniel Smith. A small man, about thirty, Jack reckoned, with neat hair and passionate eyes, he had taken the small stage, looked out at his audience and began to speak of his vision. He spoke with clarity, yet without betraying his working-class origins. His voice was that of the working man, of a shared commonalty.

To Jack, he was revelatory. His vision, Daniel Smith said, was shared – he knew – by everyone in this room. 'Oh, I know we sometimes argue—' and here he pointed out certain faces, soliciting laughter among the knowing few '—but I know we're all on the same side really. All of us. Everyone. Because we all share the vision of a new city, a new society. One in which the future isn't something to fear but something to look forward to. And we look forward to this because it's something we'll all work together to create. A city, a nation following a true socialist vision, one in which everyone is valued for the contribution he or she can make in it.

'Just think,' he said. 'What if everyone had a decent place to live? One that was warm and comfortable, well designed and, above all, affordable. Everyone, not just the lucky few. What if everyone had decent schools beside them to send their children to? Local libraries within their reach? Good hospitals with the same high standard of care whether you're rich or poor? Decent jobs that a man can be proud to come home from?'

Jack leaned forward eagerly.

'Universities for everyone of ability, whether they be rich or poor? Not only that, but what about culture? The working man's always being told that it's not for him. The theatre, the opera, the ballet. Cinema, art, music. Not for him.'

He drew breath, looked around the room, making sure he had them all with him.

'Why not? Why shouldn't they be in the working man's grasp? Why should we and our families be dissuaded from enjoying them? These are things,' Daniel Smith said, shaking his head, 'that have been denied the working classes too long. Too long.'

Jack looked around. There were nods and murmurs of assent all about him. He wasn't sure about the opera and ballet himself – he would give Mr Smith the benefit of the doubt on that one – but the rest he agreed with. He kept listening.

'Working men get together in pubs to drink beer, play darts and dominoes, to sing songs.' He looked around the room, the faces now enrapt. 'But,' he said, shaking his head, 'I know, and you do too, that there are better songs we can sing.'

More murmurs and grunts of assent from the audience.

Daniel Smith continued: 'When you look around at this city and you see some of the places and the conditions that people live in, you wonder how they manage. I'm talking about places like Byker, Heaton, my own Wallsend, Longbenton, Scotswood—'

Jack's ears pricked up.

'—Benwell. And plenty of others.' Daniel Smith sighed, shook his head. He looked as if he had personal experience of these impoverished areas. A silent yet palpable expectancy hung in the air. He continued: 'You look at these places and you think, We've just won a war. I'll say that again. We've just won—' he stressed the word hard '—a war. We're supposed to be the victors.'

Jack found his head nodding to the words.

'As you know,' Daniel Smith continued, eyes alight with passion, 'I'm anti-war. I'll have no part of it. And I don't believe in all that sloganeering that went on either. Let's wipe the Germans off the face of the earth. The only good German's a dead German. Rubbish, all of it. What myself and my colleagues in the Independent Labour Party believe in is a united socialist Europe. We've just won a war. We have a massive opportunity to do something truly different in our society now. All of us. We've got to get on to Attlee, tell him not to lose the advantage he's got. Make him work for his money. All of us.'

He stopped talking, gave a self-deprecating smile, placed his hands on his chest.

'Now, I'm just one person standing up here. You down there are the many. So with that in mind I leave you with one final question: that future I was talking about earlier. Do you want it?'

Nods and murmurs from around the room.

'Do you? Well, so do I. But if change is to happen – and it has to – then it'll have to come from you. Not just me. Because we're all in this together. All of us. We've got to pull together on this. Stop having dreams and visions. Start turning them into reality. Thank you.'

He stood down to rapturous applause.

Jack, like everyone else, was on his feet. Convinced. Converted.

Dan Smith stepped down from the podium and found himself immediately surrounded by people: handshaking, backslapping. Jack wanted to move forwards, tell the man who had spoken that he could have been directly addressing him, the words could have come from his own mouth. He found himself swept along by the throng. He stopped in front of Dan Smith, who was reaching out his hand to shake. Jack took it.

Jack opened his mouth to speak, found there were no words there.

Dan Smith smiled at him. Jack smiled back.

'New face?' he asked.

Jack nodded.

'Good. Good to see you.'

Dan Smith smiled warmly and moved on to the next person.

The crowd surged, Jack floated away, bobbing like driftwood on an open sea. He allowed himself to be eased to the back of the throng. He stood there, alone, wishing he had said something, cursing his lack of education, thinking of all the pithy one-liners he could have come out with, now lost to

the moment. He looked at the other people talking to Dan
Smith, saw how easily they made conversation. He shook his
head, sighed.

'Enjoyin' yourself?'

Jack looked up.

'Aye, you.'

The man smiled at Jack.

'Ralph Bell.'

The man stuck out a big, meaty hand. Jack took it, said his
name.

'He's good, isn't he? Dan Smith. The speaker.'

Jack nodded. 'Aye. Aye, he is.'

'More than a speaker, though. A doer. Great things are
expected of him.'

Jack looked at Ralph Bell. He was a big man, stocky and
tall, but not fat. Arms and chest enlarged by manual work.
Brown hair greased back, suit and tie functional. Moustache.
He looked about thirty, thought Jack, although given his
ruddy, leather-weathered face, that figure could have been
revised upwards.

'Aye,' said Jack. 'When he spoke, I wanted to tell him
everythin' he said was true.'

Ralph Bell gave a small laugh, looked over to where the
throng still surrounded Dan Smith.

'But you couldn't find the right words. Well, don't worry.
He's here often. You'll get your chance. This your first time
here, is it?'

Jack nodded.

'Thought I hadn't seen you here before.' He pointed to
Jack's hair, smiled. 'I'd have noticed.'

Jack felt himself redden.

Ralph Bell gestured around the room.

'They're a good bunch, as this lot goes. Everybody argues.
But we're all on the same side. Really.'

Jack ran his fingers self-consciously through his hair. It was now claiming Ralph Bell's attention.

'Where you from, then?' Ralph Bell asked.

'Scotswood.'

'You workin'?'

'Got job in one of the slaughterhouses down there.'

Ralph Bell grimaced.

'Rather you than me. I couldn't do it. Must be horrible, that.'

'Aye, it is. Horrible. Lookin' for somethin' else.' Jack knew he was mumbling his words.

'That what turned your hair white, then?'

Jack looked at him, mouth working up to a reply.

'Nuh – no,' Jack stammered. Words came to him only in meagre clumps at the best of times, but they were practically nowhere to be seen tonight. 'That's from . . . the war. I saw some things . . .'

He trailed off, hoping the memories wouldn't invade his head again. Not here. Not now.

Ralph Bell nodded.

'Don't want to talk about it, eh? Best way, probably.'

Jack nodded. He suddenly wanted to be away from the group, out of the Royal Arcade.

'I'd best be off.'

'Listen,' said Ralph Bell, 'there's a few of us goin' for a pint afterwards. Want to come?'

'No, I'd best . . .' He gestured vaguely towards the door.

'Please yourself. Next time, perhaps.' Ralph Bell stuck out his hand once more. 'Nice to meet you, Jack. You comin' back again?'

Jack looked around the room. Dan Smith still had an audience. People were still chatting animatedly. It seemed warm, welcoming.

'Aye . . . aye, probably.'

'Good. The more the merrier.'

Jack turned to go.

'Oh, before you go.' Ralph Bell spoke as if a thought had just struck him.

Jack turned back.

'You said you were lookin' for somethin' else. Instead of the slaughterhouse. That right?'

Jack nodded, slightly wary. 'Aye . . .'

'You ever done any buildin' work? Labourin' an' that?'

'In the army, I did.'

Ralph Bell smiled. 'I might be able to help you, then. I'm a builder. Run a buildin' firm in Walker. Oh, I know what you're thinkin'.' He laughed. 'What's a builder doin' here with all these socialists? Well, you shouldn't believe what you hear. We're not all Conservatives. But we are always lookin' for lads who aren't afraid of hard work. You like the sound of that?'

Jack thought, but not for long. Anything would be better than murdering animals.

'Aye, I do,' he said.

'Can you start tomorrow?'

Jack nodded.

Ralph Bell gave him the address. 'Be there seven thirty. Hope you've got an alarm clock. Now, you comin' for that drink?'

'I'd best not,' said Jack and smiled. It was a rare event. It felt alien to his face.

'Why?'

'Got an early start in the mornin'.'

He exited the Royal Arcade.

Dan Smith still had a crowd around him.

'Howay, man, look. There she is.'

The first boy pointed down the darkened alley. The Essoldo picture house on one side, offices the other. At the end, propped against the cinema wall, half claimed by shadow, stood a girl.

'Told you she'd be there, didn't I?'

The first boy looked around to the others. There were four of them, three between ten and eleven, the fourth younger. The first boy shook his head, pointed an angry finger.

'What did you bring him for?' He spoke to the third boy, finger stretched towards the fourth. 'He's a fuckin' bairn, man.'

'You kna' why, Lukey,' said the third boy. 'It's wor Brian. Me mam said I've got to look after 'im when she's out, man.'

The little boy, Brian, stood between the two older boys, watching words bounce between them as if at a tennis match. Not that he had ever seen a tennis match. His clothes were old; he was not. Grey shoes, black socks and short trousers, a shirt that may have started its life white, black duffel coat a size too small for him. Face dirty, hair untidy. Seven years old.

The first boy, Lukey, looked at Brian.

'You shoulda left 'im home, Nabs. We're not bairns.'

In the darkness, Nabs's face reddened.

'I'll look after 'im, reet?'

Lukey sighed, reluctantly nodded.

The second boy wasn't listening to them. He was staring straight down the alley. He grabbed Lukey's arm.

'How, she's lookin' down here,' he said.

Lukey turned to him, away from Nabs.

'Have you got the stuff, Fenny?' Lukey asked.

The second boy, Fenny, felt in his pocket. He had done so every five minutes. 'Aye,' he said.

Lukey swallowed hard. He was aware that his breathing had become more laboured. 'Howay, then,' he said.

The three boys looked at each other, looking for signs of weakness, looking for their own reflections. Lukey, having elected himself leader, began to move slowly, the other two following tentatively. Brian looked between the three, shared none of their apprehension, tagged along. Nabs, Lukey and Fenny were all breathing hard now. Their hearts felt too big, worked too fast for their chests. The alley, and the girl at the end of it, seemed to stretch out for miles. Nabs reached down, found Brian's hand, pulled him along.

They had first seen her nearly a week ago on one of their evening reconnaissances of the town centre. They knew what she was straight away. Why she was where she was, what she was doing. They had stared at her and she had smiled at them, talked to them, asking them why they were out so late, what they were doing in town, where they lived. They had mumbled their replies, telling her they were from Byker. She had tolerated their presence for a while longer until she told them she had to get back to work. They had drifted off then, each of them nursing an uncomfortable, yet not unpleasant, erection that had lasted for the best part of a week.

This time would be different. This time they had a plan.

She turned, saw them coming. She smiled at them.

'Hello, lads,' she said. 'You're out late again, aren't you?'

They stopped walking, stared at her. She had blonde hair, curled and bobbed, just tidy enough. Blouse and skirt, stockings and heeled shoes, black overcoat. The blouse had been opened to reveal the tops of her small breasts. She wore heavily applied make-up, a child's approximation of how an adult should look.

'Wuh – we've got somethin' for you,' said Lukey. He could barely speak, barely breathe, his heart was racing so heavily.

She looked around quickly, making sure there were no prospective punters hoving into view, then smiled at the boys.

'That's nice,' she said, a laugh in her voice. 'What is it? A diamond ring? A fur coat? Something to wear when Cary Grant escorts me from the back of his Rolls-Royce into some posh restaurant?'

She closed her eyes. The boys looked between themselves, not knowing what to do next.

She opened her eyes again, saw the boys. Their intense, nervous faces must not have been what she wanted to see. She sighed as if a great weight had been placed on her chest.

Lukey cleared his throat.

'Naw,' he said, 'nothin' like that. Sorry, like.'

He turned to the boy behind him, gestured. Fenny dug into his pocket, handed him something. He gave it to the girl. His hands were shaking. She picked up the package, examined it. A battered box of Players No. 6.

'Thanks, lads,' she said and smiled. 'That's kind of you. Keep me warm when the nights are cold.'

'It's cos, y'kna' . . .'

Lukey tried to speak, found the words wouldn't come.

'It's cos we wanna fuck ya.'

Fenny had spoken. Lukey put his head down quickly. Even in the shadows he could feel himself blushing again.

The prostitute smiled at the boys again. They were too nervous to notice its condescendingly maternal qualities.

'That's sweet,' she said. 'Listen, lads, thanks for the fags, but you'd better run along now cos I'm workin'.'

Disappointment hit the boys with an almost physical force. Nearly a week of planning, all for nothing. They stood there, unsure whether to stay or walk. Lukey turned to the others, planning to walk, trying to find as much dignity as possible.

'That's not fair,' said Nabs.

The others, including Brian and the prostitute, turned to face him.

'We bought you those fags. If we're not ganna get nowt for them, we want them back.'

The prostitute opened her mouth to speak.

'Aye, 'e's right, y'kna',' said Fenny, emboldened by Nabs's words. 'It's not fair, we should get somethin'.'

The prostitute closed her mouth again, her words dying in her throat. She looked side to side, hoping the noise hadn't put off any potential punters. There were none. She sucked her bottom lip, thinking. Red lipstick stained her teeth. She ducked back into the alley, mind quickly made up.

'Come on, then,' she said, her voice weary beyond her years, yet brisk and businesslike, 'but be quick.'

The three older boys followed her into the shadows. Brian toddled slowly behind them. Nabs, Lukey and Fenny exchanged excited smiles, amazed and not a little apprehensive that their plan had worked.

The prostitute stopped, stepped back against a darkened doorway. The boys stopped also. She began unbuttoning her blouse.

'You can all have a look at me tits,' she said, unhooking her bra from behind and pushing it up her chest.

They stared. The prostitute had small breasts with small nipples. They felt their erections rising.

Brian looked between the woman's breasts and the boys' enrapt faces. He knew something was happening but was unsure what it was.

'Can I touch them?' asked Nabs.

She sighed. 'If you must. But quickly.'

Nabs stepped up and ran his hands over them. Tentatively at first, then more assuredly as his confidence grew. He began to probe harder, breathe heavier. He took her nipples between his thumbs and forefingers and pinched.

'Ow!' She slapped his hands away. 'They are attached, you know. Right, that's your lot. You next.'

Lukey then Fenny took turns fondling her breasts.

'That's enough. I reckon that's a packet of fags' worth.' She began to reattach herself then looked down at Brian. He was staring up at her, eyes wide, blank.

'What's the matter?' she said. 'You want a go?'

'Aye, gan on, Nabs,' said Lukey. 'Let your Brian have a go.'

The prostitute kneeled down beside him.

'Well?' she asked and smiled at him. 'Do you wan' to squeeze my lovely titties as well?'

She laughed when she said it. Playful and taunting, yet with a cruel edge.

Brian looked up, his hands staying by his sides, his eyes locking on to hers.

'Are you a slag?' he asked.

The prostitute stared at him, open-mouthed.

'My mam's a slag. My dad calls her that. A fuckin' slag. Then he hits her. An' takes her money off her. Is that what happens to you?'

The prostitute stood upright and moved backwards all in the same motion. She looked like she had just been slapped in the face.

'Right,' she said, pulling her clothes back together, 'piss off, all of you. I'm workin'.'

She began to walk away, back up the alley. The boys didn't move; just stared at her. She reached the mouth of the alley, turned back to them.

'Go on, piss off!'

The boys turned and reluctantly began to walk away.

Brian reached for Nabs's hand. Nabs batted it away.

They walked home to Byker. It was a long time before any of them spoke.

Jack didn't want to go home.

Highs were heading to lows. The joy of the meeting, of getting work, was receding. As the night had darkened, so had Jack: shadows were assuming substance, fears becoming more tangible.

Memories returning in pinpoint focus.

He tried to ward it off, use the night's positives as a counterbalance, but it was no good. He could feel the mood descending, as it always did, like an old, damp army blanket thrown over his head. The harder he struggled, the firmer its grip.

He didn't want to go back to the house he used to call home. Like everything else, it now seemed so alien to him.

And so small: narrow doorways, cramped rooms, compacted hallways. Too small for the amount of people it contained. Too small for Jack. He felt as if he was always bumping into things, having to squeeze between gaps in the furniture and bodies, fight for tiny, territorial increments. He thought years of army living would have cured him of that, but even there, in that strictly regimented existence, he had more space than he had at home.

He was also sharing a bedroom with his younger brother, Tommy. A very cramped bedroom. Although Tommy had never said anything, Jack got the impression that Tommy believed he should never have returned from the war. Perhaps a hero's death fighting the Nazis, perhaps an indefinite stay in Colditz. Anything, in fact, that would have given Tommy his own room.

While Tommy snored, Jack would lie awake staring at the darkness, trying not to see tangible shapes in flickers of half-light. And if he did sleep it was the same dream. His bed was a sea, the water black, oily, treacherous with hidden currents, hungry to pull down unwary swimmers. The Tyne as it ran through Scotswood: stinking of the waste of industry. Jack would lie on the surface, floating, imaginary balls and chains shackled to his hands and feet. The balls were stuffed full of memories, of images, names and places. All heavier than lead. They were trying to drag him down, drag him back. Jack would struggle, fight to keep his head above water, to keep breathing. Then he would wake, gasping. And the dream, in one form or another, would continue. That was not the only dream, but it was probably the worst. There were others. Waking or sleeping, nights – all nights – would pass like this. The only respite was that moment of waking dislocation, of temporary amnesia as the dream fell away and reality took over. He savoured those moments. Luxuriated in them. Wished they would last for ever.

Every night he would put off going to bed but ultimately he knew he was postponing the inevitable. So he walked. Tried to tire himself out, reach a state where his body would accept sleep but not dreams.

Newcastle fascinated him. It described itself as a city but felt more like a market town. Nine thirty at night and the streets were virtually deserted. He passed pubs, glimpsed men inside drinking, playing darts and dominoes, talking, not singing. Mini communities dotted on corners. The men Dan Smith had mentioned. Jack considered entering, buying himself a pint, striking up a conversation. But he couldn't do it. He would just want to talk about the things he tried not to think about. He would be spotted, shunned as different. He would be alone in there.

He walked, not thinking, not noticing where he was going. Head down, cap pulled tight, hands in pockets, eyes narrowed.

''Scuse me, have you got the time?'

The voice, playful, singsong. Local inflections, universal cadences.

He looked up. He was standing in front of the Essoldo cinema. He had walked to the bottom of Westgate Road. The woman who had spoken to him had blonde hair, curled and bobbed, just tidy enough. Blouse and skirt, stockings and heeled shoes, black overcoat. The blouse had been opened to reveal the tops of her small breasts. She wore heavily applied make-up, a child's approximation of how an adult should look.

She smiled at him.

'Pardon?' he said.

'I asked,' she said, pushing up the playfulness in her voice, 'if you've got the time?'

Jack fumbled back his sleeve, looked at his watch. Then the penny dropped. He looked up, straight at the girl.

'Sorry,' he said, 'I'm not interested.'

They looked at each other. The girl smiled.

'Are you not?'

Jack shook his head.

'Sure?'

Jack nodded.

'Only you haven't walked away yet.'

She moved towards him, legs slow, hips gyrating languorously. She pulled her coat away from her sides so he would have an unimpeded view of her figure.

'Have you?'

Jack swallowed, his throat parched earth.

'I haven't . . . haven't got any . . . much . . . money.'

The girl smiled.

'We'll see what we can do. What's your name?'

'Juh . . . Jack.'

Her fingers stroked his jacket lapels, his shirt. The movements were well practised, clinical. Jack ignored that. He concentrated only on her fingers. The feel of another person touching him. He began to get an erection.

'This your first time, Jack?'

He began to shake his head – no – then stopped. He had been with whores in the army. They had been in every country, in every town, outside every barracks. His regiment, roaring boys all, had used whores as they had used drinking and fighting: a natural way to relax, to let off steam.

But that was in a previous life. That had happened to a different person.

'Yes,' he said, 'first time.'

'Come on, then,' she said and took his hand, leading him down the alley.

'No,' he said, stopping. He looked at the dark, the shadows. 'Not down there.'

'Where, then? You got somewhere?'

He thought of his bedroom. Tommy all snores and resentment. His bed drowning him in black, oily water. Dragging him down with the weight of memories.

He shook his head. 'No.'

She stopped moving. He felt an immediate disappointment. He wanted this woman. Or at least the use of her body for a short while. The way she had touched his jacket, his chest . . . He was hard now, built up with frustration, wanting release. Wanting her to give him release.

'Haven't you got somewhere?' he asked.

She looked at the cinema.

'We could go in here.'

'Yeah? Wouldn't they mind?'

The girl laughed.

'I don't think so. Come on.'

She led him into the lobby. Tarnished Art Deco coated with dust and loveless disrepair. Jack glanced at the lobby cards: *Things To Come*. Produced by Alexander Korda. Directed by William Cameron Menzies. It showed rocket ships, skyscrapers, spacemen. It was an old film, ten years or so. New films were as rationed as food in Newcastle.

The girl walked to the counter, Jack in tow. The man behind the counter was short, round, greasy, with more hair tonic than hair plastered across his shining pate. He gave her a smile. It curled with knowingness, unpleasantness, lasciviousness.

'Hello again, Isobel.'

'Hello, Howard. Two, please.' She hugged herself into Jack's arm. 'Me boyfriend'll pay.'

'Course he will,' said Howard, pulling two tickets off a large drum.

Jack fumbled in his pocket, brought out the correct coins, slapped them down on the counter.

Howard handed over the tickets and the change.

'Enjoy yourselves.'

'We will,' said Isobel.

They reached the doors, about to enter. Isobel stopped.

'Let's get the money sorted out first.' The playfulness had dropped out of her voice. She held her hand out. 'Twenty bob.'

'What? Twenty bob?'

'Ssh. Don't raise your voice. All right. Make it ten.'

Jack's erection was larger than his unwillingness to part with what little money he had. He fumbled in his pocket, brought out the money, handed it over, his hand shaking.

She pocketed it, plastered on her fake smile again. She gave a small shrug.

'Let's go in, then.'

Isobel entered the darkened cinema. Jack followed. She led him to a section of the cinema, beneath the projectionist's window, away from the rest of the seats. Cigarette smoke and dust curled and bounced in the shaft of light. She sat down in the shadow. Jack sat down next to her. Other customers were dotted about in twos and ones, all watching the screen. No one paid any attention to Jack and Isobel.

Jack's seat felt well sat in, the crimson velvet threadbare, springs threatening to poke through and into him, the seat hinges dropping down at an uncomfortable angle. He squirmed, tried to find a position he could settle in.

He thought of his earlier walk around Scotswood. Watching from the back of a deserted cinema. Unable to follow, unable to join in. This was different. He felt it. He hoped it.

Isobel leaned over to him, whispered, 'Excited, are you?' She placed her hand on his crotch, gave an exploratory squeeze.

'Ooh, you are.'

She kept on squeezing, pumping, building him up.

He looked around nervously.

'Don't worry,' she said, 'no one can see us here.'

She opened the buttons on his trousers, pulled out his penis, made some approving remark about it. Jack didn't hear her. He was concentrating on the feel of her fingers on himself. He opened his eyes, looked at her. She smiled at him and, with another well-practised movement, slid to her knees and licked her lips theatrically.

She bent in, started to suck.

His head rolled back. He felt the flood of sensations through the tip of his penis travel down the shaft. It was an intense, immediate feeling, a stimulation the like of which he hadn't experienced for a long time.

He gasped, closed his eyes.

And the images were back. The slaughterhouse.

The bull he had helped kill earlier: fighting for life as two inches of heavy metal were punched into its brain.

Grunts and moos, howls and squeals. Communicating their fear, their terror. Pushing and jostling, trying to escape, throwing themselves against their bars, stumbling, legs quivering, collapsing from terror and exhaustion. Knowing one of them would be next.

Then they came, unbidden: other slaughter, other carcasses.

'No . . .'

Jack hadn't realized he had spoken aloud.

'Don't worry,' said Isobel, her mouth full, 'I've got you.'

The images again, the Pathé horror newsreel.

Jack couldn't stop them, flickering back to half-life against his closed eyelids.

The stick people. Men, women and children. Skin shrunken down to their bones. Faces skeletal, eyes filled with terror.

Squashed into bunks smaller than veal crates.

Bodies piled high, bulldozed into graves.

Bones and flesh just ashes in the furnace.

People no longer human. Just meat and bone.

Walking meat.

He smelt carcasses, blood, skin.

Expertly cut, blowtorched to remove hairs then stripped from the dead animal. Waste, meat by-products, turned into coats, shoes, watchstraps, belts, anything. No limit to human ingenuity.

The bull staggered, dead but not yet realizing it.

Metal sparking off metal. Eyes lit by butchers' gleam.

Grunts and moos, howls and screams. Communicating their fear, their terror. Knowing one of them would be next.

Lambs to the slaughter.

The slaughterhouse. The abattoir.

Belsen.

'What's up with you?'

Jack opened his eyes, looked down. Isobel was holding his limp penis in her hand.

'Don't you fancy us?'

The question was asked teasingly, but her eyes held a grain of truth.

'Ye – yes.'

'Then show me.'

She began pumping him again, head bobbing speedily up and down.

He put his head back, kept his eyes open. Stared at the ceiling.

He heard voices, looked.

A celluloid Ralph Richardson talking to Raymond Massey. Both dressed in white jumpsuits. He wondered what they were saying, didn't listen. White actors in white clothes on white sets.

White.

The future.

Isobel's pace increased, head bobbed faster. He forced the other images away, concentrated on the screen, on Isobel's actions.

Cut to: the city. Huge, gleaming buildings.

White.

Images washed over him: he saw skyscrapers, tower blocks with walkways linking them, cars flying between them.

The future. He was seeing the future.

He felt movement in his body, moving towards a release.

Dan Smith's earlier words:

Stop having dreams and visions. Start turning them into reality.

He relaxed, comforted by what was before him.

Isobel's head bobbed faster.

The future.

White, gleaming.

Skyscrapers, tower blocks.

White.

He felt it, then: his body bucked, springs, wood complaining.

The future.

White.

Gleaming.

He came.

June 1956:
My Baby Love, My Baby Love, My Baby Love

Monica Blacklock lay on the bare boards, the wood cold, worn and splintering. They smelled of age and neglect. She didn't notice. She screamed and gasped: a serrated spasm of pain knifed through her belly, up her spine.

Her left hand twisted the old, threadbare, green candlewick, her right scrabbled for purchase on the floorboards. Her nails caught the wood, splinters embedded themselves under her fingertips, into her naked back and buttocks, increased the pain. She didn't notice. The pain in her belly consumed her.

Gradually it subsided, washed away. Her body regained its equilibrium in slow waves. She loosened her grip, stretched her fingers. Gulped air down, gathered herself for the next wave, hoped she would have the strength to ride it. She tried to prop herself up, support her torso and swollen abdomen. But she couldn't. Her arms trembled and shook. Bones felt brittle enough to snap. She lay back on the floor breathing deep, conserving her energy.

She hadn't felt well all day. She had woken up with pains in her back. Bad ones. She had thought it was just the strain of carrying a baby inside her. She had spoken to Brian, told him she didn't feel up to working today.

'You've got punters.' He had shrugged. 'They mean money. Don't fuckin' start with yer whingin' again.'

But Brian, she had wanted to say, it hurts. When they put it inside. It hurts. She rubbed her stomach as she thought this. She looked at his hands: knuckles pink and deflating, twitching and jumping to be reddened and reinflated. She read his mood from them. Said nothing.

It was often wise to say nothing. Brian was deaf in one ear, and Monica often found herself saying things she thought he couldn't hear, only to be painfully reminded that he had heard and fully understood.

He sat at the small kitchen table while he waited for Monica to boil the kettle, make him his morning cup of tea. He looked away from her, not even acknowledging her presence. She spooned tea from the carton into the brown pot. She set the spoon down, turned to him.

'Please, Brian. I'm eight months pregnant. This could . . . could damage the baby. Come on. Please.'

Brian looked out of the window. Grey sky above Scotswood. Black soot on the buildings.

'You've got a job to do,' he said, eyes beyond the glass. 'Do it.'

She crossed to him, stood before him, cowering slightly.

'Brian.' Her voice was fragile and small. 'Just let me use me hands. Just me hands. Or even—' she swallowed, her saliva bitter '—me mouth. I'll use me mouth.'

She looked at him, eyes flickering between his face and the table, pleading and timorous.

He looked at her, eyes fixed and direct, alive with anger and revulsion.

'They don't pay for that. If you want to do that, do it extra. But they pay to fuck a pregnant lass. An' that's what they're gonna do.'

The kettle let out a shrill, insistent whine.

'Make the tea.'

Monica turned, switched off the gas, poured hot water into the teapot. Her hand shook, water spilled on to the wooden benchtop. She kept her back to him, willing herself not to cry.

She heard the chair move behind her, the scrape of wood on lino, footsteps moving towards her. She felt hands encircle her waist, rest on her swollen abdomen. She tried to keep busy, put the lid on the teapot, but those hands, not hard yet not soft either, persistent, the only hands she allowed herself to be touched by without paying first, stopped her. She sighed the fear, the fight from her body, sank back against Brian. She felt his strength through his shirt; his frame wiry and taut, muscles like coiled, knotted rope.

'Not for much longer,' he said. 'Not for much longer.'

She sighed again, drew what comfort she could from his body, his words. She nodded, resigned.

'I'll make the tea.'

She pulled gently away from him.

He resumed his place at the table. She wiped at the corner of her eye with her thumbnail.

She poured his tea.

And that was how her day had started.

The front door had slammed shut. Her last punter leaving. There seemed to have been a long time between her first contraction, when her features contorted from faked pleasure to unchecked pain. Between him withdrawing, suddenly shrivelled and disgusted, and him leaving the flat, she had asked him for help, implored him to go and get someone. He had said and done nothing, just watched, fascinated at what was happening, mesmerized by Monica's body. But after a while it had all become too real for him. Sex and birth combining in a way that left him appalled and horrified. He had gathered his clothes about himself and left.

Any other time, Monica would have laughed. Asking help from a middle-aged, middle-class professional. Asking him to deliver a baby. A seventeen-year-old prostitute's baby. Just a child herself, really, someone whose body he had paid to use for a while.

She breathed deeply, looked around the room. It was bare, neutrally coloured. No warmth or life. Not clinical, not even neglected. Just functional. Where the punters got what they paid for. She tried to look out of the window, down into the street, but couldn't see anything beyond flat, grey sky.

She felt another wave of pain build inside her. She braced herself, gripped the candlewick hard with her left hand, just had time to notice the blood pooling beneath the fingernails of her right hand, leaving tiny trails of red on the bare boards.

The wave hit, crashed within her.

He was handsome, no doubt about that. That was the first thing she had noticed about him. And he looked like he knew what to do. Not like the other boys in the area, all fingers and panting, roughness and trembling. Not like the men, either, gropers and talkers, their pathetic lust counterbalancing their shame. He was younger than Monica, too, although he seemed much older. Like he'd had more life than he had years. She recognized that in him, knew a kindred spirit when she met one.

And the way he cocked his head to one side, listening when she talked. She liked that a lot. It made her feel like he was listening to her and her alone. Made her feel special. She didn't know it was because of his partial deafness.

She remembered their first meeting well. Nearly a year ago. She had been sitting on a bank staring at the Tyne, the factory chimneys and gasometers of Low Elswick all around her. The soot-black Scotswood bridge stretched over the slow, lapping, dark water like a huge drawbridge over some medieval moat. She imagined it could be pulled up, keeping thing she wanted inside, banishing those she didn't. This was her spot: her special place where she came to think. Straighten things out in her head.

Keep things she wanted inside, banish those she didn't.

She screwed the top off her father's hip flask, took a mouthful. She often took his flask without him knowing it. She liked the feeling of taking something from him. Cheating him. She wiped her mouth with the back of her hand. The gin was neat, and it burned as it went down. She liked it that way. She replaced the flask in a pocket within a pleat of her skirt and looked across the river to the Redheugh breaker's yard, at the piles of old metal. Scrap, worthless to anyone, she would have thought, but deemed valuable enough by someone to hang on to. She looked at the shapes the metal and shadow cast and formed, imagined not things deemed useless but a strange, new jungle populated by new and exotic beasts. A land that existed only in her head, but a land that was wholly and exclusively hers. Not scrap, not worthless, but precious and priceless. Just waiting to be seen that way.

'This private, or can anyone join in?'

Monica jumped, the voice startling her. She turned around, ready to run in case she was about to be told off for trespassing. But this was no factory worker. Dressed in a suit with a fingertip-length drape jacket, shirt and tie and crepe-soled shoes. Tony Curtis DA. A boy dressed as a man, carrying himself as a man. Smiling at her like a man.

She smiled back, suddenly aware of her bare arms, of the way the hazy white sun and the gin had made her skin, her head, tingle.

'You made me jump,' said Monica.

'You were miles away.' He looked around. They were alone. 'Can I join you?'

Despite the warmth of the day, Monica trembled.

'Uh-huh,' she said, nodding.

He sat down beside her, following her gaze to the river.

'What you lookin' at?'

'Nothin'.' She crossed her legs at the ankle. The top foot bounced off the bottom foot. 'Just thinkin'. I come here to think.'

'What about?'

She shrugged.

'All sorts. Just come here to think.'

She lay back, propped on her elbows, body stretched. The boy watched her.

'What's your name, then?'

'Monica. What's yours?'

He looked at her, smiling again. She looked up at him, his shadow looming over her, blocking out the sun.

'Brian.'

She smiled, pleased at not having to squint.

'Pleased to meet you, Brian.'

Brian lay down beside her, back flat on the grass, hands pillowed behind his head.

'Haven't seen you around here before,' said Monica.

'I'm from Byker.'

'Long way.'

'Aye.' He turned to her, smiled. The sun danced on his eyes. And Monica saw something in those eyes, something kindred. In that moment a connection was made. Monica felt warm yet shivery.

'But if I'd known you were here then I'd have come sooner.'

She giggled and blushed, turned herself away from him.

'I mean it,' he said, laughter in his voice.

She didn't reply.

'Can I kiss you?' he asked.

Monica laughed. 'You don't waste time, do you?'

Brian rolled over on to his side, body propped on one arm, legs crossed at his ankles. He was giving her that smile again. She smiled back.

'All right, then.'

He moved his head forward. Their lips met. She lay back on the grass, closed her eyes. Her head was swimming with more than the gin. She felt his hands, his legs, his body flowing over her.

And that was how their relationship had started.

She tried to breathe, to speak, use something that would help her regain control of her body and retain it. Use words instead of screams. Keep focused instead of scrunching her eyes into darkness.

'Brian . . .' she gasped through clenched teeth, strained lungs, 'Brian . . . you bastard . . .'

Another wave. Back arching in spasm, serrated knives stabbing.

'Where are you . . . you bastard . . .'

The pain dissipated. She gasped in air, felt her body unclench, unlock. She lay flat on her back. She imagined herself beached, washed up on a shore, saved from drowning in dark, oily waters, drowning in pain.

Monica blinked, felt water gather in her eyes. Salt water, threatening to spill over into tears. She gritted her teeth. She wouldn't cry, wouldn't give in. Brian would be back soon. He would help her. He would sort her out.

She felt guilty about what she'd said before, about what she'd called him. It was the pain making her say that. He'd understand, he'd know she hadn't meant it.

She sighed. Not crying, not giving in.

He'd be back soon. He'd help her. He'd sort her out. He'd look after her.

Her father hated him. Monica knew he would. She knew him well enough by now, better even than her mother did. She could tell what he was thinking, what he was feeling. She had studied his moods for years. She knew how to spot them.

Her father didn't come right out and say it; confrontation would have scared him. But she knew it. Her father hated Brian's name to be mentioned. Her mother seemed quite relieved by Brian's presence. Her two younger brothers liked him – he always gave them chocolate.

'Bloody wide boy, bloody spiv.'

Her father's rote response whenever Brian's name was mentioned. Mumbled and grumbled, never said aloud, never openly stated.

Then one day she told her father: 'I'm movin' out.'

'You're gettin' married? To that spiv?'

'No,' she said, 'I'm not gettin' married. But I'm movin' out.'

Her voice was small, hesitant.

'Where you goin', then?'

Her father put down his paper, sat looking at her from his armchair. She looked at him. Sleeveless pullover over his shirt, trousers carrying a few days' dirt. Expanding stomach, disappearing hair.

'I'm goin' to live with Brian.'

She dropped her head, looked at the floor, waited for the explosion.

Her father was out of his chair and on his feet.

'You're bloody not! You little . . . I'm not havin' you doin' that. Folks'd think you're a right little hooer.'

'Folks can think what they like.'

She surprised herself. Her voice was stronger than she imagined it would be.

Her father looked at her, shocked.

'Folks can . . .? Now, look. People hereabouts already know about you. Drinkin' an' hangin' around, an' that. People are sayin' things. There's rumours flyin'.'

Monica felt herself becoming angry.

'People round here don't know how to enjoy themselves. I do.'

'Now, listen to me. This is a respectable family . . .'

Her father was towering over her. She looked up at him, caught his eye with hers. As the look connected, some of the fire went out of his face, replaced by something else. Monica wasn't sure, but it looked like fear. She drew strength from that.

'I'm listening,' she said.

'You cannot go an' live with him. You're just a lass.'

'I'm goin'. I love 'im.'

The word 'love' hit her father like a dart. He physically recoiled from it.

'Love?' He spat the word out. 'What does he know about love?'

Monica felt the anger rising within her.

'A damn sight more than you.'

Her father looked at the floor, seemed to be staring at the pattern in the carpet. He sighed.

'Look, Monica, don't be like that. Stay here, eh? With me. Eh?' There was begging, pleading in his voice.

He made a clumsy grab for her hands, caught them. His hands felt like two enormous worn, cracked leather gloves. They were wet and shaking. He pulled her over to his armchair, sat down, still holding her hands.

'Come an' sit on me lap, eh? Come on, we'll talk about it.'

'I'm too old for that, aren't I?'

Her voice dripped vitriol.

He kept pulling at her, tugging at her wrists. She resisted.

'Come on, pet, sit down.'

His voice all warm and paternal, yet shaking below the surface.

She resisted.

He pulled harder.

'Don't be like that . . .'

'I told him, you know.'

Her father stopped pulling. He looked at her.

Monica's voice trembled. Her legs were shaking. She suddenly wanted to go to the toilet.

'Brian. I told Brian what you used to do to me.'

She felt wetness in her eyes. She blinked it back.

Her father stared up at her, his face clouded and crowded with emotions. All of them unreadable.

'He said . . .' She swallowed. Her throat had gone dry. 'He said if you touch me again, he'll fuckin' kill you.'

Her father stared at her. Beyond shock.

'I'm leavin' now. An' I'm goin' to live with Brian.'

She turned and walked out of the house, body burning with a heat more than embarrassment, more than rage.

She set off down the street. Inside, in her heart, she felt a change. The heat of her inner crucible was forming a new person. A stronger, happier one that could look to the future.

She found a wall, sat down, stared at the Tyne. She put her hand in her coat pocket, felt something in there. She drew out her father's hip flask. She shook it: liquid sloshed inside. She opened it, lifted a shaking hand to her mouth and drank. It burned.

She stared down at the Tyne, looked to the future.

And let the tears fall.

'Aw, no. I've pissed mesell . . .'

Monica looked at the bare boards. Wetness blossomed from her body, spreading wide, soaking into the wood. The backs of her legs, the base of her spine were wet.

She began to panic. This wasn't urine. It didn't smell right. It was another rebellion by her body, another piece of ignorance about the way she worked.

She wished Brian was there.

Another spasm.

Followed by an urge to push, to confront the pain, the terrible strangeness of her body, and face it down. The urge was overwhelming. She couldn't fight it.

She gasped, grimaced.

And pushed.

Brian wasn't the first. But she wished he had been.

There were all the men in all the rooms, curtains drawn, smelling of enforced loneliness and unhealthy obsession. Her father's friends and acquaintances. They had used her, hurt her, scared her. Sometimes they had been kind to her afterwards, sometimes cruel. Most times they would just turn away from her, turn inside themselves. Ignore her. In time she had come to accept it.

Her mother never asked where she had been. Not once. Monica would always go up to the room she shared with her brother and hope he wouldn't be there, hope she could be alone.

At night the dreams came. Her daytime experiences relived through a subconscious, nightmarish filter. The men from the rooms would be in hers. Repeating their terrible acts. Starting on her again. She would wake, sometimes screaming. Sometimes her father would be there. Sometimes she would be alone. Never would there be any comfort.

This stopped when hair and breasts began to appear. Then her father and his friends didn't want to know her. The rejection was so sudden and so harsh she was wounded by it. She didn't know what to do. She blamed herself. She felt undesirable, unattractive. She felt spurned.

She started going out. Hanging around pubs, getting men and some of the older boys to buy her drinks. In return she let them touch or even have her if they were nice enough.

In back alleys, in other men's houses while their wives were out. Down by the Tyne, at the backs of the factories. They took her everywhere. She would urge them to push into her hard, to make her feel it, and they would oblige. But the harder they pushed, the deeper they went, they never touched her inside. She would hold on to them, push herself against them, feel their rubber-sheathed thrusts, but it never happened. It never went deep enough.

Sex but not love.

In deep, but feeling nothing.

Until she met Brian.

He felt like the first.

He talked to her, wooed her even. Looked at her in a different way from the others. Like he really knew her, what it felt like to be her.

Love. That's what it felt like to her. She told him often that she loved him. He just smiled. She expected that. Men weren't good about saying those sort of things, she knew.

He took her out, bought her presents. Told her she was special, different. She responded, fell for everything he said.

After she had moved in with him and had the memory of her father's displeasure happily lodged in her mind, things began to change.

The presents stopped coming. The compliments stopped being given. Things began to be expected of her. Duties had to be performed.

Brian shared a house in Fenham with two others, both like him. She didn't know what the three of them got up to when they went out, how they made their money, what arrangement they had with the landlord about living there. She didn't care. As long as he came back to her. As long as he gave her money, kept her. That was the important thing. She was also expected to cook, clean and look after the three of them. She had her reservations, but she put them to the back of her mind. This was for Brian, this was for the man she loved. It was what was expected of her.

Then there was that one night. And afterwards nothing was the same.

The three lads had come in well after dark in high spirits, laughing and joking, alluding to what they had been doing, carrying the smell of the night on them. Whatever they found funny had been at someone else's expense. Monica didn't listen. It didn't concern her.

They had wanted music. She had turned on the wireless, but they wanted records. She had reached for her new Alma Cogan disc, 'Banjo's Back in Town', but they didn't want that.

'Vincent,' said Brian.

She swallowed a sigh, re-sleeved the disc. She liked the song. The melody was simple but hummable. Bright. It made her happy. She reached for Brian's choice. Gene Vincent – 'Be Bop A Lula'. It was all the things Alma Cogan wasn't. Dark. Complex. It didn't make her happy. It stirred up unpleasant feelings within her. She imagined it did the same to Brian. She imagined that was why he wanted to hear it.

She put it on.

'Hey,' said the oldest, Eddie, slumped in an armchair and dropping an empty beer bottle on the carpet, 'I wanna 'nother drink. Monica, gerrus another drink.'

Monica got up, picked up the fallen bottle, crossed to the sideboard, took out another bottle. She picked up the opener.

'Nah,' Eddie said. 'Whisky.'

She put the bottle opener and bottle back, took out the bottle of whisky and a glass, took it Eddie. She stood in front of him pouring.

'I'll tell you when.'

The whisky reached the halfway mark.

'When.'

She passed him the glass. He took a mouthful, swallowed, grimaced.

'Me an' all,' said Brian, holding up his empty glass. He was one whisky ahead of Eddie.

Monica crossed the floor, filled up Brian's glass. She knew the level he liked his drink to be at. He winked at her when she had finished. It was a cold gesture, impersonal. The kind a tightfisted gambler gives to a cloakroom girl in a casino. Service rewarded. She smiled back at him, hesitantly. She had become as adept at reading his moods as she had been her father's. He was drunk. Mean drunk.

Gene Vincent yelled more, more, more.

Brian gestured to Brimson, the third man, then to the bottle.

'Nah,' Brimson said, shifting in his seat. Monica could see he was already very drunk. He looked her up and down as she stood in the middle of their sitting room holding the bottle, smiled. It was a smile she had seen many times before. Not just on him. 'I wan' somethin', but not that.'

Brian stared at Brimson, his hollow eyes boring in to him. Brimson slipped from drunkenness to sudden sobriety. He swallowed hard. At first he wasn't sure Brian had heard him, but looking at Brian's expression he knew he had.

A grim smile split Brian's face, like a hard blade slicing through soft flesh.

'Cost you,' he said.

Brimson looked at him, tried to gauge Brian's seriousness.

'All right,' he said eventually. 'You're on.' He dug into his pockets, brought out crumpled notes, tarnished coins. Brian plucked the notes from him.

Brian turned to Monica, pointed.

'Go on.'

He nodded at her. She stared back at him, unmoving, unable to speak.

Gene Vincent sang that Lula was the one that loved him so.

'Go on.'

Brian was becoming angry at not being obeyed. Monica didn't want him to get angry. Moving slowly, as if her life had just tipped over into an unbelievable dream, she crossed to where Brimson was sitting in the armchair. He was already unbuttoning his trousers, slipping off his braces. She looked around the room, felt her face flush with embarrassment and humiliation.

'I love you, Monica,' said Brian, his voice harsh, like flesh dragged over broken glass. 'If you love me, you'll do it.'

She looked at him, the knife-like smile still in place on his face. She kneeled down in front of Brimson, took his semi-limp penis in her hand.

'That's right, pet,' Brimson slurred, laughing, 'give it a good clean.'

The other two laughed.

She bent into his crotch, took him in her mouth. He tasted as if he hadn't washed for several days. She did as she had been bid, working at keeping his drunken erection, holding him in place until he came.

She tried not to think about what she was doing. It became secondary. She thought of the word. It was the first time Brian had said it to her.

Love.

'Me next,' said Eddie. His trousers were already down to his ankles.

She repeated the act with him, all the while trying to ignore the taste and the smell, trying to absent herself from her actions. Trying to focus on the one word:

Love.

That's what Brian had said.

She finished off Eddie, grimacing and trying to hide it, and stood up. She turned to face her boyfriend, found a smile, put it on.

Gene Vincent sang of his baby love, his baby love, his baby love.

Love.

'What about you, Brian? Your turn now?'

He turned to her, eyes as cold and hard as the stone their house was built from.

'Whore.'

A whisper. A venomous, disgusted whisper.

'Fucking whore. Slag. Fucking slag.'

The words long-drawn-out, every syllable enunciated to its twisted maximum.

He lifted his arm, drew it back to strike her. Monica dropped her head, cowered in fear before him. She let out an involuntary whimper.

'Howay, Brian, man.' Brimson. 'Divvent hit 'er, man. She'll not do it again.'

Brimson's voice cut the tension in the room, broke the spell. Eddie tried to laugh. Brian turned to him as if seeing him for the first time. The laugh died on Eddie's lips. At that moment Monica became aware of the relationship between the three men. Brian was the boss. Brian was the one the other two feared.

Brian turned back to Monica, blinked.

'Get to bed.'

Monica just stared at him.

'Bed.'

Her lower lip trembling, her eyes beginning to moisten, she turned and made for the stairs.

Alone in the bedroom she let it all out.

She was still awake when, hours later, Brian came up to bed. She was on her side staring at the curtains, watching the new day appear, hoping that it would bring with it enough light to illuminate the dark corners.

The bedsprings creaked as Brian slid beneath the blankets and sheets, moved in to her. She felt his erection poking in to her back, his hands roughly working their way between her buttocks, her thighs. His fingers probing her vagina, pulling it open. His penis forcing its way inside her. Skin on flesh; for the first time no rubber between them. The rough friction of his back and forth thrusts. The tremble in his abdomen, his thighs as he came inside her. The instant withdrawal and squeal of bedsprings as he flopped on his back. The tickle between her legs as his semen slowly trickled out of her. She heard his snores as he fell into instant sleep. She sighed. She didn't move.

She lay on her side staring at the curtains.

He had said the word. He had told her he loved her. And even rough love was better than no love at all.

She was watching the new day appear, hoping that it would bring with it enough light to illuminate dark corners.

But doubting it.

They all slept in the next day. Brian woke Monica, told her to get up, make him his breakfast. Fearing what would happen if she refused, she did as she was told.

Downstairs in the cramped kitchen, she cooked him bacon and egg.

Brimson and Eddie didn't stir.

'I've been thinkin',' said Brian, forking a load of egg into his mouth, sucking the yolk in.

She turned from the sink to face him. Stood expectantly.

'What you did last night.'

Her stomach turned over.

'I've been thinkin' you should do that. Make some money.'

He put his knife to a slice of bacon, tore a strip off, pushed it into his mouth. He chewed, swallowed, looked up.

'D'you reckon?'

Monica stared at him.

'D'you reckon.'

Malice and menace had entered his voice. Not a question this time.

Monica didn't know what to say. She couldn't agree with him, and she didn't dare argue. Instead she heard herself say: 'You said love.'

Her voice was tiny and frail, like a bird not daring to fly.

'What?'

She cleared her throat, preparing her wings.

'Last night. You said love.'

'So?'

He shrugged, went on eating.

'Love. It's the first time you've said it to me.'

He finished his breakfast, rimmed the plate with his fried bread to sop up the juices, crammed it into his mouth. Chewed. Swallowed.

Monica remained standing, staring at him.

'You've never told me you love me.'

Brian took a mouthful of tea, looked up.

'I've never told you I love you?'

The words sounded foreign, alien to his mouth.

'No.'

Brian stared at her, blank-faced. Then he smiled. As he did so, his eyes seemed lit by a strange light.

'So if I tell you I love you, you'll do it?'

Monica stared at him.

He gave a small, snorted laugh, shook his head.

'I love you.'

He took another slurp of tea, set his mug down.

Monica stared at him, her eyes unreadable.

'I'll do it, then.'

Then, a couple of months later, the news. The news that she thought would end that part of her life, usher in a new, happier one.

Illuminate the dark corners.

'I'm gonna have a baby.'

She smiled when she told Brian.

Brian looked at her.

'So?'

'So I can stop working.'

Brian shrugged.

'You won't show for a while. You can keep goin'.'

She felt herself reddening.

'And then what? What about when I start to show?'

Brian shrugged again.

'We'll just have to find some punters who like pregnant lasses.'

He shrugged on his drape, checked his quiff in the mirror, walked out of the house.

Monica sat there alone in the living room. She looked around. The sun streamed in through the windows. Dust motes danced in the light. But there were dark corners the sun couldn't reach.

There would always be dark corners the sun couldn't reach.

She was gasping, panting, as the baby's head began to emerge.

It poked out from between her legs, purple and gnarled, covered in blood.

Blood. It was everywhere. Pouring out from between her thighs, darkening the wooden floor, dripping down between the boards. Covering her hands and arms, making them slippery. She wiped them on her body, left long red streaks.

She pushed, gasping again, groaning through gritted teeth, propped up on her arms. The pain was intense. She had experienced nothing like it before. As if her body was being ripped apart, flesh peeled off the bone like the skin peeled from an orange. Like trying to shit a melon.

She pushed again.

The baby was head and shoulders out now.

She had to stop, to rest. She was exhausted; she could push no more.

She looked down, the baby half in, half out of her body.

Panic again gripped her. She didn't want to go on, but she couldn't stop. She screamed in frustration. Wished for somebody to make it stop, take it all away. Deal with it for her.

She had the sense at that moment of being alone. Not just in the room, on the floor, but in her life. No one there to help her, to reach her. Alone.

Apart from this thing sticking out of her.

She pushed again, sobbing, wanting the ordeal to be over.

The baby moved further out, further then, almost with a pop, slipped fully out and lay there on the floor.

Monica breathed deeply, gasping, relieved as if she'd just run twenty three-minute miles.

The baby moved its arms and legs, its head. Lay there on a bed of blood and boards.

She looked at it, at the cause of all her pain, at the cord that joined her to it.

She felt something else move inside her and gasped again as the red and purple mass of afterbirth appeared.

Monica looked again. At the body lying there. Helpless.

And wondered what Brian would say. What kind of wedge it would drive between them?

She didn't want to, but she knew she would have to pick it up. Hold it.

Then cut that cord as soon as possible.

Brian leaned over the table, stick in hand, one eye closed. He lined up his shot, white on red, drew back the stick, pushed it forward. White rolled heavily into coloured – *clack* – like bone brought down on bone. He liked that sound. Drew comfort from it. He watched, eyes narrowed, lip corners twitching, anticipating the smile signal from his brain. The red rolled to the corner pocket, overhead light reflecting and bouncing from its surface as it travelled, to disappear silently into the black-leather-trimmed string pouch.

Brian allowed a smile to reach his face, but not of joy: one acknowledging natural superiority, offering the pocketed ball as evidence. He straightened up, resisted the temptation to run his comb through his Tony Curtis and lined up the next shot.

Behind him on the far wall, the jukebox was belting out 'See You Later, Alligator', Bill Haley and the Comets.

Brian heard it through his one good ear. Fat old bloke, thought Brian. Ought to be ashamed of himself cavortin' like a kid at his age.

The song clattered to an end to be replaced by Elvis Presley: 'Heartbreak Hotel'. Now that bloke knew the score. Brian would have sung along if he were the sort who sang. He would have danced or at least shuffled his feet, but that just wasn't him. Instead he took his smoking Woodbine from the ashtray, dragged deep, replaced it, narrowed his eyes at the table again. Calculated the angles.

Black off left-hand side cushion, in at the right-hand middle pocket; not too much spin, only shave the corner of the coloured ball.

Perfect.

He leaned over, lined up, drew back, pushed forward. Hit. Left side cushion to right-hand middle pocket, shaving the corner of the coloured ball. And in.

He stood up, took a drag. Elvis Presley declared himself so lonely he could cry. Brian blocked the sound from his ear, focused on the table.

Brimson sat at the table keeping score, his cue unused at his side, working his way down a John Player and a pint of beer. Resigned to sitting there a long time.

Brian looked at the table, worked out his next move. He stared at the balls, confident of winning; confident enough to let Presley in, let his thoughts stray towards Monica. Monica, Monica, Monica. Monica without a kid was fine. She serviced the punters. Brought in money. Kept the house clean and tidy. Monica pregnant and swollen was even better. In that state she broadened her appeal to two types of punter: those who wanted her like that, and those who didn't care either way. Of the two, the first type was less plentiful but that was good. They paid more. Brian liked that. Enjoyed selling something rare.

She was due to have the kid soon. A son and heir. That's what it would be. He had heard that babies were hard work, needed a lot of looking after. Made demands, drained energy and money. That wasn't his problem. Monica was the mother. That was her job. His was to bring in money. And once it had arrived and Monica had got used to it, she could carry on working. In fact, he might even get her pregnant again. He liked the extra money.

Contemplating the green baize angles, he became aware of a figure moving quickly towards him in his peripheral vision. He instinctively grabbed the cue, turned, ready.

It was Eddie. Hurrying, sweating, shirt untucked from the waist of his drainpipes, quiff collapsed on one side of his head like a dirty blond wave breaking against the shore of his forehead.

'Brian . . .'

He stood breathless, back bent, palms on thighs, mouth clutching at air.

Brian grabbed for his drape, pulled it on. Brimson did the same, struggling his fat frame from the chair, shrugging his jacket over his meaty shoulders. Eddie's condition could mean only one thing, Brian thought. The Bells.

Brian mentally inventoried his pockets: brass knuckles. Sweeney Todd knife. Back-up blade in case he lost Sweeney. Comb, so he looked good while he was working. The tools of his trade.

The Bell brothers and the Mooney brothers went back years. Brian's older brother Nabs, or Noel as he preferred to be called now, and his gang had declared the Bells potential rivals. No real reason: Noel's chief employment was cigarette hijacking, debt collecting and protection strong-arming. The Bells, he said, wanted a piece of all that. The Bell brothers, Kenny and Johnny, were informed. Whether it was true or not, they had been more than ready to fight. So it became a turf war. Pecking order. Respect. This town ain't big enough. All to play for.

'The Bells?' asked Brian.

Eddie nodded.

'Where?'

'Goin' into the Ropemakers. I ran straight here.'

'Good.' Brian thought, mind flicking through possibilities, seeking UN-like justification for intervention. 'On our turf. Let's go.'

Brian made for the door, a panting Eddie following. Brimson drained his pint glass and rolled behind them. The three left the snooker hall.

Elvis Presley sang that he'd been so long on Lonely Street he wasn't able to look back.

*

They walked down Raby Street in Byker, all the while looking behind them for a bus that would stop. They were keyed up, tense. Building themselves up for a fight. Brian's intensity was deepest. He moved like he had a sci-fi film force field around him, a plastic bubble; he could see out but he couldn't be touched.

No bus in sight; they had a walk ahead of them. Eddie and Brimson smoked, talked. Pumped themselves up. Brian said nothing. His face gave nothing away: blank, smooth and hard like stones on a beach. But inside, his guts squirmed like a snake pit: serpents of different sizes, weights and aspects, all writhing, biting, fighting for prominence.

Eddie and Brimson left him alone, assumed he was thinking of the impending ruck. But he wasn't. It was Monica again. Impending birth and imminent fatherhood; the two songs on the jukebox. He knew he should dismiss the thoughts: they were dangerous; they'd weigh him down in the fight to come, make him heavy when he should be nimble.

But to dismiss the thoughts he had to confront them. Honestly.

Monica. And his guts churned further. And there were the doubts again. Not just doubts – fears. That she was turning into his mother. That he was turning her into his mother.

A slag. A whore.

Brian had grown up in a house of hate. He hated his father, because of or in spite of the fact that he left them early. His mother had never given him any romantic, embroidered excuses as to his absence: just that he was a bastard who had left them. Brian had speculated for years, the younger he was the more fanciful the explanation: a fighter pilot shot down and taken prisoner during a secret mission after the Second World War, about to walk through the door at any moment. And then, when that didn't happen: not missing, but heroically killed in action. As Brian got older, his heroes changed: maybe his dad was in prison for a daring jewel robbery. Maybe he was an undercover policeman who couldn't reveal his identity. Maybe he was in the secret service, spying in an exotic foreign country. Then with age came gradual realization: he was living with another woman. He didn't care about Brian, Noel or his mother. He was in prison, but not for anything glamorous. He was drunk in a gutter somewhere. Brian didn't know what was worse: knowing or not knowing. It didn't matter. He hated both equally.

He hated his mother because she was a slag with no love in her body. She would never give them anything of herself, never even tell them anything. Brian didn't even know whether he and Noel shared the same father. He could never remember his mother looking happy. Always shouting and hitting him. It didn't matter what he did, whether he was good or bad, the result was the same. He tried to be good, tried to make her love him by doing things to make her smile, make her happy. He would tidy up the house, wash the dishes. But it didn't work. She would still shout at him, still hit him. After a while he stopped trying.

Sometimes she would get upset and give him a hug, cry and say she was sorry. That she was going to be good to him and Noel, look after them properly from now on. Brian used to smile and hug her back. Tell her he loved her. Wait for the next day to come, hoping everything would change, life would get better. But it didn't. Next day would be the same. And the day after that. He cried at first, but after a while even that ceased.

She had a powerful arm on her. He would carry with him a ringing memory of that for his whole life. She had once smacked him with her open palm on the side of his face for some imagined upset. The blow left a livid, red handprint on his skin that took nearly a week to disappear. It also caught his ear full on, bursting not only his eardrum but causing so much internal damage that his loss of hearing in that one ear became permanent.

She never apologized: something else to add to the hate list.

And gradually he became the person she turned him into.

Then there was his brother. He hated Noel for many reasons. His two working ears, his constant attempts to get his mother's attention. The fact that he might have had a different, better father. The fact that he knew Brian better than anyone else, knew his secrets, had seen him cry.

His mother had brought Brian and Noel up alone. Brian knew where the money had come from, what his mother had to do to earn it. And he hated that. His mother never discussed, never explained. Sometimes she would go out smelling of cheap perfume and come back reeking of cheap booze, fag smoke and other people's bodies. Brian didn't like that, but disliked it even more when she brought the men back with her. Brian and Noel hated them. All of them. They would stand and stare at them, eyes angry the first few times, but over the years that passion dulling. Eventually they just stared blankly at the men or just ignored them. But they never stopped hating: deep inside the fires kindled, the embers smouldered. At first his mother would send the boys outside, but after a time she stopped worrying about their presence in the house, although she never fucked in front of the boys, not even if a punter wanted to. And she never let the boys join in, even if the punter was offering very favourable terms.

She always took them through to the back room and closed the door. The boys could still hear through the walls. They would turn the radio up – *Educating Archie*, Arthur Askey – but the jokes weren't funny and the laughter made him sick. It was the sound of a world without worries enjoying itself. Brian knew that world existed; he just didn't have a clue how to get into it.

The men were all different: tall, short, fat, skinny, hairy, bald, smelly, clean, and everything in between. But they all made the same noises. Grunting, sweating, shouting, begging. Sometimes they sounded funny – funnier than that stuff on the radio. His mother's sounds were always the same too: quick and sharp, gasping and sighing. Like the men were punishing her and she was taking it.

The years passed. Brian tried not to be in when the men came calling. He hated them and all that they represented. His mother didn't notice the absence of her sons, and Brian and Noel began to see how the world really was, how things worked. The necessity of making a living. How important money was, and it didn't matter what you had to do to get it. Brian began to understand what his mother was doing and why she was doing it. And he still hated her for it. He hated the world for it. But he wasn't going to let the world do that to him.

Then there was Monica. He had thought she was different at first. But she wasn't. Just another slag, another whore. Another woman.

Just like his mother.

They crossed Walker Road towards Glasshouse Street.

The snake pit squirmed: different sizes, weights and aspects, all writhing, biting, fighting for prominence.

Mental confrontation had helped. He hadn't solved his problems, but the memories had stoked him up. Given him anger and ire. A focus for the fight.

'Nearly there, lads,' he said.

The Ropemakers Arms. Out of the city centre towards Byker, down Glasshouse Street in among old factories and wasteland. A person had to have a reason to visit, or no reason to leave. Grim enough in the daytime, but the night gave it a layer of almost impenetrable blackness, the large buildings

creating deep, dark shadows. The Tyne curved away from the
city towards the North Sea, giving oily slaps at the banks,
chugging away its accumulated debris. The Ropemakers sat
squat and ugly on the last corner before the river. The
windows were dark, a faint light barely discernible from
within. The walls once whitewashed, now sooted and dusted
down to a dull grey, the wooden door closed, rotting from the
base up. No attempt made at enticement or invitation. A
casual drinker would have had to be very, very thirsty to
enter.

Brian, Eddie and Brimson were not casual drinkers. They
were purposeful. They stopped outside, slid brass knucks
into place, practised easy blade access. They pushed open the
door, entered.

The air was thick with smoke, stale beer and grime. The
few drinkers in the place were old and tired-looking. There
because they had nowhere else to go. Dotted about were
small, shifty individuals, human rats scurrying about in the
skirting boards of society. They all looked up. Hands quickly
replaced objects in pockets. They recognized Brian and his
two lieutenants. Guessed what was about to happen. Froze.

Brian looked around, scoping for the Bells. He heard
laughter from the back of the pub, looked at the other two.
They nodded. As one, they made their way through the pub.

'Aw, now, lads . . .' said the barman. 'Not here, not again,
lads, leave them be . . .'

They ignored him, kept on walking.

A ratty old curtain partitioned the back room from the
main bar. Brian pulled it back. Dust rose from it along with
the smell of decay. Revealed were Kenny and Johnny Bell
plus two of their cronies. Kenny hard-faced, lip curled in a
perpetual snarl, Johnny the softer, more thoughtful, sneakier
of the two. All dressed in teddy boy thug chic, DAs shining
and perfectly crafted, winkle-pickers and brothel-creepers

shined, cigarettes perched on ashtrays. Kenny Bell was at the snooker table, lining up a shot. Blond and mousy, small and smug. He looked up in surprise.

'What the fuck—'

He stopped, saw who it was, straightened up. Saw the light glinting off the brass knucks. Didn't smile. Behind him the others stiffened, ready.

'Hello, Kenny,' said Brian. 'You're trespassing.'

Kenny looked at him.

'Fuck off, Mooney. This isn't your patch an' you know it.'

No messing. Straight down to business.

'That's where you're wrong, Kenny. This *is* my patch. An' I'm askin' you all to be gents an' leave.'

The barman put his head around the doorframe.

'Listen, lads, not in here. Take it outside, will youse? I mean it. I'll call the police.'

Everyone in the room ignored him. They knew he wouldn't call the police. They would ask him too many uncomfortable questions.

Kenny held the snooker cue across his body, grasped it in both hands.

'No deaf little cunt tells me where to go.'

Brian balled his fist, felt the metal around it, his body charge, swung.

Kenny Bell ducked to his left, the swing went right, catching him on the shoulder. Ignoring the pain, he turned, arcing the air with his cue. Brian stepped back out of range.

'Right, lads, that's it. I'm callin' the police.'

With that, the barman made his exit.

'Howay!' said Brian.

Eddie and Brimson waded in. Kenny's brother Johnny picked up his cue and swung. It connected with the side of Brimson's head. Brimson hit the filthy floorboards with a crash and a moan, hair exploded, a DA atom bomb.

Johnny allowed himself a small snigger that annoyed Brian all the more.

Kenny Bell was coming at him again, swinging the snooker cue at his face. To his left, one of Kenny's gang was making his way quickly towards him. Brian darted around the side of the snooker table, laid a quick punch to the advancing gang member, catching him in the throat. His hands went towards the injury, Brian was in again, another punch. Same place. The man went down.

Brian's head was yanked swiftly back. He couldn't breathe. He put his hands to his throat, found Kenny's cue constricting air, Kenny pulling hard, pushing his knee into Brian's back. Air and spit gurgled in Brian's throat.

'Cunt . . .'

Brian heard Kenny Bell's voice in his ear, smelled his beery, tabby breath. Black spots danced before his eyes. He was choking; air cut off from his lungs, blood from his brain. He had to do something.

He felt up his sleeve for his blade. Sweeney, hidden in his sleeve. He worked the blade out, let the handle fall into his palm. Turning it backwards, he thrust it with as much strength as he had left. It connected with Kenny's thigh, sunk in. Nothing for a few seconds, then, as the pain hit, Kenny screamed and let loose his grip. The cue fell to the floor. Brian pulled the knife free, turned. Kenny was standing, both hands on his leg trying to stem the blood with his fingers.

'Fuckin' 'ell, man. Look what you've done . . .'

Brian heard movement behind him: breaking glass, feet. Johnny Bell was charging at him, the jagged neck of a brown ale bottle stretched outright in his hand, anger twisting his face. He lunged.

Brian sliced the knife at the air in front of him, missing the bottle's arc. It caught Johnny on the arm. He dropped the broken bottle. It hit the faded baize of the snooker table and rolled away, clanking lightly against the white.

Johnny grasped his arm where the cut had been made. Brian swung again. Johnny put his hand out to ward off the blow. The knife caught the palm of his hand. Blood spurted. Brian, seeing that, seeing the expression on Johnny's face, laughed.

'Ha! Like that, eh? Want some more, do you?'

He sliced again. Johnny stumbled back, dodging the impact. Hit a stool, fell.

'Not so fuckin' big now, are you, cunt?'

Brian aimed a kick at Johnny's balls. He tried to move away but was too slow. The kick connected. Fear etched itself on Johnny's face, fear and pain. Brian kicked again. And again. Not caring where he hit, only that he connected. Again. And again.

And then a searing pain lanced across the small of his back. He fell to his knees, dropping the knife on the floor as he went. He turned his head. Kenny Bell, blood soaking through his suit trousers, running up his arms, stood there, cue in hand.

'Leave him alone, you bastard.'

He swung the cue again. Brian dodged out of the way. The cue landed painfully on his leg. He pulled his leg away, rolled under the table. He saw two pairs of legs at the other side, saw Brimson's prone body on the floor, saw the unconscious body of the Bell gang member he had felled. He made out one of the pairs of legs as Eddie's. He couldn't make out who was winning. He reached into his sock, expecting to find his back-up blade.

But it wasn't there.

It must have fallen out when the pool cue hit his leg. Breathing hard, swallowing down panic, he surveyed his options. With nothing to lose, he rolled out from underneath the table and attempted to get as quickly to his feet as his injured leg would allow.

Kenny was kneeling by his brother. Brian saw the broken brown ale bottle lying on the table, picked it up.

'Oi!'

Kenny turned. Brian swung the bottle, felt it connect with skin. With Kenny's face. Kenny's hands went up. Brian swung again. And again.

Kenny curled into a foetal ball. Brian, seeing no retaliation coming, dropped the bottle.

He was aware of movement behind. He turned. The Bell gang member had seen what had happened to Kenny and made his way out of the door, quickly. Eddie, out of breath again, bruised and dishevelled, came over to join Brian. Johnny looked at Kenny's face, looked up.

'Get an ambulance!' he said.

'Fuck off.'

'Look what you've done to 'im, man! Look at his eyes! Call for a fuckin' ambulance, man!'

Brian and Eddie looked at the mess left of Kenny Bell's face. At his leg, the blood pumping out.

'Hell's teeth,' said Eddie. 'You've done it now, Brian.'

Stars of hate were still dancing in Brian's eyes.

'He asked for it, he wanted it . . .'

'I think you'd best make yourself scarce.' Eddie looked at Brimson. He was lying on the floor, twitching. 'I think we all should.'

The barman appeared in the doorway.

'I've called the police an' I want youse all out. Youse bastards, you've done it again . . .'

He stopped, saw Kenny. Kenny had stopped moving, his breathing shallow.

'Oh, my God . . .'

'Call an ambulance,' said Johnny. 'Please.'

The barman turned away.

'Please!' shouted Johnny to his retreating back.

'You'd better go,' said Eddie to Brian. 'I'll get Brimson.'

Brian looked around.

'No, I should . . .'

'Just fuckin' go, man. The coppers'll be all over this place soon. They'll have you. Doesn't matter what me an' Brimson say. They'll have you.'

Brian nodded, seeing sense in what Eddie said.

'See you, then. I'll lie low for a bit. An' I'll see you soon.'

He turned and walked out of the pub. The drinkers watched him go.

Jack Smeaton looked in the mirror, straightened the knot of his wool tie. He fastened the top button of his shirt, fitted the tie snugly up to the collar. Checked the symmetry, smoothed the tie down. Picked up his comb, ran it through his hair. The dye was working well. Holding the colour, almost back to the brown it used to be. He shrugged on a zip-fronted, woollen, collared cardigan, pulled the zipper halfway up, adjusted it. He stepped back, looked again. The evening was to be casual, not formal. Jack reckoned he had pitched it just right.

Sharon came downstairs, adjusting the earring in her right ear. Blonde and slim, well dressed. Jack watched her approach, saw her calf muscles sliding slowly up and down beneath her skin as her stockinged legs moved, the fabric of her dress rustling and swaying. Married over three years now, and he still experienced the same mix of emotions as when he first met her: shafts of love, pangs of lust. Intermingled, intertwined, indivisible. He wanted her in every way.

'You ready?' he asked her.

She nodded, picked up her handbag. She crossed the hall and stood next to him, looking in the mirror. She raised her finger to her bottom lip, rubbed an invisible smudge of lipstick from her chin.

Jack watched her do it: the movement of her fingers, the slight pout. He watched and found perfection. He still couldn't believe she was his wife. That it was him she had chosen to marry. His colleagues and friends had joked that she was too good for him. That he would never keep up. Jack had smiled, not replied, but he knew they were right. She was too good for him. And he hoped he could keep up.

She was all he wanted. A nation of two.

She saw him in the mirror, looking at her. Turned to him.

'Do I look all right?' she said, smiling, guessing she knew the answer.

He took her in. Hair styled perfectly. Dress all Dior New Look ruched extravagance, Grace Kelly elegance. Heels the right height. Jack felt something melt inside.

'You look wonderful.' He felt himself blush as he spoke.

Sharon smiled, moved in close to him.

'You don't look so bad yourself.' She put her arms around him. 'You big, chunky man. My big chunky man.'

Jack smelled her perfume. Something French and expensive. She had been so happy when he bought it for her. Her happiness had made him happy.

He inclined his head to kiss her. She let his lips brush lightly against hers.

'Not too much,' she said. 'I don't want you to smudge my lipstick.'

She laughed as she said it. He laughed too.

Sharon looked at him, opened her mouth ready to speak, then closed it again.

'What?' said Jack.

'Nothing.' Sharon smiled.

'Is there something you wanted to say?'

She shook her head.

'It's nothing. I'll tell you later.'

She kissed him on the cheek, leaving a faint, red O. She smiled, began to rub it off.

'I've marked you,' she said.

Jack smiled.

'I don't mind.'

'No, but I'm sure Ralph Bell wouldn't want to see you wearing lipstick.'

'I hope not.'

They both smiled, eyes locking.

A nation of two, he thought, the words feeling warm within him.

'Let's get going,' he said.

He grabbed the car keys from the hall table and, hand on hand, they left the house.

Ten years. Since Jack first met Ralph Bell. And T. Dan Smith. Ten years. Sometimes it felt like a long time; other times it felt like no time at all.

The two men had changed Jack's life. Along with Sharon, saved Jack's life.

Jack had turned up at Ralph's builder's yard the morning after the night in the Royal Arcade. Ralph, good as his word, had set him on. Labouring at first: mixing cement, carrying bricks, transporting goods, erecting scaffolding. Jack had done anything and everything asked of him. The work was physically demanding and tiring, but Jack enjoyed it. It blotted out the memories during the day, and at night he went home too exhausted to dream.

He was a good worker and this didn't go unnoticed. Ralph found Jack honest, trustworthy, reliable. He began entrusting more and more tasks to him, responsibility mounting incrementally with each one. Jack rose to his challenges, more than equal to the work.

Gradually the nightmares visited less and less frequently, the flashbacks dimmed, became smaller. Things became manageable. He was able to box the memories away, contain them. Face the future.

And there was Ralph Bell: 'I've got two sons,' Ralph had once told Jack on a boozy night out, 'and, to be honest, neither're much cop. I won't say this any other time, mind, because they're still me sons, and I have to do the best for them. One pretends to be interested in the firm, but I know he's just payin' lip service, man. The other . . . you know what he's like. He's a waster, man. Couldn't care less.'

Ralph had given a deep, alcohol-fuelled sigh.

'I don't know which is worse. But I tell you. When I've got a lad like you workin' for us, why should I bother givin' the firm to them?'

Another sigh.

'I dunno . . . I dunno . . .'

Jack had said nothing, but inside had felt a huge yet conflicted pride.

Eventually Jack became second in charge of the company in all but name. With responsibility had come confidence and with confidence had come success. He was building the future. Living the future. The traumatized boy he had once been was no longer visible. Buried beneath fine clothes, hair dye and strong, positive living.

Jack was a changed man. A lucky man – he never stopped thinking how lucky.

And a card-carrying Labour Party member.

Dan Smith had been elevated to personal hero status in Jack's life. He had followed Smith's rise closely, felt connected to him. Felt his life mirrored his own. Smith had gone from Independent Socialist firebrand to council chairman in less than a decade. That pivotal night in the Royal Arcade when Dan Smith had stood before an audience opened windows and doors to Jack: showed futures, made faith, built strength. Smith was one of the greatest orators Jack had ever seen. He watched him whenever he could after that. But it was in the soapbox arena that he really excelled: holding forth down the Bigg Market in Newcastle, Hedley Street in Wallsend or the Market Place at Blyth. Smith would stand there and, armed only with a brain, a heart and a voice, turn an open space into a crowded one. Then he would hold that crowd, take it on a journey, tell it the way it was, the way it could be. Then let them go, disperse them back into their lives, leaving them thinking and discussing.

Smith had joined the Labour Party, standing for Walker in Newcastle's municipal elections in 1950. He had got in. By 1953 he was chairman of the City Labour Party.

Jack knew that Dan Smith still carried with him a vision. A radical agenda. Jack knew that Smith had been trying to push it through. Jack also knew that he and Ralph Bell would be heavily involved. That, he thought, was what dinner at Ralph Bell's that evening was all about.

'I suppose I'm going to be exiled to the kitchen again, am I?' Mock annoyance laced itself through Sharon's voice.

Jack shrugged.

'Dan's going to be there. He wants to talk to Ralph and me. It's business.'

'Isn't it always?'

Jack looked at her, taking his eyes off the road momentarily.

Sharon managed a smile. 'It's just . . . it gets very boring for me, sometimes. I know I have to support you, and much as I like them, Jean Bell and Dan's wife aren't really my cup of tea.'

Jack faced front. Looked at the road. Stared at it. 'Why not?'

'Oh, nothing big. They're just so much older than me. Than us. I don't have anything in common with them. Nothing to talk about. That's all.'

Jack sighed. Sharon had said similar things recently. Not the right kind of people. Wanting more. Should be doing this. Should be doing that. Nothing huge, and always politely stated. But the refrain seemed to be uttered more and more frequently.

'I know, pet,' he said tentatively. 'But I think this is going to be important. I've got a feeling. This could be the big one we've been waiting for. So please. Put up with it for one night. For me, eh?'

He risked taking his eyes off the road again, smiled at her. She smiled back.

He drove on. Carefully and expertly.

He looked over at Sharon, smiled again. She smiled back. Hesitantly, thinly, but a smile nonetheless. Jack drew what comfort he could from that.

He looked again at the road ahead, smile still in place.

Dinner was lamb in a cream and brandy sauce with potatoes and vegetables, bread-and-butter pudding, German wine. The meal was now over and the tinkle and chime of wine glasses, the bubble and simmer of polite conversation and the scrape and clink of steel on bone china had faded from the dining room along with the wives. The men had been left to talk.

'Fabulous dinner, Ralph,' said Dan Smith.

Ralph smiled. 'Thank you, Dan. We aim to please.'

'Jean's a marvellous cook. Never tasted lamb like it.'

Jack nodded, the movement setting off his heartburn again. He wondered how much of Dan's remark was politeness.

Ralph, Jack and Dan Smith sat in the lounge of Ralph's four-bedroom house in Gosforth. The furniture was comfortable, the décor mahogany reproduction. The room smelled of food and furniture polish.

The wives, along with Ralph's eleven-year-old daughter Joanne, were in the kitchen washing up.

Brandy and cigars. Ralph was doing things properly.

Dan Smith sipped from his snifter, swallowed. Inhaled, exhaled a long, controlled line of blue smoke.

'To each according to his need,' he said, relaxed and comfortable in the armchair, 'and my need at the moment is for a touch of luxury.'

The other two men smiled, drank from their glasses. Jack sipped, hiding his grimace; Ralph almost gulped the burning liquid down, his already red face deepening. It looked like only the latest and not the first brandy of the evening.

'Business good, Ralph?' said Dan Smith.

'Can't complain.'

Dan Smith smiled. 'Good. Because if everything goes to plan, it could be a lot better.'

Jack and Ralph exchanged glances. Dan Smith savoured the moment; drawing deeply from his cigar, exhaling slowly, his sense of theatre and presentation to the fore. 'I suppose you're wondering why I asked for a dinner invitation tonight.'

Get on with it, thought Jack. Just say it.

'In about two years' time—' Dan Smith had taken the cigar from his lips, was examining the glowing end, watching the curling smoke '—by my reckoning, we should be in a position to redesign this city.'

Jack knew the tone, the pitch. Dan Smith was building to oratory.

'It's radical stuff. If we get backing, we're going to demolish Scotswood. Clear it away. And Byker too, hopefully.'

Ralph and Jack exchanged glances once more. Dan Smith smiled.

'You're going to demolish it?' said Ralph, a smile birthing on his lips. 'Then presumably you'll want someone to build something in its place, then?'

'Exactly.'

Another exchange of glances. Jack saw something dance behind Ralph's eyes.

'So where do all the people go?' said Jack.

'Don't worry about that. Just leave that to us.'

Jack smiled. 'You mean you don't know yet.'

Dan Smith smiled in return. 'Not exactly, but we're working on it. The important thing is,' he said, 'that we demolish those slums and replace them with something better. Something people will be proud to live in. You've probably heard rumours about suchlike. Well, they're all true. But hey—' he looked between the two of them '—mum's the word, eh? We're not ready for it to be news yet.'

'For what to be news yet?' said Jack.

'What we're going to replace them with. I've been talking with artists and architects, and we should have something really amazing to show soon. Really put Newcastle on the map.'

'What?' said Jack.

'Tower blocks,' said Dan Smith. 'Cities in the sky.'

A shiver ran through Jack. A ghost of a memory.

'Cities in the sky?' said Ralph.

Dan Smith placed his brandy glass on the table, left his cigar to smoulder elegantly in the ashtray.

'Yes,' he said. 'Instead of terraces that go along and down, these go up and up. Come on, Ralph. You must have seen pictures of them in magazines. In Europe and America.'

'Yes,' said Ralph, 'but that's Europe and America. This is Newcastle.'

Dan Smith's eyes kindled, caught fire, his fervour increased. 'Imagine whole families,' he said, 'living in state-of-the-art, push-button housing. All mod cons. And around them playgrounds for the kiddies, parks, sculpture parks, even. Bringing beauty and life. There'll be garages. And shops. And libraries on their doorsteps. And schools, good schools, where they can be proud to send their children. That's what I want to build. That's the way this city should be. The North should be. The country should be.'

Dan Smith talked on, communicating his plan, sharing his vision. New roads for Newcastle. New hotels. An international airport. A university that would become a centre of excellence and access, so young people from every level of society could be educated.

He talked on. His plan. His vision. Communicating it, sharing it. Infecting Ralph and Jack like an airborne virus, so that they, too, would carry it. They listened, agreed, were swept up.

'And you want my firm to do the building, is that right?' said Ralph.

'I do,' Dan Smith said, looked at them and smiled.

Like a preacher to willing converts, thought Jack.

Ralph was fidgeting in his chair, as if unable to sit still.

'I think we're in, don't you, Jack?'

'Absolutely,' said Jack, not entirely still himself.

'Good,' said Dan Smith, picking up his brandy glass. He swirled the liquid, watched it catch the light.

'Marvellous play at the Royal last week,' said Dan Smith, looking up. '*Rules of the Game*. Pirandello. Did you catch it, Ralph?'

Sharon dried the plates, stacked them carefully on the patterned Formica work surface. The other two women were at the sink, talking: houses, theatre, schools and children. Sharon stood happily apart from them, claiming autonomy through the tea towel.

Joanne, Ralph and Jean's eleven-year-old daughter, danced between the three of them, smiling. Supposedly helping by putting things away, in reality staking a claim to be the centre of attention.

'What now?' Joanne said to Sharon, putting bone china sideplates in a cupboard.

'That's it for now,' said Sharon. 'Why don't you go and ask the men if they'd like their glasses topping up?'

Joanne made a face. 'It's so boring in there. All they do is talk. And those cigars stink.'

'That's what men do,' said Joanne's mother, Jean, from the sink. 'And you'd better get used to it. Go on, now.'

Joanne gave a reprise of her face and stomped from the room in mock annoyance.

Sharon watched her go. Her mind slipped tracks.

'You all right?' said Jean.

Sharon blinked.

'Sorry,' she said. 'Miles away.'

'I'm making tea. Would you like one?'

Sharon nodded.

'Thanks, yes.' She turned from the kitchen. 'D'you mind if I just go for a sit down?'

'Are you all right, pet?'

Jean crossed towards her, concern etched on her face.

'Yes, I'm fine, honestly. Just felt a little dizzy there.' Sharon smiled. 'Must be tired or something.'

Jean looked at her, expression unreadable.

'Yes, dear. Go in the other sitting room so as not to disturb the men. I'll bring you your tea when it's ready.'

Sharon smiled and did as she was bidden.

The sitting room air was cool yet stale, as if the room wasn't used much. Dinner smells had seeped in, lingering on in the rest of the house. The heavy wooden door kept the sounds of the house from reaching her. The room was crammed with the same highly polished, dark wood furniture and walled with the same heavy flock paper as the rest of the house; its pristine, preserved quality, its silence and the chill on the air gave it the feel of a mausoleum. She sat down on the settee, stretched her legs out, sighed.

She had met Jack at a dance. He had been there with others from work. Even then he had stood out from them. With them but not of them. Either possessing something or lacking something the other men in the group didn't have. All beer breath, Brylcreemed hair and tight suits they looked like they couldn't wait to shrug off, their eyes roved the dancehall hungrily.

But not Jack. He was different. Going along with the game, playing by the rules but not caring if it was ladders or snakes. She and her friends had already attracted the attention of several in the group. Sharon was used to attracting men. She knew how good-looking she was, thought it pointless to hide the fact. She didn't believe her looks were God-given, though. She put it down to parents who had fed her well and brought her up accordingly. She was secure about her looks, her body.

'Hey,' one of the young men beer-breathed at her, 'you look just like Marilyn Monroe. Anyone ever tell you that?'

Sharon sighed. Yes, she thought. Often. If not Marilyn then Diana Dors. Or Grace Kelly, or Kim Novak or any blonde film star.

'Marilyn Monroe?' she said. 'That's nice. Thank you.'

The young man smiled, swaying as he did so. 'D'you wanna dance, then?'

'No, thanks. Not at the moment. Maybe later.'

'Aw, c'mon . . .'

'No, I've just sat down. I'm just talking to my friends here.'

The young man looked at her, mentally decided what he thought of her, then turned back to his friends. Sharon wasn't sure, but above the dance band's cheerful tune she thought she heard the word lesbian.

She smiled to herself, head down. Better that, she thought, than him.

She looked back up, still smiling. And saw another one of the group looking at her. Here we go again, she thought, but on catching her eye he looked away.

Sharon looked again at the young man. Tall, dark-haired and good-looking. Dressed smartly, but with an air that set him apart from his companions. He didn't exude that desperation, that hungry-eyed, sexual need.

Intrigued, she looked at him again, deliberately trying to catch his eye this time. She did so, smiled at him. He almost smiled in return, but turned away quickly, blushing. Sharon was surprised. A big, handsome man like that? Blushing?

She smiled at him again, mouthed the word 'hello'.

He smiled back, mouthed the same word in reply.

Sharon sat there, waiting for him to move towards her, her body language neutral, inviting. He stepped, hesitantly at first, over to her.

Away from his pack, she got a good look at him. Tall, fit beneath his suit, good-looking with dark, shining hair. But his eyes drew her to him. They seemed to hold things she knew nothing about, tell of life seen in places a world away from her own. But those things seemed hidden, as if he only wanted to see his present world, only believe in what was around him, rather than look at the other one.

She smiled again.

The band struck up.

'Hello,' she said, for real this time.

'Hello,' he said.

She glanced side to side, waited.

He looked around as if he couldn't quite believe what was happening, what he was doing, then back to her.

His companions were watching him. Sharon's friends were watching her.

'Would you like to dance?' His voice was dry and dusty, his face red again.

Sharon stood up. 'I'd love to,' she said and held out her hand to be escorted on to the dance floor.

They walked there together; he took her in his arms and, gently at first, swept her away.

That dance, that night: Sharon hadn't gone out expecting anything. Just a night out with her girlfriends, a meal, a few drinks, a few dances perhaps. An opportunity to catch up on lives lived in separate directions since school.

School for Sharon had been Dame Allens, a private girls' school on the outskirts of Newcastle. Her parents had wanted the best for her, so they found the money to afford it. She was bright, an only child, and she loved her parents, had been happy to go along with their wishes. On her eighteenth birthday, her birthday card contained a poem her mother had clipped from one of her magazines. It told how they had sacrificed holidays, new cars, consumer goods and a better house for Sharon and her private education. It was given with love, but it just gave Sharon something to live up to, to be grateful for.

All her friends either had good jobs, university courses, or husbands in waiting to support them. Sharon had none of this, because Sharon had not known what she wanted. Her parents had been very supportive but, she suspected, had privately despaired of her. She enjoyed reading, so they enrolled her for a degree in English at King's College, which meant they could still have her living at home. She had gone along with the plan so as not to upset them but didn't know what she would do at the end of it. Teach, perhaps.

And then Jack Smeaton had waltzed hesitantly into her life. And suddenly she wanted to live her own life and not the one that her parents were vicariously living. Here was a man who was so different from the students on her course, who was doubtlessly intelligent but didn't feel the need to grow a wispy beard and talk incessantly about Kerouac and Ginsberg in order to prove it, who didn't need to spout beat poetry and existentialism to impress her into bed. He was a builder, and unashamedly so, but not what she expected a builder to be like. He believed he was doing an important job, creating a new future, a new environment, a new city. He was just as passionate about his politics. When he spoke on these subjects, his hesitancy fell away, revealing a strong, committed individual, both inspired and inspirational.

He had fire inside him. That fire began to burn within her. She fell in love.

She told her parents, explained she was leaving college before the end of the first year to marry a builder.

Her parents were horrified; saw their years of investment and abnegation coming to nothing. Their high expectations horribly lowered. But once they had met him, once they saw how happy he made her, how determined she was, their doubts evaporated. Or if not evaporated, then retracted to a size manageable enough to be boxed and withdrawn from view whenever the happy couple were in sight.

The wedding came soon after. Sharon's father gave her away, Ralph Bell was best man. Jack's own family marginalized from the proceedings. Both sides seemed happy with that.

Then, afterwards, life as a married couple. True New Elizabethans. A newly built starter home in Jesmond Dene. Their arrangement: Jack would bring in the money, Sharon would make all the decisions about the home. She read magazines and newspapers, visited shops, made informed decisions. The décor was up to the minute, Festival of Britain modern. She refused to live in the past; no dark reproduction furniture in her house. Look forward, always. Never back. Jack went along happily with her. He didn't want to look back either.

Jack: sometimes she caught him looking at her with so much love in his eyes it embarrassed her. Gave her something impossible to live up to. Other times his eyes would be vacant, gaze distant, off in another world she was denied access to, a time in his life in which she played no part. She had asked him about the war, about his life before her.

On the war: 'You don't want to know. And you certainly don't want to have to go through it.'

On life before her: 'I had no life before you.' Then that blush again.

On growing up in Scotswood: 'As rough as you could imagine. But as you say, we're going forwards, not backwards.'

She regarded him as an egg: hard, brittle exterior, holding softness within. Or an awful mess that, once released, could never be put back.

She respected his boundaries, left what was his alone.

At night he dreamed and thrashed, or sometimes clung hard to her – fingernails digging in, waking her, like a drowning man clinging to driftwood and wreckage.

She enjoyed her life with Jack on the whole, though found it a challenge to live with such a complex man.

Challenging in a positive way. On the whole.

'Here you are, pet.'

Jean entered, carrying a bone china teacup and saucer. Balancing it carefully, so as not to spill a drop, with her other hand she extricated the smallest of a nest of three tables, all darkly carved, bandy-legged mahogany, placed it down next to the arm of Sharon's chair, opened the second drawer down in the sideboard, reached in, withdrew a thick crocheted doilly, placed it on the table, set the cup and saucer down without any spillage.

'Just so it doesn't mark,' Jean said with a smile of well-worn domestic triumph.

Sharon smiled her thanks.

Jean pointed to the hot brown liquid. 'Make you feel better, drinking that. Can get a bit hot in the kitchen. Cooler in here.'

Sharon smiled again.

Jean returned the smile, a glint of something more than concern in her eyes.

The shock of the look hit Sharon. Her stomach flipped over. She knows, she thought. She knows what's the matter with me.

Jean opened her mouth to speak.

The doorbell rang.

Sharon breathed a sigh of relief.

'I'll just go and get that.' Jean stood up, smiled and left the room.

Sharon reached for her tea, lifted the delicate cup to her lips.

Noticed how much her hands were shaking.

A commotion came from the hall. Even through the heavy wooden door Sharon heard it. Voices, hurried footsteps. An added chill undercurrent wafted under the door as the front door let in the night air. She put her tea down and went into the hall, following the noise. There stood two uniformed policemen, blank faces verging on graveness. One of them looked up as she entered, gave her a cursory physical appraisal, drew a favourable conclusion for himself. She ignored him.

Jean was opening the door to the other sitting room, calling to Ralph. He came to the door.

'What?'

Then saw her expression, the policemen. Stopped.

'Mr Bell?' said the older of the two policemen. 'I'm afraid we have some distressing news. Is there somewhere we could talk?'

Ralph looked between them, uncomprehending.

'In here,' said Jean, and led them into the room Sharon had previously occupied. The police followed, the younger one again running his eyes the length of Sharon's body as he passed, Sharon again ignoring it, and closing the door behind them. Joanne appeared from the kitchen at her side.

'What's happening, Sharon?'

'The police have arrived. They want to talk to your mam and dad.'

Joanne turned immediately, made for the closed door. Sharon stopped her.

'No, don't,' she said.

'But I want to go in.'

Sharon thought of the room, mausoleum-cold. Her undrunk tea.

'Better wait a minute. See what they have to say first.'

Tension seeped from Joanne's body. Her shoulders fell.

'I bet it's my brothers.' Her voice was low, mumbling. 'Bet they're in trouble again.'

'Is this a regular occurrence?'

'Thought they were getting better. Johnny's all right. He can be quite kind. But Kenny is nasty. Really nasty.'

She looked around hurriedly in case anyone in earshot should berate her for bad-mouthing her brother.

'It's all right,' said Sharon. She touched Joanne's shoulder. Joanne almost smiled.

'Sorry, but it's true. If it wasn't for Kenny, Johnny would be OK. But Kenny . . . I don't know. Can you say that about your own brother?'

'I suppose so. If you think it's true.'

Joanne nodded, confirming the opinion for herself.

Sharon knew about Joanne's brothers. Everyone did. Kenny was wild, angry at something no one, least of all him, could identify. Johnny was the simpler, kinder of the two. He didn't possess Kenny's vicious streak, but then again he didn't have Joanne's strength either. Sharon had met him a few times and found him affable enough on his own, less so when Kenny was around. But, like a maggot-ridden apple, she thought his surface undamaged but inside she felt there was something soft and rotten at his core. It was a feeling she hadn't been able to share with Jack, knowing how close he was to Ralph but, nevertheless, it was a feeling she couldn't shake.

Neither of them were good workers, Jack had told her. They were happy to coast along, doing the bare minimum in the firm in the jobs their father had arranged for them. Virtual sinecures, in fact. The boys were Ralph's soft spot, and they knew it. They could get away with anything, and Ralph knew it.

The door behind Sharon and Joanne opened. Jack and Dan Smith stepped into the hall.

'What's happening?' said Dan Smith.

Sharon told him.

'Right.'

He walked to the closed door, knocked and entered. They heard his voice.

'Hello, gentlemen, I'm Councillor Smith. Can I be of any help?'

The policeman explained. Jack, Sharon, Joanne and Dan Smith's wife listened. The policeman's voice was muffled by the door and Dan Smith's body. They picked up key words, filled in the rest themselves: brothers hurt. Fight in a pub. Hospital. Critical. May lose his life. If he's lucky he may just lose his sight. Damaged hand. Hospital will see what they can do. Still looking for the attacker.

Joanne pushed the door open, knocking Dan Smith aside, rushing into the room. Her mother opened her arms, numbly enfolded her.

'They're good lads, really they are,' Ralph was repeating, mantra-like, but no one was listening.

'We'll have to go and see them,' said Jean, her words urgent, her voice sounding like it came from the opposite end of a long tunnel.

'Of course,' said the first policeman. 'I know this isn't a good time, but I'm afraid we'll need to ask you some questions.'

Ralph and Jean nodded dumbly.

'Can't that wait, constable?' said Dan Smith. 'These good people are suffering a great deal.'

'I appreciate that, councillor, but if we're going to catch whoever did this, we're going to need as much help as we can get.'

'Of course, of course.' He turned, addressing the room. 'Well, we'll give these good people the time they need.'

He motioned with his hand, gestured everyone but Ralph, Jean and the two policemen from the room. Outside in the hall he turned to his wife.

'I think we'll all have another cup of tea.'

She nodded, went to the kitchen.

'I'll help,' said Joanne. She followed.

Dan Smith looked at Jack and Sharon.

'Shall we have a sit down?'

The three of them entered the living room. Sharon coughed slightly at the cigar fug, the brandy fumes, waved her hand before her face.

'Sorry about the smell,' said Dan Smith, concern in his voice. 'That's men for you, I'm afraid.'

Sharon smiled out of politeness and sat down. Her head spun from slight nausea. Jack sat on the settee beside her, rubbing his stomach. Dan opposite in an armchair. He sighed but said nothing. None of them spoke. There was nothing to say. Silence hung in the air, more pungent and sickening to all of them than the cigar fumes had been to Sharon. To speak would have been to dissipate the hanging silence, weaken it, dilute its gravity.

The door opened. Ralph entered. His face was ashen. When he spoke, it sounded like ashes had lodged in his throat.

'We're going to the hospital. We've told them what we can. Which wasn't much. They wanted to know if anybody . . . if they had any . . . enemies . . .'

The words fell from his mouth as heavy as bricks. He shook his head. The others waited.

'Sorry,' Ralph said.

Dan Smith stood up, crossed to him, placed his hand on Ralph's arm.

'You've got nothing to apologize for, Ralph.'

Ralph gave a weak smile.

'What a way to end an evening.'

'Don't worry about it. Look, if there's anything I can do, anything at all . . . I'll make some phone calls. Ensure they have the very finest care.'

'Thanks, Dan.' Ralph sighed again. A huge, tectonic shift of a sigh. 'They're not bad lads. They're good workers. They're just . . . a bit wild.'

'I know,' said Dan Smith, voice dripping sincerity.

Jack remained silent.

'Listen, would somebody mind staying here to look after Joanne? She's got school in the morning.'

'We will,' said Sharon, deciding before looking at Jack.

'Thanks, pet,' said Ralph, his voice quiet, wheezy. 'You're a good 'un.'

A policeman's voice came from the hall. Ralph turned towards it.

'Aye, I'm comin'.'

Then back to the room.

'Look, I'm sorry, I've got to . . .' He made a feeble gesture towards the front door.

'You do what you've got to do,' said Dan Smith. 'Everything'll be all right here.'

Ralph nodded.

'And don't worry about what we were talking about earlier,' said Dan Smith. 'The offer still stands. That's your job, Ralph.'

Ralph looked at him as if he didn't know what he was talking about, then backed out of the doorway. They heard the front door close. They looked at each other.

'Well, what a night,' said Dan Smith. He looked at Jack. 'I was hoping it would be memorable for other reasons.'

Jack nodded, said nothing.

Sharon looked between the two men.

'I'll go and see where the tea's got to.'

'You do that, pet,' said Dan Smith.

Jack and Dan sat slowly down.

'Dear, dear, dear,' said Dan Smith, and made to retrieve his cigar from the ashtray.

'Oh, no,' he said, examining it. 'It's gone out. Got a match, Jack?'

Jack shook his head. He said nothing.

Outside, the air seemed colder, the night darker than when he had entered. Brian stood on the pavement, looked around. He either heard, or imagined he heard, sirens in the distance growing louder. Not wanting to find out if they were real or not, he turned away from the pub and began to walk briskly up the hill and back to the city.

His heart was slowing down, adrenalin dissipating throughout his system, coming down. He began to see things more clearly. Grasped for perspective. Kenny Bell dying, perhaps dead. Johnny injured. The other one he didn't know about. Eddie and Brimson injured. A pub full of witnesses who he knew would talk. Fighting was one thing, along with handling stolen goods – something else the Ropemakers was famous for – but murder was another thing entirely.

He walked on, trying not to let the panic, the sense of hopelessness well within him. Halfway up Glasshouse Street the sirens became real.

Brian looked around, tried to find somewhere to hide. A warehouse was on his left, fenced and gated. Chained. He looked at it, looked up the street, saw nowhere else to run. He took a run at the fence, managed to get a grip, began to climb. Reaching the top, he hauled himself over and fell to the ground. The sirens became louder. He ran around the side of the warehouse, away from the road. He pressed himself up against the brickwork and waited, breathing heavily.

Panic set in again, along with a new thought: what if there were guard dogs on the site? He hadn't thought of that. He stood still, allowed the sirens to come nearer, listened for growling or barking. The sirens approached, became louder, then receded as they sped to the pub. Brian breathed a sigh of relief. He waited until he thought the police and ambulance had passed then pulled himself over the fence and back on to the street.

He walked briskly, sticking to shadows and backstreets, hiding in the patches of dark between streetlights, staying away from other people. As he walked he thought.

He couldn't go home. That would be the first place they'd come. He couldn't go to Noel's for the same reason. He couldn't go back to his mother's. Ever.

He walked into the city centre. The streets were not particularly full; cinema- and theatre-goers mostly. Brian tried to keep away from them, keep his face hidden. He had to get away. Leave. He checked his pockets. He had money but not enough to get him far. He couldn't bargain, a bus driver would remember him. He couldn't steal a car as the owner would report it and wherever it was found would bring the police searching for him. He stood in the middle of Grainger Street, considered his options.

And had an idea.

He walked down to the Central Station, keeping an eye out all the time for police cars. He reached the station: tall, imposing, built in a neo-Georgian style to blend in with the rest of the area. He walked along the front, not wanting to go through the main entrance, and made his way around the side. The fencing was low. He hauled himself quickly up and over, looked around. Trains were slowly making their way in and out of the station. Only a handful; the service was winding down for the night.

He checked them out, ticking off items on a mental list of suitability, until he came to the one he wanted.

The mail train.

He crossed over to it, looking out for station staff all the while. Bags were being thrown on, men standing around drinking mugs of tea. No hurry, no urgency.

No security.

Brian waited until the mail workers and station staff moved away from the train then put his head around the door. The mailbags had been thrown into a large carriage. It was full of sacks.

Perfect, thought Brian.

He climbed aboard, stepped through the bags until he had found a particularly high pile, then began to burrow his way into them. Eventually he had bags piled up on all sides of him and he was safe, cocooned within.

He heard the door shut, felt the train move off. He breathed a sigh.

Newcastle was left behind. And not just Newcastle: Monica.

Kenny Bell. His mother. They were all gone. His past, behind him.

He allowed himself a small smile, felt the train rock on the tracks.

His future, ahead of him.

'She off?'

Sharon closed the door quietly behind her. The well-oiled click sealed them off from the rest of the house.

'Yeah. She was worn out, poor dear.'

Sharon sat on the settee beside Jack. She sighed.

'I made you a cup of tea,' said Jack.

Sharon gave a wry smile.

'Well done,' she said. 'I didn't know men could do that.'

'Very funny.'

She picked up her cup, drank, replaced it in the saucer, set it down.

'Ah,' she said, 'society's palliative. The real opium of the masses.'

'Don't start all that university talk with me.'

Sharon smiled.

'Once a student, always a student,' said Jack.

'Don't be a grump.'

They looked at each other, smiled. Jack put his arm around Sharon. She snuggled in.

'Kids, eh? Who'd 'ave 'em?' Jack's voice aimed for levity, shook with heaviness.

Sharon said nothing.

The Smiths had left soon after Ralph and Jean had departed for the hospital. Sharon, Jack and Joanne had continued clearing up, then Joanne had got ready for bed. Sharon had sat with her, settled her down into what would be an unsettled night's sleep for the girl. Sharon had promised to stay the night.

'You'd better go home,' she said to Jack. 'You've got work in the morning.'

'I can go from here,' said Jack. 'It's no problem.'

She snuggled in further. She was glad he had said that.

'Dan was right,' he said. 'What a night.'

They sat that way for a while in companionable silence, listening to the old house settle.

A nation of two.

'What did you want to talk to me about?' said Jack drowsily. He was beginning to drift off.

Sharon stiffened.

'What?' She knew what.

'Before we came out, you said you had something to tell me. What was it?'

'Oh,' she said, 'I'll tell you later. This isn't the best time.'

'You may as well tell me now. Everything else that's happened tonight.'

Sharon couldn't see his face, couldn't read his expression. She took a deep breath.

'Well,' she said, 'it's not a hundred per cent certain, but I'm fairly sure.'

'What?'

'You've probably guessed. I'm pregnant.'

Jack hadn't guessed. His stomach flipped over, his mouth dried up.

Jack said nothing.

PART TWO

The Brasilia of the North

At night he dreamed the city.

No vast, Technicolor pans, no panoramic swoops. He just found himself there, posited in the centre, standing straight at the heart. Feeding off it, feeding into it.

He looked around: lights in the darkness, colour, speed, noise. Colour: neon and electric brilliance, a dazzling, artificial day for night, the adverts brighter than the stars. Speed: heart was right. It was pumping, living, sending tin and steel and expectant people around its body, arteries all tarmac and pavement. Noise: voices raised, shouting, laughing, screaming. Music wailing and thumping, rhythm tuned in to the city's beat. And at the centre, surrounded by movement, Eros, Greek god of love. Still and frozen in time, bow raised, arrow flying. Aiming for anyone, everyone. Love in the city, love at the heart.

He stood there, beneath Eros, arms out, and slowly rotated, head up, eyes sucking in everything, mouth wide, grinning. Alive. No cars hit him, no one shouted at him to get out of the road. Everyone smiled, laughed as they passed. Because he belonged here. He was part of the city as the city was a part of him.

He gave a sigh of pleasure, turned, and walked back on to the pavement. He was protected. Charmed. He walked down backstreets, darker now, the contrast greater: the neon and electric light still bright, but sparser, more strategic, the darkness and shadows between now deeper and wider. He began to feel that familiar tingle, that thrill in the pit of his stomach. The thrill of the streets. These streets. His streets.

He walked. His mind could see behind doors, down alleys, up and down stairways. Through walls. Could see the flesh sold cheaply but bought dearly. Could see the drinks drunk, the pills popped, the hop inhaled. The moods altered. The money eagerly parted with, gratefully taken. The money. The love. The love of money. He smiled.

He walked. Looked through walls and doorways into other places, darker ones. Saw the flipside. The underside. What happened when the money ran out. When they wouldn't or couldn't pay. The lonely, sad chairs in empty basements, waiting for their next incumbent, showing the strains and stains of tens, or perhaps hundreds, of bloodied, broken bodies. The chairs: taken the weight of those bodies that had given up, attempted to dodge the pain, crashed to the hard, cold, uncaring floor. The chairs: acted as a brace for the kicks which inevitably followed. Brass rings, knives, cricket bats. Small electrical generators, electrodes and water if they were feeling inventive, pliers and Stanley knives if they wanted to be direct. The chairs were there now, some in use, some waiting to be used. He knew this. Because he had used them many times.

Back here, away from the brighter lights, was where he found his Eros, his love. Was where he felt he truly belonged.

But as he walked, the streets began to shiver. His reality began to blur. The pavement turned to solid water, his feet sending out ripples as he walked. He looked down. Another pavement could be glimpsed beneath. An older, shabbier one. He knew what it was. Where it was.

He looked around. The buildings were shimmering, hopes appearing as other buildings, other places, began to show through.

An earlier time, a darker time. The past breaking through to his present. He felt himself in flight again, running away. Over walls, down streets. On to a train. Away. He blinked, tried to focus.

It was recurring, the same dream. Each time increasing in strength, each time the older, darker, shabbier streets getting more of a hold. He wanted to run again, over walls, down streets, get on to a train, escape. But he couldn't. His legs turned dream-slow, his arms flailed but were useless. Each time he had given in, let the dream – the old city – claim him, wake him. Not this time.

He stood still, closed his eyes, concentrated. Willed the old city to disappear, let the new one take its place.

And it did.

He opened his eyes, looked around. The new city was gone. His city. And in its place was the old city. And the old city was new again. New, like the city whose heart he loved. Where there was once black, white and grey, it was now neon- and electric-light bright. Where there had been silence, there was noise, slowness there was now speed. And, he knew, he had made it all possible.

He smiled to himself. He looked around and proclaimed it good. The old city was gone, into the past. There was only the new city, now, only the future.

He walked, enjoying it.

The dream held no terror for him now. He smiled to himself. He knew what he had to do.

Where he had to go.

June 1962:
Terms of Human Happiness

The city was alive. Excitement flitted from person to person, buzzing and humming like a swarm of bees in a flower field, hopping plant to plant, flower to flower, but not to gather: to impart. Excitement. And like some highly contagious germ, everyone had caught it.

There were flags and bunting adorning lampposts and telegraph poles. Streets were closed to cars, their places taken by tables and chairs laid out for communal gatherings, street parties, the first since the Coronation. Fireworks were dryly stored, waiting for darkness. Pubs were licensed for day- and night-long drinking. The party was on.

Saturday 9 June 1962. The Blaydon Races Centenary. The event, immortalized in song by local bard Geordie Ridley, concerned a raucous coach journey from the centre of Newcastle, west down the Scotswood Road, then over the bridge to the unlicensed flapping track at Blaydon to watch the races. The song had propelled the event itself. For years it had been sung and celebrated. Now it had become a cornerstone for North-Eastern identity. And had to be honoured.

Dan Smith stood on rough planking and looked around at the crowds before him. The city council boss, the local boy made good, the firebrand maverick clasped uneasily but hopefully to the city's heart. He looked beyond the crowds to his own work. The work done in his name.

Old Scotswood was nearly gone, just mud and rubble. Bulldozers and wrecking balls doing what Hitler and the Luftwaffe had failed to do. He had ordered the wholesale demolition of Scotswood. Slum clearance. Drastic measures for Newcastle's drastic housing shortage. Some people moved out far away to new housing developments in Newbiggin-by-the-Sea, some not so far, to Longbenton.

From out of that, phoenix-like, came the new Scotswood. The Elms. The first of six blocks of fifteen-storey flats. Conceived in imagination and hope, midwifed by scaffolding and cranes, borne aloft on confidence and pride. The future.

A new way of living, Dan Smith had called the tower blocks. Parkland homes for whole communities, he called them, a countryside showpiece of imaginative municipal development. Taking parks to the people, he said. Landscape architecture with centrepieces made from different-coloured brick, vitreous-enamelled panels below windows, roughcast glass for balconies. Underfloor heating, electric cookers, wash boilers, stainless-steel sinks, plentiful cupboard space. Copper-roofed lifts to get up and down. Four adventure playgrounds for children to play safely. They have to be visited to be appreciated, he said.

Dan Smith's plan for a new city. A new region. The first step. The future.

'Newcastle is doing the best job of any city council in the country.'

Hugh Gaitskell, leader of the Labour Party. Standing next to Dan Smith in front of a tall, sheet-covered object, speaking to the assembled crowd before them. Reporters, photographers and inhabitants of Scotswood.

'The rebuilding of any city must include the preservation

of the past with planning and thinking for the future.
Something Newcastle is doing supremely well.'

Dan Smith nodded, glad he got that bit in. Not that there
had been any doubt. The Blaydon Races Centenary had been
Dan's idea. Opening the new flats on the same day his idea
too. Giving the illusion of looking backwards while in reality
looking forwards. Dan smiled, pleased not to have missed a
trick.

'It's always a pleasure,' Hugh Gaitskell went on, 'to be asked
to open a new block of flats or any housing scheme because
they mean so much to people in terms of human happiness.'

Dan Smith looked at the Labour leader. He was sweating,
breathing hard. Everything seemed an effort to him. That
morning he had planted a tree, become a member of
Newcastle's Tree Lovers' Guild, seen an example of Dan
Smith's imaginative use of architectural space, a children's
play area built on top of a car park, opened the Elms, now
this. Later they were due to go to Balmbras, the newly opened
old-time music hall, and start the grand parade. Dan Smith
had doubts about Hugh Gaitskell's stamina. He thought it
best not to voice them.

'Newcastle has one of the most dynamic and impressive
town planning schemes in the country. I said that at a
planning conference in London when architects and
planners from all over the country were present.' His eyes
swept the crowd, made sure he had contact. 'That took some
courage.' He smiled. 'So I'm sure I can say it here.'

He acknowledged the polite laughter, turned his attention
to the sheet-wrapped object before him. It was over twice his
height, solid and angular. Hugh Gaitskell tugged at the cloth,
huffing and puffing, Dan Smith having to step in to help
him. They struggled, but together got it uncovered. It was a
huge, reinforced-concrete block with a rough patina of
bronzing. Gaitskell looked at all twenty-five hundredweight

of it, panting, his face twisted with distaste. It looked like an ugly, abstract totem pole, he thought. The kind John Wayne rescued kidnapped white women from. Knowing his place, he looked towards the sculptor, Kenneth Ford, who was hovering on the fringes of the crowd, and managed to find a smile for him. Ford looked nervous, uncomfortable, his wispy hair, ragged beard and pinched features lending him an air of a pained D. H. Lawrence.

'Mr Ford,' said Hugh Gaitskell, 'is more or less unknown.' He paused for breath. 'But extremely talented.'

He looked around at the crowd. Every negative emotion from apprehension to open hostility, derision to incredulity was being mentally flung in the direction of the sculpture. He found his politician's smile again. Plastered it over the cracks.

Dan Smith stood beside him, smiling proudly. He understood the sculpture. What it meant.

'I understand any concern which might have been felt about the attitude of the city to this symbolic work,' Hugh Gaitskell was saying, 'but no art can be creative if it is purely imitative.'

A beaming smile, then the start of applause led by Dan Smith. The crowd joined in, realizing this was the end. They had waited all this time for that.

Then handshakes and photos: Smith and Ford, Gaitskell and Ford, Smith and Gaitskell.

'Well done, Dan,' said Gaitskell, inaudible to anyone else. 'You've managed to persuade people that that pile of bloody rubbish's a sculpture.'

'It's art, Hugh,' said Dan Smith, smiling. 'The first, probably, that people around here have seen. The trick is not to give the people what they want, Hugh. Or what they think they want. Give them what they don't realize they want until they get it.' He looked around at the unsmiling faces. 'Then they'll love you for it.'

Hugh Gaitskell said nothing, just stared at him.

'This is only the start. Wait and see.'

Hugh Gaitskell smiled, nodded. 'Where to next?'

'Balmbras. The parade.'

'Dancing girls and free beer, eh? Lead the way.'

Dan Smith turned to a collection of men accompanying him. They were all talking in a self-congratulatory way, Wilf Burns, his chief planning officer, looking particularly pleased with himself. He picked out one face that wasn't joining in.

'You coming, Ralph? The cars are waiting.'

Ralph Bell looked around at the mention of his name. He had been staring at the tower blocks, the square-cut concrete, steel and glass edifices. He was looking at the windows, small and distant, imagining small and distant lives taking place behind them. Wishing his was one of them.

Ralph shook his head.

'No, I've . . . I said I'd meet Jean.'

Dan Smith crossed to him. 'There's a place on the coach for you. The parade. These new homes didn't build themselves. You should be proud of what your company's done.'

Ralph nodded absently.

Dan Smith looked at him, his face etched with concern. 'Come on, Ralph. Take the day off. You and Jean. Enjoy yourselves. You deserve it.'

Ralph Bell sighed. 'No, I've got to . . .'

He gestured with his hand, index finger outstretched, shaking his head.

Dan Smith nodded.

'I understand, Ralph.'

He looked at Ralph. His clothes looked shabby and smelled of too many wearings, not enough washings. His hair managed the feat of appearing to be both dry and simultaneously greasy. His face held blotches of red, broken skin and prominent, livid purple veins. His eyes were black rimmed and deep set, watery and yellow, like stagnant pools. His breath was rank. His moustache a stained grey.

'I'd better . . .' Ralph gestured, a vague oscillation in the direction of the road.

'Good to see you,' said Dan Smith. He shook his hand, clasping it in both of his. 'Send my best to Jean.'

Ralph Bell nodded and stumbled off, not seeming to care whether his feet came down on mud or planking.

Hugh Gaitskell watched him go.

'Bit of a state.'

'He's had a lot of hardship in the last few years. Left him somewhat broken. But what can you do? You can't just let a man go. Besides, it's his construction company.'

'I'm surprised he can still manage to run it.'

'He can't. But his right-hand man can. Quite brilliantly, in fact.'

Hugh Gaitskell nodded.

'Come on, then.' He clapped Dan Smith on the shoulders. 'Let's not keep those dancing girls waiting.'

The waves rolled in to Bamburgh beach. Some crashing: greenish water turning to oily foam, landing noisily. Some quiet: a gentle roll, the merest edging of froth. But the follow-up always the same: the tide ebbing, clawing back water from the land, reshaping the beach, indiscriminately depositing shells, seaweed, stones, crustacean skeletons, all manner of seaborne detritus, creating a newly sanded topography.

Jack Smeaton sat on a spread rug and watched, fascinated by the tide's random, passionless beauty. Inexorable, unchanging. Creating, destroying, creating again. He looked at the sky, willed the sunshine to break through the thin cloud covering, justify his choice of clothes. But wishes didn't matter, no matter how fervently he made them: the sun was as arbitrary as the sea.

Sharon Smeaton lay next to him, stretched out, stomach down, elbows propped as she read a paperback novel. *Doctor Zhivago*. Boris Pasternak. A cold love story.

They seemed a perfect couple: Jack tanned, muscled and handsome, in shorts, shirtless. Sharon beautiful and body sculpted, seemingly unmarked by childbirth, in a black one-piece swimsuit that gripped and curved and showcased. Sunglasses hid their eyes from observers, from each other.

Between them was Isaac. Their son. He crouched at the water's edge, gathering sand, beach debris and water, collecting it in his bucket and spade, carrying it back to a castle and moat complex that he was building in the sand. Talking to himself as he rearranged his finds, imagining not sand before him but some vast, elaborate castle, existing only in his mind's eye. Occasionally looking up for parental approval. Jack smiling and nodding at him in return.

Jack thinking: my son.

Feeling strange forming the words, even in his head, even after five years.

He loved the boy, no question. He just couldn't admit it to his son or his wife. To himself. He felt love for Isaac, he felt pride. He struggled to show it. But he couldn't make that final leap. Couldn't just let go and love him unconditionally. There was still too much fear inside Jack.

Even after five years.

Jack looked at Sharon, watched her turn a page, wilfully oblivious to him. To Isaac. To everything.

A cold love story.

Jack knew why. Saturday 9 June 1962. The Blaydon Races Centenary. The unveiling of the Elms. Ralph and Jean Bell with invitations on to the podium, seats on the dignitaries' coach in the parade. Sharon and Jack: nothing. Just a rank-and-file invitation. Jack wasn't bothered, didn't want to wave and smile, be waved and smiled at in return.

Sharon was bothered. She regarded those things as just rewards for hard work. Credit where it was supposed to be due.

Jack remembered the recent argument word for word:

'So where's our invitation, then?'

Sharon in the kitchen at home. Just off the phone with Jean Bell. Her weekly call to see if there was any news, if things were any better. Or at least no worse.

'What invitation?'

Jack had been making himself a cup of tea, thinking, half an hour with the paper then I'll cut the lawn.

'You know what invitation. For the Centenary. The opening.'

'We've had it. The dinner on the Saturday night. You've read it.'

'I'm not talking about the dinner on the Saturday night. I'm talking about the opening of the Elms. The procession. Ralph and Jean have had theirs. So where's ours?'

Jack shrugged. 'Well, Ralph would have. It's his company that built the flats.'

'It may be his company,' said Sharon slowly, as if explaining to a child and not her husband, 'but who liaises with the architects? And the surveyors? Who chooses the men? Who's in charge of the whole blasted operation?'

Jack sighed in exasperation. 'You know who. Me.'

'That's right, Jack. You do all the work. If anyone were to be invited from Bell Construction it should be you and me. You know that.'

Jack sighed. 'It's not that simple.'

'Isn't it? It seems simple enough to me. Ralph drinks himself to death, you do all the work. Where's your reward? Where's your acknowledgement?'

Jack turned to face her, put his tea down. 'The name of the company is Bell and Sons. Not Bell and Smeaton.'

'Only because Ralph's too soft and guilt-ridden to change it. And you're too soft to challenge him about it.'

'That's below the belt, Sharon.'

Sharon looked away. 'You know what I mean.'

Jack sighed again, shook his head. His tea would be cooling now.

Sharon looked up again. 'We should be further on by now, Jack. We should always be trying to better ourselves. Advance ourselves. And we're not advancing fast enough.' She sighed. Anger replaced by pleading. 'Ralph should give you a partnership. He knows he should. I'm sure he does. I mean, Johnny's gone; he won't be back. And Kenny . . . It's touching that Ralph's holding out so much hope. But let's face it: things aren't going to get any better, are they?'

The same argument. From every angle in every tone of voice. The same argument. And always the same conclusion. Jack had heard it before.

Sharon looked into Jack's eyes. He saw hope in her gaze, a bridge built, waiting to be crossed. 'Look,' she said, 'why don't you call Dan? Ask . . . no, tell him you want us to be there. Why don't you do that?'

Jack turned away from her. He gripped the kitchen worktop. His knuckles were white.

'Aren't you forgetting something?'

'What?' she said.

'A question. To me. Do I want to be there?'

'Well, of course you do.'

'Do I?'

Sharon looked at him again. He saw hope die, the bridge crumble, uncrossed.

'Jack . . .' She couldn't find the words. 'What's wrong with you? Aren't you proud of what you've achieved? Especially in the area you're from?'

'You know I am.'

'Well?'

He looked around the kitchen. His tea would be cold by now. He felt himself getting hotter.

'D'you think I want to be there? Do you?' Sharon didn't reply. He sighed again, this time from exasperation. 'Well, if you think I do, you don't know me very well. Yes, I'm proud of what I've done with the flats. Hugely proud. But what has standing on a bus, grinning like an idiot with all the other idiots and waving to do with building flats? Nothing. That's why I'm not going to be there.'

'Everyone prominent will be there.'

'Prominent to who? Yes, Dan'll be there. True. But I wouldn't bother with the rest of them.'

Sharon turned away from him. He could spot a sulk when it was about to happen. He turned her round.

'What I'm doing is important. And it's going to be even more important in the next few years. It's a pure, Socialist vision. A chance for a new future. I don't work for the praise. I work through the praise.'

Sharon looked at him again, searching, willing a different answer from him. He knew what she had given up – her place at university, her potential career – to be his wife, Isaac's mother, their homemaker. He knew how difficult she found that. She had subjugated her ambitions to Jack's own career. Any achievements and successes experienced vicariously through Jack.

'So I'm sorry,' he said. 'But we won't be standing on that bus.'

Sharon turned away, marched from the kitchen.

Jack placed his arms protectively around his body, hugging himself. He shook his head. He couldn't explain it to Sharon. He didn't understand it himself.

He looked at his cup, picked it up, sipped.

Stone cold.

He tipped the tea down the sink, left the kitchen.

Bamburgh had been the compromise. The attempt at appeasement. If they couldn't be where they wanted to be in the city, then get out of the city.

He looked at Isaac, playing happily in the sand. The clouds were beginning to move, the sun break through. He smiled. And in that unguarded moment felt something stir within him. A shifting, like the sand of an hourglass running through, something previously hard-packed softening.

His heart.

Isaac played on.

Jack checked himself. Sitting on the beach, the sun shining, his wife beside him, his son before him, he felt happy. Content. Contentment he never felt in the city.

He reached out his hand. Laid it on his wife's back. She jumped, flinching at the touch. Jack chose to ignore it.

'Sharon . . .' His voice sounded strange to his own ears. As if he had gone too long without using it.

Sharon murmured, granting him permission to continue, without lifting her head from her book.

'Shall we move?'

'Where?' The reply was automatic, her attention still with her book.

'I don't know. Away from Newcastle. Into the country. I don't know. Somewhere like here.'

Sharon sighed, triangulated the corner of her page, looked up.

'And what would we do?' she said. 'How would we live?'

'We could . . .' He looked at the waves, seeking inspiration. 'Buy a farm. Live off the land.'

Sharon snorted. 'If you think I'm going to become some lumpen, red-faced, welly-wearing farmer's wife, you've got another think coming.'

'Well . . . we'll do something else, then. I'll get a job.'

'You've already got a job. And you're very good at it. I just wish you'd try harder with it, that's all.'

She unfolded her page, returned her attention to her book, the matter closed.

Jack said nothing. He looked again at Isaac, at the sea.

Clouds rolled in over the sun. Not dark, storm-rich and ominous, but thin, pale grey. The effect was the same; they still stopped the light, the heat shining through. Jack hoped they would dissipate, not build up into something heavy and threatening.

Isaac didn't notice, though; he just kept playing. Unaware.

Jack hoped he never would notice.

The celebrations were in full flow.

At one thirty, the parade left Balmbras in the Cloth Market, renamed from the Carlton, redesignated an old-time music hall to coincide with the venue in the original song. Modern cars pulled up; 1862-attired drivers and passengers disgorged. The Balmbras cancan girls danced in the streets.

The band of the Coldstream Guards struck up 'Blaydon Races', led the way. The parade began. Old horse-drawn buses and coaches, local dignitaries in period costume. Over a hundred and fifty floats. Over sixty bands. All playing, all singing 'Blaydon Races'. Over and over again.

Down Scotswood Road, crowds filling the streets. The people on the pavement roaring, cheering and clapping. All singing 'Blaydon Races'.

The same song over and over again.

Hotels and pubs along the route set up bars on the pavement, dressed for a century previously, dispensing stotty cakes and clay pipes along with the ale.

And still the same song.

On the open-topped coach: T. Dan Smith and Hugh Gaitskell. Both waving, grinning.

'Gets to you after a while, doesn't it?' said Hugh Gaitskell to Dan Smith, still facing outwards, still waving and grinning. 'That same bloody song, I mean.'

'Don't let them hear you say that,' said Dan Smith to Hugh Gaitskell, still facing outwards, still waving and grinning. 'They'll have your guts for garters round here.'

Hugh Gaitskell nodded.

'But I know what you mean,' said Dan Smith. 'As much as I love it, I quite agree with you.'

'Still, though. It's a marvellous achievement. A whole festival based on the event. On the song.'

'A defining cultural moment for the North-Eastern man,' said Dan Smith. 'Very important. Even more so since it never actually happened.' He kept waving, grinning.

'Oh, really?' said Hugh Gaitskell.

'Absolutely,' said Dan Smith. 'I mean, it may have done, it may not. It's the song that everyone remembers.'

'Do they know that?' said Hugh Gaitskell, gesturing to the crowds, waving and grinning.

'Does it matter?' said Dan Smith. 'Do the people care one way or the other whether it happened or not? Whether it was real or not? No, they don't. We've kept the pubs open all day. They're happy enough with that.'

'True enough, I suppose,' said Hugh Gaitskell.

'Just keep waving and smiling, Hugh,' said Dan Smith. 'Just keep waving and smiling.'

Dan Smith and Hugh Gaitskell kept facing outwards, waving and grinning.

And the same song over and over again.

Johnny Bell stood on the pavement. In the crowds but not of them.

They milled all about him, beer-buoyed, laughing, watching the procession, cheering. Whole families in shared experience. Johnny observed the spectacle up close but with an air of distance, a lack of comprehension and communication. The same song, old buses, marching bands. Trivial rubbish. Give them all-day drinking and a day off work and they would cheer anything. Here they were proving that. It confirmed what he already knew: people, collectively, were stupid.

He hated Saturdays, even without the celebrations. The slaughterhouse closed for the weekend. He would usually ask for extra shifts, overtime when there was any. But there was nothing today.

He loved his work, felt truly calm and at peace only with a knife in his hand: slitting open carcasses, the innards slipping and slopping out all warm and steaming, Johnny taking in a lungful of that before getting his hands inside and scooping out the remains. He would be given other tasks and did them well, but that was his favourite. He would have happily done that without pay.

Johnny pulled his coat tightly about him, stuck his hands deeply into his pockets. He was the only person, apart from the idiots in the old-fashioned clothes, not in shirtsleeves. Johnny didn't care about the heat, about what he looked like or smelled like. He just cared about keeping his coat about him, keeping his hands sunk into his pockets. Drew solace and comfort from what he had there.

His family had wanted to see him today. There was somewhere his father had wanted him to go. Joanne had been dispatched to inform him. He knew it would be Joanne. Always Joanne. He had listened, shrugged non-committally at the end. She had laid out where they were going, what they were doing. She hadn't asked him outright whether he would be joining them. They both knew he wouldn't be.

He smiled to himself at the memory of Joanne, his sister, sitting uncomfortably in his cramped bedsit, the smell of sweat, other secretions and frustrated desires permeating every surface, the walls adorned with pictures of his heroes, newspaper articles, with paintings and symbols he had done himself.

The swastikas. Hitler. The concentration camps. Nazi graffiti on Jewish family homes in Newcastle suburbs.

'You've always had something rotten inside you,' she had said to him before leaving, her face red, her voice cracked, 'but I always thought you kept it contained. Now it's broken like an egg. And it's seeped out. Contaminated every part of you.'

Johnny smiled, impressed. 'You should have studied English instead of art,' he had said. 'You've got a gift for language.'

She had walked out. He knew what answer she would give their parents.

He stood: Blaydon Races, cheering and clapping, tuned it out. That night, he thought. The Ropemakers Arms, Brian Mooney and his gang: a superheated crucible, the base elements combining to create something new. The night everything had fallen into place for him. Afterwards came soul-searching and, as weeks stretched into months, decisions were reached. Conclusions arrived at.

Johnny could not continue as he was doing if he was ever truly to fulfil his potential. Be who he wanted to be. Who he needed to be.

The first move: sever all ties with his father's company. His father, slack-jawed and impotent, had not stood in his way.

The second move: a job that suited him. Jack Smeaton had told him about his time in the Scotswood slaughterhouse. The conditions, the work. Jack had been trying to communicate the dreadfulness of the experience, but when Jack spoke horror Johnny heard pornography. Theory he wanted to put into practice. Had to put into practice.

And it hadn't disappointed him. At first he would stand and watch the animals die, fascinated by how quickly and forcefully their spark of animation, of life, was removed. And then the cutting. That first time, sliding his diamond-sharp blade into the hanging animal carcass, the hiss of escaping gas almost an orgasmic sigh, had given him an immediate erection. When the guts dropped out he wanted to grab them, smear himself with them, luxuriate in their dissipating warmth, roll around in them, feel their slippery smoothness on his naked skin. Bathe in their blood.

He remembered torturing and killing Joanne's pet cat when he was small and getting a thrill out of that. Out of seeing it suffer and die slowly, knowing the rest of the family were looking for it, out of knowing that it was his secret against Joanne, whom he hated because she was his mother's favourite. A thrill. But nothing like as great as this one.

He had hurried back to his bedsit after work and masturbated himself to the best orgasm of his life.

Work became a joy after that.

Sometimes as he worked, he thought of Jack Smeaton. About other stories the man held within him.

About the war. About Belsen.

Johnny had asked repeatedly but Jack had refused, beyond supplying bare facts, to tell him anything. The rest he had had to find from books. Photos. And that had grown into almost as big a thrill as slaughtering animals.

Combine the two and his life was complete.

Almost complete.

There were other aspects, areas that still troubled and worried him. Things he needed to sort out. But it would come. He was on the right tracks at last.

And he had to thank that night at the Ropemakers for everything. Brian Mooney for everything.

He walked through the crowd, hands plunged deep inside

his coat pockets. Fingers resting on the handles of his blades, the metal encased in home-made leather sheaths. Sewn-up skin, straight from the slaughterhouse.

His fingers curled and uncurled, stroked the shafts playfully.

His blades were his friends. His best friends.

His only friends.

Playfully stroking the shafts of his blades, he felt the stirrings of an erection.

Johnny looked around. The pack was all about him, red-faced and laughing. That inane song, again and again. What would it be like, he thought, to cut one of these? They were just cattle. Unintelligent animals. The unimaginative herd. He could just pull his knife out and slit the man next to him, the one with the short-sleeved shirt and thin black tie, greased-down hair and heavy, black-framed glasses, slit him right down the middle from chin to pubis and disappear into the crowd before anyone could stop him. What was stopping him from doing that?

Nothing. Nothing at all.

And that was why Johnny felt so superior to the crowd around him.

Because he had the power of life and death over them all.

And that knowledge made him a superman.

He walked on, erection pleasantly impeding speed. He wanted gratification. It was becoming imperative.

He walked on, excited.

He knew exactly where he was going. Who would be there. Even today, with all this going on.

And what would happen when he got there.

Everywhere she looked, Jean Bell saw ghosts.

Or, more specifically, a ghost. The same one.

It was there in the bathroom mirror that morning. It was

in the hall mirror when she had straightened her hat and buttoned her coat before going out. It had been looking into the passenger side window of the Zephyr as she sat in the passenger seat, hand feeding Polos to Ralph, listening to him nervously crunching them as he drove.

The ghost was with her all the time. Everywhere she went, everywhere she looked. All the time.

The ghost was her.

When she looked at herself in a mirror, reflected back would be a woman with grey, almost translucent skin, hanging in shrunken, papery folds against an angular skull which threatened to show through completely. Her eyes were faded green, deep sunken. Tear-watery and tear-ready. Her brow was frown-creased, her lips small, pursed and rigid. Her hair limp, dead colourless strands.

This was the woman Jean Bell had become.

The ghost of her former self.

Everything was so hard. And getting harder. Just keeping the house going, keeping Ralph fed, showing him which clothes to wear, was an effort. And all three of her children gone from home. She and Ralph used to dream about that, of the day when they would leave, taking with them parental blessings and accumulated wisdom. The things they would do, the places they would go. Dream.

Not like this. Not this way.

Never this way.

They pulled up before a grand, imposing building. A textbook example of Georgian architecture. On their first visit it had seemed an impressive edifice but now familiarity had dulled that thrill. They no longer looked at it for what it had once been, but for what it represented to them now.

They had given their names to the gateman, who had to verify their visit with his clipboarded list before allowing them access, locking the gates behind them. Then up the gravelled drive, flanked by blooming flowerbeds and green grass, all at unnatural, cartoon brightness. Jean knew what the money was going on, but didn't dare say it to Ralph. The car was parked in a small car park at the side of the house, where once had been operational stables. The three of them disgorged. Jean and Ralph from the front, Joanne from the rear.

Jean looked around. Despite the cheerful trappings, it still reminded her of a prison and her first view of it on every visit was accompanied by a sinking in her heart.

A prison.

Some prisons were subtler, more complex than others.

The three walked towards the front door, feet dragging slower with each reluctant crunch over the gravel. They slowly climbed the steps, rang the bell.

A woman wearing a stiffly starched white nurse's outfit and a brittle, too-bright smile gave them admittance.

'Mr Bell?'

Ralph Bell nodded.

'And Mrs Bell and . . .' The nurse struggled to find Joanne's name. '. . . Miss Bell. If you'll follow me, please.'

She set off down a lino-floored corridor. The Bells followed.

The interior of the house showed very little of the exterior Georgian splendour. It looked as institutional as any hospital.

'Huh . . . how is he?' said Ralph Bell, his tone indicating he didn't want to hear the answer.

'Oh . . . fine,' said the brittle-bright nurse. 'As well as can be expected. We do our best, you know.'

'I'm sure you do,' said Ralph.

They want to, the amount of money we're paying. The thought came unbidden into Jean's head. She quickly ushered it out with a guilt-ridden mental swipe.

'He's been cheerful lately,' said the nurse.

'Good, good,' said Ralph.

As they walked, Jean felt hot. The heating must be turned up, she thought. Keep the patients drowsy. It was too warm for what she was wearing, but she didn't feel she could unbutton her coat, take it off. The act might make her feel too comfortable. Too familiar in her surroundings. And she didn't want to encourage those feelings in herself.

'I didn't think you'd be coming today,' said the nurse, 'what with the centenary and everything.'

'No . . . we . . . we thought—' Ralph had gone red in the face '—we . . . we should.'

'That's nice. We're all hoping to go down later. When we finish our shifts.'

Ralph nodded absently, not hearing her.

'Will Dr Shaw be here?' said Ralph.

'I can ask for him if you need to see him.'

'Yes. Yes, please.'

They turned a corner, the nurse still leading. They walked through a large, open-plan white room in which a handful of pyjama-clad people sat reading, talking, playing draughts or just staring.

Jean tried not to look at them, tried not to think.

They crossed to a set of French windows. The nurse produced the key, opened them. They stepped out into the garden. She locked the windows behind them.

'Can't be too careful,' she said.

Prisons, thought Joan, subtler, more complex than others.

They turned a corner. A figure clad in institutional pyjamas sat on a bench at the back of the building. He wore dark glasses and a distant expression. Head cocked, listening to something. Or acting as a receiver, waiting to pick something up.

'There he is,' said the brittle-bright nurse. 'Say hello, Kenny.'

Kenny turned at the sound. Something unintelligible came out of his mouth. His expression changed slightly.

'Look at that!'

Ralph turned to his wife and daughter, eyes alight with reckless hope.

'Did you see that? He recognized us! He turned.'

The nurse gave a professional smile.

'I'll go and find Dr Shaw. If you need anything, just call.' She walked off.

Ralph crossed to him, sat on the bench next to him.

'Hello, son. Hello, Kenny. How you doing, ay?'

It was the most animated Jean had seen Ralph all day. The most animated she had seen him in a long time. Probably since their last visit to Kenny.

He had put on weight, Jean noticed. Unused muscle turned to fat. And they'd given him an institutionalized haircut to match his institutionalized pyjamas. It was a crude job, more like a monk's tonsure than a professional barber's effort.

She looked at her son. If she hadn't become used to it, if each visit hadn't leached a little more emotion, a little more mother's sorrow each time she came, then she could cry. As it was, there were no reserves left to draw on. So she just sighed.

Ralph was talking to Kenny, telling him things Jean knew he couldn't hear, would never understand. Kenny was gurgling in reply, rocking backwards and forwards, making random, inarticulate noises.

She couldn't look at him without thinking of that night. The night when everything changed. When they stopped living the lives they had planned and expected and started living this way instead.

Shadow lives.

Kenny and Johnny had been taken to the hospital. Johnny's injuries had been relatively easy to patch up, but

Kenny had been different. A major artery had been severed in his thigh. The first job had been to stanch the flow of blood, stop him bleeding to death. They had done so, but not without the pumping of blood around his body stopping completely. Only for a few seconds, but those few seconds had been crucial. The flow of blood to his brain had ceased.

The doctors struggled to save his sight, but to no avail. The optic nerves were shredded, corneas useless. He was blind.

When he did regain consciousness a few days later, the doctors' worst fears were realized. Kenny, in addition to his blindness, now had irreparable brain damage.

The Bells took the news badly. Johnny's behaviour was becoming increasingly erratic, his attitude estranged. Joanne had been wonderful. Rolling up her sleeves, both physically and metaphorically, and getting on with things. Keeping things going. Jean thought it was Joanne who was keeping the family together.

Eventually the hospital could keep Kenny no longer. He had to come home. Jean faced the prospect of looking after him, steeled herself for the unexpected and unwanted responsibility.

But Ralph wouldn't hear tell of it.

'My boy's going to get the finest treatment money can buy. We'll prove these doctors wrong. We'll show them he can get better.'

Jean had said nothing. Just nodded.

They, or rather Ralph, had chosen the Elms, a privately owned hospital on the border of Northumberland that knew the value of discretion and understood the meaning of money.

And there he had stayed. And there he would stay, thought Jean, until he either died or the money ran out. Whichever happened first.

My son, thought Jean.

She sighed again.

Ralph had been a much more devoted father since Kenny's injuries. Jean didn't delve too deeply into that. Guilt affected different people in different ways. He even insisted to Dan Smith that the first block of flats to go up be named after Kenny's hospital.

The Elms.

Jean just let him get on with it.

And there he sat on the bench, talking to Kenny. Unable or unwilling to believe Kenny couldn't see him. Couldn't understand him. Couldn't communicate with him.

The brittle-bright nurse reappeared.

'Sorry to interrupt,' she said, sounding neither sorry nor not sorry, 'but Dr Shaw is waiting if you'd like to see him.'

Ralph quickly stood up, excused himself to Kenny, bustled off, the nurse following.

Jean and Joanne looked at each other, looked at Kenny.

He didn't seem to be aware that someone had stopped talking to him. He sat making the same noises, head cocked, listening for a signal only he could hear.

'Are you coming back home tonight?' said Jean.

'No, thanks. I'll get Dad to drop me at the halls. Some of us are having a bit of a get-together tonight. The centenary thing, you know.'

Jean nodded.

'Just as long as I know how many to cook for,' she said.

They stood in silence again. Eventually Ralph returned. He was folding up a piece of paper, popping it in his inside jacket pocket.

Jean didn't ask what it was. She didn't want to know.

The nurse was following behind Ralph.

'I'm afraid visiting time's over now,' she said, her brittle-brightness tinged by a professional sadness. 'If you could be making your goodbyes.'

Ralph made loud goodbyes, telling Kenny when he'd see him next and to be good until then. Telling him not to worry, just get better, there was a place for him back at the firm.

Jean and Joanne both said in turn, 'Goodbye, Kenny.'

He responded in neither greater nor lesser degree to any of them.

They were escorted back to their car, wished a pleasant journey home. They got in, Ralph started the engine. They swept down the drive, past the cartoon flowers, out on to the road.

'Shame Johnny couldn't have been here today,' said Ralph. 'He'd have enjoyed himself.'

Jean and Joanne said nothing. Jean noticed Joanne shudder despite the heat.

'I thought he was looking better, didn't you? He recognized us when we got there.' Ralph smiled. 'Yes, I think he's turned a corner. It'll be a while, but I think he's on the mend.' Another smile. 'Ah, yes. Definitely on the mend.'

Jean and Joanne said nothing.

Jean turned to the window, sighed. The ghost woman was still there, looking at her.

Jean stared right back at her. Held her gaze.

All the way home.

Next came galloping and trotting.

Competitors from all over England and Scotland arrived for the racing at Blaydon in the afternoon. Showhorses and racehorses. Crowds oohing and aahing, clapping and cheering.

All over the region, street parties sprang up. Streets closed off. Battered bunting, last seen during the Coronation, had been dragged from damp cardboard boxes and given an airing: strung between lampposts, wrapped around telegraph poles, draped from windowsills and eaves, they flapped, bringing a faded ghost-colour to the soot-blackened streets. Tables dragged from kitchens and parlours formed higgledy-piggledy lines down the centres of streets. Chairs as mismatched as tables lined up alongside. On the tables: white triangular sandwiches filled with egg and tomato or tinned meat, orange squash in various kinds of cups, crisps, stodgy cakes. Children ate, shouted, laughed. Adults ministered, poured squash, replenished plates, helped themselves. They stood in their street, drank tea or bottled ale, chatted. Seeing their surroundings through different eyes: the sun, the gathering, the temporary dispensing of working ritual made their street, their world, a happy place of spirit, of love, of opportunity.

Mae Blacklock sat with the other children her own age, slowly chewing on a chopped-pork sandwich, swallowing, washing the taste away with orange squash. Repeating the actions until her plate and cup were cleared and empty. Between mouthfuls she looked around, saw the other children making up jokes, play-fighting at the table, carrying on, earning mock admonitions from their parents, calling to their friends.

But not to her. Never to her.

She sat with the other children her age. They talked over her, around her. She had seen something on telly once about a boy who had to live in a plastic bubble. There was something wrong with him. It looked great at first: a huge, see-through tent stretched over his specially adapted hospital bed in his specially adapted hospital room. He had toys and attention. It was an adventure. But as the programme went on, it began to look less great. He couldn't laugh with the other children, breathe the same air as them, run and play with them. The toys he played with had to be specially disinfected. They could only be small. Everything, his whole world, had to fit into the small space inside the tent. He couldn't reach out and touch.

Mae thought about that boy a lot. She often found her six-year-old mind wandering; she imagined reaching out, touching only plastic. Imagined stepping outside the bubble but finding the air poisonous and having to step back inside, choking but safe in her see-through tomb.

She was the boy, the bubble her house. The other children beyond that. She could reach out but never connect; call, but never be heard. She was always pulled back, gasping and choking, to the bubble. Her house.

Back to her mother.

And the things she couldn't talk about.

Her mother. In the room with Jesus in pain. And white walls with dark shadows. Too many shadows.

Of prison.

Then, thought triggered, thinking back: the time Mae had been talking non-stop, clowning. Wanting attention, wanting her mother to listen to her.

Playing her up, her mother had said, being wilful.

Clips around the ear, cuffs around the head, no use. Mae kept talking.

'You see that?' her mother had said.

Mae stopped talking and looked, followed her mother's pointed finger, pleased that her mother had noticed her at last, had wanted to share something with her.

They were in the centre of Newcastle, walking back home from shopping. Her mother was pointing at Grey's Monument, the imposing stone edifice at the heart of the old Georgian Grainer town. Earl Grey's statue stood atop the huge stone column. Mae looked at it.

'There,' her mother said.

Mae nodded.

'That's a prison. That's the tower where they send the naughty children who won't do what their mams tell them.'

Mae froze and stared. Her eyes travelled from the door in

the base right up to the statue on the top. A small, railed walkway ran around the base of the statue.

'They put the naughty children in there and lock the door. And leave them. The only way out is for them to climb to the top and jump off.'

Mae stared. She could well believe it. She did believe it.

They walked on in silence after that, Mae not daring to speak lest her tiny heart break and she start to sob, lest her mother lose patience and put her in prison.

They had finally reached their house in Scotswood, Mae's feet hurting but not daring to complain about them, gone inside, Mae in fear and silence. Into the place she called home.

Her mother there all the time.

She remembered times, dimly, when her mother hadn't been there. A time in hospital when she was very small: unpleasant at first as they had forced her to drink a sour, salty liquid, then stood by when she had been violently sick, smiling and helping her to clean up. After that, they had been as nice as anything: the nurses in their stiff clothes that creaked and rustled like kicked leaves when they stood up or sat down. The smiles they gave her as they tucked her up in her hospital bed. The way they sat and talked to her, laughed at her jokes, listened to her as her mother never had.

Then there was the nice woman. She had taken Mae shopping, buying her lots of pretty clothes, lovely dolls and toys. The nice woman had taken her for lunch in a café. The woman had made promises, told her about the house she would be living in and how it would always be sunny, the friends she would have. Her exciting, beautiful future.

And the other time in hospital, after the fall. Mae didn't remember much about that, just how amazed the nurses were at her lack of injuries. 'God's marked you for something special,' said one of them. Mae got a warm feeling when the nurse said that. They had asked her questions then, questions Mae didn't know the answers to. They kept asking them, and she tried to make things up just to make them happy, but they told her not to do that. She still enjoyed it, though, with the rustling nurses playing with her and talking to her.

There were other stories, other times dimly remembered, but all with the same conclusion: her mother turned up and took her home.

Back to the things she was told not to talk about. Her mother in the room with Jesus in pain. On the cross, mouth pulled back in agony. Dying. Crown of thorns, head wreathed in golden light. Mae could reach out to him but never connect, call but never be heard.

The room with white walls with dark shadows. Too many shadows.

The other children were still playing, still laughing. Mae reached for another chopped-pork sandwich, took another small handful of crisps.

She was a pretty little girl, she had been told that enough times, but had trouble believing it. Brown hair and green eyes that looked deep into people, tried to see beyond their skins and into their hearts. To see who they really were, to see what they really wanted.

From her.

'Hello, me darlin'.'

Mae looked up. She recognized the voice at once. It brought an instant smile to her face.

'Hello, Bert,' she said.

Bert looked at her, returned the smile. Dressed in an old suit, belt and braces, a collarless shirt open at his neck. Battered old boots on his feet, similarly scarred cap on his head. He could have been any age from late thirties to early fifties. He was the kind of person who seemed to have been born at a certain age and stayed there.

'Y'enjoyin' yourself, pet?'

Mae nodded through a mouthful of crisps.

'Champion,' he said. 'Good to see the bairns havin' a day out like this.'

'Where's Adam?'

'Tethered up in the yard. Haven't done the rounds today. No need.'

Mae turned round, her face lit with a rare excitement.

'Can we go and see him? We could join the parade to Blaydon.'

Bert smiled.

'They wouldn't want us in the parade, pet. I'm just an old rag an' bone man, an' Adam's too old for that lark.'

Mae's face fell.

'Can we still go round and see him, though? Can we still go to the yard?'

Bert sighed.

'You don't want to spend the day with an old duffer like me, do you, bonny lass? Not when you've got all your friends your own age to play with.'

Mae looked down the length of the table. Children ate, talked, shouted, laughed.

But not with her.

'Please, Bert,' she said. 'Can I go down the yard with you?'

Bert looked at her, smiled. He loved this little girl. This sad-eyed little girl who seemed to have no friends.

He drained his bottle of brown ale, placed it on the table.

'Come on, then, bonny lass, let's go an' see Adam.'

He held out his hand. She quickly jumped from her seat and took it, a rare, beaming smile lighting up her face.

'Mind, we cannot be too long. Your mam'll be wonderin' where you've gone, like.'

Mae shivered, as if a cloud had passed over the sun.

'Are you cold?' said Bert.

Mae shook her head.

'Let's go and see Adam,' she said.

Bert's yard. The only place in the whole wide world where Mae felt safe.

Really safe.

Fridges, tables, chairs, settees. Shelves and ornaments. Tin baths and old tyres. Everything old, worn and unwanted by others. Everything new, exciting and dream-like to Mae. A place of possibilities and adventure. On her first visit, Bert had given her a tour, told her what was potentially dangerous, told her never to get inside a fridge and close the door, to beware of sharp and rusty objects, that kind of thing, but also let her play there.

'Hello, Adam,' said Mae. She crossed to the horse, patted his flank. The old nag swished his tail.

Bert closed the gates, followed her in. He found his old armchair, dragged outside to catch the good weather, and sat down in it, pulling a bottle of brown ale from his coat pocket and uncapping it with the bottle opener he had tied to the arm of the chair by an old piece of string.

He was happy to let Mae play in his yard. He knew she didn't get on well with the other kids and needed somewhere to go. Somewhere to get her out of the house, away from her mother.

Bert was a widower. He had no children of his own and had never remarried after Winnie's heart attack had claimed her. He had needs, obviously, and had found himself having them taken care of by Monica. But then she started to get rough and he didn't like that. But he liked her. So he still kept in touch, took her out sometimes, down to the pub, for a walk. He liked to think of himself as her boyfriend, but he didn't know what Monica thought.

He had been on his rounds one day and Mae had seen him.

She had walked alongside Adam, stopping when he did, moving when he did. Not saying a word, just looking at the horse.

Gradually she had begun to speak, and eventually he had invited her to sit with him. He hadn't been comfortable with her at first since he had had no children of his own, but Mae wasn't the kind of child who said much anyway. That suited him fine. Soon she was accompanying him on his rounds when she wasn't at school. She seemed to like that.

Bert became fond of the silent little girl. Pretty, yet quiet and intense. He knew it must be difficult being brought up by her mother when her mother was with a few different men every night, but still she seemed as if she had no joy in her life. If coming on his rounds made her happy, then good. He enjoyed the company. She seemed more like a small person than a little girl. She was, as his wife would have said, an old soul.

He watched her play, sipped beer from his bottle.

Mae chatted away to herself and her imaginary friends, talked to Adam more than he had ever seen her talk to another human being.

Bert checked his watch. Getting on for six.

It wouldn't be long before he would have to take Mae back home. Then she would become sullen and monosyllabic, dragging her feet ever slower the nearer she got to her house.

Bert didn't enjoy that bit at all.

Seeing the look on Monica's face when she saw her daughter. Like someone had just attached a dead weight around her neck. Bert would try and be cheery, see if Monica wanted to go out somewhere, all three of them even, but he didn't hold out much hope. Her mother had moods. Especially when Mae was brought back to her.

He had seen the child with bruises, sometimes gashes on her legs and arms. Made him wonder what was going on in that house. What Mae was experiencing.

Best not to think of it. Not just yet.

Because that wasn't for an hour or so. Let the lassie enjoy herself while she could.

He watched her play, sipped his beer from the bottle.

Best not to think of it. Not just yet.

Let her enjoy herself while she can.

Ralph Bell parked the car, switched off the ignition, sighed.

Balmbras would be starting its evening of entertainment by now. Old-tyme music hall. 'Cushy Butterfield'. 'Blaydon Races'. 'The Lambton Worm'. All flat cappery and fake nostalgia.

And why was 'time' spelled 'tyme'?

Ralph didn't know. Cared less.

The further away from Kenny, the nearer he had got to home, the darker his mood had become. His initial prognosis on Kenny's condition had become riddled with holes, clouded by doubts. His optimism draining as his son's face faded from his mind.

His prognosis was based on guilt and blind hope. The realization hit him like a wrecking ball to his chest. Kenny wouldn't get better. He knew that. Then felt angry with himself for thinking that.

And round and round his mind went. Faster and faster, deeper and deeper. Further and further down. He couldn't help it.

Fingers trembling, he reached into his jacket pocket, pulled out the piece of paper Dr Shaw had given him. He looked at the words written on it. His breathing became heavier.

'It won't solve all your problems,' Dr Shaw had said to him, 'but it will alleviate them for a while.'

Ralph had nodded.

'I think you'll enjoy it, though,' Dr Shaw had said. 'I can always spot a fellow—' he put his head back, staring at the

ceiling, searching for the right word; he found it, returned his
head forward, locked eyes with Ralph '—enthusiast.'

'I . . . I'm, I don't think, I'm not . . .' Ralph had said. His
face had flushed red.

Dr Shaw smiled.

'Not yet,' he said, 'but you will be. Like I said, I can always
spot them.'

Ralph looked again at the paper.

'What's this line here for?' he said.

Another smile.

'My little joke. That's the line you cross. Once you've gone
over it, there's no going back.'

Ralph had nodded, folded the paper, pocketed it.

Now he looked at it again.

The line.

He had dropped Joanne off at her halls of residence. She
had smiled, kissed both Jean and himself goodbye, not able
to mask the concern in her eyes as she did so. She had
stopped short of expressing it, though, gone forward into the
Leazes Terrace halls to her new friends, her new life.

Ralph had driven Jean back home. He hated that house
now. With its chunky, dark furniture and its dead, stale air, it
was like living in a mausoleum. He tried to spend as little
time there as possible. And Jean had changed too. Drifting
around the house, her clothes drab, shapeless, shroud-like,
she was like the living shadow of the woman she had once
been. A spectre looking to be reunited with its corpse, hoping
for a spark of reanimation. And Ralph felt guilty.

He looked again at the piece of paper.

'It's a wonderful experience,' Dr Shaw had said. 'Very
cathartic.'

Ralph had nodded. He didn't know what the word meant.

'But be warned,' Dr Shaw went on. 'You won't just be able
to go once. It's very addictive.'

'Good,' Ralph had said. 'That's what I'm hoping for.'

He folded the piece of paper, put it back in his pocket. Looked around. No one could see him.

Good.

'I'm going straight out,' he had said to Jean, dropping her off at the mausoleum.

She had just nodded, expected him to say something like that.

'Got to meet somebody,' Ralph had felt compelled to explain. To find something that would fill the spaces between them. Words. Small words.

'Has to be tonight,' he said. 'Only time that's free.'

Jean had just walked up the garden path. She hadn't looked back. He didn't see her enter. One minute she was there, the next she was gone. Like the house had just silently drawn her in.

He had driven away.

Now he hauled himself out of the car, locked it. He felt uneasy about leaving the car in the area he was in, but he had no choice. This was where he had to be.

In the distance, down the bank, he could see the fledgling tower blocks: surrounded by scaffolding, loomed over by cranes. He expected his heart to be filled with pride at the sight.

It wasn't.

His heart was too full of other things for that.

He checked the address on the piece of paper again, even though he had committed it to memory.

He started walking.

Monica checked her face in the mirror.

The make-up was powdery-thick and stuck to her skin. She brushed it on as tenderly as she could, hiding the bruising on her cheekbone. She applied the last touches, put down the brush, looked in the mirror again. The bruise was covered but the swelling was still noticeable. It made her face look lopsided, misshapen.

Her eyes left her cheekbone, wandered in mirror image around the rest of her face.

All she saw was make-up. A fake skin, a false face.

Her eyes were surrounded by pale skin, fringed by long, dark lashes. The dark rings were gone, the skin no longer grey, dead and putty-like.

Her nose was prim and pale. No spidery capillaries tracing from her nostrils.

Her cheeks were heavily shaded, accentuating her bone structure. The broken veins, the splotches of ruddiness, the sunken hollows, gone.

Everywhere, her tallow skin was hidden, enclosed. Her inner self camouflaged. Monica looked, she thought, as best she could.

She checked her wig, a peroxide beehive, tucking in any limp strands of hair. She stood up, smoothed down her skirt. Her body was still bruised from an earlier punter's overenthusiasm. She found it difficult to stand fully erect, to walk without wincing.

She slowly made her way to the kitchen, half-filled a glass with gin, topped it up with tonic from a screw-top bottle. She took two full mouthfuls, sighed. That felt good. That erased the pain.

For a while.

She checked her watch. Mae would be back soon.

Mae. Behind the mask her heart sank, spirits deflated. Mae. Monica's constant reminder that she wasn't getting any younger. Nothing ages a mother, or makes a mother feel aged, like a daughter. Other women could accept that fact, even live a vicarious life through their offspring.

But not Monica.

Mae was a child born out of hate and abandonment.

And Monica had never allowed her to forget it.

At first she had tried to mother her, look after her until her father came back. Until they could be a proper family. But then she saw the news. Heard the stories. And realized Brian would never be coming back.

Then everything coalesced: the loose threads of Monica's despair at her situation, anger at Brian for abandoning her, fear for her future, all gathered together and wrapped themselves in a tight knot of seething hatred and resentment around the baby Mae. Monica wanted Brian back. She wanted Mae to disappear.

His old friends had come round, Brimson and Eddie. Supposedly seeing how she was but really just wanting to use her body. And she had let them. Thinking that would make her feel closer to Brian, connected in some way. Instead it just made her feel further apart, more alone. After a while they stopped coming.

She kept working, putting out. The only thing she knew how to do. She watched younger girls coming up, getting her trade. Prettier faces, fresher flesh. She looked at herself, having to work harder just to keep up. Twenty-three but looking thirty-three. Or forty-three in a bad light. Life using her up, wearing her out. Ageing. Fast. Mae the constant reminder.

She wanted Mae to disappear. So she plotted. She planned.

An accident. That would work best.

First there were the sleeping pills. She spilled them over the living room floor.

'Look, Mae,' Monica had said to the one-and-a-half-year-old, 'Smarties. You love Smarties, don't you?'

Mae had looked at her, wanting to trust her but even at that age expecting some kind of punishment.

'They're lovely, Mae. Your favourite. Come and get them.'

Hope triumphing over experience, the toddler approached

the sleeping pills and slowly chewed them up. Her mother smiled at her. Mae, trusting, returned it.

Monica watched as Mae had slowly fallen asleep, staggering at first as if drunk. Monica had laughed out loud, finding that very funny.

She watched as Mae slipped away.

It was working. The further Mae went, the more Monica felt the burden lift from her.

And then there was a knock at the door.

Monica had acted quickly, picking up the near-empty pill bottle and placing it on the kitchen table. She rushed to the door, opened it. There stood Shirley, a neighbour from two doors away. Without waiting to be asked, she entered.

'I'm not stoppin' long,' she said, then launched into a monologue about the problems with her husband.

When she reached the living room she stopped dead.

'What's happened?' Shirley said.

She looked down at the little girl lying on the floor.

Monica knew that she had to act convincingly. If she didn't she would be in big trouble. That was no problem, she thought. She had faked enough emotions in the past.

'She's sleepin', isn't she?' Monica said.

Shirley looked around, saw the pill bottle on the table.

'Go an' call an ambulance, Monica. Look.'

Shirley held out the bottle.

Monica's hand sprang to her mouth.

'Oh, my God . . .'

'Quickly!'

Monica ran out of the house to Shirley's to use the phone.

The ambulance arrived, took Mae to hospital. They pumped her stomach, brought her round.

Saved her life.

Monica had closed the door on the questioning policemen for the last time, stood with her back against it, heaved a huge sigh of relief. She had acted relieved, deflected questions as to how the pills came to be there, where she was at the time. Played the distraught mother. Played dumb. She had got away with it.

But the door closing had also ended her attempt to be free of Mae. The familiar weight descended again, her mood blackened. Mae was only a small child, but the house seemed too oppressive, too small for them both.

She would have to think of something else.

She did.

She gave Mae away.

She had avoided the adoption agencies. She didn't want some middle-class, middle-aged woman looking down on her, making judgements about her life. Keeping her at arm's length in case they caught something from her. She had to find another way.

She had heard of a couple who were emigrating to Australia. They were childless and desperately wanted a baby. She knew they lived locally, at the top of West Road in a bungalow in Denhill Park. Walking distance. She put Mae in her pram one afternoon, went up there. The whole street was one of well-tended front lawns, painted doors. The kind of house Monica would have liked to live in. But she had something they didn't. She would have gladly swapped. She rang the bell. A woman, early thirties, pleasant looking, answered.

'I hear you're looking for a baby,' Monica said.

The woman looked at her, open-mouthed.

'I hear you're goin' to Australia.' She pointed at the pram. 'Take her. She's yours.'

Before the woman could speak, Monica turned and walked away up the road. She heard the woman calling after her. She never once looked back.

Walking home, she again felt the burden lift from her. She

smiled to herself. Then mentally kicked herself. She should have asked for money. She should have taken cash for Mae. She stopped walking, almost turning round to go back, but deciding against it. The woman might have changed her mind, tried to give Mae back to her. It wasn't worth the risk.

She went back home, back to work. That night she was in the Crooked Billet, drinking and laughing. She turned down all offers to spend the night with her, wanting instead to wake up alone in her own house. Plan her new-found freedom. The next morning she woke up with a stinking hangover and was sick on the way to the toilet. No matter, she was happy. For a day or two she hardly faked any emotions with her punters.

Then on the third day there was a knock at the door. Thinking it was a punter, she opened it quickly. It wasn't.

Mae was returned to her. A neighbour of the couple's had heard rows between the husband and wife, seen a strange girl in their company, called the police. They had asked around, someone had mentioned Monica bragging in the pub about getting rid of Mae. The couple's solicitor managed to smooth everything over. The woman had wanted to keep Mae, her husband hadn't. If the child were returned safely to her mother, no charges would be brought. Against either parties. Mae was delivered to the doorstep clutching a caseful of new clothes and toys.

Monica closed the door, looked at her daughter. A wave of anger built up inside her, threatened to crash out through her fists on to Mae's body.

'Get upstairs,' she shouted.

Mae did so. But as she turned, Monica glimpsed her daughter's eyes. They were hard and cold, pupils tight little kernels of hatred. Directed at Monica. Mae went to her room.

Monica had never considered it before. Perhaps Mae hated her as much as she hated Mae.

A two-way street of loathing.

Monica had sat down then, the invisible burden on her shoulders too heavy to keep her upright. This was it. For ever. So she had better get used to it.

She had made her way to the kitchen, helped herself to the gin bottle.

There had been another knock at the door then. Her punter. She had sent Mae out to play, robotically serviced the punter, pocketed his money. Afterwards, she sat in the front room, counting, drinking and looking at the case Mae had brought back with her. Feeling the tide rise within her again, she picked it up, dragged it to the back door and heaved it into the rubbish in the yard. Then went back to her drink.

That was that.

She gave up planning after that. Became more opportunistic.

Monica had some friends round the house one day: Shirley, Bert too, and others. Monica had put Mae out of the way, playing upstairs. As Bert came to go, he looked up the stairs. And stopped dead. Mae was standing by the open window, dolls on the windowsill. She stretched out, overbalanced. Bert saw that and ran, two at a time, up the stairs. He reached the child just in time, pulling her back into the window, into the house. Hurting his back in the process.

Monica started: she didn't know how that happened, Mae was a naughty girl for playing there. Reprimanded the child, smacked her. Mae started to cry.

Mae's legs were scratched and cut where Bert had pulled her in. Bert was struggling to get up, his back spasming in agony. Shirley was shouting at Monica, telling her she was irresponsible. Monica just wished they would all go away, leave her alone. Let her find some peace.

It blew over. No lasting damage, apart from Bert who was off work for two weeks.

After that, Monica had given up. It was a sign. She couldn't get rid of her daughter, so she had to accept she was stuck with her.

And that, her heart heavy with acceptance, was that.

She looked away from the mirror, took another swig, checked her watch. Mae would be home soon. With Bert. He wanted to take her out to the Crooked Billet tonight. Enjoy the celebrations. She didn't mind. As long as he was buying.

He had been round a lot lately. Ever since the incident with Mae and the window. She knew he liked the child, tolerated her where Monica wouldn't. That was fine, she let him. As long as she herself didn't have to do that.

He liked to think of himself as her boyfriend. That was fine too. As long as he was paying. And didn't want sex.

She looked at her dressing gown, at her watch again. Plenty of time to get dressed. She drained her glass. Enough time for another drink. She fixed it, returned to the mirror.

She was ageing. No match for the young girls. She had had to diversify, specialize.

Pain. Domination. Humiliation. A smaller market but more lucrative if you were good at it. And Monica was good at it. She could dispense and receive suffering as if born to it. She got a lot of repeat business. She got referrals and recommendations. She didn't have to deal with a pimp. She had cuts and bruises, but she thought the odd whip scar or mouthful of piss a small price to pay. She was careful not to damage her punters too much, leave them able to heal quickly, return speedily. And she got paid for it all. And more often than not got some kind of enjoyment out of it.

In the room. With Christ in pain. With the bright white walls and the deep dark shadows.

She knew Mae would stand at the door, listen to the sounds of pain and humiliation, pleading and power that came out of there. She knew they scared the girl. But she didn't care. It was her house. If she didn't like it, Mae could live somewhere else.

She looked in the mirror again, saw the make-up covering the bruise on her cheekbone. Her last punter. Entering into the celebration spirit, getting a little too overenthusiastic. She had felt her face, tender to the touch, checked her teeth, found a couple slightly loose. She had charged him extra for that.

A knock at the door.

Mae, she thought, back from the street party. Bert to take her out. Her heart heavy, she drained the last of her gin, went to answer it.

There stood a man she hadn't seen before. Middle-aged with thinning hair, a moustache, a red face and a beer drinker's belly. Good clothes – Harris tweed jacket, collar and wool plaid tie – but worn for too long without a wash. Holding a piece of paper. Hands shaking.

First timer, thought Monica.

'Hello,' the man stammered. The red of his complexion deepened.

Monica looked at him, his silence encouraging him to speak.

'I believe—' he swallowed hard '—that you offer certain . . . services.'

'Yes,' said Monica.

'Are you . . . available?'

'How did you find out about me?'

'Someone told me.' His voice was dry. Sandpaper over rough bark. He cleared his throat. 'An . . . acquaintance of mine. A Dr Shaw.'

Monica ran the name through her memory. She knew the man. He always made her uneasy. Had a creepy side to him, a barely tamed one. And knowing what his preferences were, he was the last person she would consult on a medical matter.

'I know him,' she said, voice neutral.

'He said you were by appointment only, but ...' He shrugged. 'I just wondered.'

Monica checked her watch. No sign of Mae or Bert. Stuff them. Money was money.

'Come in,' she said, and stepped back.

As she closed the door, she sized the man up. Wondered what to wear, what he would like.

And how much she could get away with charging him for it.

The day was finally dying. Saturday begrudgingly becoming Sunday.

Drunks were everywhere. Their bodies were exhausted but still moving, unused as they were to over twelve hours of dedicated, solid alcohol consumption. Some staggered through the streets like zombies from a cheap Hammer horror flick, their progress landmarked by pooled vomit, dropped chips, broken bottle glass, let blood. Some were laughing and raging, voices and emotions heightened in the night air like declaiming Shakespearean hams. All were determined to wring the last few drops of enjoyment from the day, cling tenaciously to its fading life or half-life, be the last to leave the party.

The King's Cross train, the last of the night, pulled out of Newcastle Central Station heading for Edinburgh. The few disembarking passengers hurried through the station concourse and out into the night, off to their homes. One man stood silently, case beside him, looking around. He smiled.

His suit was Carnaby Street mod-sharp, hair brushed forward, long and stylishly trimmed. Black-rimmed glasses gave him an air of gravity. He stood like an important man, a serious man. Strong, confident, expensively tailored and groomed.

He picked up his case, walked out of the station.

'Taxi, mate?' asked a cabby at a nearby rank.

'No, thanks,' the man said. 'Think I'll walk a bit.' His accent was undeniably London, Thames estuary softened at the edges.

The cabby, no lover of Southerners, turned away. The man walked on.

He cocked his head on one side, listened through his one good ear. So strange yet so familiar. That was how the city seemed to him. Same buildings, same trolley bus lines, but the energy was different. It seemed more in tune with what he was used to. More alive.

London was his city. The city. And Soho the only place to be in that city. But he had gone as far as he thought he could. Climbed that ladder, reached the top.

And learned a lot. Things he couldn't wait to put into practice in his new manor.

His old manor.

It was all about control. Control, direction and patience.

He had learned that.

But not endless patience.

He walked the streets. There seemed to have been some sort of celebration.

So they've finally found out how to enjoy themselves, he thought. Good. I can help them on their way.

He checked his shirt cuffs, made sure there was an inch of white brilliance below his jacket sleeves. He picked up his case, kept walking.

He needed to find a hotel. A good one. But first he wanted to walk.

It had been another person from a previous life who had hidden himself on the mail train six years ago. A frightened, wild boy.

Brian Mooney.

But he was dead now. Had died the moment the train had pulled out of the station.

Ben Marshall.

That was the name on his luggage, his passport. The monogram on his clothes. Ben Marshall was very much alive.

He walked the streets, so strange yet so familiar.

The energy was different.

More alive.

Ripe. Ready to move from black and white into colour.

Perfect. For him.

He breathed in a lungful of night air, held it, let it go. Then went to find a hotel.

February 1963:
Grip of the Strangler

The audience cheered, whistled, stomped, clapped.

'Thanks a lot.'

The lead singer growled rather than spoke. Deep, Northern. Almost feral. It fitted with the atmosphere: the room was lit by a primal energy. Rich with sweat and physical excitement. Neo violent, almost sexual.

He wiped his brow, swigged from a bottle, grabbed the mic.

'Good, eh?'

The crowd cheered. He acknowledged them. Spoke like one of them.

'Fuckin' aye.'

He put the bottle down, turned to the rest of the band, nodded. Then back to the audience.

'Boom Boom,' he shouted.

The crowd, Mod-sharp and soaked in sweat and adrenalin, knew what to expect, cheered in anticipation. The band charged right in, a tight, beat-driven combo, music forceful, fist-like, stripping whatever small amount of finesse the John Lee Hooker original had once contained, reducing it to its basic hot, grinding components.

The crowd responded: picked up the energy coming towards them, flung it back at them.

John Steel and Chas Chandler: drum and bass in pounding rhythm; Hilton Valentine: cranked-up guitar squalling and squealing; Alan Price: heightening Hammond poured over like beautiful, dirty cream; Eric Burdon: voice ripping through the song with ragged authority.

Friday night, February 1963. The Animals rocking the Club A Go Go.

Ben Marshall stood against the back wall of the cramped club, unobtrusive but available. He had seen the Stones here, and they were good, but he liked this band. Even hearing them with only one good ear, he knew they had something. If they could excite the boys and girls nationally the way they did in this room, he thought, they would be huge. Another Beatles. Another Stones.

Not that he cared about music; he cared about money. Guitar bands were the next wave. There was a supply and demand market for them, and this band, the Animals, would make a lot of money for the right person. He had been tempted to manage them but decided against it. He didn't want it to interfere with his long-term plan.

He scanned the crowd. The crowd knew him. Or at least what he sold. And he loved the Club A Go Go. Fitted right in. The nearest thing Newcastle had to match Soho.

Brian Mooney had arrived in London lost, penniless. Seven years ago.

Another person, another life.

He had jacked and mugged his way to a room, a few clothes, food and drink. But he needed more.

He drifted into Soho, attracted by the bright lights, the dark shadows. He loved it there. And things were happening to him, realizations dawning. This wasn't Newcastle. He couldn't go on as he had there, relying on energy and anger to carry him. He needed more. Subtlety. A strategy. A long-term plan. Soho might provide it.

He studied the area, saw how it worked, how he could make it work for himself.

Then, a piece of self-engineered luck, the right place at the right time: a man he spoke to in a Soho pub was looking for someone to do some work. Mr Calabrese, the man said, a Maltese businessman, owned a string of bookshops. He was having trouble hiring and retaining staff. He needed help.

Brian knew the score, heard truthful words between the spoken ones. For Mr Calabrese, Maltese businessman, read Big Derek Calabrese, Epsom Salt gangster. For bookshops, read porn palaces. For trouble hiring and retaining staff, read shop managers skimming profits, then doing a bunk.

Brian could barely contain his excitement. It was the break he had been looking for. Strong-arm stuff, people to be found, lessons to learn.

Brian found the managers, taught the lessons. Enthusiastically. He impressed, was paid. Was used again. Impressed again. Then put on the payroll.

Big Derek found him special jobs. Ones that utilized his particular skills. Grasses and singers were picked up, stuck in a basement, forced by Brian to express love and fidelity to Big Derek. To see the error of their ways. Sometimes they just disappeared completely. Those were the kinds of jobs he liked best.

Then there was the day-to-day stuff, the bread-and-butter stuff: collecting rents from girls in flats, making sure they paid what Big Derek said they owed. Working the door in clubs, security in brothels. Keeping the shop managers in line. He would pay off the bent coppers, the ones with blind eyes and greedy pockets. Dirty overcoats, even dirtier souls.

Brian loved Big Derek like a father. He listened to him,

remade himself in Big Derek's image. Big Derek loved Brian in return. Like a wayward, psychopathic animal he had tamed and housetrained.

Brian loved Soho too. And Soho, it seemed, loved Brian. Made for each other.

But.

Dissatisfaction began to creep in. He had gone as far as he could with Big Derek. He knew that. But working there had allowed him to see the future. He built up ideas, formulated plans.

But not for London.

Newcastle.

He told Big Derek, explained his plans, expounded his vision. His old scores that needed settling, his new way of doing it.

Big Derek didn't want him to go. Found him too useful.

Brian talked, showed his heart was set. Offered, as a last resort, a cut to Big Derek.

Big Derek relented, gave his reluctant blessing. Even gave him a contact.

But. Another thing:

Brian insisted on a new identity. New clothes, glasses, hair colour. Polish the accent Brian was already using.

And off he went. Home.

Newcastle had changed since Brian had left: the city was all new to Ben.

He had found the Club A Go Go, based himself there. Beat kids and Mods, wanting to get high on anything they could get hold of. The club had energy. Ben could give it more. He identified a market, cut himself in, started dealing.

Uppers. Downers. Weed for the hopheads. Black bombers and purple hearts; demilitarized iconography given a post national service meaning.

And there he stood: the hatred, anger and impetuosity of

his earlier incarnation now varnished with the veneer of a suavely confident entrepreneur. The spiritual son of Big Derek Calabrese. A patient man. A planner.

Anticipation making the eventual outcome taste all the sweeter.

The Animals finished 'Boom Boom'. One more song, then the set would end. Ben left the room, went to the bar. Authentic blues played from hidden speakers. Muddy. Howlin'. Elbowed his way to a lime-green bar stool, ordered a scotch on the rocks, looked at the painted walls. The jazz greats stared down at him in huge monochrome relief. He sat directly below Earl Hines. Next picture along was of the Emcee Five, a home-grown jazz group. All the paintings were by Eric Burdon, the Animals' lead singer.

Ben sipped his scotch, waited. Let the raw sounds wash over him.

Waited for customers wanting to extend the high the music had just given them, mellow out away from it. But more important, waited for the signal that would enable him to move his plans along to the next phase.

Joanne Bell had been in the club a few times with her college friends. He had even sold some hop to them once or twice. But she hadn't recognized him. Good. Even given him the glad eye. He had almost reciprocated, noting how her curves had developed, imagining her naked and under his control, but had stopped himself.

It would have been fun, but not enough fun to jeopardize his plans.

Then the door opened and in she walked. As if on cue.

Sharon Smeaton and her girlfriends.

His target.

Perfect.

It wasn't accidental. He had made enquiries, investigated. His information was good, bought and paid for. He knew the

Smeatons' marriage was under a strain. Knew who the weak link would be. Knew who the best target would be.

He watched Sharon and her friends enjoy themselves. He knew that most of them had met at school, had married, had borne children. He knew they got together every few weeks to go for a meal or a film. He knew they considered themselves young and fashionable enough for the Club A Go Go. Knew which one to bribe to make sure they came there, and pay for her silence.

Sharon had lost none of her looks. She was older, of course, but that seemed to add to her appeal. Her looks weren't the kind to fade with youth; they were more durable than that. She still took pride in her body, her whole appearance. Tasteful make-up, fashionable hairstyling and Quant clothing. Ben noticed the amount of admiring glances she was attracting. Also noticed that she wasn't quite ignoring them as much as she would have done a few years ago.

When she and Jack were happier.

Through investigation and supposition, he had concluded that Sharon Smeaton was frustrated and stifled by the circumstances of her life. Circumstances rich for exploiting.

Ben saw the club's bar manager, Martin Fleming, at the opposite side of the room talking to a patron. He beckoned him over, told him what he wanted, slipped a note from his roll, handed it over. Martin Fleming walked off, smiling. Martin Fleming, Big Derek's contact.

Champagne was rare in the Club A Go Go. Soon a bottle of it made its waitered way over to Sharon's table. Ben saw heads turn as it went, heard the gasps of delight from the women, the sender's identity questioned. The waiter, as he had been told to do, informed them that the gentleman in the corner had wanted the beautiful blonde lady and her friends to enjoy themselves at his expense.

They all looked over, smiling, wanting a glimpse of this exotic stranger. Ben raised his whisky glass in return.

Sharon smiled, made eye contact.

Ben smiled, returned it.

Bingo.

He waited a while; made sure they were enjoying themselves, then slipped into the live music room to make some money.

The warehouse was blazing.

The old, timber frame fed and supported the flames, the corrugated roof collapsed inwards. Two fire engines were on the scene, ladders up, spraying the blaze, attempting to contain it.

A small number of Byker residents looking for local entertainment watched the fire, along with several homeward-bound pubbers making a detour to take in the spectacle, share the warmth. They stood, coats buttoned, collars up, hands thrust deep into pockets

Among them, Johnny Bell.

Johnny Bell loved to watch fires, the bigger the better. Loved to see the flames leap and jump, tried to guess which way they would dance next, how high they would climb. Fire was power as well as beauty: natural, barely tameable or containable. It could warm or it could hurt.

Hurt badly.

The moment when a fire started to take hold, switched from being manageable to uncontrollable, was his favourite time. It gave him an erotic charge when that happened, a sexual thrill.

Johnny Bell loved to watch fires.

Especially ones he had started himself.

It had started out as a thrill. A dare. An assertion of himself over a structure or an area. But then whispers started, names were mentioned. He was fearful that he would be caught, put in prison. But people heard of his skill. Asked if he worked to order, took commissions. Money became involved. And that made it even more fun.

As well as a lucrative sideline, it became a challenge to Johnny. How to make it a work of artistry. How to make it accidental enough to fool an insurance company. How to make sure that, in this case, an ailing stationery wholesaler got compensated for his tragic loss.

Because that was how Johnny got paid.

He loved the feeling of entering the chosen building, sensing the quiet, knowing he was alone, was going to be the last person to see the building looking the way it did. Knowing the power he held.

The erotic charge it gave him.

Johnny watched, hands deep in coat pockets, stroking his erect penis through the lining, as the firemen struggled to tame the blaze. The firemen seemed to be winning. The charred, wooden frame of the warehouse was beginning to supplant the darting flames as the dominant image.

The fire was abating. The fun draining with it.

Johnny turned, started walking away.

A good night's work.

His cock was still erect. He still wanted release.

He knew where to go.

La Dolce Vita. Private dining room.

Ben Marshall and Sharon Smeaton having dinner.

Steak and all the trimmings. Hers well done. His blood-rare.

'Modern,' Ben was saying, washing a mouthful of meat down with a hearty French claret, 'is good. New is good. Take this place. The owner, who's a good friend of mine, was telling me this is the first of its kind in the whole region. You

can eat, dance, drink, gamble, watch live music, anything.'
Another mouthful of claret. 'Of course, you get places like
this all the time in London, but it's rare up here.' He smiled.
'Why I'm drawn to it, I suppose. Must be homesick.'

Got her again, he thought. At the mention of London, her
eyes had widened fractionally. Not much, but enough for
someone trained to look for the signs to notice an inner
excitement.

Ben noticed.

It had been a relatively easy matter to get her to agree to
dinner. After the champagne had been drunk, Sharon, at her
friends' insistence, had come over to thank him.

'If you really want to thank me,' he said, his faux London
accent pushed to the fore, 'you could do me the honour of
having dinner with me.'

Even in the dark, he knew she had blushed.

'I'm with my friends. I can't just leave them. What would
they think?'

Ben smiled. His practised, killer smile.

'They'd be jealous it wasn't them,' he said.

She smiled back at him.

Their eyes locked.

The lazy, sensuous bossa nova beat all around them.

He had her.

'Just a minute,' she said and returned to her friends.

He watched their faces as she told them his request. Heard
the incredulous laughing, the giggling. The looking round to
see him. Then the smiling. It was what they all longed for. He
knew that. It was why he had planned it this way. He saw the
faces, mock stern, as Sharon's friends told her why she should
accept his offer. But how she should lay down certain rules
first. Make him aware where he stands.

She came back to him.

'I'd love to join you for dinner, Ben.'

'Thank you.'

'But I just want you to know that I'm a wife and a mother. And I'm not looking for anything else.'

Her eyes left his when she spoke those last few words, darting away, ending up on her handbag from where she removed an invisible speck of fluff.

'Please don't get the wrong impression,' said Ben, brow furrowed, voice dripping with sincerity. 'I'm new to the area. Up here for work. If I have to make new friends, I'd rather they were beautiful ones.'

She blushed again.

And he escorted her to a table in the private dining room, La Dolce Vita.

She had been to the pictures with her friends, she said. Not much on: a toss-up between *The Longest Day* and a double bill of *Grip of the Strangler* and *Blood of the Vampire*. She hated war films, so they had decided on the horror double bill, just for a laugh.

'And was it?'

'Boring,' Sharon said, and smiled. 'We walked out before the end. Came here for some proper entertainment.'

They ate, drank.

'So,' said Sharon after a while, 'what is it you do, exactly?'

He flourished his wine glass.

'I'm an entrepreneur,' he said.

Sharon smiled. 'So what is it you do exactly?'

Ben gave a small laugh. 'Very funny. I take small business opportunities and turn them into large ones. I did it in London with a few things and thought I'd chance my arm out in the provinces.'

'What kind of things in London?' said Sharon, looking at him over the rim of her wine glass.

Ben shrugged. 'Anything, really. Import and export. Nothing glamorous. Anything there was money in.' He caught her eye, smiled. It was suggestive with possibilities. 'Legal, of course.'

She returned the smile, sipped her wine.

'So what about you?' said Ben. 'What do you do?'

'Oh, nothing much.' Sharon broke eye contact. 'Housewife and mother, mostly.'

'The most underrated profession in the world,' said Ben. 'So easy to be taken for granted.'

'Isn't it, though.' Her words were edged with bitterness.

Ben leaned forward.

'But that's not true with you, surely?' His voice was all solicitous concern.

Sharon sighed. 'I wish it wasn't. But it's the same every day. Cleaning. Shopping. Getting Isaac ready for school. Picking Isaac up from school. Making sure a meal's there on the table at night. Trying to be as creative as possible about it.' She sighed again. 'Not that it's ever appreciated.' She looked away. 'Sorry. You shouldn't have to hear those things.'

Ben gave a look of apparently genuine concern.

'Don't worry. You've got to tell someone. Sometimes it's best to tell these things to someone you don't know. You can often be more honest.'

'I wouldn't want to bore you.'

'You wouldn't be boring me.'

Her hand was resting on the table. He placed his over it.

'That's often how friendships start.'

She looked up. Their eyes locked. Their hands gripped.

Then Sharon remembered where she was, whom she was with. And pulled her hand away.

She looked around, nervous, slightly embarrassed at her behaviour. She found her wine glass, took a hefty mouthful. Ben played along in scene, mimicked her actions.

'Sorry,' he said eventually.

'It's all right,' she said, her voice small and wavering. She sighed again. 'Sometimes I just want . . . more. And then I feel guilty for thinking that.' She looked at him, tried to smile. 'I've got nothing to complain about. Not really. I should be grateful for what I've got. Sorry.'

Her words, even to her own ears, sounded hollow.

Ben nodded sympathetically.

'No need to be.'

The waiter came to clear the plates. He asked if there was anything more.

'I'd better be getting back,' said Sharon. 'My friends'll be wondering where I've got to.'

Ben looked at his watch.

'I should think they'll be long gone by now.'

Sharon looked at him, her eyes reflecting both fear and anticipation.

Ben smiled.

'Don't worry,' he said. 'I'll make sure you get home safely.'

Her eyes widened.

'I'll get you a cab.'

She smiled, barked a short laugh. He couldn't tell if it was of relief or disappointment.

He paid for the meal in cash, helped her into her coat. She buttoned it, turned to face him.

'Well, thank you for a lovely evening,' she said, smiling.

'The pleasure was all mine,' he said. 'It isn't often I get to dine with such a charming and attractive companion.'

Her cheeks reddened again.

'Oh, before you go,' said Ben. He dug into his jacket pocket, brought out a card. He handed it to Sharon. 'That's my business card. If ever you want to give me a ring, feel free. It'll be nice to talk to a friendly voice in this town.'

'I will.'

'Listen,' he said, his voice sounding hesitant, 'we could

formalize this, you know. Perhaps dinner again? A drive in the country some time?'

'I don't know . . . .'

'I'm also going to be needing someone pretty soon.'

'Pardon?'

He looked from side to side, as if to check that no one was listening.

'If everything goes according to plan, and it seems like it is, I'm going to need an office manager. Someone I can trust.'

He looked right at her.

Sharon laughed.

'You hardly know me.'

Ben emptied his eyes of everything but the appearance of honesty.

'But I'd like to know you better. This might have prospects. It might lead on to bigger things. Are you interested? Can I contact you about it?'

Sharon turned away, thinking. Ben waited, timing the moments.

'Do you have a pen?' she said eventually.

Ben could barely contain his excitement. He wanted to laugh out loud, punch the air. Instead he said,

'Right here.'

He dug inside his jacket pocket, handed over his gold-plated fountain pen. He also gave her the receipt of the meal.

'Write on this,' he said.

She looked quickly up at him and for a second he thought he had overplayed her. Been too cocky, too sure of himself. He smiled to cover the cracks.

Wordlessly, she took the pen and paper. She didn't seem to have picked up on what he was thinking. He breathed a sigh of relief. She handed the pen and receipt back.

'That's my home number,' she said. It was her turn to look around, check no one was in earshot. 'If you want to call me, make it after nine and before three on a weekday. Not evenings or weekends.'

'Whatever you say. You make the rules.'

Ben smiled, Sharon smiled, a look of incredulity and disbelief at her own actions on her face, and a waiter arrived to tell them the taxi had arrived.

They walked through the main body of the club. The night was winding down. Chairs were being placed on tables, till rolls added up, the few hangers-on drinking up and thinking of leaving.

Outside, the cold air hit them like a slap in the face from a concrete glove.

'The winters get cold up here, don't they?' said Ben, laughing.

He opened the car door for Sharon. She turned to him.

'Thanks again for a lovely evening.'

'Again, the pleasure was all mine. I'm glad I met you.'

She kissed him on the cheek, then got quickly into the car.

She smiled and waved until the car disappeared up Percy Street, Ben returning the waves and smiles.

Once she was out of vision, he gave a sigh of satisfaction and headed back to the Go Go. Coat pulled around him, fighting the cold, he elbowed his way past the scooters parked before the narrow double doors, made his way into the club.

The band were propping the bar up, deciding which groupies to favour with their attention. Martin Fleming gave Ben a small smile as he entered, made his way to the bar, ordered a drink, waited.

To see if there were any punters who needed helping on their way.

He laughed to himself.

It had been a good night's work.

*

Four bulbs, three blown. The remaining one cast a dim light, accentuating rather than illuminating the darkness. Cold water drip-dripped on stained porcelain, bounced a frigid echo off the grubby white-tiled walls. The urinals stood tall and heavy, the wooden, paint-chipped cubicle doors hung half-open, the shadows within almost tangible, sending out threads and tendrils to ensnare the unsure, entice the wavering. The shadows made promises. The air was cold and still: morgue air.

Johnny stood before the heavy porcelain urinal, the wet of the dirty concrete floor soaking through his shoes, expelling breath as warm steam, trousers unzipped and erect cock in hand.

He pulled his foreskin back and forth, slowly, fingers smoothing up and down his shaft, taking pleasure from his own touch. He was waiting. Anticipating greater pleasure.

He always came here after a fire. Here, or somewhere like it. He had a mental map of amenable amenities, a lust-charged undergrid of the city. He wanted instant gratification, secret sex. Illicit, forbidden thrills. And he got all that here. Here, or somewhere like it.

It was quiet tonight. He had dismissed two offers, one for being too old and out of shape. The man had smelled of cheap booze, cheap aftershave. He had been too desperate, too demanding. Johnny had turned away, pointed his cock in the opposite direction. The man had implored, pleaded almost, but Johnny hadn't budged. The man had soon taken the hint. The other had been too arrogant, too cocksure. Demanding in a different sort of way. Well built, good-looking, but his eyes held promises of cruelty and pain. That had both turned Johnny on and repelled him in equal measures. Johnny had been tempted but scared. Eventually he had said no. The man had left. So he stroked himself and teased himself. Waited.

But not for long.

A man, no more than twenty Johnny reckoned, his eyes wide, his step hesitant. Johnny could almost hear the man's heart thumping like a runaway train. Well dressed. Probably a girlfriend somewhere, a wife even. Not an obvious homo, thought Johnny.

Just right.

Johnny let the man approach. He always let them make the first move; that way he knew they weren't coppers. Or at least not on-duty coppers.

The man came and stood next to Johnny, looked down at his cock. Johnny looked at the man, saw fear in his eyes, anticipation. An attempt to smile. Johnny looked back at his cock. The man did too. Slowly, the man slid out a shaking, nervous hand towards it. Touched it.

Johnny let out a small sigh, allowed the man to grasp it, move his hand slowly up and down on it.

That was good. That was what he wanted.

Nearly what he wanted.

He placed his hand over the other man's, stopping his action. The man looked at him, startled, suddenly fearful that Johnny might be a copper. Johnny nodded his head in the direction of the cubicles, made to move. The man turned and, relieved and eager, followed him.

Johnny let the man enter first, closed the door behind him. The shadows enveloped them. Wind whistled through an airbrick in the tiled wall, whispered softly, like the erotic promises made by new lovers.

It was cramped in there for the two of them. Their bodies were pushed up close together. The man made to kiss Johnny. Johnny turned his head away.

'Suck it,' he said. His voice was a snarling, desperate, whispered rasp.

The man kneeled down, found it easier to sit on the toilet seat, and put his mouth over Johnny's cock.

Johnny put his head back, sighed. This was it. This was what he wanted. Women could never do this right. Not even when he paid them.

The man was young. Inexperienced, but eager to please. Just the way Johnny liked them.

His head was bobbing up and down. Mouth enthusiastically slurping.

The pleasure was building within Johnny. Images were forming, transporting him. Erotically charged images:

Bodies: hard naked male hairless cruel powerful

Dominant

Fire: blazing licking burning dancing leaping uncontrollable

Beautiful

Punishing burning perfect flames hard powerful

Nearly there nearly

Cruel naked flames

Then a new image:

Blades: shining powerful beautiful

Perfect. Nearly

He pushed the man's head back, mouth away from his cock.

The man looked up in surprise. He opened his mouth to speak. Johnny beat him to it.

'Turn round,' he said, his voice low and guttural. 'Bend over.'

The man smiled, did as he was bid. As he bent over he began loosening his belt, undoing his trousers. Johnny took over, ripping at them, desperate to get the man's flesh exposed.

The man bent forward, straddled the toilet bowl, arse in the air.

Johnny, near to exploding, thrust his cock inside the man's anus.

The man screamed. It hurt.

Johnny pumped away, grimacing.

Burning entering

The man gasping.

Johnny pumping. Blood lubricating his cock.

Dominant cruel blades perfect naked flames

Burning. Nearly—

There.

He came.

Bucking and thrusting, pushing in pain.

The man gasped, took it.

Johnny didn't let him move away, controlled him, shouting, riding out the wave of his huge orgasm.

Hitting the peak, too intense, seeing stars behind his eyes. Gasping down air. Slowly coming down, gliding. The slope subsiding away, tailing off.

Johnny opened his eyes, loosened his grip. He saw the shadows, tangible, moving, saw the warm clouds of his breath, heard the frigid echo of the cold water drip-dripping. Heard the whisper of promises unkept. He was back.

The man stood up. He looked exhausted but happy. In pain but turned on.

'Did you enjoy that?' the man said, smiling. 'I did.'

He put an arm around Johnny, his other on Johnny's cock. He swallowed hard again.

'You going to do something for me now?'

Johnny looked down at his cock. Glistening, engorged. Covered in shit and blood, like abattoir offal.

Johnny looked at the man, felt panic rising, tried to back away. His body hit the cubicle door, banging it firmly shut against the doorframe. Keeping him in.

It was always the same. Every time. The anticipation, the exultation, the repulsion. Johnny hated how he got his pleasure, the needs he had that built inside him until they screamed for attention, for release. And he would give in willingly, wallowing in it, loving it, every time. And afterwards: self-loathing, guilt and revulsion would fall on him like a sudden, heavy rain shower.

Putting out the fire.

And the higher the mountain, the deeper the valley.

He hated it. Hated himself. What he'd become.

The man was still looking at him, thrown by Johnny's abrupt lack of enthusiasm but still smiling hopefully.

'Can I do that to you? What we've just done?' Hesitancy began to creep into the man's voice. 'I mean, if you don't want to, that's fine. We could do something else.'

Johnny's pulse was quickening. He had to get out of the cubicle. He felt trapped. Sweat prickled his forehead and body. He pushed his cock back inside his trousers. It was difficult: his erection was still too prominent. Betrayed by his body, he shoved it painfully inside his underpants, turned to the door again. He tried to open the cubicle but couldn't. His own body was blocking his only exit. The harder he pushed, the less it budged.

Trapped.

'Leave me alone,' Johnny said, his voice high and desperate. 'Don't touch me. You homo. You queer.'

The man stopped moving, looked at Johnny. Confused, quizzical.

The man laughed a little. 'What does that make what we've just done? What does that make you?'

'Get back.'

Johnny was shaking, sweating hard now.

'Look,' the man said, holding his trousers up with one hand, 'I've got a girlfriend. She doesn't know about this. I like it. It's fun. Gives me something I want I can't get from her. There's no problem. You're probably the same as me.'

'Shut up! I mean it. Now get back and let me go. Or you'll be sorry.'

'Look—'

The man moved forward.

'Don't touch me!'

Johnny pushed the man backwards. His legs hit the toilet bowl. He stumbled, sat down. Johnny advanced towards him.

'Homo. Queer. Think I'm the same as you, eh? Think I'm one of you?'

He kicked the man in the legs, hard. Viciously. The man, hurting, couldn't understand what was happening. How he had reached this point. How things had led to this.

'I'm not a homo . . . I'm not . . .' Kick. 'Think this is a bit of fun, eh?' Kick. 'I'm not . . . homo . . .'

'Wait . . . please . . .'

'No wait. No please. You make me sick, you lot. All of you.'

Johnny reached inside his pocket, produced his blade. One of his precious slaughterhouse blades. He wasn't supposed to be carrying it, but he loved having it near him. A boner and a skinner. It made the shadows jump with clean steel light.

'This is what I think of you lot. Homos . . . Queers . . .'

He slashed the man across the chest. The blade penetrated his thick winter wool coat, the layers of clothing beneath, drawing forth a slowly seeping, dark blood.

'Homo.'

Another slash. The man put his arms up to protect his face.

'Queer.'

Another slash. Johnny's blade tore through sleeve fabric.

'Fuckin' pervert, hate you . . .'

Slash. Slash. Slash.

Johnny, worn out, gasping for breath, found the door of the cubicle, pulled it open.

He stood in the centre of the toilet, breathing hard, the blade hanging bloodily loose in his limp hand. He was spent, exhausted. He looked down. His coat was splattered with blood. His hands red.

He put the knife back in his pocket, wiped his hands down the front of his coat. It was dark, heavy, woollen. Once the blood had stopped glistening and began to sink into the fabric, it would hardly show.

He looked back into the cubicle. The man was moving, groaning. Good. A relief. At least he wasn't dead.

Guilt began to creep over Johnny. Guilt and fear. He had to do something. Someone might enter the toilet. See him. He couldn't have that. He didn't want to go to prison. Didn't want to be blamed.

His mind flashed back to a night seven years earlier:

The Ropemakers Arms. Brian Mooney. His brother Kenny.

Kenny.

And now:

He felt he was about to vomit. To cry.

He swallowed it down. Kept it in. He had to think.

He needed a plan. Quickly. He thought hard. Ideas came to him. Not brilliant, but the best he could come up with, thinking like this.

He left the toilet. He would find a public telephone and make a 999 call. Tell them he'd found someone bleeding in a public toilet in Byker, on his way home from the pub. That he'd seen a man running away from the scene, looked like an Indian. Tell them where in Byker it was, what to expect. Tell them he wouldn't hang around in case they tried to pull him in for questioning, called him a queer.

Then run. Home. And get rid of his coat.

He did so.

And left cold water drip-dripping on porcelain, bouncing a frigid echo of grubby white-tiled walls. Left the air cold and still: morgue air.

Left a warm, deep, red pool, draining slowly away across the dirty concrete floor.

Left whispered promises unkept.

Sharon pushed the key into the lock. It slid in with a grating rasp. Her stomach flipped over. The noise seemed huge. She was sure it was loud enough to wake Jack.

And she didn't want to speak to Jack tonight. There was too much going on in her head.

She opened the front door. It swung silently back. She entered, shoes in hand, stockinged feet softly pad-padding on the carpeted hallway. She closed the door. The merest of clicks. She moved stealthily down the hall.

There was light coming from under the living room door.

Oh, God, she thought, he's waited up for me.

Her stomach lurched.

She moved towards it, resigned to talking, but not wanting to. Drawn: a moth to a flame that could burn her wings.

She pushed the living room door open. Jack was sitting on the sofa, head back, asleep. Next to him Isaac, body curled into his father's, head resting on his father's lap. The TV a black screen. Crisps and juice on the coffee table before them. Paperback open on the sofa arm.

Sharon felt an involuntary smile creep on to her face. Jack and Isaac had been getting along much better lately. Jack had taken steps, tentative at first, to admit his love for his son. Once he had surmounted that hurdle, things had been a little more relaxed.

She should have been happy, but she was still dissatisfied. Jack was doing more and more work for Ralph Bell with no increasing recognition. He was holding both the company and the man together and not getting his due reward. And Jack seemed fine about that. And that annoyed Sharon.

The familiar litany:

We should be further on than we are.

You're too nice to people.

You should stand up for yourself.

Said over and over again. Jack had stopped hearing it, she was sure.

Sharon looked at Jack. Tried to see him dispassionately, as a stranger would. He was looking old, worn. Always thin, he was now stringy. His hair was not as well dyed as it used to be. The white shone through, like bleached bone beneath a skin or cloth covering.

She wondered what she had once seen in him, then felt guilty for the thought. She was only thinking that because of Ben Marshall.

Ben Marshall.

She smiled at the name. At the memory of her night.

He had been trying to impress her, she knew that. Sounding like a big shot. And it might have worked. It was years since a man had found her attractive enough to buy her champagne, take her to dinner. Listen to her when she talked. Men had always found her attractive, and she had often rebuffed those who wanted to have flings and affairs with her. But no one had gone to the trouble of making her feel special, unique. Not for a long time.

She looked over at Jack and Isaac on the sofa again.

Safe. Homely. Familiar.

Overfamiliar?

She put that thought out of her mind. She felt the happiest she had for a long time, and that had nothing to do with her husband or son. And everything to do with a man who bought her champagne and dinner. Who wanted to take her driving in the country.

Who wanted to offer her a job.

With prospects. That might lead to bigger things.

She closed the door of the living room, leaving the side

light on, not wanting to disturb them. She made her way slowly upstairs and undressed.

Before getting into bed she opened her handbag and took out his card again. She looked at it, smiled. She ran her fingers slowly over the embossed lettering. Felt his name as it stood out. She smiled again, replaced it in her bag.

She crossed to the bed, pulled back the blankets and climbed in, snuggling herself down.

She felt happy. Confused, but happy.

She heard a small, feathery tapping on the window, gave a small start.

She looked.

It was a moth. Only a moth. Drawn to the bedside light.

She turned off the light, settled down to sleep.

Only a moth. Drawn by the bedside light.

A moth to a flame that could burn its wings.

August 1963:
The Great Escape

'There you go, pet.'

'Thanks.'

Ralph Bell took the cup of tea. His hands were still shaking.

He was sitting on the edge of the bed in Monica's back room. Her workroom.

White walls. Deep shadows where the light couldn't reach. Crucifixes. Christ in agony: nailed, bloodied, cut. Dying. The sinners watching.

Ralph was perched uncomfortably on the edge of the bed. He couldn't sit fully on; it still hurt too much from his session with Monica.

But hurt him good. A purging, cleansing pain.

He took a sip of his tea. Too hot. Scalded his lip. He placed it on the floor, straightened back up painfully.

Monica sat down next to him, cup of tea in her own hand. She had covered her work clothes with a dressing gown of pink, frilled, faded nylon. What she usually wore between punters. Her blonde wig sat rat-tailed and askew on her head. She sipped her tea. Found it bearable.

Ralph smiled at Monica. She automatically returned it.

He enjoyed this part. Almost as much as the sex. Sometimes

found himself racing through the session, he looked forward to it so much.

'Thank you,' he said.

Monica smiled. She didn't know whether he meant for the sex or the tea.

'You're welcome,' she said.

She knew what she had to say next. Which role to play.

'So how are things for you?'

Ralph sighed.

'The same, I suppose. Kenny's . . . well, I think he's making progress. The others, Jean and that, she tells me I shouldn't . . . y'know. Have hope. But I do. I have to.'

Monica nodded.

'I mean, last week I was there and—' he gestured with his hands, formed them into small, atomic cradles; held atoms within '—I'm sure he knew it was me. Sure of it. He smiled at me. Nodded.' Ralph sighed. Opened his hands, split atoms asunder. 'The staff say he does it all the time and that I shouldn't read anything into it. I don't know. He's my son, y'know? I should know him.'

Monica nodded, kept her mouth closed to stifle a yawn.

'What about your other son?' she said.

Ralph shook his head.

'Still never see him. I know he works down the abattoir, got one of the new flats in Scotswood. I helped him with that. Well, Dan sorted it for him. He wouldn't take any offers of help from me. I had to make it look like I had nothing to do with it.' Ralph sighed, lost in his own thoughts. 'Fancy. Your own son. And I don't know what he's doin'. Dan asked if I wanted to get someone to keep an eye on him. I said no. I was tempted, but I said no. He's grown up; he can do what he likes. But I don't even know what he's doin'. Where he is half the time.' Ralph sighed again. 'Like I've lost two sons. And they're not even dead . . .'

Monica nodded, affecting understanding.

'I'm amazed Joanne turned out as well as she did.' Another sigh. 'I've been a terrible father. Terrible. I was either working or meetin' people, tryin' to fix up deals. Work, though, always work. Or at meetin's. Giving me time to the party. Labour, y'know.' He gave a bitter laugh. 'That was just work as well. If I'm honest. Socialism's all well and good and that, and it's a nice idea, but . . . it was where the deals were made. Relationships cemented. Everyone knew Dan Smith was going places. Everyone wanted some of that. Well, I got it. I was lucky.' Another bitter laugh. 'Lucky. Well, not really luck. I mean, Dan might like to think of himself as a visionary, a Trotskyist even, but he likes money as much as the next man. I got the contracts, all right. But I had to make sure he was taken care of too. Mind you, I saw meself all right. On the Elms. But then everyone does. Cuts corners, y'know, we all do, pockets the difference. Mind I didn't tell Jack. He's too honest. He'd have left. And he's too valuable, too good at his job. I need him.'

The same speech every time. Monica had been listening to it for over a year now. She knew where the gaps came, what her lines were, what prompts she needed to give. It was as much a part of the ritual as the sex. She was still acting out a part.

She knew what was up next: guilt and indulgence.

'I used to spoil them, you know.' He smiled distantly. He was lost to Monica now, adrift on his own.

Monica nodded, no longer even pretending to listen, just a movement out of habit. She sipped her tea.

'It was guilt, I suppose. I had to indulge them, especially the boys. Because I was always out. Like I said, work, meetings. So when I saw them I'd spoil them. Take them to the football, the pictures, anywhere. Let them have anything they wanted. Anything. Jean didn't like it, but then, as I told her, it wasn't her as was going out to work every day. Wasn't her bringing the money in. First few times she would argue, but a quick slap soon shut her up.' Ralph nodded to himself. 'You have to, though, sometimes, don't you? Keep them in line.' His words were for himself. Monica sipped her tea. 'It's different hittin' a woman than it is hittin' a man. Different. But it worked, though. She didn't argue again.'

Monica drained her teacup, placed it on the floor. Ralph hadn't touched his. It would be cold by now.

'I even gave them jobs in the firm. Ones they didn't have to work at. I knew it was wrong. Even at that time I knew it was wrong. But I had to do somethin'. They turned out bad. I know they did.' Another sigh. 'And look where it got them. Look where it got me.' He shook his head. 'One's a vegetable and one's . . . I don't know what. And look at me. Look where I am.'

Monica looked up. This was her cue to tell him that things weren't so bad and that he was a good, successful man. Not a failure, as he saw himself. Once that was said and he believed it, she then had to tell him how much he was loved.

She opened her mouth to speak, summoning up the feeling to say her usual lines with conviction.

I deserve an Oscar for this, she thought.

Ralph turned to her.

'No,' he said. 'Don't say it. Don't.'

There was a strange fire in his eyes, a curious light.

Monica looked at him. Her mouth closed on the words she would have said.

'Listen to me,' he said. 'I mean, really listen. This is important.'

Monica looked at him, slightly startled at the script deviation.

'You've got a little girl, haven't you?'

Monica's heart skipped a beat. She nodded.

'Does she know what you do for a living?'

Monica made to stand up.

'I don't think this is—'

Ralph grabbed her wrist, pulled her down again.

'Please, just listen.'

Monica sat down. She had lost control of the situation.

'Do you love your daughter?'

Ralph was looking at Monica, eyes intensely boring into her. She wanted a drink. Needed one.

'She's me daughter.'

Monica's voice was dry despite the tea.

'But do you love her?'

'I . . .'

'Be honest.'

No, Monica. Mae had just always been there. Since her father disappeared. There. Holding Monica back, being a burden, in the way. Not even going when she tried getting rid of her. No. She had hated Mae, told her so. Screamed it into her face.

Love?

'I . . . I don't . . . know . . .'

Ralph grabbed her hands. Held them within his own.

'Love her. Let her know it. Don't do what I did. It's never too late to change. Never.'

Monica's heart was racing. Beneath her nylon dressing gown, her stiff, unyielding working clothes, her body was sheened with a cold, prickling sweat.

'I . . . I think you'd better go now.' She tried to pull her hands away but he had them firmly. 'I've got someone . . . someone else. Coming.'

Ralph sighed, shook his head. He slackened his grip. She pulled her hands quickly away.

'Sorry.'

He couldn't meet her eyes. He stood up.

'I'd better go. I'm sorry.'

Monica nodded. 'It's all right.'

'I shouldn't have . . .'

'It's all right.'

Ralph nodded, made his way numbly to the door. He turned.

'I didn't mean . . .'

'I know.' Monica's voice was calm, even. Held the veneer of control. 'I said it's all right.'

'I'll see you again, I hope.' Ralph was mumbling, red-faced.

'Soon.' Monica tried to invest the word with steadying warmth.

Ralph opened the door, left the room. She heard him go down the hall, open then close the front door. Gone.

She breathed a huge sigh of relief. Sat back on the bed.

Love. All that talk of love. Where did that come from?

She gave a small laugh.

'Love.'

She laughed again. It rang metallic and hollow around the empty room.

What was he on about? Poor addled man.

Love.

She looked around the room.

White walls. Deep shadows where the light couldn't reach. Crucifixes. Christ in agony: nailed, bloodied, cut. Dying. The sinners watching.

Love.

She went in to the kitchen to pour herself a drink. Gin. A large one. Very large.

Mother's ruin.

She gulped it down.

Her hands were shaking.

Ben Marshall couldn't believe his luck.

He'd always thought luck was something you made for yourself, but here he was being proved wrong.

The evidence: Ralph Bell and Monica Blacklock.

Together.

Talk about the proverbial. Two birds and one stone.

This was brilliant.

He had been trailing Ralph Bell for months. All part of the long-range plan. Ralph's work, his play. Ben building his findings into a chain, looking for the weakest links.

He'd just found another one.

He had been thinking of Kenny, something to do with Kenny. But this was even better.

This could be the one.

In all the time of trailing, it was the first time he had recognized Monica. She had been there, greeting him at the door. And he had recognized her. The wig and sometimes the dark glasses had thrown him off. Her body had changed its shape too: fat deposits shifting, settling in new, permanent places like undersea topography. Her face, when not made up, was gin-blotched, alcohol-inflated, but it was her.

And still on the game. Specializing in pain and humiliation.

And the kid. He'd seen the kid.

Small, with dead eyes. Staring at her mother, hiding her emotions, masking her fear with a film of indifference. But Ben knew what lay behind it.

Because that's how Brian had been.

That was where the family resemblance ended. She was Monica's kid, not his. Brian Mooney was dead. Monica's kid's father was dead.

Ben Marshall had nothing to do with it.

Ralph Bell and Monica, though.

Ben smiled. He had to think. He had to plan how to deal with this. How best to turn it to his own advantage.

He turned the key in the ignition, put the Sprite into gear.

Turned the radio on.

'Devil in Disguise'. Elvis Presley.
Number one.
He drove away, smiling to himself.

Monica tossed. Monica turned. She clenched and stretched. But it was no good. She couldn't reach the kind of sleep she wanted. She wanted peacefulness. Stillness. Black dreamlessness. But its reach exceeded her grasp.

She sighed, threw the bedclothes back from her body, stood up. She checked the bedside clock. Nearly twenty-past four. Hours before her usual rising time. She crossed to the window, pulled back the curtains. The street was dead. The world was dead. Everyone else was asleep. Monica was the only person awake.

Monica's heart felt like a locked, weighted coffin sinking to the bottom of a cold, cold lake. She hated being alone. And this was the worst time. Nights she could drink herself to bed, mornings she could lie about the new day's possibilities. But at this time in the morning there were no lies she could tell herself. Only harsh, painful truths.

Her reflection looked back at her from the glass. She was startled: she looked so old, so used up. Her face was drawn: dulled, grey eyes sitting above black sacks, ringed by an accretion of lines and creases that had nothing to do with laughter. Her hair, free of her wigs, hung dead and lank. Her body looked old, used, tired, as if it had become a repository for more than her punters' semen and sadism: their twisted desires, their controlled rages, their disappointments, failures and self-hatred. Given incrementally, with each thrust, lash and humiliation. Her life written on her body. The men used her and left, temporarily soul-cleansed, sated. Until those twisted desires returned, those rages threatened to slip from control. Then they would return. And Monica would receive them. Again, in the white room with the dark shadows. The crucifixes showing Christ's love and Christ's agony, Christ's love. Taking on the sins of the world, dying for them, being set free to live again. A few had asked why the religious icons were there, some taken offence. But Monica insisted they remain. A reminder.

Monica sighed, turned away from the window. Faced back into the room.

It was a mess: clothes, plates, bottles and glasses left lying around. No real pride, no real care. Not really home. Her sleeping bed – as opposed to her working one – indented only on one side. She usually slept alone.

Bert considered himself her boyfriend. Monica regarded him as a sad, obsessed punter, dreaming up a fantasy involving her to replace the memory of his dead wife. And she was happy with that. He occasionally stayed with her but rarely wanted sex. When he did it was straightforward and over with quickly, which pleased Monica. She had other boyfriends, too, which Bert knew about but never mentioned. They didn't usually last long. Her profession repelled those she would have liked, attracted those she didn't. They fell roughly into two categories: those who were turned on by what she did, and those who felt it was their right to never have to work, just live off her money. She tried hard to convince herself she was happy with these men, reinforce that feeling with alcohol, but it never worked. They drifted away after a while, on to someone easier, cheaper or more desperate. Leaving Monica alone. Again.

Monica didn't have a pimp. Didn't need one. She paid protection, like all the working girls in the area, and she had referrals. That did for her. She made a living.

Ralph Bell's words had cut into her. Verbal knives. Making her think.

About Mae.

Four thirty in the morning, honesty continued. It wasn't the girl's fault. Mae hadn't asked to be born. It was all Brian's fault. And he was so long gone and so far away; he may as well be dead. Perhaps he was dead.

All his fault. But past the point of blame now. Time for action.

Ralph Bell's words again: *Love her. Let her know it. Don't do what I did. It's never too late to change. Never.*

Monica looked around. Her room. Her bed. Her body.

Her life.

Not Mae's.

She turned, walked down the hall to Mae's room. Her daughter's room. Furnished almost as an afterthought: furniture and belongings sparse.

Mae lay in bed, asleep. Eyes closed, breathing shallow. Clutching her toy rabbit. She looked contented, at peace.

Never too late to change. Never.

Monica had to get Mae away from this life. Give her a new one. A better one.

That's what she would do. That's what she had to do.

Decision made, she yawned. Tired. She went back to her own room, lay down on her bed, pulled the covers over her body.

She knew what she had to do.

With that thought in mind, she slept.

It was past ten o'clock when she woke again.

Monica opened her eyes, looked at the time. With a start she flung back the covers, got out of bed. Her sleep had been dark and deep, like floating down a restful river in an underground, pitch-black cave.

Lovely.

She took that as an omen. Things were going to be all right. Peace would come to her.

Peace almost prematurely halted when she wrapped herself in her dressing gown and made her way into the kitchen. Mae had helped herself to cornflakes: a debris trail of cereal and milk stretched from the Formica work surface to the kitchen table.

Monica felt the familiar anger rising within her. She pulled back her hand to strike Mae, opened her mouth to bellow at her. Mae, spoon on the way to her open mouth, gave a routine, ritualistic flinch.

No, thought Monica. Not this time. Things are going to change. New day. New start.

She put down her hand, closed her mouth. Mae, spooning in cornflakes and milk, eyed her mother warily.

'Eat that and hurry up,' said Monica. 'We're going out.'

The adoption agency was in first-floor offices above a row of shops on Clayton Street. It was one of the few private agencies operating in the North-East.

Monica had put on her best clothes, her most restrained make-up, her most modest wig. She sat there in the drab, brown-walled office before the heavy functional desks and chairs, a cup of cooling tea perched on her lap. Two women looked at her from across their desks. On the wall behind them was a crucifix. Christ taking away the sins of the world. Monica knew: she and these women would see things differently.

She had put aside her prejudice, tried to calm her fast-beating heart on walking into the agency. She knew she would have to be cunning. Lie if need be.

The attitudes of the two women, brittle and superficially solicitous, had put her in mind of trips to the headmaster's office at school. The feeling went further: the form she had filled in had only highlighted her lack of formal education. Her handwriting was bad, letters ill-formed, sentences poorly constructed. The two women were looking it over. She felt she was going to be given marks out of ten, told she had failed the test, asked to leave.

The two women finished looking at the form, gave a barely perceptible nod to each other, put it down, looked at Monica.

'So,' the first woman, the one with the round cheeks that gave her a smug, self-satisfied air, said, referring to the form, 'Miss Blacklock.' She made a hiss out of 'miss'. 'Why do you want to give up your daughter to adoption?'

Monica opened her mouth, but sound was a long time in coming.

'I . . . I just . . . I can't cope. Any more. I think she needs . . .' Monica lowered her head, mumbled.

'Pardon, Miss Blacklock?' The second woman, the slope-shouldered, flat-chested one, spoke. 'We can't hear you.'

Monica knew her face was flushed.

'I said I think she needs something better.'

The two women looked at each other, exchanged small nods of concurrence, as if the words were expected.

'And you live in . . .?' Smug Cheeks again.

Monica cleared her throat. 'Scotswood,' she said.

The two nodded again at each other.

Flat Chest scrutinized the form.

'You haven't put down what you do for a living, Miss Blacklock,' she said.

Monica opened her mouth. Nothing emerged but a stuttering sound.

The two women looked at her again, expectantly.

She hadn't planned for this. Such a simple thing, and she hadn't thought of it. She had expected to just walk in, leave Mae and walk out again with their gratitude ringing in her ears. Then she would be left to get on with things. With life.

She didn't know what to say for the best. They were already being judgemental about her. Would the truth make them more so? Look further down their noses at her? Would a lie if found out make them return Mae to her? She decided to take a chance.

She cleared her throat.

'I've got a job,' she said.

The two women looked at her, silently encouraging her to keep talking.

'It's . . .' Monica swallowed hard. 'I have to be careful. I'm signin' on. You might shop us to the social.'

The two women looked at her.

'Best say I'm just signin' on.'

Monica looked down. The tea in her cup was cold. She was shaking, wrinkling the skin of the tea in the cup like a mini tidal pool.

The two women exchanged glances again. Then their eyes moved down the form.

Monica felt elation. She had done it. The first hurdle. Got one over on them.

She tried to keep the smile from growing on her lips.

'So, Miss Blacklock,' said Smug Cheeks, 'what we'd like you to do now is tell us in your own words why you want to give up your daughter for adoption.'

The two women sat back. Monica felt like a Christian in the Colosseum, waiting for a Roman emperor to decide her fate.

'Well, I . . .' Monica cleared her throat again. 'I just think . . . Mae deserves better than I can give, that's all.'

The two women held their gaze, expecting more.

Monica looked at them, wondering how much she could say.

'I can't cope with her,' she said, defeat and exhaustion in her voice. 'She's just . . . Her dad ran off before she was born. I've brought her up on me own since then.'

Flat Chest raised an eyebrow. Monica picked up on it.

'I've had other men since then, course I have. But I've still brought 'er up on me own. But I just . . .' She sighed. 'Sometimes I want to just throttle 'er, you know? She just annoys us.'

'And how does she do that?' said Flat Chest.

'Just by bein' there. Makin' a mess. Getting' in the way. Under me feet. I just want shot of her.' Monica sat forward, the tea nearly falling off. 'I mean, I can't go anywhere or do anythin'. She's there. Under me feet. On me nerves. There. Constantly.' Monica sighed. 'I just want shot of her.'

She sat back. It was the most she had spoken concerning Mae for months. Years, perhaps.

Smug Cheeks smiled.

'Well, that seems to be everything, Miss Blacklock. If you could just wait in the room outside until we've made our decision.'

Flat Chest was on her feet, around the desk and opening the door before Monica had time to put down her cup and saucer and stand up.

She was ushered out, the door closed behind her. She looked down at Mae playing on the floor with old, worn-out toys that were too young for her. She looked happy. She looked up, acknowledged her mother, almost smiled. Then returned to her game.

It's best for Mae, Monica thought. She'll be as happy as that all the time.

Monica thought she had acquitted herself well in there. They had accepted her lie about what she did for a living and listened as she spoke in an impassioned way about Mae. She felt a stirring of hope in her chest. Things were going to work out all right.

The door opened. Monica looked around.

'Could you come back in now, please, Miss Blacklock?' said Smug Cheeks.

Monica resumed her seat in the office. The door was closed behind her. Smug Cheeks sat back down.

The two women looked at her again.

Monica waited.

'Well,' said Smug Cheeks, 'my colleague and I have deliberated. And we have reached a conclusion.'

Monica sat forward expectantly.

'I'm afraid,' said Flat Chest, 'that we will not be recommending your daughter for adoption. We will be turning your application down.'

Monica gasped.

'What? But . . .' Her voice trailed off.

'For various reasons,' said Smug Cheeks. 'While we naturally think that two parents are always the ideal in regard to bringing up a child, it seems to us like you're trying very hard to make a good life for your daughter. You're willing to risk breaking the law by taking an undeclared job. Now that may well be illegal, and of course we can't condone that, but it demonstrates your maternal love if you're prepared to do that.'

Monica sat there, letting the words sink in. They had believed her lie. She opened her mouth to speak, to tell them she had lied, but stopped herself. Because then she would have to tell the truth. And that would only weaken her argument, not strengthen it.

'Now we understand,' said Smug Cheeks, 'the pain and disappointments you have to go through, the resentments you have to endure in bringing up a child alone. It's perfectly natural to feel that way. You're not the first, and you won't be the last.'

'You have to remember that your child is a gift from God,' said Flat Chest. 'Hard work sometimes, true, but oh so rewarding.' She smiled. 'So with that in mind, try not to look so downhearted. Always look on the bright side.'

'Although,' said Smug Cheeks, 'if things do get too difficult, call the council. They could place your daughter in a foster family until you felt well enough to take her back.'

'A much better solution.'

'And also,' said Smug Cheeks, 'there's your daughter.'

'We're afraid,' said Flat Chest, 'that she's just too old to consider. We normally deal with babies or very small children. Your daughter is nearly seven. The older a child is, the harder it is to find a home for them.'

'We are sorry.'

The two women sat back, a veneer of sadness on their faces.

'Very sorry.'

'We do hope you understand.'

They gave Monica what appeared to be a consoling smile.

Monica didn't move. She was physically stunned. Walking there in the morning, she had told herself this was the start of a happy new phase in her life. She had told Mae that too. And now, because these two frigid old harpies had made a decision, that was that.

Monica felt emotions rising inside her: the trapped suffocating feeling of knowing this was it. This was her life. All she could hope for, tied to a daughter who every day was reminding her mother how fast she was ageing, what she was missing out on, what was slipping by her.

She felt anger rise rapidly inside her. It wasn't going to happen. She wouldn't let it happen.

She snatched up her handbag and made for the door.

The two women were on their feet, placatory remarks on their lips, but she ignored them. She pulled open the door and ran, not even looking back at Mae playing on the floor.

Down the stairs and on to Clayton Street.

She ran.

As far away from the adoption agency, from Mae, as possible.

She ran.

And never once looked back.

They caught up with her, of course. Later. At home.

Because she had nowhere else to go.

She had walked around the city centre, in and out of shops. Looked at clothes, tried some on. Imagined herself in new, exciting situations, imagined accessories for her new life. She found a couple of pubs she knew. Had a couple of gins and tonics. Told anyone within earshot she was celebrating her new-found freedom. Her new life. People ignored her, moved away from her.

Trying too hard to be happy.

Eventually, hope and money spent, she had gone home. And waited.

Resigned.

She poured herself a drink, put the TV on. A new programme about an old Edwardian grandfather and his granddaughter in a spaceship designed as a police box. They could go anywhere in space and time with it, and it was much bigger on the inside than the outside, like the size of a house.

It was rubbish, she thought, kiddies' stuff, but she kept watching it. They were on an alien planet where a race of beautiful blonds were being menaced by some evil robot pepperpots. The old grandfather, this Doctor, was going to help them.

Monica wished she were there with them, the blond, beautiful people. It was obvious they were going to win out, defeat the robots. She would even love to be in the police box, free in time and space. She would even put up with the bad-tempered old grandfather trying to fuck her. It would be worth it.

But she knew it wouldn't happen. So she sat there, emptying

gin into her glass, topping it up with tonic, knocking it back, waiting for the knock at the door.

It wasn't long in coming.

She moved to answer it, swaying unsteadily as she made her way down the hall. There stood a young police constable, next to him, Mae.

'Miss Monica Blacklock?'

Monica nodded.

'Got something here belonging to you.' He gave a cocky grin. 'Seems you left it behind.'

He ushered Mae into the house. She went mutely, eyes down.

'Now, they're not pressing charges,' he said, a sternness in his voice, 'but they will if you try that again. OK?'

Monica nodded.

'Righto. I'll be off, then.'

She closed the door, looked at Mae, who stared back at her.

Monica knew she didn't love her daughter. She had just experienced a passing guilt, tried to farm her out as a result of that. Guilt told her Mae deserved a better chance. Guilt told her Mae didn't deserve the life she would grow into.

'Guilt can fuck off,' said Monica aloud.

Mae looked at her quizzically.

'And I don't know what you're lookin' at.'

Monica felt the familiar tide of anger rising inside her. She tried to head it off. She was too drunk, too tired to deal with it.

'Go upstairs. Go to bed.'

'But it's only—'

'Don't fuckin' argue with me—'

Monica made to cuff Mae about the head, but Mae anticipated the blow and moved. Monica overbalanced. She grabbed the banister.

'Just fuckin' get upstairs!'

Mae went. Monica made her way back to the living room, poured herself another drink.

'Cheers.'

She drank. She noticed that the bottle was nearly empty. She would need a new one soon.

Monica sat like that, berating her past, commiserating with her future, for at least two more hours. Or more. Or less. She didn't know. She lost all track of time.

She fell asleep in her chair, the TV broadcasting to no one while John Steed and Cathy Gale smashed yet another spy ring.

Then, a knock at the door.

Monica opened her eyes, closed them again. She wasn't working tonight. Must have imagined it.

Then another knock. More insistent.

Her eyes opened again, this time stayed open. She wondered where she was, who she was. She imagined herself spinning around a black and white universe in a police box spaceship, the grumpy old grandfather not so bad after all.

Another knock. Harder this time. They weren't going away.

Monica stood up. Too quickly. Her head swam. Nausea welled up from within. She stood still, swaying slightly. It passed. She made her way slowly to the door.

'I'm comin', I'm comin' . . .'

She opened the door.

'Hello, pet.'

Recognition didn't come immediately, but when it did it was with a much deeper wave of nausea that owed nothing to the alcohol.

He had thickened around the middle, his hair was greyer and sparser, his face redder and his style of clothes hadn't changed. His eyes had stayed the same.

Her father.

'Aren't you going to invite your old dad in, then, eh?'

She moved numbly aside, let him enter. He stank of beer and cheap whisky.

'You've been drinkin',' she said.

He turned to her, sniffed.

'So've you,' he said, then smiled. 'Saturday night, eh? S'what it's for.'

He walked into the house. She closed the door, followed him down the hall. Steed and Cathy Gale were involved in an elaborate fight with some black-polo-necked villains. Monica turned the TV off.

'What d'you do that for? I was watchin' that. That Cathy Gale's a bit of a one, isn't she?'

Monica stared at him. Her head was beginning to clear.

'What d'you want?' she said.

Her father laughed.

'Is that any way to talk to your old dad?' He sat down in her armchair, picked up her empty gin glass, held it out to her. 'Good idea. I'll have one an' all.'

Monica took the glass, crossed to the sideboard. She made two gins and tonics, handed one to him.

'Cheers,' he said, and drank.

Monica said nothing but drank also.

'So why are you here, then?' Monica said eventually.

'Can't I come and see me own daughter some time?'

'You never have before.'

Monica perched tentatively on the arm of the other chair.

Her dad smiled. 'Waitin' to be invited, love. Just waitin' to be invited.' He took another mouthful of gin, stretched his legs out. 'When whatsisname – Brian – left, I thought you'd be back like a shot. When you didn't come I thought it'd only be a matter of time.'

'And I never did.'

'So I thought I would come to you.'

Monica knocked back most of her gin.

'Right,' she said. 'Now you have. You can drink up and go.'

Her heart was beating fast. She was still frightened of him. She hoped it didn't show.

Her father sat there, drank, looked as if he hadn't heard her.

'Hear you're on the game now,' he said to his glass, then looked up and smiled at Monica. That cruel look she always feared was back on his face. 'You any good?'

She felt herself shivering and shaking as if the temperature in the room had dropped. She didn't trust herself to speak.

'I'll pay,' he said, offhand. 'I'm just curious, like.'

Terror welled within. Her heart pounded faster, breath quickened. The terror broke as anger. She knocked the glass from his hand. Gin and tonic soaked into the carpet.

'Get out! Just get out!'

She hit him. Small fists dealing small blows. The impact barely registered on his arm, his chest.

He stood up. She stopped, took a step back.

'Got brave suddenly, have you?' He smiled, eyes aglow with that old, cruel light. 'Maybe I should hit you. Be rough with you, eh?' He crossed to her, stood directly in front of her. 'I hear you like it.'

She closed her eyes, cowering, expecting the blow.

'What's happenin', Mam?'

Monica opened her eyes. Mae was standing there, eyes full of sleep, wearing a nightie that needed a wash, clutching her toy rabbit.

'Hello, there.'

Monica's father had bent down, switched his attention from his daughter to his granddaughter. Monica couldn't move. She just watched.

'And what's your name?'

'Mae.'

'That's a lovely name, Mae. Well, d'you know who I am?'

Mae shook her head.

'I'm your granddad. How old are you, Mae?'

'Seven.'

His eyes lit up. The cruelty intensified.

'Seven, eh? That's a great age to be.' He looked up, smiled at Monica. 'A great age.'

Monica looked at him. Watched as he stood up, crossed back towards her. He smiled at her.

'How much?' he said.

Monica felt her body tremble again. She was going to tell him to leave, to physically attempt to throw him out, make him stay away from her daughter.

But then she looked at her daughter.

Black, dead eyes staring up at her. Undisguised kernels of hatred directed at her.

Monica didn't love her. Didn't even like her. Certainly didn't want her. But she was stuck with her. And if she was stuck with her, she may as well pay her way.

'Fiver.'

Her father laughed.

'A fiver? D'you think I'm daft?'

'You'd be the first. You'd be breakin' 'er in. Fiver.'

'I haven't got a fiver on us.'

Monica smiled. She had the upper hand. She was beginning to enjoy herself.

'How much you got, then?'

He rifled through his pockets.

'Nearly a pound.'

'And your wallet.'

He sighed, opened it.

'Another pound.'

'I'll have all of that. You can owe me the rest.' She smiled again. 'And I'll collect. Or I'll tell the polis what you've done.'

Fear flickered in his eyes. Monica got a thrill from that.

She also knew he wanted Mae. Monica loved the control she had over him.

Finally.

She took his money, pocketed it.

'Mae, go with your granddad. Next door. He's got something to show you.'

Mae and her father went into the room with the white walls and the deep shadows, the crucifixes showing Christ's love, Christ's agony.

Monica poured herself another gin and tonic, one that was nearly all gin, and sat herself in the armchair. She drank.

Her father's soothing words came through the wall.

She drank.

Her daughter's cries and sobs came through the wall.

She drank.

The noise continued.

She talked, shouted, tried to drown the noises out in her head, make them go away:

'I never wanted you anyway . . . Never . . .'

She drank. Drained her glass. Filled another.

'Why didn't you go away, eh? Why didn't you stay away?'

The noise: soothing words, cries and screams.

'Why did you have to come back?'

She drank. Looked down at the floor. Saw the dropped toy rabbit. She drained her glass. Grabbed the bottle.

'Why, eh?'

Cries and screams. Soothing words.

'Why don't you just die?'

Mae, next door, white and crucifixes, crying and screaming.

Monica sitting there, drinking, tears streaming down her face, crying and screaming.

Crying and screaming.

PART THREE

Downbeat

At night he dreamed the city.

A panoramic swoop: down from the heavens and through the clouds, through the cold air, the grey sky. The city becoming larger, getting closer: various shades of black spreading out from the centre, staining the surrounding greens and browns. Small twinkles of light, like strings of lost diamonds in mud.

Closer still to make out landmarks: Grey's Monument. Royal Arcade. Grainger's New Town: Grainger Street and its covered market, Grey Street and the Theatre Royal. The theatre showing, in this dream, nothing but Victorian spectacle and Edwardian tableau. Then the bridges: the Tyne. The Swing. The High Level. The King Edward. The Redheugh. And further along: Scotswood Bridge. Familiar objects. Dependable. A feeling of comfort and warmth: seeing things where they should be.

Swoop down into the city itself. Familiar still, but now different. Dream different. A city cobbled and stitched together from fragments of previous dreams. Buildings griddled with streets leading to skewed destinations. Follow them: along, around, down. Never emerging quite where expected. The routes become disquieting. A feeling begins to grow, low-level fear:

things are not where they should be. How they should be. He realizes, with some concern, that perhaps he doesn't know the city as well as he thought. A discomforting, disturbing feeling.

He gives up trying to follow the roads, to make sense of them, and instead lets them lead him where they will. He doesn't trust them, yet can't change course. He's directionless, powerless. Panic begins to rise within him. He tries to quell it, concentrate on following the roads.

He sees people in the streets, unfamiliar, but also known to him. Dream known. He waves as he passes, tries to talk. He feels he knows them wholly, can tell life stories just from sentences.

They pass, drifting away. He tries to move faster, but the more he tries the slower he becomes. Like his legs have turned to stone, the streets to treacle. So he goes on, the roads leading him.

And then his destination is reached. The roads stop moving. Feeling returns to his legs. Before him is a building. Huge, cathedral-like with vaulted ceilings and archways, supported by massive pillars. All in soot-blackened Victorian red brick. Smooth, worn cobbles under foot. Daylight can be glimpsed through some of the archways, mist and fog rolls in. Huge chimneys belch out clouds of grey smoke. Furnaces around the walls blaze within great iron grates.

It is an abattoir.

Hanging from hooks suspended from ceiling and walls are carcasses. Hundreds, perhaps thousands of them. Blood-drained racks of meat. No individual animals: all individual animals. The place is alive with activity, like flies on a dead dog. Men dressed in cloth caps and bloodied aprons wield sharp blades, toil before the meat. Bleeding. Skinning. Carving. Removing heads, guts and hearts. Some taking the parts away, others feeding them to the furnaces. The carcasses moving along, the racks creaking, groaning.

Further in he goes. Up close, the pillars and archways seem made of candlewax: run off and set solid. Pooling on the floor.

He walks through. The men, oblivious to his presence, get on with their work.

He reaches a door. Large, heavy, studded with bolts. This, he knows with dream logic, is the centre. He opens the door, steps inside.

The door closes behind him. The heart is clean, bright. Soundless. The walls are dazzling-white ceramic tile. Decorated only by arcs of dried blood. In the centre is a stainless-steel block. Shining blade marks and scratches glinting on the surface. Time stops in the room. Chill creeps into his bones.

The white room.

He shudders from more than the cold. From understanding. He knows what the room means, what it does. The furnaces, the carcasses. With dream logic and dream clarity, he knows.

It is the heart, he knows. The cold, clinical heart. The heart of the city. What the city was built around, built on. Beating rhythmically, regularly. The heart was the room.

He wants to leave. He turns and, expecting resistance, opens the door. There is no resistance. He is free to come and go. He walks back into the huge hall. He looks again at the melted wax pillars. This time he sees them for what they are: not wax, but waste. Animal fat, gristle and skin. Some still red-veined in places. Moulded and shaped. Waste but not wasted.

He walks back out on to the street. The dream city shimmers and moves about him. Mists and fog roll through the streets, changing the layout once again. Strange. Familiar. Strange. Familiar. He looks around. He knows exactly where he is. He knows exactly what is happening.

A truth has been revealed to him. A truth he will not remember on waking. A truth that will remain beyond his fingertips. Beyond his reach.

The city moves.

He is lost.

March 1964:
Bits and Pieces

Ben Marshall checked that the levels were high and the speakers in place. He moved the arm of the portable record player so the seven-inch single was 45rpm ready. He held the arm back.

'Mr Tyler?' he said.

No response.

'Your last chance, Mr Tyler.'

Ben cocked his head, listening. Had he heard a muffled 'Bugger off'? He shrugged. No matter.

'Ah, well,' Ben said to himself.

He dropped the needle. Crackles, bloops and hisses, then: the drums. Solid, insistent.

Boom boom boom boom ta ta ta ta ta ta ta ta TA TA.

Then the guitars, bass, keyboards. All banging down together, boxing gloves subtle.

On top of that the vocals:

I'm in pieces, bits and pieces . . .

Ben nodded his head in time to the music, tapped his foot, sang along.

He stood with his back to a borrowed flat-bed truck holding a portable generator. Wires trailed to the Vox

amplifiers/speakers he had mounted on a windowsill on 23a
Berwick Street, just off Raby Street in Byker. The portable
record player was on the garden wall.

With a final drumbeat flourish, the song ended. Ben
walked to the closed front door, opened the letterbox, shouted
through it.

'Enjoy that, Mr Tyler?'

No response.

'You ready to come out or d'you want to hear it again?'

No response.

'Ah, well . . .'

He walked back to the wall, dropped the arm in place.

Boom boom boom boom ta ta ta ta ta ta ta ta ta ta TA TA.

And off again.

Ben was aware that people were looking at him. Women
were putting down their shopping bags and staring. Talking
to their neighbours, pointing. Young children were laughing.
Older people were shaking their heads, walking past,
muttering bitterly.

Ben didn't care. Let them all gawp. Let them all stare. He
thought of playing to the crowd, courting them with charm.
But decided against it. They would know who he was, or at
least what he was doing. And they would be scared.

That fear would keep them in line. And he enjoyed the
feeling that power gave him.

He had moved into property in the autumn of 1963, on the
money he had made selling pills and puff. He had handed
over his markets, opened a gateway for Big Derek into the
North-East, been allowed to retire gracefully. Through
contacts he had made, by moving in the right circles, by
March 1964 he owned six houses and three flats, all let out at
the highest possible rental value.

Things went smoothly for the most part but, occasionally,
someone gave him trouble. Like now.

Wilf Tyler had lived in the same Byker flat nearly all his life. Ben had bought the flat, together with the one upstairs, and decided that it was too big for the number of people living in it. It could be three flats. Or even four.

He had thrown the belongings of the family in the top flat out on the street, told them since they wouldn't sign a new rental agreement with him they had forfeited their right to live there. They hadn't argued.

But Wilf Tyler had. So more drastic measures had been called for.

With a final drumbeat flourish, the song ended.

Again.

Ben sighed and smiled. Back to the letterbox.

'How was that, Mr Tyler? Any good?'

No response.

'More of a Beatles man, are you? Stones?'

No response.

'Ah, well, here we go again . . .'

Several bolts were unlocked, pushed back. An old, grey-haired man emerged, wearing a suit and overcoat. His body looked thin and frail, his eyes fiery and angry.

'Right, you bastard, you've won. You've won, you bastard.'

'Hello, Mr Tyler. Nice to see you at last.'

Wilf Tyler squared up to Ben, looked him in the eye, unblinking.

'If I was twenty years younger, I'd fuckin' have you. You bastard.'

Ben smiled.

'But you're not, are you?'

Wilf Tyler was almost vibrating with rage. He hauled an old suitcase over the threshold, slammed the door behind him.

'I'll be back for the rest of me stuff.'

Ben said nothing.

'I'm goin' to me daughter's.'

He dragged his case halfway down the path, put it down, turned.

'You haven't heard the last of this, you bastard.'

He picked up his case, resumed walking. As he reached the wall, he knocked the portable record player to the ground. It crashed, leaving a strong electric hum in the air.

'I'll be billing you for that, Mr Tyler,' said Ben.

Wilf Tyler mumbled something inaudible. Then made slow, sad, painful progress up the street and away.

Ben crossed to where the record player lay. He picked it up. It was bashed, scuffed but still seemed in workable condition. The record, however, was scratched and broken. Ben threw it into the front garden.

'Hated that song anyway.'

He began packing his equipment away, ready to move on to his next recalcitrant tenant.

Johnny chose his spot, stuck his blade in, drew it down. He stood back, anticipating the blood, stopping too much of it from going on to his clothes. He peeled back the skin, let the entrails fall into the waiting bucket.

Another animal butchered. Another bull reduced to component meat and meat products.

He looked into the bull's large, glassy eye. Found nothing there.

The Victorians, he had once read, believed that a murdered person would retain the imprint of their murderer on their eyeball after death. He wondered if that were in some way true. And whether it applied to all animals.

And, above all, how many times his face would appear.

Job done, he moved to the next carcass along, hooked on to the overhead rail, brought it into place.

He was happy in his work. Contented.

Now.

After that night in the toilets in Byker, the first time, Johnny had been terrified. He had scanned the *Chronicle* for days afterwards, waiting to see the article, expecting a knock on the door and a truncheon-rush of police at any moment.

But it hadn't happened.

Days spent scouring the paper. Nothing. He began to imagine he'd missed it and would go back to check.

Panic and paranoia seeped in. Perhaps the police knew what he had done. Were sending him coded messages to lure him out. To catch him doing it again.

He watched the TV news, waiting to see his photofit.

For days, then weeks: nothing.

He set no fires, made no more trips into public toilets. Bottled his desires.

Perhaps they were waiting for him. Staking out the toilets, willing him to enter, sending in a plain-clothes man to trap him.

Days, weeks, then months: nothing.

And then he got a grip, began to think logically.

The man he had met that night hadn't wanted to press charges. He was either unable or unwilling to offer a description. The police would have only the one Johnny had mentioned in his anonymous phone call to go on. The man wouldn't have sought publicity for what had happened. Hadn't he mentioned a girlfriend? The man must have recovered. Or not: poofs killing poofs was way down on the police agenda.

Gradually the oppression began to lift. The paranoia to dissipate. The police weren't going to break his door down. An angry, vengeful God was not going to smite him with a thunderbolt. He had got away with it. He was free. To live his life.

To do it again.

He resumed his fire-starting. That was his excellence, his

art. His biggest source of income too. And he stayed at the slaughterhouse. He had heard they were going to build a new one. State-of-the-art killing. He had to get a job there. He enjoyed himself.

But sometimes he wanted more.

He stifled the urges, knowing he had no control once it had started. But he could feel it was building. Seeking another outlet.

Until he could find one, he stayed in his flat at night. Decorating it, adorning the walls, the surfaces, until it began to resemble a shrine. Expending his energy on that.

So he was happy.

For now.

Johnny chose his spot, stuck his blade in, drew it down. He stood back, anticipating the blood, stopping too much of it going on to his clothes. He peeled back the skin, let the entrails fall into the waiting bucket.

He was happy.

For now.

The Club A Go Go.

Ben sitting at the bar with Martin Fleming, telling him of the day's events.

'You should've seen him.'

Ben had laughed, shook his head.

'Looked like fuckin' Steptoe when he came out, so he did.'

Music heard through the walls: the Emcee Five blowing up a storm.

Martin Fleming, dandified in aubergine-coloured suit, lemon tie and matching top pocket handkerchief flourish, smelling of a delicate, understated floral scent, elegantly picked up his gin and tonic and smiled indulgently.

'But he saw reason.' Ben nodded. 'He saw reason.'

Another indulgent smile from Martin Fleming.

'And the equipment's back safe and sound too.'

Martin Fleming nodded. Took another elegant sip of his gin and tonic. 'What d'you think of this lot?' He inclined his head towards the music.

'Good.' Ben nodded. 'Bit rough, but good.'

'Oh, I agree,' said Martin Fleming. 'Rough. But then I like a bit of rough. That's why I like having you around, Ben.'

Ben looked at him. Martin Fleming was smiling broadly.

'Steady,' said Ben. He knew Fleming was a poof, but he didn't want it pushed in his face. Made him uncomfortable. Martin Fleming smiled.

'So, Mr Rachman, how goes your plan for buying up this fair city?'

Ben took a sip of beer, nodded.

'Coming along.'

Martin Fleming studied him, decided whether to speak. The music crescendoed, the crowd applauded. He made his mind up.

'Don't you think,' he said, his forehead creased, 'that it's a little too undignified doing this alone?'

'How d'you mean?'

'Don't you think you need a bully? Someone to strong-arm for you?'

Ben had already given the matter thought. His first instinct had been to track down his old colleagues from the Brian Mooney days. Brimson and Eddie. He had investigated: both had done their time in prison. Time that should have been Ben's. Eddie was now married with three kids and a job at Vickers. No more brushes with the law. Straight as an arrow. Ben hadn't risked approaching him; Eddie no longer fitted the profile. Brimson had been harder to trace. Word was, since he had taken a blow to the head that night in the Ropemakers, he hadn't been the same. Unable to concentrate on one thing for too long, unable to hold down a job, a relationship. His fists and temper had got him in trouble with the law many times; stitched up many a Durham mailbag as a result of a drunken fight. But the last anyone had heard of him had been on the hoppings on the Town Moor three years previously. Brimson had got a job working on the waltzer. Then in the boxing booths. When the hoppings moved on, it appeared Brimson had too.

But Ben was looking to put someone on the payroll, someone he could trust.

He smiled.

'You think I'm not tough enough?'

'Oh, I think you are.'

'Steady. Or I'll have to get physical with you.'

'Please. No, I'm sure you can manage. But don't you find getting your hands dirty a little . . . demeaning?'

'Well,' said Ben, as if the thought had just struck him, 'since you mention it. Any recommendations?'

'Well.' Martin Fleming looked around, continued conspiratorially. 'I have a man who does.'

'Does what?'

'Plenty. Primarily keeps recalcitrants in line, teaches lessons, backs up words, that sort of thing.' His voice dropped, his features hardened. 'And fires. Insurance jobs. Best I've ever seen.'

Ben looked at Martin Fleming. The campness had fallen away and he was all business. The man he had imagined when Big Derek first mentioned him.

'Sounds good,' Ben said. 'How do I find him?'

'I'll tell him you're looking for him.'

'And what do you get out of this?'

Martin Fleming smiled, draped his hand across Ben's.

'Don't. Or I'll fucking floor you.'

Martin Fleming shrugged. 'Oh, well, nothing ventured . . . The usual fee, then. For introducing such obvious soulmates.'

Ben, his throat suddenly dry, drained his drink, stood up.
'I'd better be off,' he said.
'I'll be in touch.'
Ben left the Club A Go Go. The Emcee Five finished their set: the crowd applauded. Martin Fleming drained his glass, ordered another.
Smiled contentedly to himself.

The letter came two days later. Sharon bent to pick it up, thinking it was nothing, a circular.
Isaac was at school. She was at a loose end.
Unravelling.
She opened the envelope, took out the letter. The company name was unfamiliar: Northern Star Properties. She began to read, curious, but uninterested at first. By the time she had reached the end, read the signature, she was fizzing with excitement. She put the letter down. She couldn't wait to tell Jack.
She stopped, thought.
She picked the letter up, folded it, replaced it in the envelope. She would put it away. Somewhere safe. Somewhere Jack couldn't find it. Sharon would tell Jack, or at least let him know. But not yet. Not until she was ready to.
Not until there was nothing he could do to stop her.
He heart was pounding. She had to look at the letter again, remind herself what was written there.
She read it, smiled.
Her life was about to change. She could feel it.

Leazes Park, Saturday afternoon.
From his place on the park bench before the lake, Ben Marshall could hear the roars from nearby St James' Park as Joe Harvey led Newcastle United to what would be another glimpse of Saturday-afternoon glory ultimately tempered by

harsh teatime reality. Someone would win, someone would lose. Ben didn't care which.

He pulled his coat close around him. He sighed, his breath coming out as a cloud of steam.

He checked his watch, looked around. Waited. He was due to meet the person Martin Fleming had recommended to him. He had received a phone call giving time, date, place. Nothing else.

He waited, sighed. Whoever it was, he was late.

There came a rustle from a bush behind him. Before Ben could look around he had been joined on the bench. Ben looked at the man, surprised by his speed and stealth. Blond hair cropped short, framing his moon face. Sheepskin jacket buttoned up tightly over his large frame. Straight-creased trousers. Work boots. Smelled of sawdust and old blood. Ben scrutinized him. It took a few seconds for Ben's memory to focus but then, with a jolt, he recognized the man:

Johnny Bell.

Ben recovered his composure, tried not to smile at the irony. He was glad he had chosen to wear his glasses. Glad he had had his hair restyled along John Lennon lines.

Glad he had changed sufficiently to be unrecognizable.

'You're late,' he said, his London accent pushed to the fore.

'No, I'm not,' said Johnny. 'I was here on time. Before you. I was just makin' sure you were alone. That it wasn't a setup.'

Ben looked at Johnny. He was staring straight ahead, his eyes blank, his voice emotionless.

'It's not a setup,' said Ben. 'I'm hoping you and me can do a bit of business together.'

Johnny kept staring ahead.

'What d'you say to that, then?'

Johnny shrugged.

'Did our mutual friend tell you what I wanted?'

Johnny nodded.

'And will you do it?'

Johnny nodded.

Ben felt himself getting angry.

'Was that a yes or a no?'

Johnny turned to face Ben. His eyes were remarkable for two reasons: their vivid, robin's-egg-blue colour and their complete absence of anything approaching emotion.

'Don't piss me about, Mr Marshall. I'm sure you've been told what I can do. I've been told what you want. As long as you pay me, we'll get on fine.'

Ben swallowed hard. He had been expecting some self-aggrandizing hard man talking up his credentials. Not this.

The St James' Park crowd cheered. One side had scored.

'Is there anything you won't do?' Ben said.

'If there is, I haven't found it yet.'

Ben smiled. 'Then I think we can do business.'

Johnny nodded. 'Contact me through our mutual friend.'

'I will do.' Ben stood up, offered his hand for Johnny to shake. Johnny ignored it. Ben retracted. 'I'll be off. Got a dinner date. I'll be in touch—'

Ben stopped himself. He nearly said his name.

'What should I call you?'

'Johnny.'

'I'll be in touch, Johnny.'

Ben turned and walked away. He could feel Johnny's eyes follow him as he walked around the lake and out of the park. He shuddered from something more than cold. He remembered Johnny Bell as a follower, content to stand in his brother's shadow. This one was different. Ben was a hard man, but Johnny was something else: an ice man. Cold blew from him in waves like an arctic wind.

Behind him another roar went up. Someone was winning, someone was losing.

He pulled his coat around him, tried to get warm, tried to push Johnny Bell from his mind.

Hurried away to get ready for his dinner date.

Sharon smothered her hands over the Quant minidress, checked her reflection sideways on in the mirror. She smiled to herself. Nearer thirty than twenty, but showing no sign of losing her figure. Not yet, anyway. Her figure and her youth, or the impression of youth, were things she intended to hold on to for as long as she could. To her, they were symbols that she wouldn't give in, accept less, settle for half. Symbols that there was still plenty of life in her.

She looked again in the mirror, at her legs this time. Encased in opaque white tights, black-leather boots up to her knees. Was her skirt too short? Did it show too much leg? Would she send the wrong signals, give out the wrong idea?

What was the wrong idea, anyway?

Final check: hair, make-up, dress, legs. Her stomach gave a thrilling lurch. She looked fine.

She grabbed her coat, handbag. Made her way downstairs.

Jack was sitting in an armchair reading the paper. Isaac was at the dining room table gluing together the wings of a Spitfire from a model kit Jack had bought him. The TV was on: the small, black and white screen showing a new soap opera, *Coronation Street*. Sharon had seen it once or twice before: people in a backstreet in Manchester leading small, black and white lives.

Sharon stood in the doorway, trying not to strike a pose, unable to resist.

'Right,' she said, 'I'm off now.'

Jack looked up from his paper, did a double take when he saw her. She looked into his eyes, read them. Saw the love and lust – the dress, her legs. Saw him reconnect with what had made him love her, made him want her in the first place.

Then that look fall away as realization dawned: this – the dress, her legs – was all for another man.

Sharon watched him, daring him to speak, to challenge her.

He stood up, crossed to her. Motioned for her to step into the hall. She did so, he followed. Closed the door on Isaac.

'Where d'you think you're going, dressed like that?'

'You know where I'm going. I've got a meeting with Ben to discuss the job he wants me to do.'

'Dressed like that? What kind of job does he want you to do dressed like that?'

Sharon sighed in exasperation. 'It's 1964, Jack. Everyone dresses like this.'

'Not you. Not my wife. Not when you're going out with another man.'

His temper was rising. Sharon knew she had to stop it.

'It's not like that, Jack,' she said, her voice controlled and even. 'And you know it. It's a business discussion. We can't meet during the day, so we have to meet on an evening. People always wear their best for a business meeting. They tend to get the job that way.'

'What d'you need a job for? Don't I earn enough?'

Sharon sighed again. The same argument, over and over.

'It's not like that. You know it's not. I just want some independence, that's all. I don't just want to be Isaac's mother or Jack's wife, or the person who looks after this place.' She swept her arm around the hall. 'I want more than that.'

Jack's face was turning scarlet.

'And what about us? What about your husband and son, eh? We never get to see you. You're never here.' He sighed, exasperated. 'You belong here. With us. We need you.' His voice began to tremble. 'I need you.'

He dropped his eyes, unable to meet her gaze. She looked at him. His white hair showing through, his tired face. Her haunted husband with his wounded soul and his idealistic heart. There seemed in that moment something much bigger and older between them than six years. An uncrossable distance.

She felt anger rise within. She hated him.

'You stay here and look after Isaac,' she said, her voice rippling with barely suppressed emotion. 'It's all you're good for.'

Jack looked up, his face turned from scarlet to purple.

'You bitch! You fucking—'

He pulled back his hand to strike her. She flinched from the expected blow.

'Dad! Mam!'

They both turned. In the doorway stood Isaac, his face full of incomprehension and fear.

Jack dropped his arm. Sharon stood still. Neither looked at the other.

'Go on and get ready for bed,' said Jack. 'Time for bed.'

'But Dad—'

'Just do it.'

Jack's voice rose higher than he had expected. He immediately regretted it. The boy ran quickly upstairs without speaking.

Jack sighed. The fire extinguished, the rage abated.

Sharon looked at him.

'I'm sorry,' she said.

Jack nodded. Sharon looked around, shook her head.

'We can't go on like this,' she said. 'I can't go on like this.'

Jack looked at her, his eyes red-rimmed.

'I love you,' he said.

She knew how difficult it was for him to say that. She looked into his eyes, tired and tear-ready. She could see his heart breaking behind them.

'I love you too,' she said, then looked away from him. She couldn't face those eyes when her next words came out.

'But I'm still going out.'

She turned from him, walked to the door. She put her hand on the lock, stopped. There was something more she had to say to him. She looked around. He was still there, staring at her. She opened her mouth to speak.

But the words weren't there.

'I'll probably be late,' she said. 'Don't wait up for me.'

She opened the door, slipped out, pulled it gently yet firmly closed behind her.

She walked away from the house, bracing herself in case Jack was to shout or follow her. Try to reason with her, get her to stay.

But no sound came.

She pulled her coat collar up against her neck, buttoned her coat against the cold.

She walked away.

Sharon woke with a start, gasped and reached for the bedside alarm clock. It wasn't there.

Panicking, she sat bolt upright, looked around. The curtains were unfamiliar, the room unfamiliar. The figure sleeping next to her unfamiliar.

Then she remembered. Where she'd been. What she'd done.

With Ben Marshall.

She threw back the covers, got out of bed. She stood there naked, scanning the room for her clothes.

Sharon had known what would happen. As soon as she had walked into the restaurant, blocking her home life, Jack, from her mind, she had known. Almost as if it had been preordained.

Ben had been sitting at the table waiting for her. She wasn't late – in fact she was slightly early – but Ben had arrived before her. He always did that. She had asked him why on one occasion.

'Because it's not polite to make a lady wait by herself for a man in a bar or a restaurant.'

Sharon had smiled at that.

As he rose from the table to kiss her cheek, she noticed the appreciative look he gave her. A light, quivering thrill ran through her body. She was glad she had worn the minidress.

She moved around the room in her underwear. Even lit only by the curtain-filtered streetlight, she liked his room. It was modern, groovy. It looked like it had been designed rather than decorated. It struck a chord within her. This was what she wanted for herself. This life. She was still interested in fashion, she liked design. She would no longer allow herself to be housebound by housewifery, to be mummified by motherhood. This life. She didn't know how to get it yet, but she would learn.

She looked around the room again, trying to find her tights.

Talk had come easily at the table. As they ate and drank, Ben told her more about his new company.

'Property management,' he said, swallowing a mouthful of red wine. Sharon smiled, looked suitably impressed.

'Big money in that now,' he said. 'Take over some of those old houses in Heaton or Byker or wherever, convert them into flats, rent them out to grateful families at an affordable price and there you go. Shorten the housing queue so you look good to the council, plus we get paid for it. What could be sweeter?'

'I thought Dan Smith was going to slap compulsory purchase orders on lots of those old streets? What if he does that to you?'

Ben smiled. 'Even better. Get a good price, start up again. And make more money.'

'And who is this "we"?'

'Didn't you get the letter? Northern Star Properties. And—' he leaned forward '—I hope I'm looking at my newest company member. My office manager. The hub of the big wheel.'

He smiled at her. She smiled back, looked deep into his eyes. And knew what her answer would be.

Dressed, she looked around for her handbag and the phone number of a taxi company. Ben was lying on his side, the covers kicked off. Central heating kept his modern flat warm, temperate. His body was in good condition. Well muscled, which she liked, but more scarred than she had expected.

She sighed. The first man since Jack she had allowed to touch her, to get within her.

Their lovemaking had started in the taxi. Easily, naturally, like the fulfilment of an unacknowledged wish. First eyes, then hands, then mouths. From there, the one-way bridge was crossed, no going back. On the back seat, arms entwined, mouths hungrily began to devour mouths, fingers made covert forays, promising more; the cabby craning his neck to get a good view in his mirror.

Then at Ben's flat: falling on each other as if starved, ripping away each other's clothes, wanting to be wrapped instead in each other's skin. Hardly time to look, to take in the opposite's physiological scenery, as they raced towards their final destination. Lying on the living room floor, Sharon, legs wrapped around Ben's body, heels kicking into the small of his back, pushing him in deeper, hands raking his shoulders, Ben on top of her, chest crushing her breasts, buried as far as he could get inside her, arms locked around her torso, pulling her towards him. Biting and scratching, sweating and sucking, encompassing and devouring, they both came, lying in a pool of wet bodies and crushed clothing.

Afterwards, lying on the living room floor, Sharon's head on Ben's chest. Ben's fingers running through Sharon's hair, Sharon's fingers stroking Ben's chest. A time for shared, post-coital truths.

'I wanted you the first time I saw you,' said Ben. 'That night in the Go Go. You looked so beautiful.'

Sharon smiled contentedly.

'And now you've got me.' She felt Ben's arms hug her tighter. 'Was it worth the wait?'

Ben gave a deep chuckle. Sharon felt it through his chest.

'Oh, yes,' he said. 'Well worth it.'

'Good,' said Sharon. She returned his hug.

'So how's your husband?' Ben had said at the table between mouthfuls. 'How's Jack?'

A cloud had passed over Sharon's face. And she had told him. She looked at this handsome, suave man sitting before her, and she told him.

How she and Jack weren't getting on. About his lack of ambition, his surfeit of morality and idealism. About how tired and old he looked, made her feel. About how boring she found him. About how boring he made her feel.

It all vomited forth, as if the lobster she had just eaten had reacted against her, turned her insides out.

'I just . . . don't find him desirable any more,' she said. 'On any level.'

Sharon looked up. She had been staring at the tablecloth. She smiled.

'Sorry. I shouldn't burden you with all that. Not your problem.'

Ben snaked his hand across the table, enclosed Sharon's within.

'But it could be,' he said.

She could feel her heart thumping in her chest as if it was about to break free. She found his eyes with hers.

'I adore you, Sharon,' Ben said. 'I think you're one of the most beautiful, amazing people I've ever met in my life.' He tightened his grip on her hands. 'I desire you.'

Sharon felt herself blush. She couldn't speak.

'I can't promise you an answer to everything,' he said, 'but will you come back with me tonight?'

Sharon smiled.

'Let's get the bill,' she said.

He had made her feel special. That was what meant the most to her. Yes, she had loved what he had done with his mouth, his hands, his cock, especially the second and third times after animalism had been sated and something more refined and pleasing had taken place. But it was what he had given to her emotionally, to her soul, which really touched her. It was a long time since anyone had ever touched her that deeply. She wondered if Jack ever had.

Jack.

She had been so busy with his problems, his needs, over the years that her own hadn't been catered for. That was the picture she painted for herself. Did she feel guilty? Should she?

She looked at the sleeping, naked figure. Her lover. Lying on his bed.

She felt happy. She felt fulfilled.

She felt wanted and desired.

Any other emotions she would cope with as and when they occurred. For now she felt full: of life, of hope, of optimism.

Of love.

There was a discreet rapping at the front door. Her cab.

She put on her coat, picked up her handbag, checked her watch.

Two forty a.m.

Not too bad. Not as bad as it could have been. At least she was going home.

Home. Was that still with Jack and Isaac? Or would that be here with Ben? Something else to cope with. As and when it occurred.

She blew her sleeping lover a kiss and smiled at him. She

let herself out of his flat, closing the door as softly as she could.

She climbed into the cab, gave the driver her address. In gear and off they went.

Smiling all the way home.

Ben Marshall heard the door close, the cab drive off. Waiting until he was sure he was alone, he rolled over and stretched out, pleased to have his bed all to himself again.

As work went, he thought, tonight had been enjoyable. And he should have won an Oscar for his performance at the restaurant.

But everything was falling into place.

He rolled over, closed his eyes. He could smell Sharon's perfume on his pillow. He liked that. He could smell her body, her sex, on his sheets. He liked that too.

She had been a tiger. Up for anything, willing and wanting to give as much pleasure as she could take. And she could take a lot.

Hardly work, he thought, and began to replay some of the evening's entertainment for himself.

Between imagining Sharon and smelling her, he found himself becoming aroused.

Only one thing for it, he thought, grasping his erect penis in his hand. At least it'll send me off to sleep.

His mind turning recent pleasures into porno films, he played them again on his closed inner eyelids.

He smiled.

Everything was falling into place.

December 1964:
Point of Contact

Jack Smeaton stood on the pavement, pulled his overcoat more tightly around him, stomped his booted feet, kept out the cold. He studied the piece of paper in his hand again, matching the address on it to the one in front of him. Hoping there was a mistake, knowing there wasn't.

A nondescript street in Fenham. Stone and brick Edwardian houses mostly turned into flats for multiple occupation. The heart of studentland.

He stamped his feet again, putting off what he had to do. Sharon would have told him not to do it, had he asked her. Although Sharon would more likely have said nothing.

Communication had virtually ceased between them. No contact, emotional, mental or physical. Now exchanging only the merest pleasantries, a façade of normality for Isaac. He knew what was happening with Ben Marshall, knew it was more than just work, but he couldn't stop her, couldn't confront her with it. Because if he did that, his whole carefully built life would come crashing down like a flimsy house of cards. And he couldn't take that. So he said nothing. Impotent.

He checked his watch. Nearly six o'clock. The dark, early-winter night made it appear later. The snow struggling to fall was turning to city slush in the gutters.

Jack pocketed the paper, walked reluctantly up the short path, rang the bell. He waited, hoping there would be no answer, but the door was soon opened. The girl was blonde and surprised looking. He obviously wasn't whom she was expecting.

'Hello,' he said, feeling old and bashful in her presence, 'is Joanne at home?'

Chambers seemed to click and something seemed to open in the blonde girl's mind. She smiled at him.

'She might be,' she said. 'Who shall I say is calling?'

'Jack Smeaton. I'm a friend of hers. Well, friend of the family, really.'

'Come in.'

Jack followed her inside. She closed the door and went upstairs to look for her, leaving Jack alone in the hall. He looked around. The house appeared to have been colonized. Older, heavier wall coverings and furnishings had been covered over with posters of art exhibitions and concerts plus rock and pop groups. Mick Jagger's insouciant sneer sat opposite a cheeky-faced Paul McCartney down from a severe-looking Steve Winwood and Spencer Davis.

'Hello, Jack.'

Jack looked up. Joanne was coming down the stairs smiling, yet slightly puzzled. He didn't blame her. Jack returned the greeting.

'Didn't expect to see you here,' she said.

'No,' said Jack, 'I bet you didn't.'

He looked behind her, saw the blonde girl hovering on the stairs, curious.

'I need to have a word with you,' he said, 'quiet, like. Is there anywhere we could go?'

Joanne glanced to her side, saw her flatmate, took his hint.

'There's my room. Follow me.'

She turned, made her way back upstairs. Jack followed. As

he passed the blonde girl, she gave him a smile he could have interpreted several ways. He chose to ignore it.

Joanne reached the landing, opened a door.

'Here it is,' she said. 'Sorry about the mess. Make yourself at home and I'll get us some tea. Milk? Sugar? If we have any.'

Jack smiled. 'Milk, no sugar, thanks.'

Joanne returned his smile. 'I'll not be a minute.'

He heard her footsteps descend the stairs. He looked around. The student décor continued. Pictures of pop stars, posters for art exhibitions. Joanne seemed to favour the Beatles. Sheets and blankets were all over the bed, a heavy textbook open on top. Reading in bed. He sat down on the unmade bed. It still held an imprint of her warmth. Jack felt a strange thrill course through him. It was the first time he had been in another woman's bedroom since he had been married.

He looked at the floor. A portable Dansette record player held three singles. The Beatles, the Animals, Otis Redding. On a dressing table was the usual assortment of jars, sprays, powders, by the far wall paints, sketchbooks and frames. Something drew his attention. Propped against the wall was a canvas with an abstract design on it. The colours were bold at the sides and edges, fading towards the centre. From the blocks of colour came appendages, some fluid, some more cubic, all seemingly trying to cross the white divide in the centre of the canvas, link up with those on the opposite side. They were all failing to do so: their colours faded, their shapes lost definition. Caught static and still, never to connect.

Jack crossed to the painting, studied it. It was either very good or very bad, he thought, because it gave him some kind of *frisson*. He thought he understood it, felt it touch him.

The door opened. Joanne entered, carrying two mugs of tea.

'Here you go,' she said, handing one to him.

He took it. 'Thanks.'

She set hers down on the dressing table, drew a cigarette from a packet. Something French, Jack noted.

'D'you want one?'

'No, thanks. I don't smoke.'

She lit it up with a lighter, smiled.

'Don't tell Mam and Dad.'

Jack returned her smile. 'I won't.'

He looked at her. Jeans and a baggy jumper couldn't hide her maturing figure. Her hair was long and tousled, partially tied back by a length of silk. Barefoot, she sat on the bed with her legs curled under her. She wasn't a little girl any more.

'Sorry,' said Jack. 'It's Friday night. You're probably getting ready to go out.'

She shrugged, smiled. 'Don't worry about it.'

He looked away from her, trying to find the right words to say what he had to. She studied his expression, mistook the direction of his gaze for art criticism.

'What d'you think?'

He looked up, slightly startled. 'Sorry?'

'The painting. You can tell me. I'm a big girl now. I can take it.'

'You did it?'

Joanne laughed. 'Don't sound so surprised. I *am* studying art. They expect us to paint, you know.'

Jack turned back to look at it. 'I like it. A lot.'

Joanne uncurled her legs, crossed to his side, exhaled cigarette smoke.

'It's called *Communication. Points of Communication* originally, but I shortened it. Obviously.'

Jack nodded. 'That makes sense.'

Joanne looked at him and smiled. The years of education and sophistication seemed to fall away, and she was an eager little girl again, happy to receive a compliment.

'You get it?' she said.

'Course,' said Jack. He pointed towards it. 'At least I think so. These bits here, and here, are trying to reach across and touch each other. But this . . . this void . . . is that right? This void . . . they just fall in there and fade away.'

Joanne looked at him as if seeing him properly for the first time.

'Is that right?' he said.

'Spot on,' she said.

'You look surprised.'

'I'm amazed. At college they told me it was derivative. Just aping Victor Pasmore's style without any of his inspiration. Even the title, *Points of Communication*, just a rip-off of his *Points of Contact* series, yeah?'

Jack looked blank. Joanne continued.

'They said it had no originality or spark, or anything.'

'Then they're wrong. I like it.'

Joanne laughed. 'You're welcome here any time you like.'

Jack took a deep breath. 'Not when you hear what I've got to say.'

The smile froze on Joanne's face. A look of puzzlement replaced it.

'I think you'd better sit down,' said Jack.

There was no chair in the room, so she sat back down on the bed. Jack didn't want to stand to say what he had to say, so he sat next to her. The enforced intimacy made him feel uncomfortable. He hadn't been this close to a woman in months: for all the touching he and Sharon had done, they may as well have been in separate beds. He tried to concentrate on what he had to say.

'Your mam and dad have been trying to get in touch with you,' he said, 'but since you haven't got a phone, I know it's difficult.'

'I always go round on a Sunday, though. Well, usually.'

'I know,' said Jack, 'but this couldn't wait. They thought you'd want to know straight away. That's why I said I'd come round.'

He was aware of her eyes on him. The fear and apprehension contained within. He couldn't put it off any longer.

'It's . . . Kenny. Your brother. I'm afraid he's dead.'

He looked at the carpet, unable to maintain eye contact with her.

'Dead?' Her voice sounded brittle and small. 'How?'

'Some kind of bug he picked up in the home. Weakened his immune system. Caught pneumonia. Couldn't defend himself.' Jack sighed. 'I'm sorry.'

He felt a slight movement on the bed beside him and turned round. Joanne was nodding silently, the movement spreading out from her head, threatening to turn into a full body rocking motion.

'Hey . . .' he said, feeling he had to say something.

'I should have been there . . .' Her face was screwed down tight, but still tears leaked from it. 'I should have been there with them . . . with Mam . . .'

'Come on, Joanne, it's not your fault. Kenny would have—' he balked at the word, but said it anyway '—died whether you'd been there or not.'

She was still nodding, still rocking.

'It's not your fault.'

'I . . . know. It's just . . . Mam and Dad. It's . . .' A huge sigh escaped her body. 'I don't know. I never liked him. Kenny. Not really. Isn't that an awful thing to say? About your own brother?'

'Not if it's true. There's no reason why you should like him. Just because he's your brother.'

'He was cruel. When we were growing up. And sly. Cruel and sly. He would always try to hurt me. Try to get me into trouble. And Johnny. Do the same to him too.' Another sigh. 'But I didn't want this to happen to him. Not this.'

Jack flexed and unflexed his hands. He felt useless. He wanted to comfort Joanne but knew there was nothing he could say or do. His sense of discomfort at the closeness of their bodies wasn't helping either.

'Oh, God.'

Joanne was shaking her head. Jack thought it best to sit silently.

'Oh, God.'

Jack flexed and unflexed his hands. He felt useless.

'Oh, Mam and Dad . . . Mam and Dad . . . Oh . . .'

The tears continued. Jack watched steam rise and evaporate from Joanne's cooling mug on the dressing table.

'Oh, God.'

Jack stared at the tea. At the painting.

Communication.

'Will you hold me, Jack?'

He looked at her, startled at being addressed directly.

'Please. Just hold me. I want to be held.'

He edged down towards her along the bed. She moved her body towards his. He placed his arms around her, delicately, as if she was Dresden china, and she allowed herself to sink into him, her head on his chest. He rested his arms about her. She encircled his torso with her arms, pulled him to her.

His sense of discomfort increased. He felt her breath on the skin of his neck, the wetness of her tears. Under his arms he felt the rise and fall of her whole body.

More human contact than he had had for months.

He began to get an erection.

He moved his legs, trying to conceal it, shame and embarrassment making him blush. His wriggling had the effect of holding Joanne tighter. She responded, clung to him.

She looked up, her eyes large and red-rimmed, her cheeks tear-tracked.

Jack looked at her; saw more than pain in her eyes.

And they kissed.

Talking afterwards, neither knew which had moved first. Neither cared. Their mouths were locked, eyes closed, tongues probing, like they were trying to suck the old life from each other, breathe new life in.

Jack felt his overcoat, his jacket, being pushed from his shoulders. He undid the buttons, helped the progress. His hands went to Joanne's clothes.

'Slowly,' she whispered. 'Please don't rush this.'

Jack gently moved Joanne's jumper up her back. Felt wool on his fingers replaced by skin. She reluctantly removed her mouth from his to allow it to come off. It did so, knocking the tie from her hair. She had nothing but a bra underneath it. Jack took in her body, her skin soft, white, young, her hair falling tousled about her shoulders, her face pretty and passion-hungry.

She was beautiful. Jack felt he hadn't known true desire until that moment.

He reached forward to undo her bra, but she gently pushed him back on to the bed, slowly undressed him. He felt her fingers trail on his body, the first time a woman had touched him for years. He sighed. She had him fully naked and erect. Joanne undid her bra, smiled as his eyes went to her breasts, let it drop, slid her jeans and panties over her hips and off.

Their mouths came together again. Jack wanted to grab her, devour her like a starving man in a four-star restaurant.

'Shh,' she said. 'Not so fast. Make it beautiful.'

He listened; reached out to touch her, stroke her. Felt the warmth, the smoothness of her skin. Enjoyed letting his fingers trace her. She returned the gesture.

The pleasure intensified. She touched him everywhere, as

he had her. Soon, Jack could take it no more. He rolled Joanne over on to her back. He had to be inside her.

'Wait . . .' Her voice half-whisper, half-pant.

Joanne reached across to her bedside cabinet, pulled a small package from the drawer, threw it at him.

'Put this on,' she said, still gasping. 'I don't want a baby.'

Jack ripped the condom from the packet, rolled it on to his stiff cock. Joanne watched him.

'Come on,' she said when he was ready, opened her arms and legs.

Jack slid straight inside her. The condom barely muffled the sensation. He could feel her so vividly.

They both gasped, smiled. He locked his arms around her shoulders, she encircled him, limbs around his torso. They kissed. Jack moved slowly, almost delicately, incrementally pushing back the skein of her passion, allowing their mutual pleasure to increase. Joanne held on to him, he to her. He felt Joanne's fingernails dig into his skin. Her eyes closed. He moved faster.

'Oh . . .'

Her body tensed, locked rigidly around his.

She came, clinging on to Jack like he was the last lifeboat on the *Titanic*. Eyes closed, she smiled.

Jack felt the pressure build within him. He came, pulling her to him, holding himself inside her until there was nothing left but quivering aftershocks. He opened his eyes. And found Joanne's staring straight into his.

She smiled.

He smiled back.

Contact.

'Oh, sorry. I forgot, you don't.'

Joanne lit the cigarette, inhaled, blew smoke at the ceiling.

'Smoking,' said Jack. 'You're all grown up now.'

Joanne laughed. 'Well, I would hope so. Especially after what we've just done.'

Later, in Joanne's bed. Both naked, covered by sheets and blankets. The fire on, a candle burning. Jack's arm around Joanne, Joanne snuggled into Jack's body. 'Sketches of Spain' on the Dansette; Miles Davis blowing warmth into the room.

'You feeling all right now?' said Jack.

'About Kenny, you mean?'

'Anything.'

Another inhale, another exhale.

'I'm fine about Kenny. He's been lost for a long time, really. Should have expected something like this, I suppose.'

Another inhale.

'Like I say, it's Mam and Dad I feel sorry for.' Exhale. 'What about you? You OK?'

Jack smiled. 'Well, I can't say I'm not taken aback by what's happened. University's certainly broadened your horizons.'

Joanne laughed. They slipped into an easy silence. Content to be in each other's company.

They had made love twice. Joanne's housemate had noisily left the house to meet her friends, obviously angry that Joanne wasn't accompanying her. Night had drawn in; the two of them had stayed where they were.

'I felt a bit guilty at first,' said Joanne. 'The first time. The look on your face, it was like you didn't know what had happened.'

'I didn't.'

'I suddenly realized who you were. What you were. Married. And I like Sharon.'

'Like I said, don't worry about it.'

Joanne finished her cigarette, stubbed it out in the ashtray, an old tin one, obviously stolen from a pub, at the bedside. She propped herself up on one arm, uninhibited about her naked breasts, looked at Jack.

'Are you and her not getting on?'

'D'you think I'd be here now if we were?'

Silence fell again. Jack wasn't good at talking about his feelings. He kept too much inside himself, bottled things up. Joanne's silence told him he had said the wrong thing. Or it had come out wrong. But he could speak to this girl, he would try to say the right things. He took a deep breath, started slowly.

'Sorry,' he said, 'that didn't come out right. Sharon and I aren't getting on. We haven't spoken properly for months. Haven't had ... relations for ages. We're only staying together, I think, because of Isaac.' He sighed. 'And she's been seeing someone else.'

'And now you're equal.'

'No, that's not what I mean ... I didn't mean it like that.'

Joanne smiled.

'I was joking.'

Jack said nothing. The candle flickered, guttered, kept burning.

'I think she was going out tonight. I think I was supposed to stay in and look after Isaac.'

'Oh.' Joanne couldn't hide the disappointment in her voice. 'So you'll be going, then.'

'I don't think so,' said Jack. 'It'll do her good. Remind her what a mother's supposed to do.'

Joanne smiled. 'That's one of the things I've always loved about you. Real strength of character.'

'Always loved?' said Jack. 'To be honest, Joanne, I'm having a hard time accepting this is happening without you saying things like that.'

'Sorry.' She smiled. She didn't look it.

'It's all right. But I mean, I'm thirty-six. Old enough to be your dad, almost. Don't you have a boyfriend? Someone your own age? What are you doing in bed with me?'

'I don't like the boys my own age. They're so . . . immature.' She affected a world-weary air that Jack thought made her seem younger. 'I prefer men. Older men. I've had a few boyfriends older than me. One older than you.'

'And married?'

Joanne shrugged. 'Couple, maybe.'

Jack let the facts sink in. Older men. Married men. No commitment.

'But you're different,' she said. 'I like you a lot, Jack. I always have done.'

Her fingers began to stroke the hairs on his chest. For the first time he noticed how grey they were.

'I hope today is the start of something special,' she said.

Jack pulled her closer to him. He could feel her heart beating. He could feel the hunger for her rising in him again.

'Whenever you want me,' she said, whispering in his ear, sliding her hands down his body, 'I'll be here. You'll always have me to come to. Whenever you want me.'

'I want you now,' he said.

They began to make love again, slowly, like a symphonic overture.

He thought of her words:

The start of something special.

He hadn't answered her, didn't feel safe answering her. But there in that candlelit room, smooth, warm jazz blowing gently like soft dreams, paintings against the wall, he gave the answer to himself.

I hope so too.

Their bodies joined together, singing in harmony once again.

He put the key in the lock, turned it, dreading what lay on the other side of the door.

Jack stepped into his house, closed the door behind him, waited.

Nothing.

He went into the kitchen. A place had been set for him at the table. He checked the oven. The dried-up remains of his dinner sat in there. He closed the oven door. Whatever hunger he had felt had long disappeared or been sated.

He listened. No sound: the house was silent. It felt like it was waiting for him to speak, to tell it things, to explain himself. He looked around, saw familiar walls, appliances, cupboards. His kitchen. A place he was in every day. That familiarity felt suddenly alien to him: like he was visiting it in a dream or watching an actor playing himself in a film or play, moving around.

He checked his watch. Eleven twenty-five. He may as well go to bed.

He walked upstairs, each creak and groan sounding sharp and accusatory in his ears, checked on Isaac. His son was sleeping soundly, Thunderbirds toys, Daleks on the floor of his room. Isaac's face looked at peace, almost angelic, and Jack, for the first time that evening, felt a knife-stab of guilt. He wondered if what he had done was worth risking his son's future happiness for.

He wondered what he intended to do next.

But he didn't want to start thinking about that at this time of night. He would never sleep.

Back on the landing and into the bathroom, where he prepared for bed. He moved as soundlessly as he could into the bedroom. He made out the still figure of Sharon lying on her side of the bed, breathing evenly. He changed into his pyjamas and lay under the covers with his back to her, as he always did.

He needed to sleep, but his mind was spinning like a Catherine wheel. He tried to will himself to sleep but couldn't.

'I was supposed to be going out tonight.'

Sharon's voice was cold and clear, unaffected by sleep. Jack suspected she had been awake all along, biding her time, waiting for her moment.

He felt anger and guilt well within him, bubble grittily to the surface. He swallowed them both down.

'Sorry,' he said, as neutrally as possible. 'I had to do something. Couldn't be avoided.'

'You could have let me know.'

'I tried phoning you this afternoon. You were out.'

Sharon sighed. Jack was sure it was to expel some anger.

'So I had to change all my plans because you decided you had something to do.'

The guilt was dissipating. Jack felt only anger now. He tried to keep his voice down.

'He'll have to see you another night, then.' Jack felt bile in his chest when he spoke. Before Sharon could answer he continued: 'Kenny Bell's died. Ralph needed some help.'

Jack felt Sharon bite back her retort. Instead she asked how. He told her. Her mood subsided slightly.

'When's the funeral?' she said.

'Probably next week some time. Jean's making the arrangements.' Jack lay on his back, stared at the ceiling. 'Are you going?'

Sharon paused before answering.

'Yes.'

They lay in silence for a while.

'So what did Ralph have you doing?' said Sharon eventually.

'Letting people know. He couldn't get in touch with—' he swallowed, hoped Sharon wouldn't pick up on his hesitation, write too much into it '—with Joanne. They couldn't reach her. No phone.' He tried to keep his voice inflectionless. 'So I had to go round there.'

'So that's where you've been all this time. Round at Joanne Bell's.'

Jack felt anger rise within him again. Defensive anger this time.

'Yes, I have. She's just lost her brother, for God's sake. She needed . . . somebody with her.'

Sharon gave a short, harsh laugh.

'With the students all night. I'll bet they enjoyed that. Must have been like one of their dads visiting.'

Even in the dark Jack knew his face was flushed. His body was shaking with anger. He thought of all the times Sharon had gone out wearing clothes that he thought were too young for her, depth of make-up increasing with age, running ever faster to chase her disappearing youth.

'You—' he said, then stopped himself. He didn't want an argument. Not now. He didn't trust himself not to say something he would regret. One hasty phrase and the house of cards would come crashing down.

'What?'

'Nothing. It doesn't matter. Go to sleep.'

Jack heard Sharon sigh, settle her body down. Thinking she had scored a victory with her words.

'That's a night out on my own you owe me, though.'

'Good night.'

Jack lay there, too wound up to sleep. He knew Sharon would be doing the same. The more he thought, the angrier he became. So he tried to ignore her, let her words go. Think of something else. Something happier.

Joanne.

He smiled at the thought of her. He wondered where she was, what she was doing. In bed, probably. Trying not to be too upset about Kenny. Thinking of him, hopefully. Wondering what would happen next.

I'll be here. You'll always have me to come to. Whenever you want me.

He smiled to himself, looked forward to seeing her again.

Joanne.

Like he had been brought back to life.

He smiled again.

And was soon asleep.

Rain lashed down, wind whipped, chilled through to bone. Fell with biblical fury on the Gosforth golf courses, made them unplayable and inhospitable, spread past the greens to the cemetery.

Kenny Bell's funeral.

Dark during the daytime: black-clad figures huddled beneath black umbrellas, became indistinct, blurred shapes. The rain and wind bleached foreground and background to variously graded misty hues of grey: distant buildings, winter-denuded trees and hedges, granite headstones. Up close, the rain turned the grass underfoot into marshy, swampy mud.

Jack shivered, thought no amount of heat or light could ever warm him or dry him again. He held an umbrella over himself and Sharon, cold forcing them together. He was glad Isaac, at school then the childminder's, had been spared this. Wished he had himself.

The coffin was supported, anticipating descent. The Catholic priest, old and rotund, held his book in shaking hands, spoke in trembling tones, went as fast as decorum would allow. He was shivering beneath his frocked layers, his large face aiming for sternness, showing severe discomfort. Saying: man had but a short time to live. Subtextually communicating: in this weather, that's not short enough.

The gathering was sparse: friends and family of Ralph and Jean, staff from the nursing home. Kenny had no friends of his own.

Jack's attention wandered from the priest to the mourners. A family portrait: the Bells.

Ralph and Jean Bell stood numbly, eyes transfixed by the coffin, the hole in the ground. Jean looked paler than Jack had ever seen her: skin leached of colour and almost translucent, like a thin veil covering the dead-eyed skull beneath. She moved like an animated corpse, a shrunken physical shell from which the soul had departed. Absent to the quick: only her ghost present.

Ralph was different. His size, always large, was tipping over into corpulence. Jack knew, from the increasingly rare visits Ralph made into work, that the man was drinking heavily: his purple, blotched face and ruined nose attesting to that. But there was more: like a centuries-old oak attacked by lichen and insects, something seemed to be eating Ralph away from the inside. Guilt, Jack surmised, burning through his old friend like acid or syphilis. Jack had tried talking to the man on many occasions, losing count over the months and years, but to no avail. An iron door would descend, locking Ralph in, Jack and the world out.

Next to them, but not too near, stood Johnny. Statue-still, hands in pockets, the rain hitting his cropped blond head, rivering down his face. His expression seemed curiously beatific: like a stained-glass suffering saint. The rapture of pain. Jack shivered.

At the other side of Ralph and Jean: Joanne.

His lover.

Face tipped down towards the coffin. Radiating strength for her parents, casting secret glances at Jack. Jack returning them. Her long hair, tied with a dark, silken sash, was soaked. Her overcoat, old and mannish, had water dripping from its fringes. Every movement she made squeezed a small stream from the heavy fabric. Eyes panda-black, rain-ruined.

She looked beautiful.

Jack wanted her. Even at the graveside, cold and wet. He

wanted her. Desire incarnate. He longed for her with his body and heart. They had been together several times, proving their union to be no one off. He could dress it up with different words and emotions, but he was falling in love.

Life with Sharon had drifted into an uneasy truce. Separate lives. Never questioning each other. Marking nights out on the kitchen calendar. Holding their home together by a delicate web of shattered dreams, broken promises, marital duty and Isaac. Their marriage was work. Their pleasure elsewhere.

Sharon moved, shuffled foot to foot, reminded Jack she was still there. She moved her shivering body towards his, huddled for warmth. Joanne looked across at him, her face displaying an unhappiness that had nothing to do with her brother's burial. He looked back at her, apologizing, hoped his face, his mind communicated the fact of who he really wanted to be with.

The priest moved to the end of his address.

Ashes to ashes.

Dust to dust.

The coffin was lowered. He threw earth on to the wooden lid. Rain-sodden and muddied, it hit the wood with a wet slap, left his hand with a filthy stain.

He concluded and, after wiping his hand on his cassock, shook hands with Ralph and Jean, then quickly disappeared.

'If you'd like to come back to my mam and dad's house,' said Joanne against the wind, 'you're all welcome.'

She left the graveside with her parents.

Jack watched them walk away, both supported by Joanne. Like they had buried more than their son, he thought. A part of their past had died and an uncertain future had been born.

The other mourners followed at a respectful distance, trudging through the wind and rain like broken, failed explorers lost in an arctic blizzard wilderness, dwindling into a fog of static.

Jack sighed, rolled over on his back, smiled. Joanne stroked his chest hair, smiled also.

'I needed that,' she said.

'So did I.'

Back at Joanne's flat. Rain still pounding outside, rattling the window frames, candles and warmth inside. An incense stick burning. Keeping the world at bay.

Bottle of wine by the bed. Two half-drunk glasses.

Earlier, the wake at the Bells' house:

Lighted gas fires carried an unused smell, like burning dust.

Curtains pulled close and overhead lights increased the mausoleum atmosphere.

Wet mourners steamed and shivered.

Finger food and bone-china tea. Something stronger for those who wanted it.

In the hall, an incongruous Christmas tree stood, sad and sparsely festive.

Conversation in small, hushed tones: platitudes and clichés of bereavement.

Ralph and Jean can get on with their lives.

It's a blessing really.

They lost him a long time ago, if you're being honest.

No celebrating or mourning the loss of Kenny for his own sake. No mention or knowledge of his life.

No Dan Smith. 'Sends his regards,' Ralph had said. 'Out of the country. Some Scandinavian place.'

Everyone drinking up, eating up, hurrying off as quickly as possible.

Joanne asks Jack into the garage, the pretence of reaching down stored spirits.

They were on each other, mouths and hands devouring. Her nearness made his thighs tremble.

'I've wanted you all day,' Jack said, gasping.

'Likewise.'

They kissed again. She asked him round to her place that evening.

'Won't they need you? I notice Johnny left pretty quickly.'

'I do what I can for them, but sometimes I have to think of myself. I have needs as well,' she said. 'Enormous needs. I need you.'

They had kissed again.

Later, on the way home in the car, he told Sharon he would be out that night.

'You didn't mark it on the calendar,' she said. 'What if I'd planned to go out tonight?'

'It's not on the calendar. And I said it first.'

A little thrill of petty triumph ran through him. Sharon sat still, staring ahead, her features like an injection-moulded mask.

He checked himself. How had they reached that situation? Both lying to each other, scoring points, wounding but never going in for the kill? How? He didn't know. And he didn't know if there was any way back from it. Or if he wanted there to be.

'Hold me,' Joanne said, her small, quiet voice breaking into his thoughts, 'just hold me.'

He did so.

'Trying day,' he said.

She sighed.

'Wouldn't want to go through that again in a hurry.'

She lit herself a cigarette, blew smoke at the ceiling.

'Funerals,' she said, 'make you think, don't they? I mean, not just about Mam and Dad and that, seeing they're all right, but the really important stuff. The big stuff.'

'You mean why are we here? That sort of thing?'

'Yeah. Why are we here, what's life for, all that.'

Jack gave a small smile. The candle shadows gave his face a sad aspect. He took a sip from his wine glass.

'If you can answer that one,' he said, replacing the glass on the floor, 'you'll make a fortune.'

'Don't you have any answers at all?'

'I don't know. I thought I did.' The wine, the shadows, were loosening his tongue. Loosening the dusty chains that kept his memories locked up. 'When I was your age, I was in the army. Just coming out. Second World War. Europe.' He sighed. 'I saw some things.'

Joanne propped herself up on one elbow, interested.

'What sort of things?'

He avoided answering, made an issue of taking a mouthful of wine.

'What sort of things?'

'Belsen,' he said eventually.

'The concentration camp?'

Jack nodded. 'I was there at the end. The liberation.' Another sigh.

'What was it like?' Joanne's voice was quiet again.

Jack opened his mouth to speak, but no sound came out. He struggled with memories, found himself back there. The images again. The Pathé horror newsreel.

Cranking up again, flickering back to half-life.

He spoke as he watched.

'I couldn't . . .'

The stick people. Men, women and children. Skin shrunken down to their bones. Faces skeletal. Eyes filled with terror.

'I don't want you to . . .'

The crunch of bone underfoot. The slap and slip of boot on sun-dried, leathery skin.

'It's not fair for you . . . to . . .'

Squashed into bunks smaller than veal crates.

Bodies piled high, bulldozed into graves.

'To . . .'

Bones and flesh, just ashes in the furnace.

'Jack? You're shivering. Come here . . .'

Joanne stubbed out her cigarette, put her arms around him.
Jack went willingly, his body shaking.

'Sorry . . .' His words were whispers. 'I thought I was . . .
over . . . it . . . but the memories, they're . . .'

'It's all right.'

Rocking him.

'Still there . . .'

'It's all right. You're here now. With me.'

Jack held on to her, gripping hard to her as if she was the
last precipice of life before falling into the abyss. They lay like
that until, with a forceful sigh, the tense rigidity left Jack's
body and he flopped back against the mattress, cold sweat
pinpricking his skin.

'I'm sorry,' he said again.

'You needn't be. You're here with me.'

'I thought . . . I could talk about it. But I can't.' Another
sigh. 'I hope you never have to see what I saw then. Or
anything like it. I'd hate those visions to get inside your head.
Infect you.'

She kept her arms around him. They lay in silence for
some time.

Joanne took a deep breath. Her eyes shone in the dark.

'Always thought of you as sensitive. Like you can almost
see your soul through your skin.'

'Oh.'

'It's a compliment.'

'Oh.'

They lay wrapped in each other's arms. Not speaking.

'Anyway,' said Joanne eventually, 'you said you had answers.'

'When?'

'Seems like hours ago. To life? To why we're here.'

'Right. Socialism, I was going to say. How it saved me. How I met your dad. Dan Smith.'

Joanne looked at him.

'Socialism.'

'Yeah. I thought after . . . Belsen and everything we couldn't let that happen again. Needed to work towards a new future. Build a bright new tomorrow. And all that.'

'But?'

Jack smiled. 'Didn't happen, did it? I mean, Dan's still doing a good job and that, but . . . I don't know. This doesn't seem to be the bright new future we planned, does it?'

'Doesn't it?'

Jack sighed. 'Oh, maybe it's just me. Maybe I'm just old and jaded. Maybe I've just lost my faith.'

'Maybe you have.'

'I don't know. Perhaps it's just the way you're supposed to feel. When you're young. And idealistic. I mean, if you can't be an idealistic Socialist when you're twenty, when can you be?'

Jack saw the look on Joanne's face.

'Sorry,' he said. 'I didn't mean to sound patronizing. But perhaps that's the way it is. Life. Maybe your fire's supposed to burn out as you get older. Settle for less. Accept things for being the way they are.'

'Is that what you want?' said Joanne. 'Is that the way you want to live your life?'

Jack sighed. Then he looked at Joanne. Saw her youth. Felt her life. Her vibrancy.

'No,' he said. 'No, it's not.'

A smile crossed Joanne's face. She immediately sat upright. Jack stared at her naked body, felt a stab of lustful desire.

'Let's go out,' she said.

'What?'

'You and me.' She adopted a mock posh accent. Jane Austen of Fenham. 'Mr Smeaton, I wish to take the air. And I wish you to accompany me as my beau.'

'But ... Are you sure? What if somebody sees us? Together?'

'So what? Lots of people will. But where we're going, it won't matter at all.'

'And where's that?'

'Somewhere where you won't feel old and jaded.' Joanne smiled. 'Somewhere that'll reignite your faith.'

The Downbeat.

Newcastle's nightclubs: New Orleans, Guys and Dolls, the Oxford, even the Club A Go Go. All bright, aspirational. The Downbeat the flipside of that.

A beacon to outsiders, a gathering place for the angrily dispossessed and disenfranchised. A dark, disused warehouse now home to the beats, the peaceniks and refuseniks, the revolutionaries. The atmosphere: heat, sweat, booze and fag and dope smoke. The soundtrack: hardcore heavy R & B, reverberating through chests and heads. On the wall in white paint: BAN THE BLOODY BOMB. Around the walls in brick-built caverns and deliberately dimly lit archways, human transactions caught in furtive, sidelong glances. Half-hidden by obscuring pillars, glimpsed in the gloom:

Art. Revolution. Drugs. Sex.

An easy, natural confluence. All there. All happening. All night.

Jack looked around, listened to the music, absorbed the atmosphere. Beside him Joanne, arm linked through his, holding on to him. Claiming him as hers.

'What d'you think?' she said, smiling.

She had dressed him. Rummaged through her clothes until she found a black polo neck too big for her.

'Too long for me,' she had said, 'even with my big boobs.'

The suit stayed, as did the overcoat.

'There,' she had said. 'You look quite the French existentialist.'

He had taken that as a compliment, smiled.

Now, looking around the place, he realized that whatever he had worn would have made him overdressed. Blue and black. Denim and night. Raw.

Joanne smiled at him, waited for an answer.

'It's . . . loud.'

He smiled as he spoke. She laughed and hugged him.

'My old man. Come on, let's get a drink.'

She led him across to the bar. Figures were dancing about on the floor, working hard to the music. They walked through an alcove, away from the noise. Conversations could be overheard as they passed. Jack was surprised. People talked passionately, violently even. Art, theatre, cinema. And plenty about politics.

He was reminded of the old Socialist Party meetings in the Royal Arcade where he had first met Dan Smith.

And Ralph Bell.

Same arguments, same passion.

Different decade.

He glimpsed something more in a corner, stared. A writhing mass of cloth and flesh. Then another, further along in the gloom. Then another. Bodies having sex.

Same passion.

Different decade.

He looked at Joanne, pointed.

'Over there, they're—'

'Fucking,' she said.

He just looked at her.

'Free love, Jack. What makes the world go round.'

He just looked at her.

'Oh, come on, Jack. Don't be so uptight. You'll be taken as an undercover copper.'

He felt anger rise within him.

'Maybe it's my age,' he said. 'Your old man?'

Joanne looked at him, shocked.

'I didn't mean it like that, Jack. I'm sorry. Age has got nothing to do with it.'

'What has, then?'

'Outlook. Attitude. It doesn't matter how old you are, or what you wear. It's what you've got inside you.'

'Really?'

She put her arms around him.

'Really. You're not some boring suit. Some straight. You're like me. Like everybody here.'

'And what's that?'

She smiled again.

'An outsider. You belong here. You belong with me.'

He kissed her then, full on the mouth.

His spontaneity, his passion, took them both by surprise.

He liked that feeling.

Three hours later and he was feeling tired. He and Joanne were sitting on the floor, backs against a pillar, listening to Muddy Waters over the PA, cans of beer in hands.

'What time does it close?' he said.

'When it gets light.'

He nodded.

Jack was drunk. He knew it. And stoned.

A couple of hours earlier, Joanne had introduced him to a friend of hers. Dave, she said his name was. She thought the two of them would get on. They both liked discussing politics.

Jack had felt a wave of resentment emanating from the scruffy young man, but he thought that had more to do with the fact that he was with Joanne than any conflict of ideology.

Jack had told him what he did for a living.

'I'm a builder.'

'A builder.'

'Yeah. I suppose, if you want to be grand, you could say I implement Dan Smith's ideas. Dream the future, if you want to be pretentious.'

Dave sneered.

'Dan Smith? Bloody Tory.'

'Dan's a Marxist.'

'Aye, he likes to make out he is. An' he might have been once. But scratch 'im an' 'e'll bleed Tory.'

'I've known Dan for years . . .'

'I don't doubt it. But it's the same story every time. They always start off on the right side. An' they always have dreams. But by the time they get themselves into a position to do anything about it, they've compromised, watered down their vision so much, made deals with an' courted all the people they used to hate that it's not worth doin'.'

'I think you're wrong.'

'An' 'e sends his kids to private schools.'

'I still think you're wrong.'

'I hope I am. But I think I'm right. If he wants to be a Tory, wants to be one of them, it'll all come to nothin'. One way or the other.'

And on they argued, until the two men became just two more Downbeat figures locked in the arms of a passionate discussion.

Joanne wandered off. Jack kept glancing at her through his peripheral vision. He saw her dance a few times, chat to friends. He wondered if he should break off his discussion, keep her company. He decided not to. She seemed happy enough.

And so was Jack. He didn't know if he was intoxicated by the atmosphere, the alcohol or the close proximity to Joanne, or by the fact that he was away from his unreal, strained life with Sharon, but he felt better than he had done for a long time.

On fire again.

Just as Joanne had said he would.

He saw her coming back to join them, cigarette in hand. As she got nearer, Jack noticed the cigarette was hand-rolled, thick, giving off a pungent, sweet smell. She sat down next to him, snuggled in to him, dreamily handed him the roll-up.

'Have some,' she said.

'I don't smoke.'

'You'll like this.'

And then he realized what it was. A joint.

'Go on,' she said.

He took it, more to please her than for himself. He put it to his lips, inhaled. Held it down, tried not to cough, exhaled. Mild euphoria gently washed over him. The smoky sickness in his stomach was negligible compared with the buzz he felt. He inhaled again. A mellow, prickly heat covered his body. He smiled.

'Me next,' said Dave.

Jack handed it over. Thirty-six and having my first joint, he thought. He laughed. Better late than never.

They smoked and talked. The heat had gone from the two men's argument. They found themselves more in agreement as the night wore on.

Eventually Dave moved away, leaving Jack and Joanne alone. They drank, smoked and even danced a little. They sat back down again, backs against the wall, on the floor.

'D'you want to go home yet?' Jack was slurring his words.

Joanne shrugged.

'Happy here.' She was slurring too.

She looked at him, smiled. And in that gesture, that moment, he knew he loved her face, her body, her soul, her life. His heart about to burst.

'I love you,' he said.

She looked at him again. Searched his eyes for doubt, desperation, untruth. Found none.

'I love you too,' she said.

Then they were on one another, kissing, grappling, devouring each other in their passion. Unzipping, unbuckling, unbuttoning.

They shuffled along the floor, joined the other writhing shadows as a dark corner claimed them.

Jack threw his overcoat over them.

Then he was inside her.

They gasped together.

They moved together.

Same passion. But deeper now.

Jack: his heart about to burst.

January–August 1965:
Paradise

Ben Marshall walked through the double glass doors of the Newcastle civic centre feeling like a character in a science fiction film.

It was all so modern: blond wood, marble and steel in clean, geometric designs. Pristine. A huge, primary-coloured mural behind the main desk drew his eye, gave the lobby its focus.

He felt a thrill within. This was Dan Smith's design writ large. Un-English. Un-Northern. The future.

Ben loved it. Belonged to it.

He walked up to the main desk. A pretty brunette looked up expectantly. Ben assumed a winning smile.

'Can I help you?'

'Ben Marshall. Here to see Dan Smith. He's expecting me.'

She checked the diary before her.

'That's fine, Mr Marshall.'

She gave him directions to the private lift. He gave her another winning smile in return. She giggled.

He walked around the corner to the lift, which was inlaid in a huge wall of interlocking geometric wooden designs. Stepping inside, he pressed the one button. He straightened his tie in his brushed-steel reflection, glinted his cufflinks in the overhead light, smiled to himself.

Feeling good.

The doors opened. He was greeted by a suited and bespectacled middle-aged man.

'Mr Marshall?'

The man stuck out his hand. Ben accepted it.

'I'm Terry. Mr Smith's personal assistant.'

His handshake was warm, dry and firm.

'If you'd like to follow me.'

Ben followed down halls, through corridors. Modernist wood and leather panelling on the walls. Green leather and chrome banquettes dotted about. Ben was led to a hall filled with glass display cases.

'If you'd just wait here a moment,' Terry said. 'I'll tell Mr Smith you're here.'

He disappeared through a doorway.

Ben looked around. The display cases contained items of regional significance dating back centuries. Ceremonial swords, gestures of friendship between countries and regions, trophies, cups and awards won. History. Highly polished, on display but ultimately compartmentalized and locked away. That fitted with what he had heard about Dan Smith.

The door opened. Terry stood there.

'Mr Marshall?'

Ben turned.

'Mr Smith will see you now.'

Ben entered Dan Smith's office. Stark white walls, the only colour being the blond wood desk and matching filing cabinets, the green leather office chair and matching sofas. On one wall, near the floor-length window overlooking the city, was a model of what looked like a miniature city in white and grey cardboard. Sweeping, multi-level roadways, huge, monolithic office blocks. A science fiction city, not one Ben recognized.

Dan Smith, suited, hair slicked back as usual, was seated behind his desk. He rose as Ben entered, extended his hand.

'Happy New Year, Mr Marshall,' said Dan Smith.

'And to you too,' said Ben.

'Let's hope 1965 brings us plenty of things to be cheerful about.'

He directed Ben to a green leather armchair facing the desk. Dan Smith resumed his seat behind it.

'Would you like something to drink?'

Ben asked for coffee, was informed he could have something stronger if he wished, insisted on coffee. Dan Smith asked for tea. Terry, closing an adjoining door behind him, went to get the drinks.

'Lovely building,' said Ben once the two men were alone.

'This your first visit to the civic centre?'

Ben told him it was.

'It's not finished yet,' said Dan Smith, smiling, 'but we put a lot of planning into it. I like to think of it as a people's art gallery. Something the whole city can be proud of.'

'It's wonderful,' said Ben. 'I'm sure they will be.'

'High praise indeed, when a Southern gentleman such as yourself can appreciate what we're doing up here.'

Ben smiled.

Terry arrived with the tea and coffee, set it out, left.

'So,' said Dan Smith, sipping his tea, wincing from the heat, 'what can I do for you?'

Ben set down his coffee.

'Well,' he said, 'I'm from London, as you can tell. But I prefer to be based up here. More of a sense of optimism in Newcastle. And that's in no small part due to you.'

Dan Smith almost blushed.

'Well, we've got a good team around us. We have to get rid of the old, flat-cap image of the grim, industrial North. Replace it with a new, international one. That's the only way we can attract new business. The only way we can move forward.'

'I agree,' said Ben. 'That's why I wanted this meeting.'

Ben took a sip of coffee, crossed his legs, continued.

'I'm an entrepreneur, a businessman. I own property, rent it out. Walker, Byker, that way. Heaton.'

The quality of light in Dan Smith's eye changed, but his face remained the same. He kept listening.

'I'm moving into property development. I'm buying up buildings, land. I've got an expanding portfolio. I'm moving into redevelopment. However . . .'

He looked straight into Dan Smith's eyes.

'I want to make sure that my vision can sit alongside yours. Otherwise there's no point.'

Dan Smith nodded, kept listening.

'Now I may not be, politically, the kind of person you normally deal with . . .'

Dan Smith showed amusement.

'But I think we can agree on this.'

Dan Smith scrutinized Ben, then stood up.

'Come over here.'

Dan Smith crossed to the corner of the room, where the model city lay. Pristine white towers thrust from the ground. Shining, multi-level walkways and driveways encircled the city. Old buildings were depicted as flat, low and grey. The new, modernist white-hot city rising from the ash-coloured old.

'This,' said Dan Smith, 'is the shape of things to come. This is going to be the city of Newcastle.'

Ben looked at the plan, saw potential. Saw money. He turned to Dan Smith, smiled.

'I think you're a man I can do business with,' he said.

They sat back down, talked. Dan Smith brought Ben up to date with his plans. Le Corbusier brought in to design.

State-of-the-art housing. A new international airport. Hotels. A whole city precinct devoted to education with an extended university. Massive cultural initiatives making the arts accessible for all. A huge, indoor shopping centre in the middle of the city. Existing stores and banks asked to change their branded images to black and white to fit in with the city colour scheme. Complete redevelopment. A whole new environment.

His vision.

'So you see,' said Dan Smith, 'although my roots are in Marxism, I prefer to see myself as a progressive. From what you say, I think you're the kind of young man I could see eye to eye with.'

'I've got a vision too,' said Ben. 'Not as grand as yours, though. The vision for my company is to create one that can offer a full service. Look at the way you do things at the moment. You want a building put up. Or a road, whatever. That involves surveyors, consultants, town planners . . . there would have to be costings made, studies taken. Now, assuming this goes ahead, you'd need an architect to design it, engineers, builders to build it, then it's up. Then you need managers . . .' He shrugged. 'Lot of planning. Lot of dealing with different companies. Wouldn't it be better just to deal with one company?'

Dan Smith smiled.

'That's an audacious concept.'

'It is. And I'm working towards it. I'm starting by moving into construction.'

'Well, you'll have to go a long way to beat Bell and Sons. Number-one company in the area. Our first choice.'

'Well . . .' Ben looked at his immaculately polished boot. 'Not going to be around for ever, are they? Not the way Ralph Bell is.'

Dan Smith sighed sympathetically.

'The man's had a lot of misfortune in his life,' he said. 'Especially recently.'

'Perhaps he won't be in business much longer.'

Dan Smith shrugged.

'Perhaps you'd be open to a bit of . . . competitive tendering.'

Dan Smith looked at Ben, gauging him. Then he nodded.

'If the time comes, we'll talk about it then. I'm open to offers.'

Ben smiled.

The two men talked more. Ben found himself liking Dan Smith, being swept along by his vision. A visionary bureaucrat.

Accent on the visionary.

Dan Smith stood up.

'Well, if you'll excuse me, Mr Marshall, I'll have to be getting on.'

He stood up, offered his hand. Ben took it.

'Pleasure to meet you.'

'Likewise, Mr Smith.'

'Call me Dan.'

'Dan.'

'I like your ideas. I'm sure we can do business together. Let's keep in touch.' He gestured to the door. 'Terry will see you out.'

Terry did see Ben out, all the way to the lift. He made his way across the foyer, giving the brunette receptionist a wink, getting a giggle in return. Once outside in the fountained courtyard, he took a deep breath of cold, January air.

'Let's hope 1965 brings us plenty to be cheerful about,' he said out loud.

He walked to the car park to pick up his car.

He had an appointment with his solicitor.

Mae Blacklock opened her eyes. But the nightmare was still with her.

Waking or sleeping, the nightmare was still with her.

She wanted to get out of bed, get a drink of water. Go to the toilet.

But she didn't dare.

Her mother might be waiting for her. Might have things for her to do.

She clutched the stuffed rabbit close to her chest. The toy was threadbare, dirty and well handled. It was the only protection she had. It was no protection at all.

At least she hadn't wet the bed this time. She hated that. Her mother would hang the mattress on the line so that the entire street could see what she had done. And rub her face in the wee on the sheets.

She lay there, covers pulled up tight, staring at the ceiling. Trying not to breathe, not to exist.

After that first night, that first, horrible night, her mother had started in earnest. Men would arrive at the house specifically to see Mae. Mae would be taken into the white room with the crucifixes on the wall, the expressions of love and agony, and made to greet the men. Mae didn't want to do it, refused at first.

'Remember the prison,' her mother said, 'where they send the naughty children who won't do what their mams tell them.'

Mae looked at the man, at her mother. Terrified. She nodded.

'Well, that's where you'll be if you don't do what you're told.'

Her mother nodded at the man, who handed her some money and began to undress.

And he had her.

And he hurt her.

Sometimes her mother was there. Holding her down, forcing her mouth or legs open.

This just got the men more excited.

Sometimes the men would tie her up, blindfold her.

Sometimes they would hit her with things. Hard things. Soft things. It didn't matter. They were all used with force. They all hurt.

Sometimes her mother was there, laughing and joining in. Sometimes she wasn't.

It didn't matter.

Sometimes her mother would take her to another woman's house where the same things would happen.

Afterwards, Mae would have to wait while her mother drank gin and went to bed with the other woman.

She would hear them laughing together. Swearing together.

Mae retreated to a small place inside herself. A small cell that she couldn't escape from but at least nothing could get in to hurt her.

She felt tiny, powerless.

She felt like she was dying slowly, a piece at a time.

The girl in the bubble. The small, dark bubble.

Other children seemed further away than ever.

Mae desperately needed a wee.

Slowly, she flung back the covers, swung her feet to the floor. She pad-padded over the lino, down the hall and to the toilet. The cold made her shiver through her nightie.

She finished up, wiped herself off. Gently, because she was sore all the time. Then she debated. To flush or not to flush. The sound might wake her mother. Make her angry. But then if she didn't flush the toilet, her mother might be angry about that too.

She took a deep breath, pulled the chain. Kept the door tightly closed until the last of the water echoed away.

Then tiptoed back to her bed.

She risked a glance around her mother's bedroom door; careful not to make the door creak, she pushed it open.

Her mother sprawled naked across the bed, bedclothes twisted and tangled about her body as if she were roped down. She was snoring loudly, head back, mouth open.

Booze-snoring, Mae called it.

Mae wondered what day it was.

Saturday.

Good.

She hurried out of her bedroom, began to get dressed.

Hopefully, she could be out of the house before her mother woke up.

She knew just where to go.

Bert sat at his kitchen table with a mug of strong tea, a Woodbine and the *Daily Mirror*.

Breakfast.

He turned to the back page, began to read the football news, planning on studying the form, too, put a bet on later. There was a knock at the door.

Bert pulled on his Woodbine, set it down in an ashtray and, pulling his braces up over his vest, went to answer it.

He opened the door. There stood Mae. Fully dressed in her winter coat, clutching her battered old stuffed rabbit.

She's too old for that, he had thought on several occasions. Too old to be carrying a little kid's toy around. He hadn't said anything, though. He had heard that some of the kids at school had taunted her about that. He had also heard that at least one of them had required hospital treatment as a result.

Bert had said nothing about it.

'Hello, pet,' he said to her now. 'This is a surprise.'

Her dark eyes bored into him.

'Can I come in?'

'Course you can, pet. In you come.'

She went into the kitchen. He closed the door, then followed her.

'There's tea in the pot still, if you want some,' he said. 'Or I've milk if you'd prefer.'

Mae didn't reply, just helped herself to a cup of tea, sat down.

Bert looked at her. Mae was still a little girl, but sometimes she seemed so grown up. Drinking tea. What was she now? Nine or ten? Something like that, he thought. Maybe even younger. And she carried herself like a grown up. Talked like a grown-up. When she talked at all. Mostly just sat there. Stared.

Bert often found that unnerving.

'Can I stay here today?' she said.

'Well, for a bit, aye. I'm goin' out later, like.'

'Where?'

'The pub. At dinnertime. An' the bettin' shop an' all.'

'Can I stay here?'

'Well . . .'

He looked at Mae. Her big eyes, her blank expression. There was something going on behind those eyes, inside her mind. He would get an occasional glimpse of what seemed like terror fluttering and flickering, like a caged animal desperate to escape. He didn't know what was wrong with her, but he knew she wouldn't tell him if he asked.

And it probably wasn't any of his business.

'Aye, go on then. Will Monica be missin' you?'

Mae shook her head.

'All right, then, you can stay.'

Mae gave a slight smile.

'Thanks,' she said. 'Can I go and see Adam?'

'Course you can, pet. You know where he is.'

She went out into the yard, looking almost happy.

Bert sat back down, picked up his Woodbine. It was nearly half ash. He took a few last pulls from it, stubbed it out.

Watched the smoke curl and drift to the ceiling.

He hardly saw Monica any more. She had never been a big part of his life; they were friends who had occasional sex more than anything else. In the last few months he had noticed a change in Monica. She had become harder, crueller. Maybe she had always been, he thought. Maybe, as their relationship was dwindling, he was seeing her in a more honest light.

There were other women around but, if he was honest with himself, the older he got the less interested in sex he became.

He read the paper, drank his tea and smoked for much of the morning. Mae played in the yard, talking to imaginary people, acting out imaginary scenes. Bert didn't listen.

'Mae,' he said, putting his coat and cap on, 'I'm away out now. Will you be all right, pet?'

'Uh-huh.'

'Champion. I'll be in the Shovel if you need us.'

He left the house.

A few pints, conversations, wasted bets and hours later, he returned. Took up his position in the armchair and fell asleep with the newspaper over his chest.

Forgotten Mae was even there.

Bert began to feel an unfamiliar sensation in his groin. Unfamiliar, but not unpleasant. Behind his closed eyes, he saw Ava Gardner appear before him. He was surprised to see her there but, as he had always liked her, he didn't mind. She was wearing a black, see-through negligee, and seeing the outline of her body, the curve of her breasts and thighs, gave him an erection. He watched as she smiled at him, then bent over before him.

He felt Ava's lips around his erect cock. Pushing up and down. Up and down. He smiled, opened his eyes.

And froze.

There was Mae. Kneeling on his legs with her mouth over his penis.

'What you doin'?'

He jerked away. The movement sent her crashing to the floor. She looked up at him, eyes spinning different emotions, going round like fruit machine wheels: fear, incomprehension, disappointment. And more he didn't recognize. Couldn't name.

He quickly buttoned himself up.

'What you doin', pet?'

Mae scuttled herself into a corner, stared up at him. Tears were welling in her eyes.

She looked like a hurt animal.

Terrified.

He thought the best thing to do would be to play it down. Reassure her.

'Come here,' he said and held out his arms.

She stared at him, didn't move.

'Come on, pet, it's all right. Come over here.'

He managed a small smile for her. It was an effort.

'Come on.'

Slowly, she picked herself up off the floor and crossed towards him.

'Sit down,' he said.

He had meant on a chair, but she sat on his lap. It made him uncomfortable, but he didn't have the heart to turf her off. She put her arms around his neck, buried her face into him.

'Men like that,' she said, her voice a small, fragile thing. 'Men like it when I do that.'

'Not all men, pet. Not all of them.'

He felt her hug him all the harder. He felt her tears on his skin.

Bert's body was shaking. From anger or shock, he didn't know which.

'Come on, pet,' he said, his voice soothing, 'no harm done, eh?'

Mae kept sobbing.

'Listen,' he said, 'what about a nice cup of tea, eh? I'll put the kettle on an' make us a nice cup of tea. Would you like that?'

He felt her head nod slowly against his neck.

'Right, then. You sit here and I'll do it.'

She clung on even harder.

Bert forced a smile. 'Come on, pet, I can't get up if you won't let go.'

She didn't let go.

Bert sighed. 'What is it, pet? Is something wrong at home?'

He felt her body go rigid. She froze in mid-sob. She pulled her head back, stared at him.

There was that look again, he thought. That scared, caged animal look.

'All right, pet, you stay here. I'll go and put the kettle on.'

Bert stood up, leaving Mae in the armchair, and made his way to the kitchen. He busied himself filling the kettle and teapot, trying not to think about what had just happened.

Then he heard the door slam.

He went back into the room. Mae was gone.

Just her rabbit left on the chair.

He sighed, shook his head.

From the kitchen, the kettle began to whine.

Just what's going on in that house, he wondered.

'So how d'you want me, then?'

'On top.'

'You want me to do all the work, then?'

'You don't expect me to, do you? I'm paying you. Fucking do it.'

She was a whore, a cheap one. Young, but already beyond the point of redemption. Ben liked that. It turned him on, adding to her corruption.

Sweaty, dirty sex in a sweaty, dirty basement.

He loved it.

She wore a see-through baby doll nightie and giggled when she mounted him. A *frisson* ran through his body as she lowered herself on to him.

He thought of Sharon.

'Just popping out to see a client, darling,' he had said. 'You'll be all right on your own for an hour or so?'

She had smiled and nodded. Ben could still see the adoration in her eyes. He feigned it and returned it.

Sharon.

A means to an end. He had seduced her, corrupted her, and now had her where he wanted her. He still kept up the pretence of courting her, wining and dining her, but, like commuting to work or eating dinner, it was part of the routine. A workmanlike but necessary part of his day. Her ageing body no longer thrilled him, but he played along. Fucked her. Because he still had a part for her to play.

'You're smilin'. You like that?'

'Yeah, I like that. Don't talk. Just keep going.'

He had driven past his mother's old place in Byker a few days earlier. He didn't know why; he hadn't felt the need to do it previously. Must be getting sentimental.

The house had been allowed to atrophy. He could imagine his mother sitting inside. Gnarled and twisted into a hate-filled old age.

He had parked and looked at the house.

And felt nothing.

Another person, another life.

He had driven away.

He felt an orgasm building inside him. This pockmarked, flabby-thighed whore was pulling it out of him.

He thought of his plan. How near it was to completion.

And came.

*

Summer arrived. School's out.

The Animals had left the Club A Go Go, gone on to bigger things: 'We Gotta Get out of This Place' duking it out with the Stones' 'Satisfaction' and the Beatles' 'Help' for the top spot.

And Newcastle was changing. Dan Smith planned, implemented. Dan the man who made things happen:

New homes. New roads. New office blocks. New civic centre. New airport. New university.

New city.

*New*castle.

And Dan Smith everywhere: the papers. The radio. The television. Calling for more money, more employers, more leisure facilities, more jobs.

More, more, more.

And Dan getting what he wanted.

Dan loved and adored. Admired and revered. Mr Popularity.

And the city remade in his image.

Dan's Castle.

And Scotswood was changing too:

Not just tower blocks and attendant periphery, but a new abattoir. A fully automated, conveyor-belt-driven slaughterhouse. Costing two million pounds, filling eleven acres of land. Between Scotswood Road and Whitehouse Road, a place called Paradise.

Animals would be killed, bled, gutted, skinned, beheaded, dehoofed, carved, chopped. Passing down the line, being stripped back to their component meat products. Packaged and processed and freighted away. Reinforced-concrete and white-tile efficiency. No waste. Carcass after carcass.

Good for Newcastle, good for the area, good for jobs.

One lone voice of dissent: Professor M. M. Cooper, Dean of Agriculture at King's College. 'Any slaughterhouse built

within a city rapidly creates slum conditions,' he said. 'I do
not think it is a question of civic pride. Get the dashed thing
out of town.'

No one listened.

The tower blocks and attendant periphery. The abattoir.
Paradise.

Summer, and school's out:

Mae stood at the top end of her street, looked down
towards the river. Her eyes were hard, dark and empty.
Showing nothing, filmed over like emotional cataracts.

The car was there again: 1600 Cortina. Some suited man
behind the wheel. Third day now. Sitting and looking.

At her.

Mae knew what he was there for. What he wanted. Even at
a distance, she knew. A sense she had developed; forcibly
planted, and violently encouraged to grow inside her. It
enabled her to spot needs, pinpoint twisted wants. She had
become a child alchemist, had found the whore's
philosophers' stone: she knew how to turn base desires into
money.

She walked down the street. Around her, other children
played, people led their lives. She ignored them. She was
working. She reached the car. The man looked at her, his eyes
wide. She looked into them, saw what he wanted, what he
needed, before he did.

The man kept staring. Mae didn't move. The man licked
his dry lips, swallowed. Mae didn't move. The man realized
she wasn't going to go away so slid across and wound his
window down. His hand was shaking.

'Hello,' the man said. 'What's your name?'

His voice was as shaky as his hand.

'Mae.'

'Mae, eh? That's a pretty name. D'you live round here,
Mae?'

'Over the road.'

The man looked, eyes settling on Mae's house. He nodded as if confirming something to himself. When he spoke again, his voice was stronger.

'Why don't you get in, Mae, eh? Sit next to me.'

He patted the green leather of the passenger seat.

Mae opened the door, got in, closed it behind her. The car smelled of old, anticipatory sweat. She could see the man's erection through his suit trousers. He was squirming around in his seat, eyes saucered, lit by dark fires.

Mae looked at the man's groin.

'D'you want me to play with your cock?'

The man gasped. Mae almost smiled. She felt something like electricity surge through her body.

'Yuh – yes.'

He sweated, squirmed, some more.

'Cost you,' she said.

'Huh – how much?'

'A tanner.'

The electricity swelled and surged.

'That all?' he said and, laughing, reached eagerly into his trouser pocket.

Mae felt herself flush with a sudden rage. The man was laughing at her. Belittling her. She couldn't have that.

The man pulled some change from his pocket, handed her a sixpence.

'And those pennies there,' Mae said, pointing.

The man handed over the pennies. Mae pocketed the money. She leaned across and undid the man's trousers, her fingers still shaking with a residue of anger. She pulled the man's penis out and began moving it up and down, her little hand holding on tight.

He settled back in the seat, face a study of pleasure.

Mae kept pumping.

'You see that house there?'

Mae pointed with her free hand. The man reluctantly allowed his gaze to follow her finger.

'That's me uncle's house, that.'

The man grunted.

'He'll be in there now, I reckon. Watchin'.'

'That's what he does for pleasure, is it?' the man said between gasps.

Mae kept pumping.

'No,' she said. 'He doesn't like us doin' this. Tries to stop us.'

The man moaned.

'Found us with one bloke last week. I had his willy in me mouth.'

The man moaned louder.

'I told 'im it was all the bloke's fault.'

Mae kept pumping. She felt the man's penis soften slightly.

'Don't talk,' he gasped. 'Just keep going.'

Mae acted as if she hadn't heard him.

'He got a hold of this bloke, an' 'e was all "I hate perverts, I hate poofs" an' that, an' 'e was ganna cut this bloke's willy off.'

Mae kept pumping. The man's penis was rapidly softening.

'Just . . . shut up . . . keep . . . going . . .'

'Well, 'e just beat the bloke up,' said Mae. She giggled. 'Had to go to hospital afterwards.'

'Shut . . . up . . .'

Rapidly softening.

'Said 'e would kill the next one.'

Mae pumping away.

'Shut up!'

'Cut 'is willy off.'

'Shut up!'

'Stuff it in 'is mouth.'

'Shut up!'

Rapidly softening.

Mae looked up, didn't stop pumping.

'I think this is 'im now.'

'Fuck!'

The man reached across Mae, fingers scrabbling frantically, and opened the passenger door.

'Get out! Just get out!'

He pushed Mae bodily from the car, scrambled to close the door. He pulled away from the kerb, tyres screeching, trousers around his knees.

Mae picked herself up, watched him go.

She smiled to herself. Electricity lit up her whole body. She felt like some kind of Christmas tree, bright, alive and pulsing with power.

An angry, rage-driven power.

She checked the money in her pocket. Her smile widened. All hers. None for her mother. All hers.

She put it back, enjoying the weighted clink of the coins against her thigh. She walked away.

Thinking what she would spend it on.

Thinking how she could make some more.

Sharon threw the last of her tea down the sink, rinsed her mug, stood it on the drainer. She turned around. She was, all things considered, happy.

If she thought of her job and how it made her feel valued and the degree of independence it gave her, then yes, she was happy. If she thought of her lover and the fact that after all this time he could still move her and thrill her. How dynamic and uncomplicated he was. Charismatic and genuinely funny. He didn't want to move in with her or marry her but, as he had explained, that was a good thing. They would never have to go shopping together. Do the housework. Buy insurance. They would never have to be mundane; they would always be exciting for one another.

Happy.

And then there was Jack. And Isaac. And their house. She had given up with Jack. She had given him every opportunity to improve, every chance to change. And he hadn't done any of it. It was his own fault. He had brought her indifference on himself. Lately, though, he had been more relaxed, spending more time away from the house. If he had a lover, she would love to see the boring old hag who would have taken him on.

And Isaac. His school reports were showing an increasingly violent, angry child. At home he was sullen and withdrawn. Sharon had tried talking but received no response. She felt guilty but didn't know what else to do. But he was a boy. They did that. It was a phase he was going through.

The house. No longer a real, functioning home. Just a series of compartmentalized areas. The three of them living in three separate worlds. Even with the heating on in the winter, the air between them felt cold and brittle. They rarely spoke, as if sound wouldn't be carried and received from one person to the next. They had become used to it. Accepted it. It was the way they lived. She would spend as little time there as possible. Cook, clean, shop. Fuel the engine. Hope that by doing that it would need no maintenance.

Sharon tried not to think too hard about these aspects of her life.

Sharon was, all things considered, happy.

And then the phone rang.

Jack sat on the sofa, tired after a day at work.

He had seen Isaac, tried to talk to him, but the boy had just gone to his room, shut himself in. Shut everyone else out.

Jack despaired of him. Didn't know what to do. He couldn't talk to Sharon about it. Or about anything. If it weren't for Isaac he would have left by now. Walked out and set up home with Joanne.

Joanne. He smiled to himself. The best thing in his life. He truly loved that girl. Felt younger with her. Dressed and acted younger. He felt alive, on fire with life for the first time in years. And it was all due to Joanne.

The firm was doing well. Jack was running it now in all but name. He was trying to reconcile his work with his politics. Something might have to give eventually, but for now all was smooth.

He sighed.

Maybe he should just take the chance. Move in with Joanne. Even take Isaac with him. Find somewhere for them all to live together. Or just kick Sharon out and stay in the house with Isaac. Invite Joanne to move in.

So many options. For the first time in years he felt able to examine each one clearly and face the future with confidence.

And then the phone rang.

Jack waited for Sharon to emerge from the kitchen and answer it. It rang. She didn't appear. Reluctantly he prised himself from the sofa, walked into the hall and picked it up.

'Jack Smeaton.'

'Hello, Jack. How you doing?'

Jack felt his earlier good mood rapidly dissipate to be replaced by a churning rage within him.

Ben Marshall.

'She's in the kitchen,' said Jack. 'I'll get her.'

'Well, actually, Jack, it's you I want to talk to.'

Ben Marshall's falsely chummy voice grated on Jack's ears, but he was nonetheless intrigued.

'What about?'

Ben Marshall gave an irritating laugh.

'Business, Jack. What else?'

'What kind of business could I have with you?'

Ben Marshall told him. Told him where, when, who else would be there.

Jack reluctantly agreed and put the phone down with shaking hands.

Rage.

A rage he knew he'd never be able to express.

'So how are things for you?'

Ralph sighed.

'The same, I suppose. Kenny's ... you know, gone now ...'

Ralph sighed again. Stopped talking.

Monica looked at him, untouched cup of tea at his feet.

'Gone ...'

Ralph shook his head.

This was how it had been since Kenny's death. Ralph stumbling, halting, barely articulate. Monica watching him virtually disintegrate before her eyes. No script any more. Just improvization. Guesswork.

'Gone.'

Ralph sighed again.

Monica searched for words that would help, soothe. Found they were beyond the reach of her vocabulary. She settled for nods, smiles. Sympathetic looks. But not hand-holding. He had tried that once but she had shrugged him off. Sympathy, yes. But not intimacy.

Ralph had stopped talking, the words, feelings dammed up.

Monica sighed, looked at him.

Then a knock at the door.

Monica stood up, relieved at the interruption.

'Now who can that be? I'll be right back, pet.'

She left the white room, went down the hall, opened the door.

And nearly died on the spot.

The hair was a different colour, the glasses weren't there previously. The suit was well tailored and up to date and, of course, he was nearly ten years older. But it was unmistakably him.

Brian Mooney.

He spoke.

'You all right, love? You look like you've seen a ghost.'

The voice was all wrong. Cockney. Chirpy. More like Michael Caine.

Monica opened her mouth. No words emerged.

'Listen, love, d'you want to have a sit-down or something?'

She looked at him again. The hair wasn't right. The glasses. He even stood differently. And the voice. All wrong. No, she thought. It wasn't him.

'Sorry,' she said at last. 'I thought I knew you.'

He laughed.

'Sorry, love. I don't think we've had the pleasure.'

'Sorry.' It was all she could think of to say.

'No worries, darling. Listen, I'm here to pick up Ralph Bell. Got to take him to a meeting. He here?'

'Yes . . . yes. I'll just get him.'

Monica was aware that she was making vague hand gestures.

'If you could, please. We have to be there by eight.'

Monica drifted back into the house, told Ralph he was needed. He stood up numbly, followed her to the door. He looked at the other man, a quizzical expression on his face.

'Hello,' he said. 'I'm Ralph Bell. What can I do for you?'

The man repeated what he had said to Monica. A meeting. At eight.

'Oh. Who with?'

'Jack set it up. Potential new business associate.'

Ralph looked confused.

'But Jack normally deals with that.'

'Well, he needs you there this time.'

Ralph shrugged. 'Oh, well,' he said.

He apologized to Monica for the abrupt departure. She told him not to worry about it.

She watched Ralph cross the street, got into the Michael Caine man's sports car. The Michael Caine man looked back, gave her a wink.

Her heart flipped over. It's him, she thought. He's just playing with me.

And then, the engine roaring, the two men were gone.

Monica slammed the door, stood behind it, panting.

Was it him? Brian? She had been so convinced. Then unconvinced. Then . . . she didn't know what to think.

She looked around frantically.

She would follow them. Get a taxi. Go to Ralph's company offices, spy on them. Find out more.

But she would have to get changed first.

She started up the stairs. Another knock on the door. Thinking it was them, she rushed back down to answer it.

She opened the door.

And stared.

'Hello, pet,' said her father.

'Wh – what d'you want? I'm goin' out.'

'Not any more, you're not.'

Her father walked past her into the hall. He closed the door behind him.

'I said I'm goin' out.'

He looked around.

'Where is she, then? That lovely little girl of yours?'

'She's not in.'

'I'll wait.'

He walked into the living room. Monica followed him.

'I said I'm goin' out.'

He turned to her, smiled. His pupils were like razor-sharp chips of obsidian.

'And I said not any more, you're not.'

He stared at her. She sighed, slumped against the wall. He took his coat off, sat down in an armchair.

'That's better,' he said.

'D'you want a drink?'

'Well, we'll have to do somethin' to fill in the time. A drink'll do.' He looked at her. That smile again. 'For starters.'

Monica turned, went into the kitchen.

It was all she could do not to cry.

The sun was beginning to set over the Tyne. The newer tower blocks, the older, dying factories to the west of the city, all thrown into picture-postcard silhouette by the dying sun. A monochrome snapshot.

Ben drove to the site of the half-completed abattoir, parked his car as far from the main road as possible, got out.

'Ah,' he said. 'Paradise.'

He looked towards the car.

'Come on, Ralph, out you come.'

Ralph Bell did as he was told. He looked around as if not recognizing the place. Surprised to find himself there.

'This is . . . the new abattoir.'

'That's right, Ralph,' said Ben. 'It is. One of yours. Come on inside.'

'Not the site office?'

'No. Inside the abattoir. Get the feel of the new place. A progress report. Come on.'

Ben ushered Ralph inside. The building was just a concrete shell for the most part. Structurally sound yet unembellished. Dying sunlight and distant streetlights the only illumination. Shadows fell, were cast, claimed whole areas as their own.

'Watch your step here,' said Ben. 'This way.'

He steered Ralph towards an area that looked more finished than the rest. The walls were white tiled, the floor bare. Ben patted the wall, searching.

'Here we are.'

A light came on overhead. A bright, harsh, temporary working lamp, it threw the whole room into stark relief. Not warming, just clinical, deadening.

Ben let the box containing the light switch hang. He looked at Ralph, smiled.

'Shouldn't be long now.'

As if on cue, there came the muffled trips and stumbles of someone making their way through the darkened building.

'This way,' called Ben. 'Follow my voice.'

A distant shadow came nearer, took shape. Jack Smeaton.

'Hello, Jack,' said Ben with a large smile. 'Glad you could make it.'

Ben looked at Jack. Took in his long dark hair, his suede jacket and jeans, his boots. He didn't look like a building contractor at all. He looked like some ageing student ban the bomber.

Jack nodded a hello to Ralph, kept staring at Ben.

'What's this about, then?'

'Well,' said Ben, 'since we're all busy people, I'll come straight to the point.' He looked around. 'Like the tiles. Nice touch. Death just wipes away. Now, to business. I'm an entrepreneur. A property developer.'

'You're a slum landlord,' said Jack, bile on his tongue. 'The worst kind of capitalist bastard.'

Ben shrugged.

'I prefer entrepreneur and property developer. But never mind. I'll come to the point. I've been talking to Dan Smith. Giving him some ideas. He likes them. But I need a construction company. So I'm taking over yours.'

Jack laughed.

'Piss off. It's not for sale. Come on, Ralph. Let's go.'

Ralph looked up. He had been fiddling with his hip flask, trying to get the lid off. He hadn't been listening.

'Erm . . .'

'He wants the company,' said Jack, pointing to Ben. 'He wants Bell and Sons Construction.'

Ralph weakly shook his head.

'No . . . no . . .' he said. 'It's not for sale. It's for . . . it's for Kenny . . . for Johnny . . .'

His voice trailed off.

'There's your answer,' said Jack.

Ben looked quizzically at Jack.

'How d'you run that company, knowing you'll never be in charge of that company? How d'you put up with him?'

Jack stared hard at Ben.

'None of your fucking business.'

Ben shrugged.

'Fair enough.'

'So no,' said Jack. 'The company's not for sale. We'll be off now. Good night.'

Jack turned to leave.

'Just a minute,' said Ben.

Jack turned back.

'I thought you might say that,' said Ben. He reached inside his jacket pocket, brought out a brown envelope, held it out to Jack. 'So I brought this. Go on, take them. Have a look.'

Jack took the envelope, opened it. Inside were photographs. Black and white. Jack looked through them. They were all of Ralph: spread-eagled and tied; whipped by a woman with a ruined face in a blonde wig; having his genitals mauled. And more. Jack looked up.

'Not pretty, are they?'

'You bastard.'

Ben shrugged again.

'Take a good look, Jack. This is how your boss gets his pleasure.'

Jack looked at Ralph. The older man held his head down, pretended to be absorbed in the workings of his flask lid.

'Sorry.'

Ralph said it so quietly Jack didn't know who the word was aimed at.

The pictures were disgusting. But Jack wasn't shocked by them. Just saddened. They made an already pathetic man look even worse.

'Just think what would happen to those pictures,' said Ben, almost ruminatively, 'if they found their way into the newspapers. Or the hands of a rival firm. Or his wife.'

Jack shook his head. A whiplash of rage cracked through his body.

'You bastard,' he said. 'You cunt.'

Ben shrugged again.

'I just had the photos taken. Don't blame the messenger. It's not me having my balls whipped with stinging nettles, is it?'

Jack looked across at Ralph. The man looked totally spent. Completely broken. Jack shook his head. Anger tempered by sadness.

'And then there's you, Jack,' said Ben.

'What about me?'

The anger was building within Jack, threatening to spill out.

'There's your lovely wife, for starters. You know I'm fucking her, don't you? Course you do. But d'you want to know a secret, Jack? I don't fancy her any more. Never did, really. Just a means to an end. Just a way of taking over this company.'

Jack's fists began to clench and unclench. He was building himself up to attacking Ben.

'And she's getting old now,' said Ben. 'Starting to sag. Time to get a younger bird. Like you've done.'

Jack stopped moving, said nothing.

'Does Ralph know, Jack? Does he?'

'No.'

The word was reluctantly dragged from him.

'Didn't think so.' Ben turned to Ralph. 'You didn't know, did you?'

Ralph looked in a daze.

'Know what?'

'About Jack. And your little girl. About what they get up to together.'

'What?'

'Here,' said Ben, taking out another package of photos, throwing them to Ralph. Ralph dropped them, picked them up, looked at them. Eventually he looked up, eyes red and wet.

'My little girl . . . what are you doing to my little girl . . .?'

Jack gave a bitter sigh.

'She's not a little girl, Ralph. She's a fully grown woman. It's not like that, Ralph.'

'My little girl . . . I trusted you . . .'

'We were going to tell you, Ralph. We just had a few things to sort out first.' Jack sighed. 'I love her, Ralph.'

Ben gave a harsh laugh.

'Families, eh? Who'd 'ave 'em?'

Ben walked towards Ralph.

'I think we can safely assume I'm going to get my way with your company, gentlemen, yes?'

They said nothing.

'Good.' He crossed the room, reached Ralph. 'Because there's one more thing I have to say before we conclude our business here. But it's for Ralph's ears only. Sorry, Jack.'

Ben bent in close to Ralph, smelled old sweat and alcohol coming off him in waves. He blocked the smell out, leaned into his ear, whispered:

'I'm. Brian. Mooney.'

Ben stepped back, removed his glasses, looked right into Ralph's eyes. He saw the comprehension slowly dawn, the recognition come. He saw Ralph realize he was staring into the face of the man he blamed for the death of his son. The loss of everything.

'You understand, now, Ralph? Why it had to be you? Your company? How this makes it perfect?' Ben laughed. 'Best thing that ever happened to me, Ralph. Best thing. Just wanted you to know that.'

Ben snapped his fingers. A shadow detached itself from the darkness beyond the bulb's glare, entered the room. Ben moved as far away from Ralph as he could. It took a few seconds to recognize who the figure was walking towards Ralph. With a jolting shock Jack recognized him.

Johnny Bell. Ralph's son.

At a nod from Ben, Johnny walked up behind Ralph, pulled a gleaming blade across his neck, cleanly slit his throat.

Jack watched, stunned beyond word or action, as the blood arced across the tiled walls of the white room, as Ralph gurgled and thrashed his way down to the floor, to lie twitching in a pool of his own blood, his son smiling, eyes dancing to a manic tune only he could hear.

'Nice little symmetry,' said Ben quietly. 'Almost biblical. Hey, catch!'

Jack looked at him, extended his hands by reflex. Johnny's bloody knife slap-landed on his chest, leaving a grotesque red flower on his suede jacket and shirt. His hands gripped the handle of the blade, leaving his smudged fingerprints on the handle, blood on his hands.

'I'll have that,' said Ben.

He was holding open a polythene bag. Jack looked at him.

'In,' said Ben.

Johnny stepped forward, smiling.

Jack saw the movement, numbly dropped the knife into the bag.

'Thank you,' said Ben. 'Bit of extra insurance. Never goes amiss. You might have to throw the jacket, though. It's a bugger getting blood out of suede.'

Ben replaced his glasses, smiled.

'Looks like I've got you over a barrel, doesn't it? Looks like you killed your boss because he disapproved of you shagging his daughter. Or because he wouldn't hand over the company to you. Or because he's a pervert. Who knows? Who cares?'

'You bastard.'

'And I wouldn't open your mouth about this to anyone. Not if you want your son to have a mother. Or your girlfriend to keep her pretty face. Know what I mean?'

Jack stared at Ben. Ben looked around the room.

'Bit of a mess in here, isn't it? Blood on the walls, a body on the floor. Got a bit of tidying up to do, haven't you?'

'What? Me?'

'Who else? You don't think I'm going to do it, do you? And where else? This is a building site. Perfect.'

Ben laughed, then crossed his arms, attempted to look serious.

'I heard that in olden days builders used to put a live cat or something in a building when they'd finished it, brick it up, keep the bad spirits out. Or even a live woman, so I heard. Well, what about a dead man?'

Jack stared at him.

'You'd better get the concrete mixer going, add a little something to the foundations, hadn't you? Then hose the place down.' Ben sighed. 'You've got a busy night ahead.'

Jack stared at him.

'No arguments, Jack. I'm the new boss.'

Ben smiled. 'Welcome to the firm, Jack.'

PART FOUR

Deserted Cities of the Heart

At night she dreamed the city.

But it doesn't start in the city.

There's a land of sun and warmth, a fairy-tale place with castles, fields, enchanted forests, streams of jewels. And she can fly: she can soar over the hills and valleys of this rural idyll, happy in the knowledge that this is where she belongs. This is her true kingdom.

She stops to help an old beshawled beggar woman. She doesn't know what's wrong with her except she claims to be in pain. As soon as she touches her, the fairyland has gone. She can no longer fly. The old woman has somehow tricked her.

With dream jump-cutting, she's now in the city.

It's small and dark. Not always night, but always dark. Narrow streets and tall, oppressive buildings. Soot-blackened brick walls surround her. Industrial smoke and rolling fog choke her delicate fairyland lungs. Factory sirens make her shiver, glance over her shoulder. It's cold. Sparse streetlighting throws out meagre light, creates deep shadows.

And in those shadows lurk monsters.

She can hear them: whispering as she walks past, their big, pointed teeth chattering, laughing at her, planning what they would do to her. Some snake out parts of their anatomy to touch her, test her.

She walks, shivers.

Always the same walk on the same street. Always the same shiver.

She knows she has to walk down the street. If she can reach the other end without the grazing monsters grabbing her, claiming her, she will be free. She has never managed it yet.

She begins to walk, trying to hurry, dream feet not moving quickly enough.

Laughter from her left, then a grab. She flinches, feints, moves out of the way. Keeps walking.

Another to her right. This one grabs her, holds her. She struggles and pulls, bites and hits. And she is free.

She runs on as fast as her dream legs can carry her.

Then feels fingers around her throat.

She knows this monster. It's the old woman without her disguise. Shiny black carapace like an oily beetle. Yellow gorgon snake hair. Stinking breath. The monster speaks to her. Holds her captive with its words. It doesn't need anything else. It promises, it taunts. It pleads. Dream words.

She listens, allows it to cast its spell, believes its lies again. Wants to believe.

And the monster drags her away, into the shadows.

Too late, she realizes she has been tricked. Again.

The monster had her, embraced her, clutched her to its breast.

The monster has friends. Other shadow lurkers. All around, she can see eyes and teeth. Cruel eyes. Cruel teeth. Narrowed slits and bad smiles. All moving closer.

She closes her dream eyes but can still see them. Wills her dream body rigid but can still feel the touch of them on her skin. She tries to think herself small, shrink insignificantly out of their clutches. Tiny, tiny, so she doesn't exist.

Her legs feel wet. Smell unpleasant.

'You've wet the bed now,' says the gorgon monster. 'She won't like that.'

She nods. She knows she won't.

'You know what she'll do to you.'

She nods. She does.

She closes her eyes. Waits for the monsters to do what they are going to do.

Knows she will never see her real, fairy-tale home again.

August 1965–August 1966:
Bold as Love

Jack looked at the stage. On it was a man dressed in a deliberate clash of colour, all ruffles and feathers, playing a right-handed guitar in a left-handed fashion. He was a pale-skinned black man, his big afroed hair held in place by a wide silk band. He was coaxing sounds from his guitar, sounds Jack and most of the audience had never heard before. He had started playing the song with his drummer and bassist, both nearly as flamboyantly dressed as their front man, but he had left them way behind, relegated them to timekeeping observers. He wasn't much of a singer, but he gave the guitar a voice it had never had before. He was making it sing songs never heard before. It was blues, but all colours of the rainbow blues. Psychedelic.

The Jimi Hendrix Experience. August 1966.

Jack didn't know whether he liked it or not, but he was mesmerized by the sounds. Staring, transfixed, at the stage. The Mayfair ballroom in Newcastle had seen nothing like it before. It was the first time they had hosted an event like this. But then the world was changing. And with it the audience: the beatniks, peaceniks and refuseniks were coming together with the Mods. Metamorphosing. Coalescing and colliding to become a new counter-cultural entity: hippies.

Joanne had fully embraced the change. She was dressed almost exclusively in denim and printed India cotton; chiffon and silk scarves adorned her. Her hair long. Smoking dope and meditating. Reading philosophy and comparative religion. New writers: James Baldwin, Tom Wolfe, Hunter S. Thompson. And Carl Jung. Joanne loved him, read his philosophy, studied his works with an almost religious fervour. She was perfectly in tune with her times, the times in tune with herself. A revolution in the head, heart and soul. Her psyche awakening.

Jack loved Joanne. With all his heart. But he could never fully relax, never totally enjoy the feeling. Always like that, yes, but the past year had added another layer. No matter how hard he tried to forget, to convince himself that the future was bright, that he had as much right to happiness as anyone else, a thought, an action, a word, an image would send a sudden electric jolt through his body:

Ralph Bell's son murdered him / I buried Ralph Bell / I'm in love with Ralph Bell's daughter.

The same unholy triptych.

And the other one:

Ben Marshall / Johnny Bell / Ralph Bell.

That night. That memory.

Always there in his head, lurking in the back of his mind like a tumour.

Waiting, wondering when it will grow to malignant proportions, threaten his life. And Joanne's.

Jimi Hendrix joined with his rhythm section for a final crescendo, then the song ended. The audience, as if waking from a hypnotic slumber, burst into huge applause. Jimi Hendrix nodded, turned to his other two band members, grinned at them. Enjoying himself. Knowing the effect he was having.

'Thanks, man. This is, uh, this is a Bob Dylan song. This is "All along the Watchtower".'

Applause broke out at the mention of the title and the namecheck for Dylan. Hendrix started, got his guitar singing again. Jack knew the song, the Dylan version. He had never heard it sound like this before.

He looked at Joanne. She was gone, her expression enrapt. A combination of the music, plus the red wine and spliffs before they had left the flat. He envied her that ability to lose herself, connect with something else. She felt him looking at her, smiled at him. He smiled back.

They squeezed hands. Happy. For now.

That last, hard year, starting with:

Ralph's death. That night. That memory.

Jack would never forget.

He had mixed concrete, dragged Ralph's body to an area that would become a concrete-floored loading bay but was still a huge pit, rolled it in, covered it. Smoothed down the surface, let it harden. All on his own. No help from Ben and Johnny. He had cleaned the floor and the walls, hosed down any trace of murder. He worked all night without a break then, beyond tired, drove home, bathed and changed, got ready for work. Bagged up his filthy, bloodstained clothes, left them in the boot of his car. The physical demands of the night's work left him no time to think about what had happened. Sharon just thought he had stayed out for the night.

He went to work as usual. Later in the day Jean contacted him, asked if Ralph was there.

'Not today, Jean,' said Jack, swallowing the lie hard. 'Haven't seen him.'

'He didn't come home last night.' Her voice was weak, trembling. The phone gave it a disembodied, ethereal quality.

Jack said he would let her know if he heard anything.

He put the phone down. Ben Marshall was sitting next to him in the office. Sprawled in a swivel chair, feet up on the desk.

'Got to tell her something, Jackie boy.'

Jack said nothing; just stared at the phone, hand still on the receiver.

'I think it best,' said Ben ruminatively, 'if we wait till Ralph's disappearance has blown over to announce that I'm running the show now. Timing, and all that – know what I mean?'

Jack said nothing.

The police were, inevitably, brought in. They questioned Jack, who stuck to the same story. He had been due to meet Ralph to discuss a business matter that evening. Ralph never turned up. Ralph had friends in the police force. They had sympathy with him for what had happened to Kenny. They knew Jack had been good to Ralph, went easy on him, privately confided that they reckoned Ralph had got himself drunk, taken a stroll along the Tyne, fallen in. They were hoping the body would turn up eventually, but they weren't holding out much hope.

'Best to just treat him as dead, really,' the detective inspector had said. 'Get on with life without him.'

Jack could breathe a sigh of relief.

But he couldn't look Joanne in the eye.

She was taking her father's disappearance hard, needing Jack more than ever. Jack was scared of committing himself to her, scared of getting too close, scared about what he might say in an unguarded moment.

Scared of what her brother could do to her if she found out.

But she needed him. So for her sake he cast out as much fear from his soul as he could. He found that by giving her strength he was able to receive it in return.

It was a difficult, trying time. It was painful, but that pain bonded them closer than ever.

Joanne was throwing herself into studying. Gearing up for her finals, hoping for a 2:1.

Jack knew he had painful, long-reaching conclusions to come to.

Sharon was sitting in the bedroom, dressed in a pair of gym shorts and a T-shirt. She was sitting on the floor, legs apart, bending over, touching her toes. Five one side, five the other, five in the middle.

He stood watching her from the doorway, saw a sheen of sweat glistening on her bare arms and legs, like a gentle application of baby oil. She was still attractive, he would give her that. But although she worked hard at it, it seemed the image of perfect youth she was chasing was beginning to outpace her.

She hadn't noticed him there. He cleared his throat. She looked up, startled, then realizing it was only Jack went back to her workout, ignoring him.

'I think we need to talk,' said Jack.

'I'm busy.'

She kept on exercising, ignoring him.

'I said, I think we need to talk. Now.'

Something in Jack's voice made her look up. She saw how steely his eyes were. She stopped what she was doing.

'Let's sit down,' he said, closing the bedroom door and sitting on the bed.

Sharon reluctantly raised herself from the floor, sat down next to him. She was panting slightly.

Jack looked at her before speaking. Took in her face, her body, her hair. Her eyes.

'What?' Sharon said, uncomfortable with the scrutiny.

Jack smiled. It made his face look tired.

'I was just thinking,' he said, 'how much of a stranger you are to me now.'

Sharon stood up.

'If you've come to—'

'Sit down, Sharon.'

'No, Jack, I'm not going to—'

'Sit down, Sharon.'

She looked at him again. The tired smile had gone. The steely eyes were back. She sat down again.

'I'm not prepared for things to go on like this any longer,' Jack said. 'It's not good for me, you and especially not Isaac.'

Sharon nodded slightly.

'So I'm giving you the chance. And I'm going to say this only once. It's either Ben Marshall or me.'

Sharon's mouth fell open. After so long spent tiptoeing around the subject, Jack had finally brought it out into the open. The words hung between them, then dissolved. Like a great, unspeakable evil that, once named, loses its power. Sharon looked at him almost admiringly.

'Well . . .' she said, 'it's not just . . . like that. I mean . . . you have someone else too. I know it.'

'I do,' said Jack. 'But I just wanted to give you one last chance. Just to see if there's still something there. Something salvageable. A spark. Anything.'

He looked directly into her eyes. She found his gaze unnerving. Looked away.

He knew what her answer would be. Hoped what her answer would be. Jack felt nothing for her now; even the rage had long dissipated. He kept looking at her. The opposite of love is not hate, he thought: it's indifference.

'I . . .' Sharon looked up. 'I'm going to have to choose Ben, Jack. When you put it like that. Sorry.'

She attempted a weak smile. Jack ignored it, stood up.

'Fine,' he said. 'I just wanted to know.'

'Where are you going?'

'Away from here. I'll take Isaac out at the weekend. Explain it to him then. Here.' He handed her a piece of paper. 'That's where I'm staying. At least until we find somewhere together.'

'We?'

'Joanne and I. Joanne Bell.'

Sharon looked stunned.

'Joanne . . .'

'Oh, come on, Sharon. You must have heard. I thought everyone knew by now.'

'Oh, Jack . . . Joanne?' Sharon laughed.

Jack reddened. 'You think it's funny? Well, here's something else. I'll be going to see my solicitor later today to start divorce proceedings. Then I'll put the house on the market. Start looking for somewhere else for you and Isaac to live.'

Sharon had stopped smiling.

'Me and Isaac?'

'You're his mother, aren't you? You're going to take him with you, aren't you?'

'Yes . . .'

'Good. Because if you don't, I'll take him. And you'll never see a penny out of me.'

'But what'll I do?'

'You've got your job, haven't you? The one that makes you proud of your independence. Or there's always Ben. You could throw yourself on his mercy. But I wouldn't bother. He hasn't got any. You're made for each other.' Jack sighed, tried to swallow away the bitterness. 'I'm going now.'

Sharon placed a hand on his arm.

'Jack, wait—'

'No, Sharon. I'm going.' He took a deep breath, let it go. 'And I wish I'd done this years ago.'

He walked out of the bedroom, out of the house. He stood on the pavement, smiled. It was like a great weight had been lifted from his chest. He still had to deal with Isaac, and that would be difficult. But better in the long run. Maybe then he could start to have a proper relationship with his son. Be a good father to him.

He walked away from the house, off to meet Joanne, tell her the good news.

Sound wailed and coalesced. Built and subsided. Became angry and impassioned, cold and aloof. Hendrix lost to his guitar, his fingers moving almost imperceptibly, a sonic union. He threw it out, built it up, then, with a glance at the rhythm section, reined it in again. They played foursquare and tight, with just enough raggedness to make it exciting. Jack was struck by how good they sounded together.

They built higher and higher, harder and harder, and the song ended. Again, wild applause, this time from Jack too. He knew nothing of music beyond Presley, Orbison, Cash and the blues, but he knew he was witnessing a unique talent.

He looked at Joanne, smiled again. She was taking a toke from a spliff that was doing the rounds of the crowd. She passed it to him. He took a deep drag, passed it on.

'This is our last one for now,' said Jimi Hendrix, and counted the band in for another song.

Jack felt the weed hit behind his eyes. He nodded his head to the music, as lost as he would allow himself to be.

Jack let himself in to the house, looked around for Joanne. She wasn't there.

Now that Joanne's housemate had moved out, they were the only two living there. Jack was taking care of the rent. Joanne now had her own studio space, and they both had the run of the house. Much better than having to scurry off to her room any time they wanted a bit of privacy.

He took his coat off, opened a bottle of red wine, put on a John Coltrane album and settled down on the settee, waiting for Joanne. She had decorated the room herself, all Indian fabrics, knick-knacks and psychedelic posters. Jack liked it, made him feel young, not old.

He sipped his wine, listened to the music, smiled in anticipation of what he had to say.

A Love Supreme.

The door opened. Joanne entered, looked surprised to see him. He held up his wine glass.

'Got yours here,' he said.

She smiled, took her coat off, kissed him and curled up beside him on the sofa. She wanted to talk about looming exams, pressure of studying, but instead she said: 'This is a surprise.'

'You'd better get used to it.'

She looked quizzical. He told her.

She listened, open-mouthed.

'So what d'you say?' said Jack at the end of it. 'You've got me all the time now.'

Joanne looked away, smiled.

Jack looked at her, concern in his eyes.

'I thought that's what you wanted,' he said. 'For us to be a proper couple.'

'Well, yes ... but ... it seems a bit ... now that it's happened, it feels a bit ...'

'What?'

'Final.'

Jack sat back, Coltrane's sax-blowing sounding suddenly discordant.

'Oh.'

'No, I mean, it's just ... going to take some getting used to, that's all.'

Jack just looked at her. 'Are you seeing someone else?'

'Course not. It's just ... I want you to know what you've done. You haven't just swapped one marriage for another. Now that you've moved in properly, don't expect me to be a housewife.'

'I don't.'

'I've got my finals coming up, Jack. I want to get a good result. And then I want to do a postgrad course in art therapy.'

'I know.'

'I mean it. I've found one that does Jungian art therapy. It's perfect for me. I don't want to let that go. If there's cooking and cleaning to be done, then don't automatically assume I'll be doing it. Just because I'm a woman.'

'I won't.'

'We either do it together or get someone in to do it.'

'Fine.'

'Good.'

'So what's for dinner, then?'

Joanne looked at him uncomprehendingly. Jack smiled. She realized he was joking and hit him.

'All right,' he said, 'enough. I know what's for dinner. Because I'm taking you out.'

The Blue Sky Chinese restaurant, Pilgrim Street, Newcastle. Three hours, one bottle of wine and one bout of lovemaking later.

Spare ribs, satay chicken, prawn crackers and seaweed.

Sweet-and-sour pork, monks' vegetables, roast pork and fried rice.

Another two bottles of red wine.

And slight indigestion for Jack. There were things he still had to say.

He waited until the dinner was well under way, the wine half-drunk.

'Listen,' he said, 'there's something else.'

Joanne looked up, red-dripping pork ball chopstick-poised before her mouth. Jack caught her eyes. Saw Ralph in them. A dark shudder passed through him.

The tumour flexing its tendrils.

'What?'

'I'm . . . leaving the company.'

She replaced her pork ball on her plate, gave him her full attention.

'Yeah,' Jack continued. 'I don't want to run it, and your dad had already been holding talks with someone about selling out.'

'But what will you do?'

Jack shrugged. 'Don't know. We'll be fine for money, though. Since the company went public, my shares have done well. I've made investments over the years like a good little capitalist, got savings . . . we'll be all right.' He smiled. 'I could even pay for that postgrad course if you want me to.'

Her response was a beaming smile. It fell on his heart like a shaft of warm sunlight.

Then her face darkened slightly.

'What about Sharon?' she said.

'She gets nothing,' Jack said, unable to keep the bitterness from his voice. 'She's made her bed.'

'And Isaac?'

'Well, that's another matter.' Jack took another mouthful of wine. 'He's staying with her for now, but there may come a time when he might stay with us. I might want to get him out of there.'

Joanne nodded, unsmiling.

'What?'

'Well,' she said slowly, choosing her words carefully, 'I know he's your son. And I know you love him. And I know that being with you involves being with him too. That's fine. But . . . well, it goes back to what I said earlier. I don't want you to think I'm going to be a surrogate mother for him.'

Jack looked at her.

'I'm sorry. I didn't mean that to sound harsh. I know you love him and you want him to be a part of your life. Just like I love you and want you as a part of mine. And it's fine if he comes to stay for weekends or days at a time. But not full time.'

Jack nodded. 'That's what I thought you'd say.'

He took another swig of wine.

'That's fine, though. I think it's best if Isaac stays where he is. If there was ever a time when I could look after him properly or even if we both could—' he looked at Joanne; she nodded '—then, OK. But until then, leave things as they are.'

'I like just being with you.'

Jack smiled.

'Good.'

Later that night they made love in the most gentle, intimate manner. They fell asleep in each other's arms. Woke up in the same position.

'So what d'you think?' said Joanne, drink in hand, eyes glassily spliffed over. They were waiting for the show to restart.

'Never heard anything like it,' said Jack, 'in any respect.'

Joanne giggled. 'Good, wasn't he? Go far, I reckon.'

They chatted some more, spoke to people they knew in the crowd, waited for the main attraction.

Cream.

The lights went out, the cheers went up. Three instantly recognizable figures, even in silhouette, took up their places. Ginger Baker on drums, Jack Bruce on bass, Eric Clapton on guitar. Jack's favourite. No one could play the blues like Eric. And he would never have heard of them if not for Joanne. Something else to thank her for.

They launched straight in with a song from their new album. *The White Room.*

Jack smiled, clapped in recognition.

It was going to be a good gig.

Ben had been in the site office in Ralph's old chair again, feet up on Ralph's old desk again, when Jack walked in and announced that he was leaving the firm. Ben smiled.

'That might be a silly move to make, Jackie boy.'

'Too late. I've already quit.'

Ben swung his legs to the floor, sat looking at Jack, arms folded. 'You remember what I've got for safekeeping?' he said.

'What?' said Jack. 'My wife?'

Ben laughed. 'That too,' he said. 'I was referring to a certain blade with certain fingerprints on the handle.'

'I don't care,' said Jack. 'I'm not the slightest bit interested. Yes, you could make a case against me, but so what? I don't want this firm, Ben. I don't want Sharon. I don't want anything you've got. And I don't want anything to do with you.'

Ben looked at him, head cocked, listening.

'You're a businessman, Ben. You're very busy. Why would you take the time to come after me? Eh? You've got what you want, Ben. You've won. You hear? You've won. I'll sell my shares, cash in, whatever. You've won. It's all yours.'

Ben kept staring at Jack, eyes hard and unflinching, the whirring of calculations hidden behind them.

Jack swallowed hard. Tried not to let his fear show. He had brazened it well this far, but it could still turn out badly.

Eventually Ben smiled. Jack took no comfort from that. It could have meant anything.

'All right,' he said, and stood up.

The two men stood facing each other.

'I'll let you go,' said Ben. 'Make whatever financial arrangements you want.'

'Thank you.'

Ben stepped in close to Jack. Jack could see the unquenchable flames dancing in Ben's eyes.

'But if you step out of line, or so much as think about stepping out of line, I'll know about it. Don't think you've got away free, because these things have a nasty habit of coming back and biting you on the arse.'

Jack just stared at him.

'By that I mean it might not be a knife finding its way to the police. It might be a knife finding its way across your throat. Or your girlfriend's. Or your son's. Do we understand each other?'

Jack swallowed hard. 'Perfectly,' he said.

'Good. Then get off my property.'

Jack turned and left, walking out of the site and away down the street. Never once looking back. His head throbbing mildly.

The tumour, going into remission.

But reminding him it was still there.

'Thanks a lot.'

Eric Clapton acknowledged the applause.

'This one's called "Deserted Cities of the Heart".'

Nine months after Ralph Bell's disappearance, Jean Bell died.

Nine months. Grief's own gestation period.

Cancer, supposedly, although Jack suspected the real reason was a broken heart. She seemed to have lost the will to live.

The funeral was sparsely attended. Most of Jean's friends had faded away in their own way as she had in hers. Joanne clung to Jack, told him many times she didn't know what she'd do without him. He had often thought the same about her but said nothing in those instances. She needed his strength. He supplied it.

Johnny Bell turned up. It was the first time Jack had seen him since that night at the abattoir. He watched him talking to Joanne, pleased he kept his butcher's hands in his pockets. Jack knew he was only talking to her to annoy him. Unnerve him. It wasn't something he would normally do. He kept glancing across at Jack, smiling at their shared, unacknowledged secret. Almost daring him to say something, challenge him. Jack didn't. Jack couldn't even look him in the eye.

The coffin was lowered, the sparse spattering of mourners then walked back to the black car. Jack held his arm around Joanne. Johnny Bell walked behind them. The smell of old meat and stale blood billowed from him. It turned Jack's stomach, vomited unpleasant memories into his mind.

All he wanted was peace. Life with Joanne.

And he would damn well have it.

The band had finished, the encores done with. Jack and Joanne walked home, arms wrapped around each other.

'Good night?'

She snuggled into him. 'The best.'

'Want to stop off anywhere? Last drink? Club?'

Joanne shook her head. 'Got some wine at home. Let's go to bed. I want you to play me like Hendrix played that guitar tonight.'

Jack laughed. 'I thought you'd be sick of sex with me after all this time.'

'Think again,' she said.

Jack sighed. Eric Clapton and the love of a good woman. A perfect night out. He thought they would have been beyond getting excited about each other after two years. But neither was. In any respect.

'You're something special, you know that?' He felt his heart would burst with joy when he said those words.

Joanne didn't reply. But she squeezed his arm.

And he knew she was smiling.

They walked home. Jack's head didn't hurt at all.

August 1965–August 1966:
Aftermath

Monica didn't know what to do with herself.

Back and forth it came, ebbing and flowing like a sick tide in and out of her brain. Weeks turning into months. Sometimes she would forget, allow whole days to go without thinking about it. Other times it was all that was there in her mind. The more she thought about it, the more she was convinced that the man she had seen was Brian Mooney.

She couldn't concentrate, couldn't focus on her life. She was going through the motions with her clients even less than usual. She found it all so tiring, so draining. She stopped seeing some of them. Some of them sensed the change in her, found other outlets. Her trade dwindled.

She had never saved money, preferring to invest in gin rather than pensions. Her income began to dry up. She forced Mae to work harder, made a half-hearted attempt to get herself going again.

But he was there, his grinning face in her head.

Brian Mooney.

And Ralph Bell had never returned.

She was quite relieved, in a way. His self-pitying monologues had finally become too tiresome. He had probably found a more sympathetic listener. Shame. He was a good customer. Regular. And she thought no more about him.

Until one night she came across an old – months old – newspaper wrapping her post-pub fish and chips in. And there, grease-stained and vinegared, was Ralph's picture. And the headline:

MISSING: Property developer presumed
to have 'walked off into the night'

Her stomach gave a Spanish City rollercoaster flip. Missing. Her hunger forgotten, she read the article through fully. She read the date he was last seen alive, tried to work it out in her head. It took a while, but she got it. The same date as his last visit to her.

The same date she saw Brian Mooney.

With Ralph.

She read on. His company was due to be sold to Northern Star Properties, run by London-born business entrepreneur Ben Marshall.

She thought of the man again. Brian Mooney. Remembered his accent. London-born.

Ben Marshall.

Brian Mooney.

Same initials.

Another rollercoaster stomach lurch.

She had to do something; she didn't know what.

Two full days she thought about it. Two full days of dwindling clients, drying-up money supplies. She came to a decision.

She knocked on Bert's door that evening. It was a long time since she had seen the rag-and-bone man, even longer since she had slept with him. She felt he had been avoiding her. But

she didn't care. She needed an ally. And he was the best she
could do.

The door opened. She heard a TV going inside, smelled
the remains of cooked food. Normal life. Bert, standing in his
customary vest, trousers and braces, didn't hide his surprise
at seeing her there. Or the fact that he wasn't pleased.

'Monica . . .'

'Hello, Bert. Can I come in?'

She had one leg raised, mounting the step. Bert didn't move.

'What d'you want?'

Monica sighed in exasperation.

'Let us in an' I'll tell you.'

Bert reluctantly moved aside and she entered. He closed
the door behind her after looking up and down the street,
checking no one had witnessed her entry.

Monica made her way to the front room, stood beside the
fireplace and unfolded the copy of the *Evening Chronicle* she
had been carrying around for the last few days. She thrust it
at Bert, already open at the relevant article.

'Here. Read that.'

He looked at it, wrinkled his nose. 'This been wrappin' fish
an' chips?'

'Never mind about that. Just read it.'

'What for?'

She sighed in exasperation. She felt like hitting him. 'Just
read it.'

Taking the paper, he wearily began to read. He finished,
handed it back to her.

'So?' he said. 'I can't see what—'

'Ralph Bell! Ralph Bell!' Monica was almost shouting. 'I
saw him. Just before he disappeared.'

Bert nodded. 'Right. So what d'you want me to do about it?'

Monica shook her head in exasperation.

'He was there. At my house. I was with 'im. An' then

someone called for 'im. Drove 'im away. An' 'e was never seen again.'

'Oh,' said Bert. He sat down, didn't invite Monica to. 'So why don't you go to the police? Tell them?'

'Oh, don't be stupid, Bert. How can I go to the police? They wouldn't listen to me. An', anyway, I want nothin' to do with them. Especially when I tell them who he was with.'

'Who?'

Monica sat on the settee next to Bert, her face all stupid fox cunning. She looked right into his eyes.

'Brian Mooney.'

Bert looked blankly at her. 'Who?'

'Oh, for God's sake!' Monica jumped up, paced the room in exasperation. 'Brian Mooney! Mac's father. The bloke I used to live with.'

Bert frowned. 'Are you sure?'

'Of course I'm sure! It was him! Except now 'e's callin' 'imself Ben Marshall. An' talkin' with a London accent.'

'Are you sure it's 'im?'

'Yes! The initials! BM! It has to be 'im!'

'Oh.' Bert sat back thoughtfully. 'So why are you tellin' me all this?'

Monica sighed.

'Because I want to ask you a favour.'

'No, Monica.' Bert shook his head wearily. 'No. Whatever it is, no. I want nothin' more to do with you. You know that.'

'There'll be a lot of money in it. A lot. We can share it.'

'I'm not interested. No.'

'Just listen. Let me tell you.'

That night in her bed, gin and tonic on the bedside, Monica felt more relaxed than she had in ages. Relaxed and quite excited.

She had talked and Bert had listened. If Brian Mooney was now calling himself Ben Marshall, and he was a well-known businessman, then he would be worth a bob or two. And the last thing he would want would be for someone to expose his past. His illegitimate daughter. He would pay good money not to have that happen.

But they had to be sure it was him.

Her plan: because he would recognize Monica, Bert would ride his rag-and-bone wagon around some of Northern Star's construction sites. See if there was anything he could take. Then get talking to people. Find out more about Ben Marshall. And when they had enough on him, confront him with it. And get paid.

And Bert had seen the pound signs, given in, agreed. They were talking about a lot of money. She wasn't surprised at the speed with which he had said yes.

Monica took a sip of gin that turned into a mouthful that continued until she had drained the glass.

She settled down to sleep, smiling.

Brian had never given her a penny for Mae. Nothing. Well, she'd get more than a penny out of him now.

She closed her eyes, still smiling.

The Red House, the Quayside, Newcastle.

Low ceilings, dark oak beams, white walls. Uneven, wooden floors. The whole building warped and wefted by time, not a straight, vertical line in the whole place. An old shipman's tavern turned bar and restaurant.

Another Dan Smith initiative: business meetings disguised as dinner parties. Conversation flowed with the wine. Food was as plentiful as ideas. Deals were sealed in a select, convivial atmosphere. The waiters had been briefed by Dan beforehand. Food and drink weren't the important things. Conversation was. Told them to read the table: hold off on the entrées if the talk was flowing. Marinate it with Mateus if it wasn't.

Ben Marshall sat back in his seat, glass of rosé in hand. His stomach was full, his waistline expanding. He didn't mind. Wore it as a measure of success.

Nineteen sixty-six was working up to being a good year for Ben. Business was booming, development and redevelopment in full swing thanks to Dan. Ben was now one of the favoured knights in Dan's castle.

Dan was holding court at the far end of the table. Lecturing: regionalism versus nationalism. No takers for a fight, Dan elaborating: regionalism is its own nationalism.

Discuss.

No takers. Only listeners.

Sharon had picked at her food, drank listlessly, hardly spoken all evening. Ben hadn't asked what was wrong with her; assumed she would elaborate in the fullness of time.

He had spent most of the evening talking to the man on his left. Balding, with deep-set eyes that darted the length of the table as he spoke.

'John Poulson,' he had introduced himself as. 'Architect. Poulson Associates.'

'Ben Marshal.' He smiled. 'I run Northern Star.'

'Heard a lot about you, Mr Marshal.'

'Nothing good, I hope.'

The two men laughed, talked. Sharon pushed her food around her plate, sighed. Ben heard the constant, disconsolate scrapings of her knife. Ignored them.

'So what d'you think of—' John Poulson poked his fork at the head of the table '—our friend up there?'

'Great man,' said Ben, 'a visionary.'

John Poulson nodded.

'Yes. I know he puts a lot of people's backs up. About as many as admire him. But he's a good businessman. I can work with him.'

'What are you doing for him at the moment?'

'Designing. Couldn't get Le Corbusier. Got me instead.'

Ben laughed politely.

Sharon scraped her knife.

The two men talked. Business.

'You're right, though, Ben,' said John Poulson, gesturing with his wine glass. 'Complete packages. That's the thing. Course, you should take things one step further.'

'How d'you mean?'

'Them that give you the green light, put them on the payroll. You want clearance? Politically?' John Poulson's voice was hushed, conspiratorial. 'Get your MP on board. Put him on the payroll. Call him a Parliamentary Consultant. You want it to sound like a good scheme? Get the head of the council. Or whoever's a big noise in the region—' he waved his fork towards the head of the table again '—put him on the payroll. Make him your PR man. Charge what you want for the job. And then undercut yourself. Pocket the difference, no questions asked. Know what I mean?'

Ben nodded, smiled.

'So are you a Socialist,' asked Ben, 'like Dan?'

John Poulson laughed. 'A Socialist? Like Dan? I might be like Dan, but I'm not a Socialist. No. Doesn't matter if you're red or blue or even orange. There's only one colour brings politicians together.' He rubbed his thumb and forefinger together. 'And that's green.' He smiled.

They talked some more. Then Ben excused himself to go to the toilet. Inside, he looked in the mirror, fixed his tie, hair and cufflinks in place. Coming out, he found Sharon standing in the narrow corridor away from the dining room, back against the wall, smoking a cigarette.

'Hello, darling,' he said, fixing his smile in place. 'Enjoying yourself?'

'No, I'm bloody not,' she spat at him. 'You've ignored me all night. Talked to that shifty-looking architect instead.'

'It's a business dinner, you know that.'

'Business.' She gave a harsh laugh. 'D'you know, I must know every person in that room. And d'you know what they'll be thinking? There's Jack Smeaton's wife. What's she doing here?'

'Ex-wife.'

'It doesn't matter. They'll all be thinking the same thing. Whore.'

They both fell silent as a town planner squeezed past them on the way to the gents.

'Should I call a cab? Take you home?'

'A cab? I want more than a cab, Ben. I want you to marry me. Make it legal.'

Ben swallowed back anger, sighed.

'This conversation can wait until later.'

Sharon pushed her face in Ben's. 'No, it can't. No, it can't bloody wait. I don't want to walk back in there and have them think the same about me. Now I've been loyal to you. I think it's about time I got something back. It's about time I got some commitment.'

Ben looked at her long and hard, unsmiling, then spoke. His eyes were like flint.

'All right, then,' he said. 'It seems I've got two choices. I can either throw you over or marry you.'

Sharon's eyes lit up slightly, grasping the words.

'Now, if I dump you, that's that. Finito. End of story. If I marry you, then you've got to know why. D'you want to marry me?'

'Oh, yes, Ben, yes, of course I do.'

She smiled at him. His eyes remained like flint.

'Then you'd better know why. You'd better listen to the rules. Just so you can't say later that you weren't told. Now, if I marry you, it's because I want a good-looking woman to take to parties, be a good hostess, lend me a bit of respectability. Stability. Someone my own age, so it doesn't look embarrassing either way. In return I'll give you money, buy you clothes, get you a car, a Mini or something, even pay for your kid to get good schooling. But don't think I'm in love with you. Because it's not about love. Or anything approaching that. We might still have occasional sex together. But that's all.'

She stared at him, unmoving, unblinking, cigarette down to her fingers, burned down to ash.

'And that's another thing,' he said. 'Sex. I'll be fucking other women. Other girls. It's expected of me. But you can't fuck other men. That'll make me look weak. So if I so much as suspect you of playing around, you're out on your ear. And I'll make you hurt before that.'

He stood back, regarded her coolly.

'That's the deal. Call it a . . . pre-nuptial agreement.' He smiled at the good phrase he had just made up. 'What's your answer?'

The town planner chose that moment to emerge from the gents. With mumbled apologies he squeezed past them, rubbing his body against Sharon as he went.

Sharon didn't notice, didn't move, just stared at Ben.

'What's your answer?'

She remained still, staring. Ben gave a harsh laugh.

'If you didn't want to hear the answer, you shouldn't have asked the question. Don't throw some stroppy, hissy fit with me and expect me to back down. You're not with Jack fucking Smeaton now.'

Sharon remained staring. Ben sighed in exasperation.

'You going to fucking answer, or are we going to stand here all fucking night?'

Sharon looked him in the eye. She looked like she had been physically punched. Numbly, she nodded.

'Good,' said Ben. 'Now get back in that room and start smiling. That's what I expect from a wife.'

Sharon somnambulated back into the dining room.

Ben followed, shaking his head, hoping John Poulson was still there, hoping they could put a bit of business together.

The glass pane was small, square. The putty holding it in old, shrunken, hard. One tap from the half-brick and it smashed.

Mae put her hand in, felt for the snub on the inside lock. Carefully, so as not to cut herself, she found it, turned it. The door swung open.

Mae giggled, felt a powerful elation run through her body. She hadn't expected breaking into a school to be so easy.

'Howay,' she said, 'we're in.'

Behind her, Eileen gave one of her hoarse guffaws and quickly followed Mae inside.

Eileen. Mae's new best friend.

Mae's only real friend.

Eileen was twelve to Mae's ten years, but inside much younger. She was large-framed, always wearing the same washed-out flower print dress or one of its twins, her large workboots and an old overcoat. Her hair was hacked and bobbed; a hair grip bearing a small, porcelain flower kept it out of her eyes, was her only concession to outright femininity. She was always smiling, as if finding savant-like wonderment in the world or uncomprehending bafflement at life.

Mae had found her one day when she had been aimlessly wandering around the area, trying to do anything rather than go to school. She had stood and watched the wrecking ball smash into the side of a row of old terraced houses, saw the walls collapse with a force that rocked the pavement she stood on. Laughed at the amount of rats that had come running out of the rubble, disappearing into cracks and crevices of houses opposite. Making new homes for themselves.

She looked around. A girl sat on the wall watching the workmen, laughing at the rats also. Mae sat down next to her. The girl looked at her, stopped laughing, kept smiling.

'Hello,' she said. 'I'm Eileen. What's your name?'

'Mae.'

'Will you be my friend, Mae?'

Mae looked at the girl, suspicion in her eyes. Why was this older girl wanting to be friends with her? Did she want the same from her that the men did?

'Why?' said Mae, stone-faced.

'Cos I like havin' friends an' I haven't got one. So will you?' Eileen smiled. Her face open and unthreatening.

'All right, then.'

And Mae had found her first friend.

Mae had the time of her life. The first time she could remember being happy. Eileen never judged: Mae could say anything, do anything, tell her anything and Eileen just smiled and nodded.

Mae loved it. She could clown and fool and Eileen smiled and laughed. She could shout and scream and Eileen smiled and laughed.

Eileen knew all the younger children too. The little kids, the pre-schoolers. And Mae became friends with them. They would follow the two girls around, laughing, like rats to the Pied Piper. Mae loved it, played up to it.

Her first friends: the feebs and the babies.

Mae Blacklock, the Outsider Queen.

Sometimes Mae did things just to get a reaction, just to see Eileen's face change. Mae felt she had within her a vast, deep, black reservoir of rage. Unfathomed. Untapped. Sometimes a great geyser of it would belch and bubble to the surface. And Mae would direct it at Eileen. She would swear, scream, call her names; she would pinch her, poke her, hit her. Eileen would look confused, ask her what was wrong, but still offer her uncritical friendship.

The rages were becoming more frequent.

And Mae couldn't control them.

Eileen gave Mae licence to voice ideas, to do things she would never have had the nerve to do on her own.

Like break into the school.

Mae hated school, felt hated within it. Wanted to take her rage out on it. So she did. And took Eileen, smiling and giggling, along with her.

They were in. Mae looked around.

'Come on.'

Mae ran down the hall, Eileen following. She pulled over bookcases as she went, knocked objects from shelves, pulled corners of displays, ripped them down as she ran. Eileen followed her lead, echoing the mayhem.

Mae found her own classroom. Where she was supposed to be when she wasn't playing truant.

'In here.'

Eileen followed Mae.

The room was neatly ordered, everything put away, ready for the next day.

'Let's wreck it.'

Desks were upturned, contents spilled over the floor. Chairs kicked over, projects torn down from walls, objects of interest smashed on the floor, books pulled from shelves, covers and spines ripped off. Mae found the paint cupboard. She pulled the paints out, threw them at the walls. She felt a slight twang of guilt – she had always enjoyed painting – but not enough to stop what she was doing.

She stopped, admired her work. She smiled. The room was wrecked.

She smiled at the devastation. Her chest was heaving with exertion. She felt something else building within her.

'I need to do a shit,' she said out loud.

She looked around; the teacher's desk. Her teacher: always sneering at Mae, belittling her. Making her low opinion of her known.

She climbed on the desk, hitched up her skirt, dropped her knickers.

And shat in the middle of the desk.

Eileen giggled.

Mae finished, wiped herself off with a piece of paper from the desk, redressed herself.

She was still panting hard, but the fight had gone out of her, the adrenalin high fading.

'Come on, then,' she said. 'Let's go.'

They made their way out of the building, walking slowly through their trail of destruction.

Then into the night and away.

September 1966–May 1967:
Old Ghosts in the New Machine

Nineteen sixty-six and the statue had long gone.

Unveiled by Hugh Gaitskell and T. Dan Smith in 1962 as a piece of public art for the citizens of Scotswood, it soon became a target for vandals and graffiti artists. Huge metal mesh barriers were erected around it, imprisoning it in its own cage. Eventually the cage was smashed, the statue taken, the bronze sold and melted down.

No one was ever caught or blamed.

Then the tower blocks began to decline. The paucity of top-grade materials used in their manufacture became apparent. Lifts began to break down. Waste-disposal chutes became disconnected. Refuse piled up. Light bulbs on stairways and walkways would blow and not be replaced. Broken windows would go unmended. Opportunists began to emerge.

Muggers sensed easy prey in darkened alleyways. Crimes were plotted and carried out in shadows. Police became more hesitant about entering the estates. Neighbours began to mirror the decline in other neighbours, let themselves go.

A downward spiral. Starting slowly.

The new abattoir continued to thrive.

Dan Smith pressed on with his plans.

It was the same house, although no one would have recognized it as such. It had been totally transformed.

Sharon had walked without contesting. Jack had moved back, bringing Joanne with him. Gone were Sharon's clean, clinical lines; in came Joanne's warmth and softness. Her vibrancy and youth. Exciting colours replaced bare, muted tones. India prints replaced English severity. Jack was happy to let her do it, wanted her to feel at home, wanted Sharon's ghost exorcised.

They had kept a room for Isaac. He made occasional visits, stopped overnight sometimes. Always sullen, always near-silent.

He would talk to Joanne more than his father. Found her easier to approach. Joanne, diffident at first, began to enjoy his visits, look forward to them even. He didn't regard her as a surrogate mother, more as an older sister. Or a friend. Jack was pleased they got along.

Joanne got the impression Isaac wasn't happy living with his recently remarried mother and Ben Marshall at their big new house in Ponteland. So she should have expected the knock at the door.

January 1967. Christmas had been a quiet affair for Jack and Joanne. They had spent the time almost exclusively with each other. Joanne was studying her course in art therapy, and she had some nights out with her college friends. Jack was reading a lot, thinking about taking a course in something, but he hadn't decided on a subject. He was happy staying at home. They had spent Boxing Day with Isaac – Ben Marshall giving Jack a knowing smile that made his head ache when they returned the boy home – but apart from that they had been on their own.

And they had loved it.

They were true partners; they shared everything. The age difference fell away when they were together. Their love only deepened the longer they were together.

Then came the knock at the door.

A January evening, the air cold, threatening snow.

Jack put down his book, made his way to the front door, opened it. There stood a ten-year-old boy, gloved hands in pockets, duffel coat toggled up, hood pulled around him.

Isaac.

'Hello . . .' said Jack, surprised. 'What are you doing here?'

Isaac looked up at him, his eyes wide.

'Can I come in?'

'Course you can,' said Jack, stepping aside to let the boy in. Before he closed the door he looked up and down the street, expecting to see Sharon's Mini. No sign.

He closed the door, turned to Isaac.

'You on your own?'

The boy nodded. He was shivering.

'Come on inside. Let's get you warmed up.'

Jack directed Isaac to the living room. It was warm with muted lighting. Comfortable. Joanne looked up from her textbook.

'Got a visitor,' said Jack.

'Hello, Isaac . . .'

Joanne got up, crossed to him, gave him a hug.

'You're freezing. Come by the fire and warm up.'

Jack went into the kitchen, made coffee for himself and Joanne, warm Ribena for Isaac. He took the drinks in, handed them round, resumed his seat. He looked between the two of them. They had obviously been talking.

'Well, this is an unexpected surprise,' said Jack.

Joanne and Isaac exchanged glances.

'Tell him,' said Joanne.

'Tell me what?'

Isaac looked at his father, gathered strength to speak.

'I've run away,' he said. 'I want to come here and live with you two.'

Jack looked between the two of them.

'Well, that's a . . . that's a shock,' he said.

'Can I, then?' said Isaac.

'Well, I don't know. We'll have to talk about it,' said Jack.

Joanne leaned in closer to Isaac.

'Why d'you want to stay here?'

Isaac shrugged. 'Cos I want to.'

'Won't they miss you?'

'I doubt it. It's taken me hours to get here. They haven't even noticed I'm gone.'

Joanne looked at Jack, then back to Isaac. She kept questioning him.

'Are you not happy with your mother?'

Isaac, looking at the carpet, shrugged.

'Are you not, Isaac?'

He shook his head, kept looking at the carpet.

'Why not?' Joanne's voice was barely above a whisper.

'Cos . . . they hate me.'

'I'm sure they don't, Isaac. They love you. Your mother loves you.'

Isaac looked up, tears welling in his eyes.

'No, she doesn't. All she does is sit around all day. Drink. Then when she drinks she gets angry with me. I hate her.'

He began crying. Joanne moved, put her arm around him. Made words out of comforting, soothing sounds. She looked up at Jack. Jack didn't know what to do.

Isaac's tears subsided slightly.

'And . . . and they want to send me away. To buh – boarding school.'

And the tears started all over again.

Joanne held him, gently rocking him. Jack looked on, helpless. Isaac eventually stopped crying. He looked up, hope and fear in his pleading boy eyes.

'So can I come and live here? Please?'

Joanne and Jack looked at each other. Neither could commit themselves to an answer.

Jack stood up.

'I think Joanne and I need to have a little talk. We'll be back in a minute.'

Joanne gave Isaac an anxious smile, followed Jack to the kitchen, closed the door behind her.

'Well . . .' he said.

'What d'you want to do?'

'Well, he can stay tonight, obviously,' said Jack. 'But beyond that . . . I don't know. I mean, he's my son, yes, and I don't want him going back there if he's unhappy. I've never liked him being there. But it's you I'm thinking of. You told me you never wanted to be a surrogate mother, a housewife. You're too young. And I agree. You want a career. And I'm all for that too. That's the life we wanted for ourselves.'

Joanne stared hard at the closed kitchen door before answering. She eventually turned back to Jack.

'I don't think . . . I don't think it's a question of want, any more. I think it's a question of need. And right now that boy in there needs his dad.'

'And you.'

Joanne shrugged.

'I don't know about that,' she said. 'But he needs help. And he needs love. And I don't think either of us could live with ourselves if we sent him back.'

Jack looked at her, put his arms around her, kissed her.

'I love you.'

'I know. And I love you too.'

'And you're right. Again.'

Joanne smiled. 'I've been thinking a lot about my mam since she died. Thinking a lot about families. My family. How I would hate history to be repeated like that.'

Jack understood.

They kissed again.

'But I'm still going on with my course,' said Joanne. 'I still want a career.'

'Of course.'

'You'll have to do a lot of the looking after, Jack. Take responsibility for him.'

'Pleasure.'

Joanne smiled.

Good.

They kissed again.

When they went to tell Isaac the good news, they found him curled up by the fire asleep.

Ben sat back in his black leather office chair, lit his cigar. He didn't like cigars, but he smoked them. It was expected of him.

The room was stark: minimalistic, functional and very, very expensively furnished. So little cost so much. A glass wall looking out on to the city. Blown-up framed photos of developments on the other walls. A white leather bag of golf clubs in the corner the only piece of individualism or personality. He didn't like golf, but he played it. It was expected of him.

Ben was thinking. About enemies.

Dan Smith had just left. His last call before flying to London for some business meetings and a *Desert Island Discs* recording. Their meeting had gone well, businesslike. But Ben sensed Dan was not his usual ebullient self.

'You all right, Dan?' Ben had asked. 'You seem a bit . . . distracted.'

Dan sighed.

'Oh, I'll be fine, Ben. I'll be fine.'

Ben looked at him, said nothing. He sensed that Dan would elaborate. He did.

'You don't get to be in my position without making enemies, Ben,' he said. 'You know me. If someone comes out with an opinion that I know is wrong, I'll tell them.'

'Destroy them, more like.'

Dan nodded. 'If I have to, yes. I've never courted popularity. The work's too important to be a people pleaser. But there are those against me. I know that. They've been manoeuvring, trying to find a weakness. Be on your guard.'

Ben was confused. 'I will, Dan.'

Dan Smith leaned forward. 'I'm not one of them. That's what it is. Oh, yes, I've been to London. I know the way things work. I'm an outsider. I know what they think of me. Of us. Up here. They think they'll let us go so far and no further.'

Dan sat back, sighed.

'Well, we've got to prove them wrong.'

He stood up.

'I'd better be off.' They shook hands. 'Be on your guard, Ben. Be careful.'

And Dan left.

Ben sat back down, frowning. Be careful. Enemies. He didn't know what Dan had been talking about. He wasn't usually so obscure. Must have a lot on his mind, be under a lot of pressure. But the words themselves. Enemies. Be careful. That got Ben thinking. About himself.

He had gone legit now. That was the way forward. He was sometimes nostalgic for the old days, but that's all it was. Nostalgia.

He'd examined his actions, his mistakes, his enemies, his potential enemies.

Jack Smeaton. Ben had nothing to fear from him. He valued his son and girlfriend too much.

Martin Fleming and Derek Calabrese. They had parted company on good terms. Might even work together again in the future.

Johnny Bell. A good soldier. But Ben still harboured doubts about him. He could never work out what Johnny was thinking. Only on the side of the highest payer, which was fine as long as Ben was the highest payer. He was also unpredictable. Ben felt that it wouldn't take too much for him to become uncontrollable. And he knew a great deal. Too much. Perhaps Johnny's usefulness was coming to an end. Perhaps he needed more professional enforcement.

Monica Blacklock. Perhaps his biggest potential enemy. And his own entire fault. He should never have shown up on her doorstep. Smiled at her. Winked, even. And then walked off with Ralph Bell. What had he been thinking? So unprofessional.

And now she'd been heard shouting her drunken head off in public about the money she was going to make from Brian Mooney's little secret. And the rag-and-bone man had been making a nuisance of himself for months. It hadn't taken much to put them together. A little lateral thinking. A little surveillance work from Johnny. And the letters he had been receiving. Crudely written, but plainly spelled out:

You ar Brian Mooney. I know you ar. you should shar your money with yor old mates.

It was her. All her. Had to be.
Ben looked down. His cigar had gone out.
'Bastard . . .'
He reached for his gold desk lighter, fumbled his cigar lit again, sat back in the resulting fug.
Enemies. And potential enemies.
He reached for the phone. To call Johnny.

Get some work out of him before he took him off the payroll.

Get him to teach that rag-and-bone man a lesson.

Bert sat down in his armchair, lit up a Woodbine, held the smoke in, exhaled, relaxed.

That was that. Unhappy it was over in a way. He had quite enjoyed himself. Been a bit of a James Bond. Done something exciting.

But it was over. Definitely over. He had told Monica, been firm about it.

'Keep trying,' she had said.

Bert had sighed.

'What more can I do?' he had said. 'I go to the sites, I try to get some scrap from them, then make friends with them. Get talkin'. An' none of them knows anythin' about Brian Mooney. I've asked, an' they've all said the same thing. They know nothin' about 'im. 'Cept 'e's called Ben Marshall, he took over the firm from Ralph Bell, an' that's that.'

Monica didn't even try to hide her disappointment.

'Then you've got to try harder. It's him, I know it's him. You've just got to find somethin' to prove it.'

'I can't.'

'Well, next time.'

'No, Monica, there is no next time. I've done enough.'

'But—'

'I don't care. Maybe it is him, maybe it isn't. Maybe we'd have got some money off him, maybe we wouldn't. If you find another way, remember my cut.'

He had left her then, gone home.

Bert dragged, exhaled again. The Woodbine was reaching an end. He stubbed it out in an ashtray. He sighed. Wondered what was on television. He reached across for the paper, stopped dead.

A noise. Coming from the yard.

He froze, gasped.

The thought: probably just Adam. Or something falling from a shelf. Stacked badly. There was that much stuff in there at the moment, all he'd picked up from the building—

Another noise.

Someone was in the yard.

Heart beating fast, Bert slowly hauled himself from his armchair. Legs shaking, he made his way slowly through the kitchen and out into the yard. He looked around.

The night was casting streetlamp shadows over the yard. The piled-up junk was accentuated, like a miniature city of discards with its own light and shade, its own dark alleys. But everything seemed to be in its place.

Bert tried the light switch. Nothing. The overhead bulb must have blown.

Through the dim, refracted light from his kitchen, he could see Adam in its stall. The horse was pawing the ground with its hoof, shaking its head in apparent anxiety. Bert crossed to him.

'What's up, feller?' Somethin' spooked you? Was that you makin' all that noise, eh?'

'No,' said a voice behind him. 'It was me.'

Bert's heart skipped a beat. He turned, but the intruder was too fast for him. Bert was roughly grabbed, one arm around his throat.

He smelled old meat and stale blood.

He felt a knife against his ribs.

'Don't turn around,' said the intruder, voice like a dead man's, 'or I'll gut you.'

Bert stood so still he began to shake.

'If it's money you want,' he said, his voice vibrating with fear, 'I haven't got much. But if you—'

'Shut up,' said the dead man's voice. 'I don't want your

money. I'm here to deliver a message. And you'd better listen, because if you don't I'll skin and gut your horse alive right in front of you. Right?'

Bert, not trusting his voice, nodded. He stood still, hardly daring to breathe, waited.

'You've been hangin' around buildin' sites. Makin' a nuisance of yourself. Askin' about Brian Mooney.'

'I've stopped that. I'm not doin' it any more. I was only—'

The dead man's voice laughed. It was a cold, chilly sound. 'Following orders. I know. But you won't do it again. I'm here to make sure you don't.'

The blade moved away from Bert's ribs. Bert breathed a heavy sigh.

'You're right,' said Bert. 'I won't. I promise.'

'I know you won't,' said the dead man. 'But just in case you forget, here's somethin' to remind you.'

The arm holding Bert around the throat was removed. Quickly, Bert's right hand was pulled out, flattened, and the knife slid across the palm, cutting deeply. Then back again. Then the dead man gouged into the centre of the wound with the knife tip.

Bert screamed and dropped to his knees, blood pumping from his hand, pain indescribable.

'I've severed the tendons that work your fingers,' the dead man said. 'Even if you get to a hospital in time and they patch you up, you'll never be able to use it again. Not properly. And every time it fails you, remember me.'

The dead man walked out through the door of the yard where the night enveloped him.

The horse whinnied in fear.

Bert kneeled on the ground holding his bloody hand, sobbing.

He would never forget.

*

It was accidental but perhaps inevitable, Newcastle being the size of a city with the feel of a market town, that Jack would meet Sharon again. Since Isaac had moved in with Jack and Joanne, their only contact had been through the telephone. That suited Jack fine.

Jack had been making one of his regular forays into the city centre. The money was holding up, and he hadn't needed to take another job yet. Joanne was studying, Isaac was at school. He filled in the days with books. He had never used the library so much in his life. He was one of Morson, Swan and Morgan's best customers too. And he read voraciously: literature, psychology, philosophy, history. He missed the physicality of his old work, but he had never previously used his mind to such an extent. That more than made up for it.

He had looked through several university prospectuses. Was thinking of doing a degree in something. He just couldn't decide what.

He had no headaches. The tumour seemed to have disappeared.

He had just visited Morson's and bought three new books. He was on his way to the library when he saw her. Coming out of Fenwick, bags in each hand.

Sharon.

His stomach flipped over. Why? He wasn't scared of meeting her again.

He tried to turn in the opposite direction, but she had seen him. She had tried to turn away too. But it was too late. Politeness dictated that acknowledgement was needed. He walked up to her, smiled experimentally.

'Hello,' he said.

'Hello.' She smiled at him. Brightly.

They both stood there, uncomfortable, unsure of what to say next.

'You look well,' he said.

She was dressed expensively, but Jack noticed that she had put on weight. Her face was bloated, her make-up heavy, and she hadn't been able to cover up the lines around her face or the black rings beneath her eyes. Or the broken veins in her cheeks.

'Thank you,' she said. Her bright smile wavered slightly. It creased her face up but didn't touch her eyes. 'So do you.'

Jack had on a new suede jacket and jeans and had allowed his hair to grow. It was still dyed black.

Jack shuffled from foot to foot. Sharon sighed and smiled brightly again.

'How's Isaac?' said Sharon.

'He's doing well. Good at school. Good at home.'

Sharon flinched slightly at the word 'home'. She nodded.

'You all right?' said Jack.

'Me? Oh, I'm fine,' she said. 'I'm fine.'

She smiled again. Again, it failed to reach her eyes.

'Well,' he said, 'I'd best get on.'

'Me too.'

They looked at each other. Straight into each other's eyes. The moment was naked, unguarded. Jack saw through Sharon's make-up and false smile. Saw the eyes of someone who had made a mistake. Who couldn't work out how she had got to where she was. Jack wanted to get away.

'Nice to see you again,' he said.

'You too.'

He turned and hurried away.

Didn't once look back.

Monica was scared.

She could feel them on her. Everywhere she went, everything she did.

Eyes.

Staring, unblinking.

From cars. From street corners. Through windows.

Eyes.

Everywhere.

She knew when they first appeared. After Ralph Bell disappeared. When Ben Marshall appeared.

When she started to put things together.

Bert wouldn't answer the door to her. She had heard from neighbours that something had happened to him. He'd been taken into hospital. He had trouble doing his round. He was a changed man, more solitary, introspective. He wanted to leave the area, go and live somewhere else. Anywhere else, he had apparently said.

Monica thought it a sudden, strange way to behave. Then she started thinking. Bert's behaviour had begun to change after he told her he wouldn't be trying to find out any more about Ben Marshall.

Had something happened to him, then? As a direct result? What?

Hammering on his door, shouting through the letterbox. Ignoring the stares and looks from passers-by.

No reply. Nothing.

Around the corner to try the yard door. Chained up. No sound of a horse inside.

She had tried waiting for him in the street but if he saw her he either shut himself up or ran away.

Eventually she gave up with him. Left him alone.

She settled back into her routine. Tried to forget about Ben Marshall. So what if he was Brian Mooney? What was it to her?   So no more standing drunk in the Shovel, shouting out to anyone who'd listen that she had found Mae's father and was going to make him pay. No more spending his money in her head before she had it in her hand. Because that's all it was. Money. She didn't want him back or anything.

So she forgot about it. Let it go. Which was easier than she expected. Her memory seemed to be getting worse; things didn't stay in her head for as long these days.

And then she started to notice the eyes.

She would see cars parked on the street, the driver staring at her. At first she thought nothing of it. Men often parked by her house, summoning up courage to put their desires into practice. Sometimes she would smile at them, give them a bit of encouragement. Usually that made their minds up: they either came to see her or sped off. But this one just sat there, staring. No amount of smiling could move him. One way or the other.

He was a big man with short-cropped blond hair. Wearing a sheepskin coat. He would usually wait until she was inside the house then drive off. But sometimes he would sit there all night.

He unnerved her with his dead-eyed stare. She began to see him even when he wasn't there. She imagined him standing at the window staring in. Or in the room beside her. Every noise that Mae made in the house, she imagined it was him. In relief, she would take her fear out on her daughter. Beat her. But it didn't shift the terror out of Monica.

She didn't know where to turn, whom to talk to. She needed an ally. Or even someone who could get a message to Ben Marshall, tell him that she didn't care if he was Brian Mooney. She would leave him alone. Just leave her alone.

She thought of asking her father for help but rejected the idea. He would want her to go for the money.

No. She needed someone else.

Then she thought of someone.

The Prince of Wales pub, Westgate Road, Newcastle. A working man's pub, just next to the General Hospital. Not somewhere Monica usually frequented, which was why she was there.

She ordered herself a gin and orange, took a seat, sipped it, listening to the Monkees on the jukebox telling all and sundry that they were believers. Other drinkers in the pub had sized her up. They way she wore her belted black PVC coat and blonde wig gave it away. Not to mention the sunglasses despite its being cloudy outside. She settled back against the maroon padded seat, ignored them. Wondered idly whether she would meet any of her doctor clients in this pub. Wave and give a knowing smile. She decided it was unlikely. Not their sort of place.

She didn't have long to wait.

He walked in: tall, with longish dark hair. Wearing jeans, a suede jacket and an expression saying he would rather be somewhere else.

Jack Smeaton.

Good-looking, she thought, and hoped again that some of her doctor clients might see her in here with him. Get jealous.

She had remembered his name from the cutting in the paper on Ralph's disappearance. She didn't know whether he would be ally or go-between. She would have to tread carefully.

She waved to him, he walked over to her. There was a look of recognition in his eyes. She didn't know him.

'I'm Jack Smeaton.'

'Monica. Monica Blacklock. Thanks for comin'.'

She took her sunglasses off. He sat down opposite her, not bothering to order a drink. He didn't look as if he wanted to stay long.

'I didn't have much choice, really,' he said. 'You phoned me that many times saying you wanted to talk to me about Ralph Bell. How did you get my number, by the way?'

'The phone book. I tried all the Smeatons till I found you.'

'Then you kept phoning me over and over.'

'Sorry. But I needed to talk to someone. And you were the only person I could think of.'

Jack Smeaton sat back, folded his arms.

'Well, I'm here. What did you want to tell me?'

She swallowed hard, suddenly nervous. She took a large mouthful of gin and orange, started to speak.

She told him everything. From Ralph Bell to Bert. From Ben Marshall to the dead man following her. She finished, needed another swing of gin.

'So what's he look like?' said Jack Smeaton. 'This man?'

She described his close-cropped blond hair. His sheepskin coat.

'And his eyes,' she said. 'Horrible. Like a dead man's.'

'Are they blue?' said Jack.

Monica looked shocked. 'D'you know him?'

'I think I do,' said Jack.

'Is he dangerous?'

'He's . . .' Jack searched for the right words. 'You don't want to get him angry.'

Monica looked shaken.

'But don't worry.' Jack's voice searched for a reassuring tone. 'He'll go away if you're not threatening him.'

'Well, that's why I wanted you.'

'Me? Why?'

'To get a message to Ben Marshall. Tell 'im I don't want anythin' off him. I'm leavin' 'im alone. To leave me alone.'

Jack sighed. 'Well, I don't mean to sound callous, but there's not a lot I can do for you. I don't work for the company any longer. I have nothing to do with Ben Marshall any more.'

He shrugged.

'Sorry.'

Monica looked at him. It hadn't been the answer she had wanted to hear. She had wanted Jack Smeaton to take the problem away from her. Make it disappear. And he wouldn't. She stared at the table, suddenly depressed.

Jack sighed. 'I'm really sorry. But there's nothing I can do. As I said, I have nothing to do with these people any more.'

Monica nodded mutely.

'What was his name, anyway?'

Monica looked up. 'Who? Whose name?'

'This ex-boyfriend of yours.'

'Oh. Brian Mooney. Same initials, see?'

She looked up again. Jack Smeaton was staring at her as if he'd seen a ghost. Or heard a ghost's name.

'What's the matter?' said Monica. 'D'you know him.'

Jack Smeaton screwed his eyes up, rubbed his head, like he had a headache.

'I thought . . . I knew the name.' He sighed. 'Must have been mistaken.'

Monica had heard liars before. And Jack Smeaton was lying.

He quickly looked at his watch, stood up.

'Sorry,' he said again. 'Have to be somewhere. Another appointment. Good luck. Just write him a letter. That should do it.'

And he was out of the door and away.

Monica stepped into her house, closed the door. Sighing, she made her way to the living room and flopped into an armchair. She shook her head, sighed again.

Jack Smeaton had been a dead loss. She was so pissed off with him she had stayed in the pub. Flirted with the regulars. Told them he was a TV star and she knew all his secrets. They had indulged her, kept her in gin. But she had left them all, came home alone.

She stood up. Time for another.

She walked into the kitchen searching for a glass. She

flicked on the light switch. No light. She tried it again. Nothing.

'Oh, bugger,' she said. A blown bulb. And she didn't have a replacement.

She walked over to the draining board, feeling around in the shadow-darkened state. She picked up a glass and was about to move when she heard a noise behind her.

'Mae? What you doin' creepin' about in the—'

It wasn't Mae.

The figure grabbed her from behind, held her immobile in his powerful arms. She knew in a terrified instant who it was. She had only glimpsed him before he grabbed her, but she knew.

Blond close-cropped hair. Sheepskin coat. Dead man's eyes. And up close, a smell of old meat and stale blood.

'Mae's not here,' he said with a voice that matched his eyes. 'No one is. Just you and me.'

Monica heard a whimpering sound, realized it was her. She was aware of a dampness about her legs. She had wet herself.

'You've been talkin' too much,' the dead voice said. 'Talk, talk, talk. And writin' letters.'

Monica was puzzled. 'Letters?'

'Don't pretend you don't know. You've been writin' to Ben Marshall. Sayin' things. And even talkin' to Jack Smeaton. We can't have that.'

'Please . . . let me go. I won't say any more. I promise.'

Behind her, she felt the dead man smile.

'Oh, I know. When I'm finished with you, you won't talk.'

She heard herself whimpering again.

The intruder reached forward to the kitchen table, picked up a plastic bottle he had placed there earlier. Even in the gloom Monica knew what it was. Recognized it as one of hers.

Bleach.

The top was off. The intruder's gloved hand held the bottle. 'About time you got your mouth washed out,' he said.

She struggled, kicked and clawed, but to no avail. He was stronger than her. He punched her in the head. She fell to the floor.

She saw lights, stars. She blacked out for a few seconds. Dazed, she looked up.

And saw the dead man's face right in front of her. Ice-chip eyes staring into hers. She felt the bottle kiss her lips. She started to struggle again.

He punched her again.

She slowly opened her eyes.

Felt the liquid being tipped down her throat.

Felt burning agony.

Then felt nothing.

It made the papers.

Page two of Thursday's *Evening Chronicle*:

LOCAL CALL GIRL IN HORROR ATTACK

Jack nearly missed it. Ordinarily it would have been the kind of article he would have ignored, skimmed over at most. And he would have done with this, had not the name of the victim and the estimated date and time of the attack jumped out at him.

Monica Blacklock. Tuesday evening, some time after nine thirty p.m.

Monica Blacklock. He had left her in the pub at around six.

He read the article again, fingers trembling as he held the paper, picked at various key words and phrases:

Vicious attack. Household bleach. Facial injuries.

Intensive care. Critical. No witnesses.

Tragic daughter. Stay with grandparents.

Police: no leads at this time. Perhaps disgruntled customer.

His stomach lurched; his mind flipped back. Horror newsreels again:

The abattoir, that night nearly two years previously.

Blood on his hands, cement dust in his eyes.

Two psychopaths looking at him, laughing.

His head was hurting, the tumour starting up again. Like the last two years never happened.

Jack threw the paper down, began to pace the room. His heart was pumping, blood speeding around his body, breath coming in ragged gasps. He knew why she had been attacked. He could guess who had done it. But he didn't know what to do next.

He had met Monica because of her insistency. He had recognized her straight away: Ralph Bell's whore, as photographed by Ben Marshall. Then the Ben Marshall / Brian Mooney supposition. Too audacious. He had dismissed it.

He stood still, tried to bring his body under control.

Household bleach. Critical.

Write a letter, he had said. Tell him you mean no harm.

Too late for that now.

He began pacing again. What could he do? Would it be him next? How could he keep Joanne and Isaac safe?

His first instinct: run. Gather them up and get out of Newcastle. But that wasn't possible. They had lives in Newcastle. They couldn't just run without somewhere to go.

An anonymous phone call to the police. Too risky. He was already compromised over Ralph's death. Ben Marshall was a well-connected man in the city. If it was traced back to Jack that would be at least fifteen years of his life gone. Plus Joanne and Isaac.

Do nothing. His head throbbed. His head would always throb if he did nothing. Not an option any more.

He stopped pacing, ran his hands through his hair, sighed.

He knew what he had to do. Find out if Ben Marshall was really Brian Mooney. And if that was the case, tell him to leave the three of them alone. Tell Ben he had written it all down, kept it safe as proof. If anything should happen to him, it would be made public. That was it. The only plan he could think of.

But first he needed proof.

The next day Jack was down at Central Library, waiting for it to open.

He had spent the previous evening in a distracted state. Joanne had been concerned, asked him what was wrong. He had sat down on the sofa with her after putting Isaac to bed. The fire was on, the lights subdued. The room felt warm, safe. It was a lie. Nothing, nowhere was.

Jack sighed.

'Why don't you go to bed? Have an early night?'

Joanne's concern nearly broke his heart. She was sitting next to him, hand resting on his shoulder. He nearly gave in at that moment. Nearly told her.

But he didn't. Because that would have been the end of everything.

'Look . . .' he said.

Joanne listened, waited for him to say more.

'I might have to . . . sort something out.' His head was down. He spoke to the Oriental rug.

'What kind of thing?' said Joanne, her face bent forward, eyes trying to see into his.

He sighed again. 'Something to do with . . . the old firm.'

She looked at him, frowned. 'You mean my dad's old firm?'

Jack nodded.

'What kind of thing? Is it something to do with my dad? With his disappearance? Is that it?'

'I don't . . . I don't know,' he said, his eyes still downcast, not meeting hers. 'It's something . . . that should have been sorted out years ago.'

He looked up. Saw nothing but concern in her eyes, felt nothing but deceit in his own.

'What kind of thing? Jack, what's going on? Are you in some sort of trouble?'

'No,' he said quickly. 'No, I'm not. But it might be . . .' He sighed. 'Look, I think you should go away for a while. Take Isaac. Just till . . . this blows over.'

Joanne's hand dropped from his shoulder. She stood up and stared at him, incredulously, hands on hips. 'What's going on, Jack? What's so terrible that we have to get away from it? Tell me.'

Jack shook his head. 'I'm really sorry, Joanne. I honestly can't say yet. All I can say is it's something I have to get cleared up. Once that's done we'll be fine. You'll be able to come back in about a week or so.'

'A week?' Joanne's anger was building. 'What the hell is going on, Jack? What have you got into?'

'Nothing,' he said. 'I've done nothing wrong. But I have to get this sorted out.' He felt his head begin to throb. 'I can't rest until I do.'

They looked each other in the eye. Jack felt points of contact dissolving. He didn't want that to happen.

'Joanne, sit down. Come on, sit next to me.'

Joanne moved, reluctantly at first, until she was sitting next to him. She kept separate from him, her body still rigid with anger.

'Joanne . . .'

'We've never had secrets from each other, Jack.'

'And we haven't now . . .' His eyes dropped again. 'It's just something I have to find out. It might be serious, it might not. But it's best not to take chances.'

He stretched out his hand, touched her shoulder.

'Please, Joanne. Please trust me on this. I wouldn't ask if it wasn't important. Please. I'm only asking you to go away because I don't want you dragged into it. I care about you both.'

She sighed. The anger began to dissipate from her body.

'All right,' she said. 'But when we come back, I want to know everything, right?'

'Definitely.'

'Good.'

They made love that night, tenderly, gently. As if they were both badly bruised and scarred and didn't want to add to each other's hurt.

The library door was unlocked, opened. Jack was the first one in.

Up to the reference library, looking for the *Newcastle Evening Chronicle*. 1956.

It took him about an hour, but he found it. The account of the attack on Kenny and Johnny Bell. The description of Brian Mooney.

And a photo.

It was a head-and-shoulder shot. A cut-down mugshot. Features blurred and indistinct, just able to make out the staring eyes, the snarling lip, the attempted Elvis quiff.

Jack imagined glasses. Longer hair, brushed forward. The anger controlled and directed behind a forced smile.

It could have been him.

It could have well been him.

The house felt strange without them. Like the life itself had been sucked out of it.

Jack put on the fire, subdued the lights. But it wasn't the same.

Joanne had taken the car, driven herself and Isaac to a

remote bed and breakfast in the Lake District. Joanne had told Isaac it was a surprise holiday, jollying him along as if it was a big adventure, but her eyes when they met Jack's told a different story.

Isaac was sad Jack wasn't going, but Joanne told him: 'Daddy's got a bit of work to do. We'll see him soon.'

Then goodbyes.

'I'll call you,' said Joanne.

'I love you,' said Jack. 'Once this is out of the way, we'll be happy for the rest of our lives.'

They drove off.

Jack stood up. He didn't want to sit on the sofa without Joanne. He didn't feel comfortable.

He walked into the bathroom, thinking about Ben Marshall / Brian Mooney. About identity. About how image changed personality.

He looked in the mirror, saw a middle-aged man who was lucky enough to look younger. To feel younger. A father. A lover. A good man.

To do what he was going to do, to be successful, he would have to change.

He looked at his hair; saw the white poking through beneath the black. He needed his roots done. He looked closer.

No.

He found some scissors. And began cutting.

Half an hour later he was done. Black hair carpeted the bathroom floor like a falling of inverse snow. His head was now covered in short, white stubble. It accentuated his features, made his cheekbones prominent, his eyes sunken and hollow.

Like the soldier he once was.

All he needed was the dark clothes.

He felt his attitude change with the look. His resolve strengthen.

He thought of the tumour. Fuck remission: it was time to cut the cancer out.

It was time to pay a visit to Johnny Bell.

Hate and rage. Rage and hate. Sometimes Mae felt like they were her only true friends.

They were with her constantly, talking and listening to her. There were others, too, that she didn't see that often: suspicion, depression, self-pity. And fear. She used to see a lot of fear. They were inseparable at one time. But fear didn't come round much any more. They had very little time for each other. It was just a phase she was going through. Now hate was all the rage. And vice versa.

'This'll be your room here,' her grandmother had said, pointing into a tiny boxroom that hardly had space for a single bed.

The room smelled strongly of damp and stale air. Like it had been sealed up for years. The bedding looked old, seemed festering with mildew. The wallpaper peeling. Mae's grandmother looked at the girl. She seemed to be suggesting that the room and Mae were made for each other.

Mae entered, placed her small bag of meagre possessions on the bed.

'When can I go home?' she said.

Her grandmother looked away as she began to reply, as if she had more important things to busy herself with. 'Don't know yet. When your mother's well again.'

'When will that be?'

'Oh, God, girl, I don't know. Stop askin' questions. This is your room. Just be thankful you've got a roof over your head.'

She turned, went noisily downstairs.

Mae sat slowly on the bed, felt the cold of the blankets even through her clothes. She stared at the peeling wallpaper, at the old, brown-stained pattern, tried to imagine it ever looking new and bright. Failed. Not in this house. Never in this house.

She had come in from playing with Eileen one night to find the police in her house. They told Mae there had been an accident and her mother was in hospital. Very seriously injured.

Mae had looked around, thought of the house without her mother in it and laughed. Long and loud.

The police had looked at her strangely. The words 'delayed shock' had been mentioned, nods given.

They told her she would have to stay somewhere else. She said Bert's name. But Bert wouldn't have her. Didn't want anything to do with her. So it was the grandparents.

Her heart was heavy at the thought. Her granddad.

Rage and hate. And fear made a reappearance.

And after her grandma had left her sitting on the bed, her granddad came to visit.

Made sure he locked the door first.

Mae hardly went to school. She hated the teachers, how small and dumb they made her feel. So she would persuade Eileen to play truant with her. The teachers didn't complain. Mae felt they were pleased to be rid of her.

She liked Eileen. Or liked having her around. Because Eileen never complained, always laughed and smiled, always went along with whatever Mae wanted her to do.

And because of Eileen, Mae felt she could do things she wouldn't have dared on her own. Mae felt there was nothing she couldn't do.

Rage and hate. Hate and rage.

Eileen gave tacit encouragement. Legitimized Mae's actions.

One day, when they should have been at school, they watched three little girls skipping over a rope outside on the street. They were singing a skipping song as they jumped, taking turns to operate the rope and do the skipping. Their mothers had sent them out in clean, pressed frocks. They were laughing, enjoying themselves.

Mae hated them.

She felt that hatred rise within her, turn to inarticulate rage.

'Watch this,' she said to Eileen.

Mae walked across the street to where the girls were playing, caught the eye of the girl about to jump. She stopped, looked, smiled.

And Mae was on her.

Hands about her throat, snarling words through gritted teeth.

'I could kill you, you know. I could kill you . . .'

The little girl's face began to turn blue.

Mae stopped and stood up, shaking.

The little girl climbed slowly to her feet and ran home, crying. Mae watched her go, then rejoined Eileen and kept on walking down the street.

Eileen gave out her usual simple-minded smile.

But Mae was laughing. Not joyous, humorous laughing: hateful, raging laughing.

After that, Mae was often to be found hurting and hitting little children. Sometimes she got into trouble with the parents, sometimes not. She didn't care. Afterwards, she would feel so powerful inside, she felt nothing could touch her.

But something could.

Her granddad paid regular visits to her room. Mae was used to that; she could put up with it, send her mind somewhere else. At least it was just him. At least there weren't other men hurting her in the white room with the crucifixes. That was something.

But there was still her granddad. And she didn't want to put up with it any more. She wanted him to stop.

She found a pair of scissors in a kitchen drawer, secretly pocketed them and waited with them in her hands, on her bed, waited for him to enter the room that night.

He did. And she attacked, blades pointing in front of her, aiming for his heart, his veins, his eyes, anything. Everything.

She got in one good blow, felt metal slide beneath skin, before he swatted her back on to the bed, disarmed her and held her there. He was too strong for her. He laughed.

'You want it rough, do you?' His eyes glittered, lit by cruel, sickly light. 'Good. I like a bit of rough.'

And he was rough with her. Very rough.

Afterwards, Mae sat on the bed, blankets covering her naked body, staring at the door, shivering.

Rage and hate, her only true friends, coursed through her.

She refused to allow in suspicion, depression, self-pity or fear.

She refused to cry. She refused to be weak.

She spotted the scissors on the floor, light glinting off the blades.

She picked them up, caressed them, kissed them. Saw her granddad's blood on them, held them close.

Rage and hate. Her only true friends.

Now she had a third.

Jack slipped the key into the lock, turned it. The door swung inwardly open.

Breaking into a seventh-floor flat in the Elms. He knew how to slip in undetected. He knew where to find a duplicate key. He smiled to himself. He should know. He had built the block.

He paused before entering. Just another Wednesday. May 1967. Spring. A time of renewal. Jack, breathing heavily, keeping his shaking hands under control, hoped it would be a time of renewal for him too. Hoped he could do what he had to do then get on with the rest of his life.

He had phoned Ben Marshall the previous day, spent a long weekend building himself up to it. Practising what he would say, riffing on every permutation of conversation in his head. He had imagined every possible outcome, too, believing that if he imagined something bad, worked through it in his mind, planned it out, it couldn't come true.

Whatever he could imagine wouldn't happen.

It became his mantra.

He had got through to Ben Marshall eventually, endured his false, bonhomie-riddled tones as he told him he wanted to see him. Had some things to discuss.

Jack made the date and the time. Johnny's flat. Six p.m. Ben agreed. Jack put the phone down, sweating. He hadn't expected it to go so smoothly.

Then he had to prepare. Think himself back into being a soldier again. He worked out. Shocked at how much his muscles had atrophied with disuse. He needed some back-up. Insurance.

He had an old army acquaintance who ran a gun club in Darras Hall. Jack paid him a visit, enrolled for membership. This acquaintance also bought and sold handguns. Jack knew what he wanted, zeroed in on a Second World War Enfield. Hadn't seen one since 1945.

Since Belsen.

Paperwork and licence were rushed through for old times' sake. Jack bought rounds, practised on the range. It all came back to him. Like riding a bike.

Imagined Ben Marshall in his sights. Johnny Bell.

Felt like a soldier again.

He slipped the Enfield from the back of the waistband of his black jeans, cocked it, entered the flat feeling a dull throb in his head. He had got there early, knowing Johnny would still be at work. He planned to wait.

To be ready.

He closed the door behind him, noting it was reinforced steel. A paranoid's front door.

The smell hit him first. Not just stale air and sweat, but also rancid meat. He looked into the kitchen. It was a mess. In among the wilful clutter was a half-carcass of some unidentified animal, being feasted on by flies and maggots.

Jack almost retched but swallowed it down. He walked into the living room. And stopped dead.

Joanne had told him Johnny had a Nazi fixation, had decorated his flat with Nazi regalia. But this was like the Fourth Reich.

The Nazi stuff was there: a huge swastika flag dominated one wall. Before it, a table turned shrine by Nazi objects: a gold swastika lectern, on it a gold-leaf copy of *Mein Kampf*, beside it a huge photo of Hitler saluting. And other stuff, all marked by eagles and swastikas. On the other walls around the room: photos, magazine clippings, newspaper articles of Nazi-related activities, some yellowing, some more recent. The Searchlight trial. Attacks on Jewish homes and cemeteries. National Front mobilization.

And, if that wasn't enough, other images, mostly in black, white and smudgy grey, showed gay S & M porn, men hurting each other, taking sexual pleasure from agony. The pictures became more extreme: dismemberment, disease-ridden bodies, violent death, torture, autopsy.

The Fourth Reich. Built on sex and death.

Jack felt physically sick. Almost like he was back in Belsen again.

This was the past that had to be destroyed. To build the future. This was the past he thought had been destroyed.

He heard a noise, turned. Saw a blur before him.

He raised his gun.

Too late.

A pain in his head. A firework explosion behind his eyes.

And then darkness.

Mae was bored. She was always bored these days. But this was more than boredom. There was something behind it, building, pushing, threatening to break through. She and Eileen were taking another day off school. Watching the little kids play. Mae put her hand in her coat pocket, felt the scissors. Ran her finger carefully along the blade. Drew comfort from it.

The little kids were running around in the rubble of a half-demolished street. Playing chasy while the workmen destroyed the past, built the future.

They had called repeatedly for the two girls to come and join them. Eileen had wanted to, but Mae had refused. Eileen had mutely consented to Mae's wishes.

The kids called again to the girls.

Mae was going to say something, shout out what they could do with their play offer, but . . .

Something building, pushing, threatening to break through.

She ran her fingers along the edge of the scissors blade. Drew comfort from it.

One of the boys called again.

'Howay, youse two. Come an' play wi' wuh.'

Mae stood up. 'All right, then.'

She crossed the road, Eileen following excitedly. She stood among the small children in the rubble.

Mae Blacklock, Queen of the Outcasts.

'What we gonna play?' the same boy, Trevor, asked.

He had curly brown hair and a ready smile. He was four at the most, Mae thought, and popular with both children and adults. Sparky personality, infectious good humour. Mae looked at him, felt something curdle in her stomach, felt that pressure again.

'We'll play . . .' said Mae, looking among the kids, 'hide and seek. We'll count, you hide.'

The three children immediately ran away. Mae covered her eyes, watched from between her fingers.

'One . . . two . . . three . . . four . . .'

The children ran and hid. From behind her fingers, Mae tracked Trevor's progress. He ran to a half-wrecked house, went inside it.

'. . . ninety eight . . . ninety nine . . . a hundred. Comin', ready or not!'

She set off over the rubble, making for the house with Trevor in it.

Something threatening to break through.

She entered the house, started to creep around. She heard a movement from upstairs; a creaking floorboard, a little boy's giggle.

Felt her two old friends in her heart.

She made her way slowly up the half-destroyed staircase, tried room after doorless room. She found him. He opened his mouth to speak, but she put her finger to her lips.

'Ssh,' she said.

Trevor closed his mouth. Mae continued to walk slowly towards him. He stood still.

'This is still part of the game,' she said. 'We're still playing.'

He looked at her, frowning in puzzlement.

'Lie down,' she said, 'on the floor.'

His face still showing puzzlement, the little boy did as bid.

'Now,' said Mae, 'you have to lie as still as possible, right?'

The little boy nodded.

'Like you're a statue. Or you're dead.'

Trevor lay still, wanting to please the older girl.

Mae looked at him, directly into his eyes. Her stomach

writhed and coiled like snakes in a snake pit. Little stars appeared before her eyes. She tried to blink them away. She felt light-headed, giddy, shaking with power. She had never felt so strong before. She smiled. She loved it.

And slid her hands around his throat.

Trevor looked surprised, put his own hands over Mae's, made to pull them off.

'Ssh,' she said. 'Just lie still. Don't move. This is a game. This is all a game.'

Mae kept staring at him, looking deep into his eyes. Trying to see something in them, beyond them.

'You're scarin' me, Mae. Stop lookin' at us like that.'

Mae smiled at him. Blinked back the stars from her eyes. He slackened his grip, replaced his arms at his sides.

Mae felt her breath coming in fast gasps. She was shaking, quivering. A dark joyousness spread within her, like black ink injected into muscle.

She smiled again.

And started to squeeze.

Trevor began to thrash and struggle, but Mae was stronger. She kneeled on his chest, holding him down, her thumbs digging into his windpipe. Her old friends, rage and hate, dancing within her.

She gripped harder, breathed faster.

Trevor's face began to turn blue.

'I'm gonna murder you,' she gasped through gritted teeth, flecks of spittle landing on the boy's face. 'Murder . . . kill youse . . . all . . .'

Trevor thrashed and struggled, made gurgling noises in his throat.

And then Trevor's face disappeared.

Replaced by her mother's face. Wig rat-tailed and askew, eyes burning with anger, mouth spewing gin-fuelled obscenities. Mae squeezed harder. Tried to make it go away.

It did. And her granddad's face appeared in its place. His eyes glittering sharply, his smile widening as her pain would increase. Mae squeezed harder. Squeezed his face away.

Then came a variety of faces: the men who had come to her mother's house to use her body. To make her hurt and cry. They came to her in shards of memories: she remembered one's eyes, another's smile, another's breath. Ears. Nose. Broken skin. Something of all of them coalesced, blurred and shifted into one identikit of hate.

Mae squeezed. Then they were gone. Replaced by Bert. Her failed protector. Who had wanted nothing more to do with her.

Then he was gone and her teachers were there. Sneering, snarling. Belittling. She squeezed harder.

Then it was Eileen, smiling uncomprehending. Mae wanted to squeeze the smile from her face.

'I hate you . . .'

Mae grinding her teeth together, gasping the words through them.

'I hate you all . . .'

Their faces disappeared, leaving only one: her mother.

'I hate you . . . hate you . . .'

Then darkness.

Mae opened her eyes, looked around. She must have blacked out. She was kneeling on top of Trevor's chest, hands still locked around his throat. She slowly unclenched her fingers, removed them. They were sore, stiff with muscle rigidity.

She looked at Trevor. His face was blue, his lips purple. Spittle and froth trickled down his cheeks and chin. His eyes, showing white, had rolled back into his head. Hand-shaped bruising was already starting to form around his throat from where she had grabbed him.

She sat back, her spirit spent, her body exhausted.

'Get up,' she said to him.

Trevor didn't move.

She looked at him, understanding for the first time that he was dead.

She laughed.

'Get up!' she shouted, kicking him. 'Get up!'

Trevor didn't move.

She kicked him again, in frustration. And again.

'Get up!' Another kick.

She began to dance around his body, singing 'Get up' in a singsong, nursery-rhyme way. Stopping to punctuate the end of a line with a kick.

She stopped dancing, looked at the body. He was still there. He hadn't moved. She put her hands in her pockets.

The scissors were there.

Quickly she drew them out, brandished them at him.

'Get up, or I'll . . .'

He didn't move.

The power she had felt earlier was gone. She could make him lie still but not rise up again. But she still had power over his corpse. Her eyes roved his body, hate-filled, rage-fuelled, looking for somewhere to inflict damage.

She found it.

She pulled down his short trousers, his underpants, took in his small, immature genitals. And started to slash.

And slash.

And slash.

'Get up . . . I hate you . . . get up . . . I hate you . . .'

Over and over, like a nursery rhyme again.

And slash.

She finished and sat back panting, regarding what she had done to the little boy's body. And felt nothing. No feelings, no emotions. Like an empty cardboard box with the present removed.

She heard a noise behind her.

She turned. Eileen was standing at the top of the stairs. Looking at Mae, frowning. Mae dropped the scissors, stood up. Eileen looked at Mae, expecting an answer.

'Trevor's dead,' she said. 'He won't get up.'

Eileen frowned. 'Will he be coming back to play?'

'No.'

Mae crossed to the stairs.

'Let's go.'

Eileen followed her. Before she descended, Mae stopped, turned, looked at her.

'Say nothin', right?'

Eileen nodded.

'Good.'

Mae went downstairs and outside, followed by Eileen. Back to play with the other children.

Jack opened his eyes. Slowly. His head still hurt. He looked around.

He was still in Johnny's flat, lying along the sofa. He tried to sit up, felt nauseous from the sudden movement. A shape he didn't recognize hove into view. Jack flinched, expecting a blow.

'He's back,' said a rough London accent.

'Good,' said a voice Jack recognized. Ben Marshall.

Jack looked at the owner of the first voice. A big man, muscled, not fat, wearing a three-button suit, white shirt and dark tie and a history of violence on his face. Broken nose. Scars. Misshapen ears. Jack saw a bulge beneath the left side of his jacket. Gun. Jack didn't move.

Ben Marshall entered the room, usual supercilious smile in place.

'Hello, Jack,' he said. 'Bit sneaky, coming here early.' He held Jack's gun up. 'Anyone would think you had bad intentions in mind. Good job Dougie was on hand to meet you.'

'I had to,' said Jack, rubbing his sore head. 'I thought you might try something like this.'

Ben Marshall sat down on a dining chair.

'So what did you want, Jack?' He pointed the Enfield at Jack. 'To kill me? Is that it?'

'That's for protection,' said Jack. 'I just wanted to talk to you.'

'So why not make an appointment at my office? Why all this cloak-and-dagger shit?'

'Because I thought you'd try something when you heard what I had to say.'

Ben Marshall sat back, an amused look on his face.

'And what was that, Jack? What did you want to say?'

Jack swallowed hard. 'I know who you are.'

Ben just looked at him, smiled. 'Course you do.'

'I mean who you were.'

Ben remained smiling, but his eyes hardened, darkened.

'Did you work that out for yourself?' he said, 'or did that whore tell you?'

'The . . . she told me. I wasn't convinced. But you've just convinced me.'

Ben nodded.

'So, let's see . . . You thought you'd come in here, hold a gun on me, get a confession from me . . . then what? Take me to the police? Kill me? Out of a sense of revenge for Ralph Bell? Am I right?'

Jack kept staring at Ben. He sighed, put his head down.

'Something like that,' said Jack.

Ben Marshall laughed. 'That's better. Confession's good for the soul. Now if it's the former you've come for, I doubt you'd find a policeman who'd believe you. Especially with the evidence I've got on you. Were you willing to risk that?'

Jack said nothing.

'Thought not,' said Ben. 'So it's the latter. Well, just remember what the Irish poet once said: you come looking for revenge, you better dig two graves.'

Jack stared at Ben, said nothing.

'And where does Johnny fit into all this?'

'I just wanted to let him know who he was dealing with. Who you really are. See what he does then.'

Ben threw back his head, gave a sharp, barking laugh.

'You think he doesn't know? Look around you. Look at this place. You think he cares?' Ben shook his head. 'Ah, Johnny,' he said fondly. 'It's a shame. All good things, and that.'

There came the sound of a key in the lock. The front door opened.

'Speak of the devil,' said Ben.

Johnny entered the room, stood there. He looked around. He didn't look happy.

'Come on in, Johnny,' said Ben. 'Join the party.'

'I don't like people in my flat,' said Johnny, his usual dead monotone barbed with anger. 'People I haven't invited.'

'Don't worry, Johnny,' said Ben. 'We won't be staying long. Why not have a seat next to Jack?'

Johnny remained standing, staring at Ben. Ben swung around, pointing the Enfield at Johnny's belly. Surprise flickered on Johnny's face.

'Now please,' said Ben, his voice dropping ominously. 'Don't think I won't use this.'

Johnny reluctantly sat next to Jack. He kept his hate-narrowed eyes on Ben.

'Well,' said Ben, 'I'm glad it's worked out like this. Got a nice symmetry to it. Saved a lot of bother.'

Ben looked at Dougie, gave him a nod. Dougie got up, lumbered out of the room. Ben turned back to Jack and Johnny.

'Well, Jack, I thought I could trust you to leave me alone.

I really did. I'd have left you alone, you know. If you hadn't come here. Really. You were nothing to me.'

Jack put his head down, let Ben's words sink in.

Ben sighed. 'But since you're here, it obviously means I've got to deal with you.'

'If anything happens to me,' said Jack, 'I've written down everything I've got on you. People will start to investigate.'

Ben laughed. 'Really? What d'you think this is? *Z Cars*? Course you haven't. And if you have, I'll find a way around it. I always do. No, Jack, it seems I've got to do something about you.'

'Leave Joanne and Isaac out of this,' said Jack, a look of desperate pleading on his face as he began to realize just how desperate his situation was. 'They don't know I'm here. They don't know anything about this. Please.'

Ben scrutinized him, gauging the measure of truth in his eyes.

'OK,' he said. 'I believe you.'

Jack breathed a sigh of relief.

'But you, Johnny . . .' Ben shook his head. 'Well, I'm sorry. You've worked very well for me, but . . . it's time to put things on a more professional footing. Time I took things more seriously.'

Ben stood up, his eyes, the gun never leaving the two seated men.

'The time of the talented amateur has passed,' said Ben. 'And that's all you are, Johnny. A first-class psychopath, admittedly, but just a talented amateur. And you know too much too. And you, Jack, are an idealist. You believe in perfection. There's no place for either of you in the future I'm building.'

'And what kind of future might that be?' said Jack. 'A future for sociopaths?'

Ben smiled. 'Sociopath? Not me. I'm a realist, Jack, not a

dreamer. I don't believe in dreams; I believe in goals. I'm a businessman. The future belongs to me. And those like me.'

Dougie entered the room carrying two large metal cans. He opened the cap of the first one, began to slosh the contained liquid liberally about the flat. Jack could smell what it was.

Petrol.

'Not as much finesse as one of your jobs, Johnny, but then it doesn't need it. Dougie here is my new right-hand man. That's Mr Shaw to you. He's from London. I called in some favours, arranged some deals, and now Dougie works for me. He's on the payroll, he doesn't ask questions, he just gets on with his job. Businesslike. It's the way forward.'

Dougie emptied the last drops of the first petrol can on to the carpet. He opened the second, gave the flat another dosing.

'Any last words?' said Ben.

Johnny jumped up from the sofa and lunged towards Ben. He didn't reach him. Ben pulled the trigger. Twice. Johnny fell to the floor, hands clutching his stomach, blood spilling between them.

Ben smiled.

'That was a stroke of luck,' he said, looking at Jack. 'Any questions, they'll think you shot him.'

'That noise is going to get people running,' said Jack. 'They'll want to know what's going on.'

'I doubt it,' said Ben. 'They'll probably think it's a car backfiring. They're not big on community around here. Despite your best efforts.'

'You bastard,' said Jack. 'Why d'you want to do this?'

'Because I'm a winner,' said Ben, as if stating the obvious. 'And winners win.'

Dougie took out a set of handcuffs and advanced on Jack. He pulled him off the sofa by his left wrist, cuffed it, marched him to the balcony, put the other half of the cuff

around the handrail. Locked it. Then walked towards the
front door, stood waiting.

Ben crossed to him, stood over him.

'Goodbye, Jack,' he said. 'I'll leave your son and girlfriend
alone. And I love waking up to your wife. I love seeing that
sense of realization on her face every day of how she's fucked
her life up. But don't worry; I'll look after her. For as long as
she amuses me, anyway.'

Jack pulled at the chain, tried to go for Ben. Ben smiled and
moved out of reach. He followed Dougie to the door. Dougie
struck a match, began to light a cigarette. Ben threw Jack's
gun on to the carpet, then opened the front door and left.
Dougie got his cigarette lit, turned to go, threw his match on
the floor. He closed the front door behind him.

'Get the car. I want to wait here a minute. Want to watch.'

Dougie nodded and headed towards the car park. Ben,
standing in the deserted, walled-in children's playground at
the foot of the tower block, looked up. He picked out
Johnny's window from all the other identical windows,
watched. There would be smoke soon. Smoke and flames. By
then it would be too late.

He smiled, sighed contentedly. He wasn't worried about
being seen, about being connected to the fire. He was often
seen walking among new buildings. Especially ones his
company, or adopted company, had built. He liked the feeling
of power the buildings gave him, the sense of concrete
achievement he felt looking around. Knowing it was he who
was responsible. He who was building the new city.

He could feel the power coursing through him. He was
unstoppable, untouchable. He thought of Jack and Johnny.
Smiled again. It was a long time since he had disposed of his
enemies so directly. It felt good to be back in the saddle again.
Perhaps it was something he should do more often.

He looked at the window. Wisps of smoke were beginning to trail out. Like ghosts exiting the concrete machine of the block. He listened hard. Could he hear cries for help? Or was it the wind whipping around the buildings? It didn't matter either way. It was too late for both of them.

He turned, began to make his way towards the car, which he knew would be waiting for him on the main road. And saw out of the corner of his eye a blur of movement. The sound of a rushing body.

He turned. Too late. Something connected with his head, hard and heavy. Volcanoes erupted behind his eyes, engulfing him in white-hot lava. He fell, succumbing to the pain.

Ben looked up. Saw a figure standing over him holding what looked like a cricket bat. A figure he didn't recognize. The figure was speaking to him.

'Ignored my letters, eh? Think you're too good for me now, eh?'

Ben instinctively raised his hands, tried to prop himself up, fight this attacker off.

Another whack to his head with the cricket bat. Ben fell back, hitting the tarmac with a crack. He both felt and heard his skull cave in from the blow, splinters of bone embedded themselves in the soft, blood-soaked tissue of his brain. His vision began to darken. He blinked his eyes.

'Eh? No time for your old mates now. Not now that you're Ben Marshall.'

Another blow, a kick this time. Just above his ear. Ben felt the back of his head and neck becoming increasingly wetter.

Ben's focus was slipping. The man's voice winding in and out, losing transmission like a loose radio dial. Ben closed his eyes. Felt the pain ebb away. The man kept talking.

'Don't you die, you bastard. I'm not done with you yet.'

Another kick. Then another.

'Don't die. Not yet . . . not until I'm finished with you . . .'

He looked down at the prone body. Ben was still breathing.

'Don't you recognize your old mate, eh? Your old mate Brimson? The one you let carry the can when you ran off? The one you let go to prison for you? Eh?'

Another kick, this time to the body. Ben groaned, didn't open his eyes.

'You've done all right for yourself, haven't you? Think you're too fancy to share it with your old mates, though.'

He kneeled down, supported himself on the cricket bat. He leaned in close to Ben's body.

'Can you hear us? I hope so.'

Brimson stared hard at Ben, his chest burning with rage and exhaustion. He was overweight, sweating hard, his face knotted by anger and heart pains. Years of prison, of drunken, bare-knuckle fighting, of the boxing booth had taken their toll on his body.

'Came back in to town with the hoppings, saw your photo in the paper. Not so tough now, are you? Bastard.'

'Mr Marshall?'

Brimson looked up. Ben Marshall's driver calling for him. Time to go. He stood up, looked down at the body. Ben Marshall was still breathing. Brimson thought of all the wasted years he had had, all the times he had blamed Brian Mooney for what had happened in his life. And now this. Back with a new identity. A rich identity. And not sharing any of it with his old mates. Not paying his debts.

He spat. It landed right in Ben's face.

Brimson turned and left the playground.

Flames engulfed the flat almost instantly. Scuttling up walls like fiery spiders, curling Johnny's pictures black, burning them to grey ash. The carpets and furniture were quick to combust, the sofa catching immediately, belching black, acrid smoke.

Out on the balcony, Jack could feel the heat on his body, the smoke entering his lungs. He tried to turn his body, to see into other flats.

'Help!' he shouted, twisting his body towards next-door's balcony. 'Fire! Help!'

No response.

The flames increased in intensity, hungrily licking, tasting and eating anything and everything in their way. Jack saw Johnny lying on the floor, flames beginning to bite at his clothes where the petrol from the carpet had seeped into the fabric. He was still moving.

'Johnny . . .' Jack shouted, 'crawl to the door . . . get the front door open . . .'

Johnny looked up slowly, saw Jack. He looked back at the door, back to the balcony, began to painfully drag his body towards Jack.

'No . . . not this way . . . the other way . . . the front door . . .'

Johnny kept coming towards him.

A wave of panic jumped through Jack. He had to get free. He had to escape. Frantically, he began to rattle the handcuffs, tried to pull the handrail free. It was no use. It was stuck fast to the concrete.

Jack knew it would be. At one time he could have even said which British safety standard it conformed to.

Jack looked down. Johnny had pulled himself right to Jack's feet. Burning and smoking, he was attempting to pull himself up Jack's legs.

'Go to the front door . . . crawl to . . .'

Jack looked up, looked inside. The flat was now a raging inferno. A completely unbreachable wall of flame. Especially for a crawling, dying man.

Jack coughed, felt the smoke curling into his lungs, choking him.

Jack looked down. Johnny had collapsed on his feet, curled up into a bleeding, smoking, neo-fetal ball. He smelled like burning meat. Johnny looked up. There were tears in his eyes, down his soot-blackened face.

'I'm sorry,' he sobbed weakly. 'I'm sorry . . .'

Jack just looked at him. At the nearing flames. Back to Johnny.

'I'm sorry,' Johnny said again. 'It hurts . . . it . . . really . . . hurts . . .'

Jack looked into the flat. Saw the remains of the swastika flame-shrivel away to nothing. Hitler burn and disappear.

'I'm sorry . . .' Johnny looked up. 'Will you forgive me? Please . . .'

Jack looked at the approaching flames, at the man weeping at his feet.

He sighed in hopelessness, sank down beside Johnny.

'I'm sorry . . . I'm sorry . . .'

Johnny put his head in Jack's lap. Jack cradled it.

The flames had reached the petrol-soaked balcony. He could feel their heat around his legs. The smoke choked and blinded him. He closed his eyes.

Emotions he couldn't name, feelings he had never identified coursed through him. Too quick to catch, too fast to hold.

He settled on one image:

Joanne. In her bed. Candles gently glowing, Miles smoothly blowing.

Happiness. Love.

Then another:

Joanne and him looking down at the sleeping body of Isaac in front of the fire in January. Holding her hand, feeling her squeeze his in return. Realizing they had accidentally become a family.

Happiness. Love.

He closed his eyes, tuned everything else out, held on to those feelings, those images.

The flames drew nearer, the smoke choked, blinded.

Black dots danced before his eyes.

Happiness. Love.

A loud whoom as the gas cooker in the kitchen exploded, sending a fireball hunting for a way out. It found the balcony.

Jack's eyes closed, he didn't see it coming.

It hit.

Jack smiled.

PART FIVE

The Future

The Future

At night he dreamed the city.

One straight road. A high street, stretching from the past to the future. A recurring dream of a recurring city. Always the same.

He was walking. From the past to the future. But he never got there. Wherever he stopped, in the dream, he was always in the present. He looked back, saw the past all grimy and sooty. Small and shabby. Depressing and squalid. He would look to the future and see light, dazzling and shining. See huge constructs reaching up and up, aspiring higher and higher. Radiant and beautiful. A city in the sky. Made the heart sing to look upon it. Utopia. He would imagine himself there, living in it. Then he would look around. Find himself back in the present.

The present was neither the black of the past nor the white of the future. It was always grey. Everyday grey. And he would walk, sometimes try to run, towards the future, but his dream legs couldn't move him fast enough. Couldn't outrun the grey present.

Always stuck. Always now. Always looking for desperate ways to barter himself forward.

He stopped walking, looked around. The present loomed up, all around him. Towering grey walls. They began to close in.

He looked around, tried to escape. There was no way out.

The walls moved in closer.

He began to sweat. He tried to run, but his legs wouldn't move.

The walls moved closer.

Closer. He stretched out his arms, could touch both sides with his fingertips.

He tried to shout, to raise the alarm, but when he opened his mouth he found he had no dream voice.

Closer.

He tensed, anticipating being crushed.

Closer.

Then nothing. Silence. They had stopped moving.

He breathed a huge sigh of relief, then looked around. He couldn't move. He was trapped, powerless. Dream logic told him he would not be moving for quite a while. Dream logic told him this was because of his bartering. Trying to sell the present to buy the future.

He looked around, heart heavy, and tried to get used to his new environment. He had accepted his imprisonment to a degree that surprised him. He thought he would have fought. But deep down his dream self knew. He couldn't have fought these walls and won.

There was no door. But one of the walls had a window. Small, barred, high up. Through it he could just manage to see the gleaming, brilliant city of the future.

He sighed, slumped down.

The radiance of the future glowed through the bars, illuminating the cell of the present. He knew it was out there on the road, but he couldn't touch it, couldn't reach it.

He could just sit there, immobile, and bask in reflected glow of an unreachable utopia.

And that was all.

June 1974:
Sweatbox Reverie

Camera flashes, sharp and brief: a mini firework display at the small, square windows. A lurch as the sweatbox took a corner, scattering press outside, leaving running feet, jostling equipment and unanswered requests in its diesel slipstream.

Down the road and away.

From Leeds Crown Court to prison.

Dan Smith sat back, tried to steady himself against the hard metal seat, hard metal wall.

So sudden, he thought, so swift. No chance to put affairs in order, have meaningful goodbyes with loved ones, mentally prepare oneself for the contraction of one's world. Dan tried to sit still, think.

Dan knew he would have a lot of time to think.

Bribery and corruption, the judge had said. Bribery and corruption.

And conspiracy.

Six years.

Six years' loss of freedom. Of stigmatization.

Six years.

Bribery, corruption, conspiracy.

Rubbish.

Dan knew it was how the business worked. Give out cash bonuses and incentives to guarantee that the companies he represented would get the work. Make sure the contracts would go to the right companies. And they would be the right companies.

They would be the ones who shared the vision.

Dan's vision.

Building utopia.

The prosecution saw it differently:

J. G. L. Poulson – Architects. J. G. L. Poulson & Associates – Consulting Engineers. Construction Promotions. Ropergate Services – Bank and Project Coordinator. Ovalgate Investments. Open House Building. International Technical & Constructional Services. Worldwide Interiors. Water Reclamation. Science & Economic.

All Poulson's companies. All fronted by Dan.

All, as Dan insisted, sharing his vision.

Poulson already serving seven years. Andy Cunningham, former chairman of Durham County Council, getting five.

All giving money out to secure contracts.

To: BR. NCB. Gas Board. To civil servants. To other councils. To MPs both red and blue. To Reggie Maudling, the Home Secretary.

Not bribes, argued Dan. Business. He said it again: it was how the business world worked, the way things were done. Everyone did it.

But not everyone saw it that way. Not everyone shared his vision.

Dan lurched; half-fell off his seat, as the sweatbox took a bump in the road.

Sweatbox. A misnomer, thought Dan. It was beginning to get hot, to stink, true. To smell of all the men who had been in there. But not just sweat: other bodily excretions. Their piss. Their blood. Their tears. Their secret hopes and huge fears.

Trundling, bumping along.

Putting more miles between Dan and freedom.

Freedom. Losing that was bad enough. But not the most important thing Dan could have taken away from him.

Power. He had been stripped of his power.

The worst thing the court could have done, worse even than removing freedom from a man, was to remove power from a politician. Because that was all Dan had ever wanted, ever worked towards, ever craved.

Power.

His aphrodisiac. His drug of choice. His reason for living.

Power.

But not for its own sake. Not for nothing. There was no point in having it unless he could use it. And Dan used it. Felt it course through his body, flowing, like the Tyne to the North Sea.

Used it. Wielded it. Courted with it. Made it bend things into the shape he wanted them. Made his vision into reality.

The Challenge of the Changing North.

The *New*castle.

Dan's castle.

He had the knack, he had once been told, of getting inside people's minds, of making his dreams their dreams. He had never known if it was an insult or a compliment. But it was a description he was proud of.

The sweatbox rattled on its way.

Dan had had time to think. He would have a lot more.

And he would try not to be bitter.

Because he knew what had been done to him. And he knew why. To put him in his place. To remind him: so far and no further.

He had been to London, he had seen how it worked. He had been patronized, strung along, played. Subtly reminded he wasn't one of them.

He wasn't born of influence and affluence. He was a working-class lad from Wallsend. He hadn't been to the right schools, the right universities. He had left school at fourteen, gone to work. He didn't consider himself above the people. He considered himself *of* the people.

So far and no further.

Then slap him down.

There had been five previous attempts to get him this far. Five failed previous attempts.

One success.

He wasn't being paranoid; he wasn't seeing conspiracy theories where there weren't any.

Dan was sure of that.

The proof:

Poulson, Cunningham, himself: prison.

Reggie Maudling: nothing.

They would close ranks, protect their own. One law for the regions, the outsiders. Another for the Establishment. For Home Secretaries.

And he would try not to be bitter.

Bitterness didn't enter into it.

And to add insult to injury:

The Elms estate was crumbling.

The tower blocks were falling apart. Ralph Bell had cheated him, jerry-built the blocks using substandard materials. Everything needed replacing. And then there was the asbestos removal. Big, big headaches. Plus the fact that the tower blocks were becoming high-rise slums. Inner-city no-go areas.

And no Ben Marshall to clear it up. Still in a private room at the Nuffield, still not responding to stimuli, still a privately maintained vegetable. His ex-wife not having the heart or the authority to flick the switch. No clues as to his attacker. No one brought to justice.

Dan had visited him. He had expected to find Ben lying there with calmness and serenity, a hushed, reverent atmosphere. Instead he had found a misshapen-headed body, muscles and tendons contracted due to years of inertia, curled and wizened into a gnarled facsimile of agony, hooked up to drips and monitors, like the half-eaten carcass of a fly trapped in a spider's web. Dan hadn't stayed long.

Enter Dougie Shaw. The saviour. Looked and talked old school, thought and acted new school. The new owner of Northern Star. Now a subsidiary of London-based Calabrese Holdings plc. The company had been awarded the refurbishment contract. And they hoped to try to attract a new type of tenant. Or 'client', as Dougie Shaw had called them in the paper. And Dan's plan for an indoor shopping centre in the heart of the city had been given the go-ahead. With Northern Star. Likewise the underground train system for Newcastle.

Dan had seen a photo of Dougie Shaw in the paper. A black tie do, Dougie all dicky bowed and jovial, cigar elongating, waistline expanding. Beside him Sharon, his wife. Clinging on to him like a drowning woman to a life raft. Ex-Mrs Smeaton, ex-Mrs Marshall. Like she came with the company. Now nipped and tucked beyond all recognition. But stretched skin and hormone therapy couldn't altogether disguise her bloated features, her vague-eyed, clumsy coordination. Her alcohol and prescription painkillers addiction tacit common knowledge.

Looking at it, Dan had sighed, shook his head.

Heard the rumours of a knighthood for London-born entrepreneur.

He would try not to be bitter.

The sweatbox turned another corner, began to slow down.

Almost there.

Dan's heart sank.

If I've done anything wrong, Dan had said before the trial, then I deserve punishment.

He hadn't done anything wrong. He firmly believed that. There were others far worse than him getting away with far more than him.

And they had no vision.

The sweatbox pulled up; a sudden halt, air brakes hissing.

Dan Smith sighed, looked at his hands.

No more vision.

No more power.

No more utopia.

The sweatbox pulled slowly forward, through the gates.

June 1972:
Archetypal Behaviour

Joanne placed the paintings on the table, looked at them.

A glass of wine sat at the edge of the desk lamp's illumination. In the background Neil Young sang that he was still looking for a heart of gold. She liked working this way, felt more creative, in tune with her work.

The paintings. Done by a child's hand, the first showed a sea in the middle of a storm. Huge, violent, thrashing waves. Rain lashing down. Dark clouds hanging in the sky. Off-centre was a small figure clinging to a piece of driftwood. A little girl.

She remembered the conversation that accompanied it:

'The waves are huge,' the girl had said. 'They can take your breath away. Drown you.'

'And what's this little figure here doing?' said Joanne.

'Trying to cling on. Trying to survive.' The girl frowned. 'I was going to have her lying dead, but then I thought no. Let her live.'

'And her mouth's open. What's she shouting?'

'Dunno.' The girl had shrugged. 'For help, I suppose.'

Joanne wrote in the notebook she kept by the side of the paintings. Compiled her report.

The second was of a shadowy, ill-lit backstreet. Joanne thought she recognized it as the West End of Newcastle. The tower blocks gave it away. From around a corner in this urban noir landscape, the girl had painted a lion in mid-pounce. Huge, mad-eyed, its jaws dripping blood.

The conversation:

'Well,' Joanne had said, 'that's scary.'

'That's what they're like. That's what they do.'

'Why is it on the street, though? Why isn't it in a jungle?'

The girl had shrugged. 'I've never been to the jungle.'

Another few sentences in the notebook, another mouthful of wine.

Joanne's work: art therapy.

She had been practising for years, making real progress in what was becoming an increasingly respected field. She worked mainly with disturbed teenagers throughout Hertfordshire and the South-East, where she was based. Her signature work: a personality test based on the responses to a set of universal archetypes. She was highly praised for her work and for her results, but she refused to take too much credit for two reasons. The first was that Jung originally devised the test, and she had just adapted it for painted responses. The second was the fact that her clients had reached the stage where they wanted to come to terms with their predicaments, whatever they may be, and take positive steps to change their lives for the better. Joanne was the first step towards making that happen.

The first question: think of a colour.

'Blue,' the girl had said.

'Now think of three words to describe that colour.'

The girl had closed her eyes. 'Dark, swirling, blurred. I mean blurry.'

'Now paint a picture based on that.'

The colour: how the subject sees himself or herself.

Joanne looked at the painting again, made more notes.

The second question: think of an animal.

Three words: 'Fierce, scary, attacking.'

The animal. How the subject saw other people.

Joanne made more notes, stood upright. She took another mouthful of wine, stretched her back.

She loved her work. It was the one thing she could lose herself in. The only thing she felt confident enough to give herself to without fear of its being taken away from her.

May 1967. When everything changed. When Jack was taken away from her.

Jack. Seven years dead and she still couldn't let go of him. She doubted she ever would.

Jack. Some days she loved him, some days she hated him. Every day she missed him.

There had been others since then. Of course there had; she was an attractive, fit, healthy young woman. She had physical needs and had found lovers who would take care of them. But not her emotional needs. She let no one take care of them. If relationships stopped being purely physical, if lovers and partners attempted to move on to something more committed, then she would drop them. Find ways to escape. Usually it was work: she would throw herself into it; lose herself in her client's troubles, escape from her own. It was an imperfect solution, she knew, but it worked.

She still felt the wrench from the loss of Jack on a daily basis. Sometimes she examined her own feelings, wondered if he had been everything she remembered him being or whether the relationship was just something she had created out of memory. Something that had been all-consuming, all-pervading only in hindsight. She shouldn't have doubted; she knew the answer.

'You're in a state of regression,' her Jungian therapist had said at the time. 'You want to go back to a dream state, right?'

Joanne had nodded, almost totally withdrawn at that point. 'Yes,' she had said. 'That's exactly where I want to go.'

In the aftermath of Jack's death, she had come close to losing herself. Drink. Drugs. Casual sex – just to feel wanted, just to feel. Therapy had helped her cope, but it was Isaac who had saved her, who had kept her grounded. His father had been violently taken from him; his mother was a uninterested stranger loudly proclaiming she had problems of her own to take care of. Joanne was all he had, and he needed her. And, she was surprised to find, vice versa.

They had confronted the facts together. The official verdict: arson. The truth, as much as it had been gathered, as much as it could be told, was that Jack Smeaton had gone to confront Johnny Bell about the disappearance of his father, Ralph Bell. Johnny, it emerged at the inquest, was apparently a high-functioning psychopath. He was suspected of several arson attacks on warehouses. Rumours were beginning to circulate that the son had killed the father. Jack had heard these rumours, packed Joanne and Isaac off for their own safety, gone to confront Johnny. Things had escalated. Johnny had attacked Jack, overpowered him, left him to die in the flat when he set fire to it. Jack had shot and wounded Johnny, stopping him from leaving. They had both died together.

The police then received an anonymous tip-off telling them to check the foundations of the Paradise abattoir. They did so. And eventually identified the body of Ralph Bell.

It was too much for Joanne. She sold the house, found a new university course in London, took Isaac with her.

Sharon didn't contest or complain. Not even when Joanne legally adopted Isaac.

Joanne had been honest with the boy. Encouraged him to ask questions about his dad, allowed him to grieve. And in return allowed herself to grieve. She also found the strength to keep going, to shoulder the majority of the burdens. Isaac realized this, responded to this, and the bond between them grew stronger. Like survivors of a plane wreck struggling to return to civilization, they clung together, knowing that separately they would be weaker. They were both wounded, hurt. They had bound each other's wounds, strengthened each other's resolve, and carried each other along. They weren't a conventional family unit. But they found something between them that worked.

Their home was a house deep in the Hertfordshire countryside. It was old, warm. It was the only place that made her feel safe, secure. Despite that, Joanne still felt there was something missing in the house. A space, an unexpected draught of cold air. A ghost.

Joanne took another mouthful of wine, lifted another painting on to the table.

The third question: think of a body of water.

She had had doubts about asking this question, knowing as she did her client's past. The whole country knew her client's past. The case had even penetrated Joanne's life at the time.

Mae Blacklock. Child killer. The most hated girl in Britain.

Mae Blacklock. Devil child. Those unsmiling dark eyes. Satan's eyes. Demon and demonized. Mothers would say to their children at night: go straight to sleep or Mae Blacklock'll come and get you. Kill you. And the children would slip away into shivery sleep.

Mae Blacklock sold newspapers, incited opinion.

Mae Blacklock caused HATE! HATE! HATE!

The reality, as Joanne had expected, was somewhat different.

Fenton Hall was a special unit for teenage offenders in Hertfordshire. Previously a home to only boys, the unit now contained one girl. Mae Blacklock.

The state hadn't known what to do with her, so they had

sent her there. She had been found guilty of murder,
therefore some punishment was needed. But also, crucially,
some therapy had been considered necessary too. Some
method of ascertaining why she had done what she had done.

All the inmates at Fenton Hall had transgressed in some
way, either large or small. They were all deemed to have
contributory emotional problems. A couple, Mr and Mrs
Everett, who tried to look after the children as their own, ran
the centre. They lived with the children in the same big
house, ate with them around the old pine kitchen table. They
behaved, as much as possible, as one large family. It was an
approach that, by and large, yielded enormous dividends.
Despite some initial reluctance, Mae was responding well to
Mr and Mrs Everett's approach. Mae enjoyed art. Joanne was
brought in.

Joanne had tried to carry as few preconceptions as possible
the first time she had met Mae. She had read reports on
Mae's parental background, home life, friends and family.
The girl had been guarded in the information she gave away,
saying as little as possible. Any question she didn't want to
answer was met with the same reply: ask me mam. Since her
mother had died some years previously as a result of injuries
sustained at the hands of, it was assumed, a disgruntled
punter, she knew they wouldn't be able to. From what little
they had managed to discover about her mother, it was
commonly felt that she was a malevolent influence that Mae
was better off without. Given her mother's background and
Mae's own highly sexualized nature, though, assumptions
were drawn, conclusions reached.

She had found a pretty girl with intelligent, guarded eyes
sprawled in an armchair, wearing jeans and a baggy jumper,
aiming for nonchalance but watching her intently. Joanne,
wearing her brown Biba skirt and complementing dirty pink
headscarf, had smiled.

Mae had been initially wary, but it was Joanne's job to deal with children like that. They had talked, realized they were from the same part of the world, which Joanne said was why she had been asked to talk to Mae, and, gradually, week after week, became more relaxed in each other's company.

Joanne worked hard with Mae, teaching her to paint, to draw, showing the value of stillness, observation, interpretation. She found Mae lacking in self-confidence, haunted by nightmares she couldn't specify or consciously articulate. She was a much more complex girl than the tabloids had painted her at her trial, which came as no surprise to Joanne. Mae was a scared and damaged child who desperately wanted to trust, make friends, love and be loved, but whose internal wiring when it came to making these connections was hopelessly tangled.

Joanne tried her best to untangle them but felt herself failing. Mae was the toughest individual Joanne had ever had to deal with. Try as she might, she just couldn't strike up a rapport with the girl. When she thought she was on to something, Mae would clam up, elude her in some way. Mae agreed to take part in the sessions because she thought she might get released earlier if she did. That, she said, was the only reason. Joanne had exhausted all her usual techniques and was ready to do what she rarely did: admit defeat when Mae started asking questions.

'You got a boyfriend?' Mae said during what Joanne had decided was going to be their final session.

'No,' Joanne had smiled. 'I haven't.'

'Girlfriend?'

Joanne laughed. 'No.' She looked at the girl. Decided to take a chance. 'I did have someone once. He meant a lot to me.'

Mae sat forward, became interested. 'What happened?'

Joanne looked at Mae again. She knew she was breaking

Home Office rules by telling the girl anything personal about herself.

'He died,' Joanne said. 'Suddenly. In a fire.'

Mae nodded to herself. 'D'you miss him?'

Joanne sighed. She looked at the floor. 'Every day.'

And that was the breakthrough. The common ground. They talked on. About loss, about life. And coping. Over the next few weeks Mae opened up more, and Joanne began to read the signs. Little by little Mae was coming to terms with herself and her situation. She gradually admitted that she was ready to move on, to put her old life behind her, to change for the better. That she was ready for more intensive therapy.

Joanne went to work.

'A body of water,' Joanne had said. 'Three words.'

'Deep,' Mae said. 'Like you might drown. That kind of deep.'

Joanne nodded.

'Forbidden.'

Joanne nodded.

'And lonely.'

Then the painting: a deserted lake in a stunted, denuded forest. It looked misty, stagnant. Grey. To the side, hardly in the picture, were some boys. They were dressed in brightly coloured clothes. They seemed wary to venture any further in. They resembled some of the boys Joanne had seen in the unit.

Mae looked exhausted after she had finished, like the effort of painting had cost her something.

'That looks like a cold, uninviting place,' said Joanne.

Mae shivered. 'It is. It's horrible.'

'Those boys look like they want to come nearer.'

'They're scared. They want to play there. But they're worried. The water might be dangerous. Might have hidden currents. Whirlpools. Might suck them under and they'd never be seen again.'

Joanne was pleased she had decided to do the third question.

The body of water. The subject's sex life.

Joanne made more notes in her book. She straightened up again, checked her watch. As if on cue, the door opened and closed behind her. Footsteps made their way into the room. The sound of a bag being dropped. Joanne turned.

'Did you win?' she said.

Isaac smiled. 'Ninety-seven–twenty-four.'

Joanne smiled too. 'Well done. Did you score?'

Isaac looked at her as if he couldn't believe she had asked the question.

'What d'you think?' he said. He walked off into the kitchen. 'What's for dinner? I'm starving.'

'When are you not?'

Isaac loved his basketball. He was one of the stars on the school team. He was built for it. Tall, like his father had been. But Joanne didn't like to make comparisons. She couldn't avoid it but found it unhelpful. He was nearly sixteen. A strong, handsome man-child. And every day he became less of his father, more of his own person. It was sometimes painful to watch, to see Jack disappear from his son, but it was right, thought Joanne. It was the way it should be.

She followed him into the kitchen.

'I waited for you coming in to eat.'

'You shouldn't have done,' he said.

'I know, but I'm soft that way.'

Isaac smiled. She knew he was pleased she had waited. They both needed the company equally.

She crossed to the oven, began removing a casserole. They sat down to dinner, telling each other about their respective days.

Neil Young in the background telling how in order to give
a love you had to live a love.

The car window was open. She felt the warmth of the sun on
her arm. The countryside was gearing up for full summer:
birds flying in and out of hedgerows, flowers showing off
their blooms, trees full of rich green leaves. She sighed,
thought, as she often did, how Jack would have enjoyed it.

Al Green was on the car radio: 'Let's Stay Together'.
Joanne sang along. She loved the song. Thought Jack would
have done too.

It was to be the last session with Mae, the fourth and final
question.

She pulled up at the gates, went through security and she
was in Fenton Hall. She would be sad to say goodbye to Mae,
but she had other work, other clients. Other lives to get lost
in.

Joanne entered the workroom. Mae looked genuinely
pleased to see her. Joanne took a moment, smiled at her. She
couldn't believe it was the same girl from the sullen,
uncommunicative teenager she had met a few months ago.

'Hey, guess what?' said Mae excitedly.

'What?'

'Me sentence is under review. They reckon I've got a good
chance of goin' free. Or at least not goin' to prison. Goin' to
somewhere like this. You know, for adults.'

Joanne smiled. 'That's wonderful, Mae.'

'I think it all depends on how it goes with your report.'
Mae smiled. 'So make it a good 'un, Jo.'

'Talk about pressure,' said Joanne. 'Don't worry. I'll do my
best.'

They sat down, ready to start. Joanne delved into her bag,
pulled something out.

'Here,' she said.

Mae looked puzzled. 'What?'

'This is supposed to be our last session today. I got this for you.'

Mae opened the wrapped package. It was a Biba headscarf, dirty pink.

'Just like mine,' said Joanne. 'I know you liked it. Well, now you've got your own.'

Mae looked at it, nodded. 'That's not fair,' she said. 'You know I can't get you anythin'.'

'I don't want anything, Mae. I've really enjoyed working with you. I just wanted you to have it, that's all.'

Mae nodded again, slid the scarf off the table into her pocket. She was trying hard not to cry, Joanne knew that. Joanne also knew that Mae regarded crying as a sign of weakness. She pretended not to notice.

'Right,' she said. 'Let's get going.'

Mae smiled, excited.

'Right,' said Joanne. 'Let's get started. I want you to imagine a room. A sealed white room. Can you think of one?'

Mae said nothing. She sat perfectly still, rigid.

'Mae?' Joanne leaned across the table. 'Mae, are you all right?'

Mae was shaking.

Joanne looked quickly around, trying to find someone to help. No one was near.

'Mae?'

'You want three words?' Her voice was shaking as much as her body. 'I'll give you three words. Suffering. Pain. And . . . and—'

Her mouth moved quickly, as if speaking a silent litany, as if auditioning and rejecting words before settling on one she could say. That she was brave enough to put in her mouth and speak aloud.

'—hope . . .'

Her voice trembled. Tears freely cascaded down her cheeks.

Joanne moved around the table, arms ready to comfort her.

'Don't touch me . . . don't touch me . . .' Mae sprang back, recoiled from Joanne.

Mae's eyes locked with Joanne's. Mae seemed to be standing on a precipice of words, wanting to tip them over, waiting for the right time. The right person to unload them on to.

Mae snatched a sheet of paper, picked up her brush, started painting.

She worked in a frenzy, eyes locked on the paper, seeing shapes and colours, looking beyond them. Pulling something out of herself, dredging it up and spewing it out. Almost attacking the paper with paint. Grunting and huffing, lips moving in a silent, mumbled running commentary that only her own ears could hear. And the speed: Joanne had seen nothing like it. She was fascinated by the girl.

Joanne couldn't make out the image that was being created. She tried to guess but after a while gave up. Her guesses would be nowhere near.

'Finished,' said Mae eventually. She sat back in her chair, sweat beading her forehead. She looked exhausted, visibly shaken.

Joanne turned the wet sheet of paper around, looked at it. She couldn't hide her surprise.

Jesus crucified on the cross. His face twisted. Against a white background. Shadows forming at the corners.

'What d'you think?' Mae's voice again small.

'It's . . .'

'Not what you were expectin'?'

'To be honest Mae, no. I didn't know you were religious.'

Mae gave a harsh laugh. 'I'm not that stupid.'

'Then why this?'

'Because . . . Jesus died. He was made to suffer. And then he died. And came back. He came back . . .' Mae's voice trailed off.

Jung's fourth question: a white room.

The white room: how the subject sees death.

Joanne nodded.

'Comin' back from death, that means hope, yeah?'

Joanne nodded. 'Yes, Mae, it does.'

They both stood there in silence, staring at the picture.

'Are you going to tell me what they all mean?' said Mae. 'What I've been painting?'

'I said I would. I'll pass the results on to your therapist. She'll—'

'I only want to work with you.'

'Why?'

'I trust you. An' you've suffered an' all.'

Joanne nodded. 'We'll work something out.'

Mae looked at her painting again.

'There's sufferin' there,' she said. 'But hope. Hope.'

Joanne nodded. She thought of Jack. Wondered what his three words would have been. Wondered what things he would have painted.

Mae began crying again. Joanne went to put her arms around her, comfort her. She didn't rebuff her this time.

Joanne stood, holding the weeping girl in her arms.

Suffering, she had said. But hope.

Hope.

For the future.

Joanne held on tight. Not letting her go.